About the Author

Jan Carson is a writer and community arts development officer based in Belfast. She is the current recipient of the Arts Council of Northern Ireland Artists' Career Enhancement scholarship. *Malcolm Orange Disappears* is her first novel.

First published in 2014 by
Liberties Press
140 Terenure Road North | Terenure | Dublin 6W
Tel: +353 (1) 405 5701
www.libertiespress.com | info@libertiespress.com

Trade enquiries to Gill & Macmillan Distribution
Hume Avenue | Park West | Dublin 12
T: +353 (1) 500 9534 | F: +353 (1) 500 9595 | E: sales@gillmacmillan.ie

Distributed in the UK by
Turnaround Publisher Services
Unit 3 | Olympia Trading Estate | Coburg Road | London N22 6TZ
T: +44 (0) 20 8829 3000 | E: orders@turnaround-uk.com

Distributed in the United States by
IPM | 22841 Quicksilver Dr | Dulles, VA 20166
T: +1 (703) 661-1586 | F: +1 (703) 661-1547 | E: ipmmail@presswarehouse.com

Copyright © Jan Carson, 2014
The author asserts her moral rights.

ISBN: 978-1-909718-31-9
2 4 6 8 10 9 7 5 3 1

A CIP record for this title is available from the British Library.

Cover design by Karen Vaughan
Internal design by Liberties Press

This book is sold subject to the condition that it shall not, by way of trade or otherwise, be lent, resold, hired out or otherwise circulated, without the publisher's prior consent, in any form other than that in which it is published and without a similar condition including this condition being imposed on the subsequent publisher.
No part of this publication may be reproduced or transmitted in any form or by any means, electronic or mechanical, including photocopying, recording or storage in any information or retrieval system, without the prior permission of the publisher in writing.

The publishers gratefully acknowledge financial assistance from the Arts Council of Northern Ireland.

All characters in this book are fictitious, and any resemblance to actual persons, living or dead, is purely coincidental.

Malcolm Orange Disappears

Jan Carson

*for Caleb and Izzy,
the original flying children*

– Chapter One –

Malcolm Orange Disappears

Malcolm Orange was beginning to disappear.

On Monday evening, preoccupied by the tiny perforations which had just that morning appeared all across his forearms, he excused himself from the supper table early.

'May I be excused, mama?' he mumbled through a mouthful of Hamburger Helper. 'I feel sick. I think I'm going to have diarrhea.'

His mother was lying on the sofa watching her Mexican soap operas which she very rarely missed. She claimed to be learning Spanish.

'You'll thank me,' she'd explain, 'when we go to Spain and I can order anything you want to eat in the restaurants.'

Malcolm Orange had lived in nineteen different states and never eaten in a restaurant where meals could not be ordered simply by pointing at a picture on a laminated display board. He thought it unlikely that Spanish restaurants would have an ordering system significantly less sophisticated than the method favored by the United States of America but said nothing of this to his mother. His mother had never been to Spain.

Malcolm Orange was extremely relieved to see his mother pre-occupied with something aside from sniffling into her sweater sleeves and so he tolerated both the Mexican soap operas and her excruciating attempts at Spanish conversation in the local taqueria.

'Mama,' repeated Malcolm, louder now as he competed with the Mexican couple fornicating in grainy colors all over the television screen, 'can I be excused before I have diarrhea at the table, please?'

'*Sí*,' replied his mother without so much as lifting her eyes.

In the bathroom Malcolm locked the door, stripped down to his tube socks, flushed the toilet twice and turned both faucets on. (It was important to preserve the appearance of diarrhea and so he continued to flush the toilet every two to three minutes for the duration of his stay in the bathroom.)

The bathroom was pastel green and smelt faintly of Nivea cold cream and mildew. The walls, even on the hottest day of a northwestern summer, remained permanently damp to the touch like an elderly man, perspiring even in repose. In its previous life the bathroom had offered a temporary home to some thirteen senior couples who had squatted and scrubbed, pissed and plucked in full view of the pastel green bathroom suite, before being shuffled – fully coherent or comatose – to a more permanent resting place. The 'pull for assistance' cord lingered still; a subtle monument to residents now departed. It had recently been knotted up to deter Malcolm from accidentally 'pulling for assistance' whilst in pursuit of the light bulb cord.

No self-respecting elderly person, emerging from their morning shower, wishes to be greeted by a full six-foot vision of shriveling, raisin flesh and consequently the bathroom was poorly equipped with mirrors. This was a problem for Malcolm who required not only mirrors but also the privacy of the only lockable room in the entire chalet for a full and intimate examination of his disappearing parts.

Earlier that afternoon an extensive search of the chalet had revealed one compact mirror (ferreted away at the bottom of his mother's make-up purse), two wall-mounted decorative mirrors, firmly screwed to the bedroom walls and, of course, the mirrored doors of the medicine cupboard which hovered over the bathroom sink and which, despite two decades of accumulating toothpaste flecks and fingerprints, still offered a three-foot-square rectangle of reflective possibility.

Clambering on to the closed toilet lid Malcolm Orange twisted around for a good angle and began to examine himself in the medicine cupboard mirror, one sausage-colored rectangle at a time. For the purpose of medical accuracy he had stolen a battery-powered flashlight from the basement and used this to illuminate each area of flesh as it came under examination. Beginning with his shoulder blades he navigated his way southwards in three-inch segments.

Malcolm Orange had seen more than enough medical dramas, both Mexican and ordinary, to understand the gravity of his situation. There were thousands of holes, millions perhaps, all across his face and belly, speckling his knees like sandpaper. Though he was not yet old enough to look over his own shoulders, Malcolm suspected his back to be equally infested. Fully utilizing the compact mirror and a complex series of acrobatic maneuvers (perfected during the nine years he'd spent living in the back seat of an ancient Volvo), Malcolm could just about read the base of his neck. It was now blessed with an intricate constellation of prick marks.

'Good grief,' he thought, 'I'm covered in tiny holes. The water's going to get into me when I shower.'

(It would be one week and three days before Malcolm Orange – forced by the unspeakable stench emanating from both armpits

– next chanced a full body shower. Even then, anxious about the water getting in and diluting his blood or causing him to balloon like a boy-shaped water bed, Malcolm was extra-specially careful to keep his head outside the cubicle at all times and, for safety's sake, bandaged up the biggest holes with waterproof Band-Aids.)

As he considered the long-term implications of swimming, showering and torrential rain, Malcolm's thoughts were disturbed by his own mother, raising Hell outside the bathroom door.

'Malcolm,' shouted Mrs Orange, trying the door handle, 'What's going on in there? You know I don't like you locking the door when you're in the bathroom.'

'Mama!' exclaimed Malcolm Orange, hastily pumping the toilet flush, once, twice, three times for effect, 'I'm almost twelve. I can lock the door of the bathroom if I want to.'

'You could have a fit in there or fall and knock yourself out against the bath tub or drown and I wouldn't be able to help you. I'd have to call the fire department to break down the bathroom door and that could take half an hour or more. You could be dead before I get to you, drowned in the bath and dead. Please, please, please don't lock the door, Malcolm!'

Even through the bathroom door with the toilet flushing every thirty seconds Malcolm Orange could tell his mother was about to cry. Lately his mother had developed the uncanny ability to cry at almost anything from a locked bathroom door to an empty spaghetti pot or the fact that Ross, now approaching three months, was beginning to grow out of the sock drawer and might very soon require a bigger crib; an orange crate or grocery cart for example.

'Don't cry, mama. I'm not going to drown. I'm not even in the bath. I'm just having diarrhea and it's starting to slow down. I'll be out in five minutes.'

'OK, Malcolm.' A long, papery silence followed, during which Malcolm Orange considered the necessity of another alibi-grounding toilet flush. 'You know I love you, Malcolm? I only get worried because I love you so much.'

Malcolm Orange could hear his mother kissing the back of the bathroom door before returning to the living room. When she got a little crazy, as she often did in the two-hour gap between dinner and bed, it was not unknown for his mother to kiss the oddest things: freshly laundered sheets, sack lunches and tennis shoes to name but a handful of her most recent conquests. This seemed like a basic design fault for she remained chronically incapable of visiting actual, physical affection upon her two sons, choosing instead to bless them by proxy, as if attempting to leave a thin sheen of love on every surface they might possibly touch.

Malcolm Orange removed his ear from the bathroom door, climbed back onto the toilet seat and resumed his examinations. He poked at his chest, just south of the left nipple, delicately at first (expecting to experience the dull satisfaction of a fresh bruise), and then with a growing recklessness as he realized the perforations were not the slightest bit painful. They weren't itchy either. This came as an enormous relief to Malcolm, who knew all about itchy, and also scabs.

Malcolm Orange was the only child in the history of the Pacific Northwest unfortunate enough to have suffered from chicken pox on three separate occasions. The first bout had been early enough to leave not so much as the smallest dent on his memory but the second and third occurrences had stayed with him, itching like the Devil himself was trying to burrow out of both elbows.

When the third set of welts began to appear around his eight-year-old belly Malcolm Orange's mother automatically assumed eczema brought on by the recent stress of losing a grandmother in the bathroom of a downtown Dairy Queen.

'It's OK to be sad, Malcolm,' she'd explained, rubbing her own anti-aging moisturizer into his scaly belly, 'old people die and it doesn't even bother them. They just get tired of talking about the same stuff over and over. Everyone dies when they get done with not being dead. It's nothing to get stressed about.'

'I'm not stressed about Grandma dying,' replied Malcolm. 'There's more room in the backseat of the car without her.'

When it became clear that neither good advice nor Oil of Olay were having the slightest effect upon the ever-expanding patch of scabs, Mrs Orange finally realized that this was no ordinary case of grief-related eczema; her firstborn had once again been stricken with the chicken pox.

This seemed something of a miracle in reverse and, as such, more than worthy of celebration. Malcolm's mother walked to the phone booth on the corner and called the local press who quickly retaliated with thirty-two lines on the little boy who'd suffered and survived full-body chicken pox three times before his ninth birthday. 'Local Kid Shingled Out for Third Bout of the Pox', ran the headline. It had been a slow news day in the suburbs of Tucson and the miracle of Malcolm Orange featured only slightly less prominently than a truckload of cows tipped across downtown I-10.

For one long April weekend Malcolm Orange enjoyed a certain level of neighborhood celebrity. Had he been well enough to leave the living room sofa and wander down to the corner store he might have found himself plied with offers of free ice cream sandwiches and candy bars or, for the first time ever, ushered into a soccer game by the older Mexican kids who hung out on the gas station wall, spitting and scraping cigarette butts off the sidewalk.

Unfortunately for Malcolm, by the time his chicken pox had itched and scabbed its way into remission the fickle finger of local fame had passed on to a pair of twin girls, born with complete sets of extendable wings attached at the shoulder. Malcolm Orange could hardly complain. Given the choice he himself would have chosen angel babies over chicken pox any day of the week.

His disappointment was tempered somewhat when, the following Friday morning, with little more than a half hour's warning, the entire Orange family upped and moved to Kentucky.

At the time Kentucky had seemed like the sort of state worth anchoring into. To the eight-year-old Malcolm (whose only previous knowledge of the Bluegrass State had been a brief and greasy love affair with the fried chicken joint of the same name), Kentucky sounded like an enormous castle of a state, fashioned entirely from ordinary sticks, popsicle sticks and over-chewed gum. He imagined his father building a semi-permanent popsicle cabin, digging his own foundations with a disposable plastic spoon and fashioning windows from Ziploc baggies. This spit and stickle notion of a non-transient home was Malcolm Orange's own particular brand of pornography and he held fast to its elbows for the better part of a month, digging his heels into the bubbling Kentucky asphalt when everything began to slide.

It was only several months in, after the Volvo's backseat had evolved into a one-bed trailer by the sewage works; after his step-Nana had passed away, bolt upright and undetected for ninety minutes during a two-buck matinee of *Ghostbusters*; after the dust, and the flatness, and the air conditioning gone to shit and nonsense; in fact it was only after the second of three dead dogs, curdling in the storm drain, that Malcolm Orange finally began to reconsider Kentucky.

Thankfully, by this stage the bottom had already fallen out of the southern tire market. 'Let's get rolling, Oranges,' Malcolm's father had said, slapping the hood of the Volvo, careful to avoid the constellation of rust marks around the headlights. 'Let's head east. There's an honest-to-God fortune waiting for the Oranges on the east coast.' Malcolm Orange had not even bothered to plead for his second-hand bicycle, having long since come to realize the futility of asking for anything less necessary than a microwave oven.

By the time the Oranges had arrived on the east coast only the worst of Malcolm's chicken pox scars remained, bearing permanent testimony to the family's misadventures in the south. The year was nineteen hundred and ninety three. Malcolm Orange was approaching double figures and much too old for miracles. He would never again be blessed with an infectious skin disease of any kind. However, the chicken pox trilogy had left him with a lifelong wariness of prominent rashes including acne, sunburn and various trifling skin irritations.

Though Malcolm's chicken pox scabs had peeled off in increasingly outlandish shapes (giving his fingers something worth thinking about when he couldn't pick his nose), the itchiness had driven him to big time cursing and bad temper. To mark the moment, Malcolm Orange had collected and kept a matchbox full of chicken pox scabs as a permanent reminder of the cruel things God will visit on kids, just because he can.

Someday he hoped to do something useful with his scabs – make a piece of art perhaps, or bury them under a just-planted tree – but, for the time being, Malcolm held on to the matchbox and the chicken pox scabs, keeping the whole precious package bundled up inside an old pillow case. From time to time, when he'd almost got to trusting God again, Malcolm Orange took out his scabs, balanced one on the end of a finger – like he'd seen in a contact lens commercial – and thought about all the things God had taken away from him.

The list was substantial: nineteen states before his twelfth birthday, eight whole grandparents (this number, though biologically impossible, included step-grandparents, parents of grandparents and at least one older person of ill-defined relation who, for ease of use, Malcolm Orange had come to call grandparent), three dogs – one wanted, the second and third unwanted and subsequently un-mourned – fifteen thrift store bicycles (luxury items which, when it came to packing the Volvo's trunk, had been giving precedence to towels, saucepans and undead grandparents, for the better part of a decade), the entire nail of his second largest toe and one absconded father, who'd made it as far as Portland, Oregon before disappearing quietly and without warning in the general direction of Mexico.

Malcolm Orange was not yet old enough to articulate his God-rage but he did from time to wonder what the Almighty could possibly be wanting with all those bicycles and mean as Hell old folk. Right there in the chalet's pastel green bathroom, confronting the possibility of his own imminent disappearance, Malcolm began to suspect that this latest theft was yet another incidence of God's unending greed.

After several minutes of examining himself in the medicine cabinet door – backwards, side-wards, full-frontal and an ill-fated attempt at upside down – Malcolm Orange grew confident that these new holes were an entirely different form of plague, absolutely distinct from the chicken pox of his youth. They were neither itchy nor prone to scabbing. They had not arrived individually. That morning they had simply been there, prickling every inch of his body with a consistency comparable to skin itself so he felt like a kid cut from perforated kitchen towel.

The previous evening Malcolm Orange was absolutely, one hundred and fifty-three percent certain they had not been there for, during his nightly game of Wimbledon, played against the gable wall of the chalet, he had worked up enough of a sweat to necessitate a shower. After this shower Malcolm had completed his customary mustache check and was, as usual, disappointed to find his upper lip not only smooth as a hard-boiled egg but also absolutely, definitely free of perforations.

(It was this attention to detail, perfected over the previous two years of biweekly mustache checks, which would later reassure Malcolm Orange that he'd only been disappearing for twenty-four hours at very most.)

Malcolm Orange climbed off the toilet lid and began to dress himself. As he pulled his pants over his knees, buckling them firmly about his skimpy middle, his head got to considering where these holes might have appeared from.

'Perhaps,' he conjectured, 'every young man, approaching puberty, is temporarily struck down with perforations and I, with my absent father and not-quite-right-in-the-head mother, have simply never been warned.'

This seemed like a logical explanation, yet Malcolm Orange struggled to picture his father – a brick of a man even at twelve years old – all shot through with tiny holes. Furthermore, Malcolm had indulged in more than his fair share of experimental glancing in the school showers and though his left eye – Hellbent on veering permanently northeast – made it difficult to be certain of anything more complex than his own ankles, he was pretty sure none of the other junior high boys were perforated.

'Could these holes be a curse?' Malcolm then asked himself, eyeing his own reflection suspiciously. 'Could they be some kind of otherworldly punishment for all the times I've picked my nose and stuck it inside the seatbelt holder? Or, if not a curse, what about some kind of superhero power?'

This was a thought worth thinking and much more appealing than a nose-picking curse. He had read enough X-Men comics to understand the extreme, unholy coolness of a well-placed mutation. However, even Malcolm Orange, blessed as he was with the overleaping imagination of an Old Testament prophet, struggled to imagine the superhero potential in being eleven years old and perforated.

Though Malcolm was loath to consider it – and would most probably have preferred tropical diseases or even a curse – there was, of course, the distinct possibility of dreams. More likely than superpowers or the long-anticipated onset of puberty, bad dreams seemed the shiftiest-looking suspect in a long lineup of plausible causes.

Malcolm Orange did not trust dreams.

(For the very same reason he also distrusted hiccups, tropical storms, death and shopping tax, all of which had, on several occasions, been visited upon him unexpectedly and without permission at no small inconvenience to his normal routine.)

For the previous three years Malcolm had been sleeping with a wad of balled-up Kleenex wedged into each ear; a safeguard against the possibility of a particularly wily dream sneaking into his head whilst he slept. Balled-up Kleenex, it turned out, did not make for the best dream catchers and often had to be extricated over the breakfast table with eyebrow tweezers or chopsticks.

'Malcolm,' his mother would say, as she picked the sodden orange shards of the latest tissue plug from her son's ears, 'this is the absolute last time I am going to pull Kleenex out of your head. If you don't want bad dreams count sheep like a normal kid.'

Having once read a most unsettling article in a woman's magazine, Malcolm Orange had been waging war on dreams for almost five years.

It should be noted that Malcolm – averaging three to five schools per year and consequently deprived of the normal educational outlets – had gleaned most of his life skills from the back pages of the cheaper women's magazines which congregated in the waiting areas of suburban beauty parlors and hairdressing salons. Beauty parlors remained the one immutable constant in Mrs Orange's careering pilgrimage across North America and her firstborn son, even now at the almost adult age of eleven, played a non-negotiable part in this ritual.

Regardless of State or season, Malcolm Orange spent every Saturday morning of his young life waiting while his mother had her hair permed, her eyebrows waxed, her fingernails polished, painted and filed into Dracula points, her armpits mown and teeth bleached, or the hard skin on both heels sandpapered into bloody pulp and vanilla butter. Between the hours of nine thirty and twelve Malcolm worshipped reluctantly at the traveling temples of suburban beauty. A series of five-buck beauty parlors in a series of medium-sized American cities looked on with avid disinterest while Malcolm balanced his skinny butt on a series of identical orange plastic chairs (carefully avoiding the worst of the cigarette scars), and plowed his way through towering stacks of women's magazines.

By the time Malcolm reached his tenth birthday he had absorbed enough secondhand peroxide to bleach his hair three shades lighter round the ears and had learned most everything he would ever need to know about hair removal, hot flushes and what to do when one's lover runs off with a younger woman. The experimental remnants of last summer's hot pink nail polish, still lingering round the cuticle of his big toe nail, bore witness to the fact that Malcolm Orange had spent an unhealthy amount of his childhood hanging out in beauty parlors.

When you're six months shy of your eighth birthday mom and pop beauty parlors have their limits, and Malcolm Orange had quickly outgrown the thrill of eavesdropping on the birdy little chi-chats between hairdressers and their over-primped regulars. Overheard conversations of a sexual nature were a dime a dozen and no longer thrilled Malcolm as they had at five and six. Having no concept of anything more stable than the backseat of a Volvo he could not understand the appeal of gossip. 'What's the use,' he wondered, 'in knowing all this grubby stuff about people I'll never see again?'

Looking for an alternative distraction he'd sucked his way through dozens of complimentary mints, examined the underside of coffee tables for rude words or salvageable gum and made countless pictures of the ocean from the swirling offcuts of recently trimmed hair. Eventually, bored with the walls and the inevitable dust-lined blinds, Malcolm's attention had turned to the dog-eared stacks of Vogues and Cosmopolitans which balanced out either side of the coffee table.

To Malcolm Orange these magazines were like small doors opening suddenly into a world more bizarre and terrifying than anything ever experienced, conquered or annihilated by his beloved X-Men.

Over the years Malcolm found himself freshly surprised by the heights and depths of disgusting processes the female body was party to. He took to watching the door suspiciously every time his mother visited the bathroom, wondering what monsterish horrors might be playing out behind closed doors. He devoured the problem pages and true-life stories, marveling at the freakish dilemmas these women were capable of orchestrating, and thanked the Lord nightly for the simple fact that he had been blessed with both a penis and the possibility of body hair in all the proper places.

Malcolm Orange read furtively, holding his eyebrows at all times loose and sloped in a light arch of disinterest. He fully understood that these magazines were not suitable for preadolescent boys and that, by some incredible stroke of good fortune, he'd found himself privy to a wealth of top secret, womanly information; the sort of facts and fictions which could later be used as ammunition in his own defense. He was careful not to appear too enthusiastic lest his mother might suspect deviancy or, more terrifying by far, some slim-wristed Vietnamese waxer or massively armed Mexican hairdresser might catch him on, crossing the salon floor in three furious strides to address his impertinence in broken English and clip him round the ears with the sharp end of a hairdryer.

It was on one such Saturday morning pilgrimage, somewhere in the outer armpit of Chicago, that Malcolm Orange first became suspicious of dreams.

Flicking eagerly through a sizeable stack of magazines which had, in an act of overzealous artistry, been fanned across the laminated coffee table, his eye had alighted on one particular headline.

'I Gave Birth to A Dinosaur Baby'

It was just the sort of article Malcolm most enjoyed and so he popped a complimentary mint and reached for the magazine. Both the article and the publication containing it had been almost eighteen months out of date but this gave Malcolm no cause to doubt the veracity of the story.

'Tampa, Florida. June 1989. Woman Gives Birth To A Fully-Formed Dinosaur. Experts Baffled.

'Katie Overlein-Locke, a twenty-five-year-old mother of three, last night gave birth to a fully formed, fire-breathing dinosaur baby. On first examination it appears to be a triceratops but it could well turn out to be a stegosaurus. Experts are baffled. This is the first recorded case of a woman giving birth to a dinosaur in almost two hundred and fifty years. Obstetrician Dr Hugo Martinez issued the following statement, "We're baffled by this one. It's so long since we've had a dinosaur baby in the United States I think we all thought we'd seen the last of this sort of thing. It's a good-looking kid though and it breathes fire."

'Both mother and dinosaur are doing well and expect to leave the hospital in the next few days. When interviewed exclusively for *Woman's World Magazine*, Mrs Overlein-Locke said, "I never thought this would happen to me. I mean, you read about this stuff happening in African places but not here in the United States. I guess I knew though. I dreamt about dinosaurs every night for the last nine months. I just want to warn other women to be very careful what they dream about when they're pregnant."'

The article was accompanied by a small, and somewhat blurry, photo of Mrs Overlein-Locke, propped up in her hospital bed, cradling what appeared to be a tiny green dinosaur dressed in a pair of men's pajamas.

Upon reading this article Malcolm Orange was overcome by the need to have diarrhea, very suddenly in the beauty parlor bathroom. The thought of dreaming into being an actual dinosaur baby had scared the shit right out of his churning bowels.

Malcolm had never before acknowledged the faint suspicion that his dreams might have an actual, honest-to-God bearing on his wide-awake hours. It was the singular worst thought he could possibly think, for his dreams were full of curdling screams and planes crashing into volcanoes, leprosy and teenage girls tying him up in ribbons.

Malcolm Orange had once dreamt himself, in glorious Technicolor, being run over by a car whilst crossing the Golden Gate Bridge. Waking the next morning he'd discovered a bruise, exactly the size and shape of a mandarin orange, beginning to swell at the base of his skull. Having never been run over by a car or crossed the Golden Gate Bridge, Malcolm was unsure if the dream was consistent with his injuries but from this point on he'd suspected, yet never fully acknowledged, that dreams could not be trusted.

The grainy snapshot of the dinosaur baby had confirmed everything Malcolm Orange already knew to be true. He instantly determined to do his level-headed best never to dream again. It was simply too dangerous to leave himself open to the possibility of dreaming into existence a gruesome death or apocalyptic encounter with a teenage girl. And thus had begun the golden era of the Kleenex earplugs.

Having reached the believable limit of diarrhea, Malcolm flushed the toilet one final time, unbolted the bathroom door and stepped back into the living room. His mother was still seated on the living room sofa kissing the strap of Ross's diaper bag while she watched her soap operas. Between kisses she swigged Diet Coke straight from a two liter bottle. She managed the bottle one handed like a professional shot-putter.

'Better?' she asked, turning to watch as Malcolm positioned himself, cross-legged on the floor.

'Uh-huh,' replied Malcolm, and wrapped one arm round his middle in a last-ditch attempt at attention to detail, 'I feel much better now the diarrhea's out. I think I probably ate something bad this afternoon but it's all gone now. If it's OK, I think I'll just sit here and read for a while before bed.'

'OK Hon, whatever you want. Just don't make too much noise. I'm trying to learn my Spanish off the subtitles.' His mother clicked the volume up a few notches and gave the remote a quick but deliberate kiss before positioning it on the arm of the sofa.

Malcolm Orange began to flick absentmindedly through the short stack of comics which had, of recent weeks, congregated against the coffee table leg, breeding there unnoticed, until the bigger part of the table was now supported by science fiction. Malcolm wasn't reading. He was still thinking about his dreams.

Two things were looking increasingly likely; Malcolm Orange was beginning to disappear and the Kleenex earplugs had been a colossal waste of time and imagination.

Though frustrated to admit that bad dreams could not be caught and squished like garden bugs in a balled-up tissue, Malcolm took small hope in the unpredictable nature of these dreamings. If the holes were the result of some particularly pointed dream there was a distinct possibility, he reasoned, that they could be removed in a similar fashion, exorcised with some appropriate dream about cement or liquid skin.

Sitting on the living room carpet Malcolm tried not to panic.

Yes, he was disappearing. That much seemed obvious. In fact, examining his exposed parts in the limited glow from the TV screen, the holes in his wrists seemed larger now than earlier in the afternoon. Perhaps by the morning the perforations would have conspired to collide, leaving Malcolm almost entirely missing. Tomorrow evening, when the shock had finally settled into his stomach, Malcolm would have to devise some means of scientifically monitoring the progress of his holes.

Malcolm Orange was terribly good at measuring.

In the past he had faithfully recorded every Dairy Queen from the east to west coast, the changing tones of deep south sunsets and, most recently, the growing hysteria of his mother, plotted faithfully on a bar graph with his father's absence running like constant loss all along the horizontal axis. Beginning tomorrow, after dinner and his unavoidable helping of household chores, Malcolm Orange would draft a chart to monitor the progress of his own disappearance.

In the meantime he decided not to panic. He coerced his mother into surrendering the Diet Coke bottle, poured himself a tall glass with ice and settled down on the carpet to catch up on his Mexican soap operas. As Malcolm watched the screen his lips instinctively followed his mother's, invoking Spanish sentiments he would never quite understand nor pronounce correctly. Side by side, with their similar eyebrows, mother and son seemed glazed, like two penitent saints caught in the act of solemn confession.

Malcolm was miles away, settling into the sweet space between his ears where the Kleenex had filtered out all but the softest thoughts. He found himself frustratingly incapable of anything more anxious than a sideways glance.

'I'm beginning to disappear,' he reminded himself during the commercial breaks, 'I'm beginning to disappear and my father's not here to fix me.' Unsettling as this realization was, Malcolm Orange remained incapable of panic.

Worse things had happened in Texas: dead grandparents, trailer parks and the never-again-mentioned incident with the borrowed shotgun. Dreadful as each occurrence had been, individually and collectively, all Oranges capable of mounting the Volvo and skipping town had rolled on to conquer the next small city scandal. It was the Orange way to cope; just keep rolling.

Only Malcolm's mother – an Orange by marriage rather than blood – seemed incapable of getting off the sofa and trundling on to the next catastrophe.

Malcolm Orange took after his father in all matters other than eyebrows. Aged almost twelve and well-versed in the etiquette of the near disaster, he had arrived in Portland, Oregon with the belief that all things (even the enormously broken) could be fixed with just the right mix of Jesus and bravado. When all else failed and Jesus simply wasn't working, the most complicated problems could be abandoned in the dust receding slowly in the rearview mirror as the Volvo cut a quick, sharp path for the next town over.

'Mama,' he said, draining the dregs of his Diet Coke glass, 'I think I'm going to hit the sack now. I'll see you in the morning.'

'*Sí*,' she replied, reaching absentmindedly to pat the space where Malcolm had been. Her fingers met with thin air and the empty glass. Standing just inside his bedroom door, Malcolm Orange watched as his mother ran her lips lightly around the smudged rim of his empty glass. It was clear that she would have nothing constructive to contribute to his problem.

In the bedroom Ross was breathing heavily, sucking the air in and out of the sock drawer. Malcolm's mother had used parcel tape to keep him tied in, scared that his freshly stretched limbs would allow him to wriggle free of the socks and underpants, perhaps escaping forever like a liberated snake – scooching under the living room door, down the garden path and crawling south in the general direction of his absent father.

Malcolm Orange ignored Ross as he had been ignoring Ross for the last three months.

He could see himself roughly reflected in the dark sheen of the curtain-less window. The light from the living room was burrowing its way through his face and arms. He removed his shirt quickly, keeping the bedroom door open to allow the light in. The light was filtering right through Malcolm's belly. He was glowing now, luminous as tissue paper stretched over a light bulb. He turned backwards and sideways, high on the thought of being iridescent. He looked really friggin' cool – better than an X-Man by far, more like Jesus on the holy candles with hundreds of light rays coming out of his head.

Malcolm Orange removed his pants, crossed himself quickly and crawled under the bed sheets. 'Jesus, God, Holy Spirit, can you stop me from disappearing please?' he prayed, barely audible but solid enough to feel his own warm breath refracting damply off the bed sheets, 'Jesus, God, Holy Spirit, you can leave the holes for a few days but don't let me disappear entirely. In your name, Amen.'

Malcolm crossed himself again, this time in reverse, for he'd read somewhere that this was the correct way to end a prayer. Then he curled into a question mark and settled down with the very real intention of dreaming solid dreams: cement and concrete, liquid skin, the Grand Canyon, filled to the brim with asphalt and sand.

Malcolm Orange was going to imagine himself better.

– Chapter Two –

Idaho

Malcolm's father was in tires.

The Oranges moved around a lot, all across America with a backseat full of grandparents.

Papa Orange died in New Jersey. Great Grandma never made it back across the Brooklyn Bridge. Malcolm's Step Nana – a hulking blister of a woman who loved to fill the Volvo's cramped backseat with the vomit-inducing stench of pipe smoke and eggy farts – quit this mortal coil twenty minutes into a *Ghostbusters* matinee.

(By the time the movie ended, rigor mortis had set in, making it all but impossible to remove a family-sized popcorn sack from its habitual spot, nestled into the crook of her right arm. Mr Orange reluctantly buried his grandmother fully prepared for the possibility of afterlife snacking.

'It's a definite first for me,' remarked the local undertaker, viewing the corpse laid out in its enormous coffin, 'never buried nobody with popping corn before. Sure does look a little odd to me. Maybe it's one of them new-fangled ideas from China. I guess you live and learn in this business. You live and learn.'

'What can I say?' replied Mr Orange. 'My grandmother was a tremendous lover of popcorn.')

Step Nana's untimely demise came just six short weeks after Malcolm's maternal grandmother had left the dinner table to powder her nose and never returned. They'd left her propped against the bathroom wall in a downtown Dairy Queen. 'She'd have wanted it this way,' Malcolm's father claimed, and bought each of the remaining Oranges a CheeseQuake Blizzard. 'To take the edge off the grief,' he'd said, plastic spoon already poised over his cup.

Malcolm's mother never finished her Blizzard. It turned to ice cream water and dribbled all across the dashboard like a river of seagull poop. No one said anything about the Blizzard river. They just kept driving, state to state, rented room to room, swapping wheels when the tires fell off. The Oranges left their elderly relatives like signposts all the way back to California. By the time they got good and proper east only four Oranges remained: father, mother, Malcolm and his soon to be smaller brother, still gestating thickly under Mrs Orange's shirt.

'What say we get ourselves a pet?' Malcolm would ask his father every time the opportunity arose: birthdays, Christmas, funeral services. 'What say we get a big, dumb dog, or a kitty – a smart little kitty with green, grey eyes – a rabbit even? It'll take the edge off the loneliness. It'll make the backseat seem more like home.' (Malcolm Orange was not, for one second, speaking truthfully about the rabbit. While dogs and cats and killer whales roam the planet unloved, no self-respecting child will ever be properly satisfied with a rabbit).

'Nope,' his father consistently replied, and eventually bought him a substitutionary tennis racquet. 'No pets for you, young man. Pets die and I can't afford another funeral this year.'

The racquet would not hit right. It was abnormally holey, even for a tennis racquet. At the time Malcolm Orange suspected it the dumbest present he'd ever got given. Much later, when his father had finally disappeared – pointing the Volvo in the general direction of Mexico and leaving them stranded in Oregon with little more than a heap of balding tires to keep the child support coming – Malcolm got to reconsidering his tennis racquet. Resurrecting it from the laundry basket, he played endless, angry games of Wimbledon up against the gable wall of the retirement chalet which would come to pass for home, all the time punishing his racquet for the very fact that it could not talk back.

Less than two weeks after the giving (and ungrateful receiving) of Malcolm's tennis racquet, the Oranges had left town again.

Waking early one morning to find his parents already up and glaring furiously at each other over the breakfast table, Malcolm Orange was already anticipating an unsatisfactory outcome. At eleven years old (almost twelve), with eighteen states trailing behind his backside, Malcolm knew his father's moving speech better than the Pledge of Allegiance, the Lord's Prayer and the opening scenes of *Star Wars* combined.

When it arrived – one minute and forty-five seconds into Malcolm's daily bowl of Captain Crunch – the speech fell predictably flat on the kitchen floor, dropping like one side of an ill-timed high five.

'The east coast is not for us,' insisted Malcolm's father. 'There's an honest-to-God fortune awaiting us on the west coast. Let's get rolling, Oranges.' The speech, as tradition dictated, was accompanied by a peal of nervous laughter, a politician's smile and a thick, paternal hand placed on the back of Malcolm's neck; one part disciplinary pinch, one part half-assed hug.

Malcolm Orange was, as usual, unconvinced but, for the time being, eleven years old and therefore incapable of anything but forced consent.

'I'll pack my stuff,' he said, already wondering if his brand-new tennis racquet would make it into the Volvo's trunk when so many perfectly reasonable sticks and thrift store bicycles had tried, bravely pleaded, and failed.

His mother remained at the breakfast table, absentmindedly drinking from an already empty juice glass. 'It's extremely odd,' Malcolm had thought (even though these were early days, long before his absent father left, succinctly explaining all abnormalities in the Orange household), 'despite the baby growing inside her mom seems to be shrinking. With every state she appears smaller. I'm not sure if this is considered normal for pregnant women.'

Having no previous experience in this department, Malcolm Orange made a mental note to stop the very next enormously pregnant lady he came across and enquire as to exactly what was considered normal when having a baby.

That afternoon when the Volvo – heaving under the extra weight of unborn passengers, tennis racquets and antique dressers – finally left the east coast for west, Malcolm's mother was carrying nothing more than a carrier bag full of recipe books and the clothes she'd been sleeping in for the last two weeks. She was tremendously fat and very uncomfortable, struggling to wedge her belly underneath the Volvo's crummy dashboard.

'It's you or the dresser, sweetheart. We've only got room for one or the other,' joked Malcolm's father as he watched his wife slowly maneuver into the passenger seat. 'I'm guessing the dresser will come in more useful in the long run.'

It was not a very funny joke. No one laughed.

Malcolm's brother had appeared somewhere outside Chicago, struggling to make his presence known in the parking lot of a Ross Dress for Less. 'How convenient,' his father exclaimed, shaking his wife's hand wildly, 'you can buy yourself a cheap frock to fit your new flat belly.'

With no input from Malcolm Orange – who had for the greater part of his mother's pregnancy been rooting for Wolverine – they named the baby Ross. Sensing the battle already lost, Malcolm made one final stab at ownership.

'What about Wolverine for a middle name?' he proposed, mere minutes after the placenta had slithered free, disappearing forever into the bark dust beneath a parking lot palm tree.

'Shut up, Malcolm,' his father replied, turning to glare at him over the Volvo's seat back. 'This baby only needs one name. What would it do with a second one? Second names only make folks uppity and far too big for their own britches. One name was good enough for your ma and me. It was good enough for you when you were a tiny critter and it'll suffice for this little guy. You need to shut your mouth and fix your ma a cigarette. Stop talking nonsense or we'll leave you here in Chicago for good. Truth be told, that's not such a bad idea. We only ever wanted one kid anyway, didn't we Martha?'

Malcolm's mother said nothing. She was busy cleaning the goop off the baby with a packet of Kleenex and a half-drunk bottle of Evian. She had already deflated to half the size she'd been in Denny's that morning when Malcolm and his father had wedged her into a corner booth and watched, stupefied, as she clawed her way through three helpings of buckwheat pancakes and syrup. It was a mystery to Malcolm, for Ross was only one-third the size of his mother's belly. Perhaps, he eventually concluded, some of the breakfast pancakes had slipped out while she was pushing.

'I'm going to call him Wolverine anyway,' Malcolm Orange announced, pettily.

'Over my dead body you are,' his father replied. 'Call him anything but Ross and we're leaving you at the next Greyhound station.'

It was at this point in the conversation that Malcolm Orange suddenly, and without hope of retrieval completely lost interest in his new brother and turned his attention to the pursuit of a proper pet; a crocodile ideally.

Malcolm was entirely justified in his indifference.

Ross would prove to be an absolutely mediocre baby, given to neither miracles, misbehavior, nor any of the more disgusting infant illnesses which might have allowed him some room for growth in Malcolm's estimation. Ross expanded at the normal rate for an average boy child, slept a lot, occasionally barfed and developed the charming habit of smiling when spoken to. Malcolm couldn't have been more disappointed. He'd hoped for conjoined twins, a brother with tentacles or at very least a couple of extra digits, something to impress strangers with. Unfortunately the new baby's only redeemable feature seemed to be its ongoing lack of hair. Ross would remain bald as a coot 'til the day he turned three and woke freakishly and unexpectedly hairy with enough wild auburn curls to justify a ponytail.

It was five weeks and three days before the Oranges could officially call themselves west. Eight days should have sufficed, twelve at very most, but the tires came off in Nebraska, once again in Wyoming and a final infuriating time on the border of Idaho and Oregon. They were cheap tires, incorrectly fitted; the kind of tires which had kept Mr Orange rolling indiscriminately through the mid-sized towns and cities of North America for the better part of twenty-five years.

The Oranges were forced to drop temporary anchor on the Oregon border while Malcolm's father went foraging for new tires. Tires did not grow on trees, especially in the outermost armpit of Idaho, and it would take almost an entire month for the Volvo to get back on its feet. In the interim Malcolm's mother did laundry for the local folks, hauling their tired sheets and blouses down the main street in a stolen shopping cart. She washed, ironed, folded and stacked in the local laundromat while Ross dozed complicitly in a sports bag at her feet. Malcolm was now old enough to help with sorting colors and would do a full load for the reasonable price of one stick of Wrigley's gum, unchewed. Returning the freshly steamed laundry door to door with both children in tow, Mrs Orange charged five bucks more than the laundromat and though this was far from a fortune, even for the Oranges, it was enough to keep the entire family in Ramen noodles and Snickers bars.

During his month in Idaho, Malcolm Orange awarded himself an early summer vacation. Preoccupied with missing tires and other people's bed sheets, his parents simply shrugged their collective shoulders and complied.

'If someone stops you from Social Services,' his father advised, 'just tell them you've got yourself a dose of cancer. See, if you've got the cancer you don't have to go to school. You can do whatever the hell you feel like and the Social Services can't say a thing. We'll be gone before they find out you're lying.'

(Faking cancer was a trick Malcolm Orange's father had employed on several previous occasions; effortlessly wangling his way out of various responsibilities, including jury duty and several of Malcolm's own birthday parties.)

Though he often fantasized about being taken into care and forcibly placed with a family who did not live in a Volvo, though he was permanently ready to display bruises and boot marks (self-inflicted), and fully capable of lying his father into the county jail, no one from Social Services ever stopped Malcolm Orange.

Disinterested as the Social Services were – finding their time better spent in pursuit of teenage arsonists, stolen babies and those unfortunate children forced to sleep in fridges and family-sized suitcases – the elderly population of Milton, Idaho were greatly intrigued by the apparition of Malcolm Orange.

Perhaps it was the diminishing stature of the elderly, the curved spines and arthritic stoops, which thrust Malcolm Orange into eye line every time the older folk stepped over their front doormats; perhaps it was the fact that nothing of interest had occurred in Milton, Idaho since the enormous potato of '65; perhaps it was God himself, drawing the two parties together, like a pair of mismatched carpet slippers; more likely it was the ever-present nature of the boy who, suddenly shot of school routine, spent entire days lingering on the curb outside the library, flicking spit balls at the wall of the post office and rooting through the Main Street garbage cans for the last dregs of soda pop cans, but the over-sixties soon began to notice him.

At first they kept their distance, observing the boy from behind the window in the local deli, discussing him delicately over their coffee cups, their needlework and short-loan library books. The next town over had recently endured a spate of crimes against the elderly orchestrated by a seven-year-old girl with a BB gun, and subsequently the older contingent held their interest at a sensible distance of fifteen feet. Having observed Malcolm without incident for the better part of a week, their suspicion gradually turned from caution to concern.

A delegation comprised of two formidable ladies and a Golden Retriever was duly formed and dispatched to the far side of the street. At the last minute a bar of out-of-date Hershey's was added to the ensemble as a kind of peace offering-cum-conversation starter. The remainder of the elderly population congregated behind the deli's gingham curtains to offer moral support and instant back-up should an unpleasant incident occur.

The Golden Retriever led the charge.

He was a dog of advanced days – one hundred and fifteen canine years on his next birthday – and in his old age had grown excessively suspicious of change; preferring to eat, sleep and deliver his daily shit in exactly the same well-appointed spot. (A persistent yellowing patch in the grass beneath the elementary school flagpole not only infuriated the school's custodian but also bore witness to the Retriever's love of routine.)

Occasionally answering to the name 'Dog' or 'Boy', and most often 'Here You', the Golden Retriever, some six owners into his career, had managed to remain anonymous for almost a decade, carefully concealing the mortifying truth writ large on his Kennel Club papers. His first owner had greatly admired the world's favorite British Prime Minister and, in homage, had forced upon his dog the ridiculously pompous moniker of Winston. Not a single soul in Milton, Idaho had ever called him Winston. The Retriever was exceedingly glad of the fact. He had come to relish his anonymity. At some point in the not too distant future he fully intended to take this ugly little secret to the pet cemetery on the far side of town and bury it beneath an unmarked headstone.

There were several annoying constants Winston had lately come to detest. These included dry dog food (of the variety favored by younger couples and veterinary clinics), outfits for animals, and little boys in thrift store pants who, in Winston's one hundred and thirteen years of accumulated experience, were always up to no good.

Approaching Malcolm Orange at a righteous clip, Winston slid to a halt in front of the boy's scabby knees and verified his suspicions with a lusty sniff of Malcolm's crotch. As he'd expected, the sugary stench of Kool-Aid cut with piss emanated from the child's marl-grey pants. Winston lowered his snout, ready to nip the problem in the bud and scare the kid straight out of Idaho. Instead he found himself manhandled roughly by the ears, caught in mid-attack, unable to advance or retreat.

'Hello boy,' Malcolm Orange whispered, ruffling Winston's ears. 'What's your name?'

'*Grrrrr*,' slobbered Winston, still pinioned five inches above the boy's lap, '*grrrrrr.*'

Misinterpreting the dog's hostility as an invitation to instigate a long-term friendship, Malcolm Orange christened the dog Wolverine in his head and hooked both arms around its shaggy neck, hanging there like a skinny-dripped bandana.

The elderly ladies, sensing that imminent danger had been sufficiently diffused, shuffled forward to address Malcolm. Their walking aids reached Malcolm's toes two beats before their orthopedic shoes. They viewed the boy anxiously from the towering heights of five foot three and two, respectively. The second of the elderly ladies felt a keen need to come down to the child's level. She made a preliminary stab at bending and, having advanced no further than an arthritic half-inch closer to the ground, levered herself back to full height and wearily gave up on the curb. It had been almost sixteen years since either of these two women had bent in the fashion usually associated with bending.

'Son,' the first lady asked, offering the chocolate bar like a silent explanation, 'shouldn't you be in school?'

'Where's your mama?' the second lady asked and, because nerves had got the better of her and consequently erased their preplanned script, repeated the first lady's question. 'Shouldn't you be in school?'

(The Golden Retriever wisely held his tongue and lowered his backside onto the curb beside Malcolm Orange, where he made short work of the chocolate bar, still enclosed in its foil wrapper.)

'No ma'am,' Malcolm Orange replied, affecting an Idaho drawl, 'I got myself a dose of cancer and I don't want to be giving it to the other kids.'

The second lady, troubled by nerves and the recent loss of a perfectly good husband – her third of the decade – promptly burst into tears and, finding herself uncharacteristically caught without a handkerchief, dripped snot all the way down the leg of Malcolm Orange's school pants.

Twenty minutes later Malcolm found himself permanently installed in the back left corner of the Milton Deli where he held court for four weeks straight. During these halcyon days a constant stream of ice cream, expensive cheese and pastrami sandwiches made its way from the counter to Malcolm's gingham-clad table and eventually, subject to his perverse whims and affectations, the inner chambers of his ever-expanding belly.

Over the course of his month-long stay in Milton, Idaho Malcolm Orange grew fat on the generosity of the elderly. His school pants, salvaged from a Brooklyn-based thrift store, began to pinch at the middle. His T-shirts rose in resistance, crawling towards his armpits. By July Fourth both his school slacks and the second-hand Levis which completed the lower echelons of Malcolm's wardrobe could no longer be buttoned across his waist and, with no money for spare pants forthcoming, were subsequently worn hip-hop style coasting two inches beneath his pancake butt.

'Man oh boy,' Mr Wilson, elderly proprietor of the Milton

Deli, was heard to mutter over the latest in a towering mountain of handmade pastrami and banana rolls, 'if I didn't know better I'd say that kid's a darn sight healthier than anyone else in this store. Look at him there chowing down ice cream sandwiches like the Lord himself was coming back tomorrow. He's ten pounds heavier than he was two weeks ago. Funniest cancer I ever seen.'

When the muttering could no longer be ignored and Malcolm's demands for tuna on rye with barbecue sauce, though never denied, were met with increasingly resentful looks, he hopped up on the counter, feet straddling a large jar of homemade jelly, and made it known that the cancer drugs caused bloating, and his ever-expanding belly, far from being a sign of health, was in fact a sure indicator of his imminent demise.

(Malcolm Orange had, from an early age, enjoyed a laissez-faire relationship with the truth. Given the choice between honesty and the opportunity to evoke sympathy, devotion or a standing ovation, Malcolm almost always went with fantastical lies.

He had inherited this trait from his father, who at the tender age of twenty-three had developed acute appendicitis during a spring break trip to Cabo San Lucas. Chronically short of cash, Jimmy Orange (or Clem, as he'd been known in his college days, the guys in his dorm taking all of two days to make the subtle leap from Orange to Clementine and finally Clem) had found himself unable to afford a trip to the local tourist hospital. Powered by resolve and a full bottle of Mexican tequila, Mr Orange had had his appendix removed by a 'qualified' doctor who spoke only three terse words of English and operated out of a local funeral parlor.

Mr Orange latterly claimed that the Mexican surgeon, incapable of understanding his instructions, had removed not only his diseased appendix but also half a rib, two suspicious-looking moles and the small gland that controls truth-telling in all normal humans.

'Don't blame me, Martha,' Malcolm often heard his father yelling, 'I'm medically incapable of telling the truth. Malcolm too. It's not his fault. It's genetic.'

Mrs Orange's response was most often indecipherable, a whirling barrage of four-letter words and flying fists. Seemingly, despite her lifelong devotion to medical dramas, both Mexican and normal, she simply did not understand the complexities of the human body.)

In Milton, Idaho, with his flip-flopped feet balancing up on the countertop, Malcolm Orange drew breath, placed his hand on the exact spot – just below his right shoulder blade – where his father had often pointed out the missing truth gland, and lied like all future meals depended on it.

'The doctor says I've got two weeks at the most,' he stated bluntly, mumbling through a mouthful of butterscotch sundae and chopped nuts. 'I could go at any second though.'

The original ladies, those reluctant pioneers who'd first approached him on Main Street – or Etta and Letty, as Malcolm had come to know them – fished a pair of lace hankies out of their sleeves and simultaneously cried into their china teacups; salt water mixing with their old-fashioned Earl Grey. Mr Wilson, penitent in his candy stripe apron, fixed a whole plate of pastrami and banana sandwiches, exactly the way Malcolm liked them, and Winston the Golden Retriever, who was blessed with an over-developed ability to sniff out bullshit, both canine and human, retired to the front stoop to gnaw, deeply frustrated, on his own hind leg.

Thereafter, the residents of Milton, Idaho struggled to preserve a sense of normalcy, all the time aware that tragedy lurked, imminent and inevitable, just around the corner. Mr Wilson kept Malcolm's stomach constantly full, heaping fresh treats onto the tabletop every time his plate ran empty. Etta, armed with a floral notebook, helped him to compose an epitaph suitable for his coming funeral. Letty, motivated by a particularly earnest made-for-TV movie she'd recently seen on the Hallmark Channel, asked Malcolm if he'd like to have a park bench constructed in his honor. Malcolm Orange politely declined, saying he'd prefer a swing seeing as he wasn't greatly inclined to sitting still. Letty immediately left the Milton Deli, vindicated and eager to find a suitable local swing upon which to nail a commemorative plaque.

It was only on the eleventh day of Malcolm Orange's final fortnight on earth that the truth came leaking out.

Mrs Orange, who had become semi-permanently based in the Main Street laundromat, was up to her elbows in the second white wash of the day when she found herself facing down a delegation of elderly ladies with notebooks. Having spent the better part of fifteen years in the company of Jimmy Orange, Martha Orange (an Orange by marriage rather than blood) had grown adept in the spotting, and subsequent avoidance of, sticky situations, long before they became attached to her person. Without so much as drawing breath she quickly twisted her waist-length hair east, west and finally south, securing it atop her head with the help of an unpaired tube sock. After which she began to stuff dozens of vests, underpants, mismatched socks and graying brassieres, still dripping, into a pair of ancient carrier bags. Then, hooking the bags into each elbow like a set of old-fashioned water pails, she hoisted the sports bag containing a sleeping Ross into her arms and attempted to exit the laundromat.

Malcolm Orange Disappears

The Golden Retriever cut her off at the door.

(Winston, driven by the desire to see the Oranges disappear, was greatly inclined to chew the baby as it slept noisily in its sports bag. However, having realized that no one – not even the elderly, and soon to be irate, inhabitants of an Idaho backwater – looks favorably upon a dog who eats small children, he found himself acting as a tactical roadblock instead. 'A confrontation,' he concluded, 'will inevitably lead to a lynching and then things can return to normal round here.' He glanced surreptitiously at his hind legs which were chewed raw round the ankles, and his previously lustrous tail which was beginning to go the same way, and decided to stand his ground even if the Orange lady kicked him in the teeth.)

The elderly ladies shuffled forwards and grouped around Malcolm's mother. They were a terrifying breed to look upon, with eyes saucering behind their prescription lenses and corrective footwear burrowing into the laundromat floor and floral notepads poised like a gaggle of preshrunk paparazzi.

Martha Orange – who had in her pre-Orange days been an Oklahoma farm girl and, for the most part, unfenced – shook right down to her mismatched ankle socks, shook like a boxed cow and fought the inclination to bolt, scattering elderly ladies like bowling pins all along Main Street. She hefted Ross higher in her arms, silently reminded herself of the fact that she had once shot a jackrabbit at a quarter mile distance and, thus armed, gathered her resolve like a downtown bulldozer.

'Excuse me,' she said, attempting to elbow her way through the forest of walking aids, 'I was just leaving.'

The elderly ladies, resolute as the Red Sea, showed no inclination of parting.

Martha Orange stepped forward, swinging her sleeping son

with intent. The Golden Retriever, previously upright, stretched out on the graying linoleum, blocking the door. The eldest and most forthright of the elderly ladies took a step forward to meet her.

'You forgot your shoes, dear,' she shouted, adjusting her hearing aid to a more sociable level even as she yelled.

In her haste to avoid the lynching party Mrs Orange had indeed abandoned her tennis shoes by the tumble dryer. She realized, with a weariness far beyond her thirty-seven years, that the battle was not only lost but already coasting towards out-and-out disaster. Deflated, she lowered herself onto a plastic seat, gently placed Ross, still encased in his sports bag, on the seat opposite and slipped her feet into her unlaced sneakers.

Etta and Letty, anxious to block her exit route, positioned themselves on either side of Mrs Orange and introduced themselves, Etta first, and by proxy Letty, who'd been taking a supporting role since nineteen hundred and thirty-three and felt no inclination to rattle the boat in this, her eighty-eighth year. After which, having elicited no response from Mrs Orange, Etta, by way of an icebreaker, offered the young woman a Red Vine from the box she always carried in her apron pocket.

Mrs Orange accepted. The three women sat on the laundromat seats with their naked ankles extended towards the washing machine screens, sucking and slurping quietly for the better part of two minutes. From a distance Martha Orange admired her own Southern-fried ankles, two brassy doorknobs protruding from a pair of girlish shins. She had been blessed at birth with both an unfortunate boxer's nose and a pair of Hollywood legs, capable, even at thirty-seven, of shaming girls half her age as she cut up dance floors, sidewalks and, more lately, the bargain aisles of Walmarts, all across the United States. Etta glanced down at the younger lady's ankles and felt the feeble sting of fading jealousy. Etta, who had, in the summers of nineteen hundred and fifty-three and -four, won the Miss Lovely Legs Idaho competition, who had once prided herself on mile-high stilettos and whore-red toenails, who could turn the farm boys' heads with a single flash of naked heel, now tottered round town in a pair of orthopedic sandals, her ankles ham-pink, swollen and crisscrossed with varicose veins as fine and furious as spiderwebs.

Whilst the three ladies polished off their Red Vines, the rest of the delegation regrouped, forming a nosy semicircle around their feet. A reverent hush descended upon the laundromat floor, settling into the spaces between the soap powder stains and dryer fluff. Overcome by the heat and the anticipation, Emmy-Kate Barrett, a substantial lady currently located to the left of Martha Orange's shoulder, felt herself about to succumb to one of her infamous turns and, lowering herself to the floor in preparation, adopted the supine pose of a zealous worshipper; hands clenched, knees braced against the unforgiving linoleum, eyes cast heavenward in the hope of respite or divine vision. The ranks parted to make way for her mammoth backside, now angled upwards in contemplation of the ceiling fan. A fevered hum worked its way through the ranks. Cotton handkerchiefs were unfurled and raised to mop sweating lips. Dentures were adjusted, high coiled hairdos patted into place and the occasional shirt sleeve slid high to meet an eager elbow. Somewhere towards the back of the group an elderly lady, one-time photographer for the local rag, produced an aging Canon and prepared to commit the coming incident to film.

However, when the Red Vines had been sucked right down to their bloody nibs and sticky fingers wiped surreptitiously on sweater fronts, and a confrontation seemed all but inevitable, Etta rose awkwardly, leaning on Malcolm's mother for support, and shooed the audience reluctantly through the front door. They moved like soup through the summer heat, canes and sandal heels catching on the laundromat floor. Etta persevered, thin-lipped and silent, employing the same stoic thunder she had, in nineteen hundred and fifty six, used to stare down a stampeding bull. Once relegated to Main Street, the group instantly reformed, cackling like a gaggle of ill-tempered geese, veiny noses pressed against the window.

Etta Mae Wheeler, fast approaching her eighty-sixth year, had seen more than her fair share of confrontations. During the preceding eighty-five years she had been yelled at, punched, kicked, insulted and occasionally baptized with a vitriolic pint of local brew. For the most part Etta Mae Wheeler received exactly what she deserved, for, as she often said, 'Folk round here walk their size nines all over a gal if she don't give as good as she gets.' Occasionally, however, she'd found herself the innocent victim of unfortunate circumstances. As a small girl, growing up thin and filthy on the family's North Dakota chicken farm, Etta had once lost two teeth and the tip of her left earlobe in an impromptu shotgun battle between her elder brother and the hired hand. The instigating incident – something vague concerning the unjust consumption of the last pickled onion – was long forgotten in the annals of Wheeler history. The consequences lingered on, forever measured out in half sets of earrings, in prosthetic teeth and haircuts eternally swept to the left side.

An almost century of American arguments had developed in Etta Mae Wheeler a thicker than usual skin, the ability to withstand tremendous shocks – including gunfire, swinging fists and hurtling baseball bats – without so much as flinching. An argument, she'd come to realize, was a dish best served with limited sides. Neither Etta nor Letty (who was for all intents and purposes a slightly less vociferous extension of Etta, having long ago developed verisimilar opinions on all subjects including capital punishment, Mexicans and the best way to cook sweet potatoes) were cruel women. Both ladies had experienced enough home-cooked suffering to recognize their own kind. Eager as they were to see justice rain down on the unsuspecting shoulders of young Malcolm, they held no particular beef with his mother.

Etta cracked open a fresh pack of Red Vines, offered one to Mrs Orange and, when declined, cleared her throat and launched into the lynching. She started slowly, as was her policy on most everything except lovemaking, which at the righteous age of eighty-five needed to be instigated with extreme and excessive speed lest the moment pass into yet another void of senile disappointment.

'Lord Almighty, girl,' she said, allowing the air to whistle slowly through the gap in her dentures, 'them's a mighty fine pair of pins you got there. Kind of legs'll get a girl in trouble, turn the wrong kind of fella's head if you know what I mean?'

(Martha Orange nodded slowly and thought of a hay shed in Oklahoma and her overalls puddling round her ankles as two swords of blind blonde sunlight bounced from the balding pate of her father's foreman. She pictured her own blue eyes reflected enormously in his prescription sunglasses, cut as they were to resemble Elvis's.

'This is it,' she'd thought, even then, just gone fifteen and frantic to be shot of Oklahoma. 'These legs'll walk me right out of this godforsaken state if I play my cards right.'

Thereafter, she'd played her cards fast and loose and found herself twenty-five years old waiting tables in a mid-sized market town just forty-three miles from the place of her birth. By twenty-five her fresh blue eyes had turned sap gray from wishing, her breasts were beginning to slip towards her waist and her shoulders leaned perpetually forward as if angling for any escape route out of Oklahoma. Only her legs remained, peeking from the hem of a heavy-frilled waiting skirt; two towering reminders of her junior high potential. Permanently encased in a pair of sinless white sneakers these very same legs had been ready for running the precise instant that Jimmy Orange walked through the diner door and charmed her sleepy heart with the unforgettable opener, 'A slice of the Key Lime. Heavy on the cream there, honey. Show a bit more leg, and make the pie to go.')

'Don't I know it, ma'am,' Martha Orange whispered turning to face the older lady, 'there are days I wish I'd been born with elephant stumps instead of these legs. They've done me nothing but trouble, the pair of them.'

Etta placed a solitary hand on Martha's bare knee, cupping it like a mashed potato scoop, just below the skirt line. Thus situated she administered a series of slight, reassuring pats. Letty held her distance as she had been long accustomed to, twisting her cotton handkerchief silently in a gesture of unspoken solidarity.

'The Lord himself giveth and then he done turn round and take away,' Etta pronounced, using her spare hand to tug on her missing earlobe. 'You be glad of the hand you got dealt, girl.'

'Yes ma'am, I'm glad of everything I've got. There's people around here much worse than me.'

'You're speaking the truth there, honey child. You've still got your health, not to mention a fine-looking baby, and Malcolm, and a good man to support you.'

At the mention of her husband, Martha Orange colored slightly and twisted her wedding band three complete circuits of her finger. Etta Mae Wheeler – who had in her eighty-six years of toil and sorrow been blessed with more than her fair share of no-good husbands and their no-good kin – noted the problem instantly and steered the conversation well away from Jimmy Orange's doorstep.

'Let me cut to the chase, honey. It's Malcolm we come here to talk to you about,' Etta continued. 'The child's got the whole town in an uproar.'

'Lord Almighty,' muttered Mrs Orange, absentmindedly disentangling Ross from the bowels of his sports bag. 'What has he been doing now?'

'He's dying of the cancer,' interjected Letty, suddenly unable to contain her vindication. 'And I done bought him a swing set for to put a fine-lookin' plaque on after he's passed.'

Martha Orange raised her infant son to her face and moaned deeply into his bald, pink head.

'And Isaac Wilson's been feeding him up on pastrami sandwiches and root beer . . . and Etta's here's got the funeral all sorted . . . and week after next, if the child's still alive, Emmy-Kate Barrett's plannin' on drivin' up to Moscow to get the child a funeral suit,' Letty continued, firing forwards on eighty-odd years of self-contained steam.

'Oh dear,' whispered Mrs Orange, 'there seems to be a bit of confusion here, ladies.'

'A bit of confusion, my white, cotton arse!' Etta stated bluntly. 'The child's been taking us all for a ride.'

'Folks round here ain't too happy.'

'They're fixing for a lynching of sorts.'

'Best thing you Oranges can do is leave town tonight. Hell, leave the county if you can. You're not best welcome in these parts.'

Somewhere, miles above the laundromat roof, Martha Orange

allowed herself to smile, just a little, in moderation. Malcolm, she remembered for the first time in many years, in several states and three time zones, though blessed with his father's arbitrary grasp of the truth, was also the son of an Oklahoma farm girl. His world was wide and unfenced. His imagination could not be contained by an aging Volvo.

Malcolm Orange, she realized with the greatest of delight, was not quite entirely ruined just yet.

Within three hours the Orange Volvo was once more rolling, winding its way slowly towards the Oregon border. Malcolm Orange – lodged in the back seat between Ross, an entire week's worth of strangers' laundry, unreturned, and the ever-present dresser – sat gingerly on his recently pulverized backside and chewed surreptitiously on a two-day-old pastrami and banana sandwich, part of the stash he'd long been saving for the day of his downfall.

Malcolm's father, fuming in the driver's seat, had, upon hearing a greatly downplayed version of the laundromat lynching, whipped the living daylights out of his son with his own tennis racquet. The crisscross pattern would remain embellished upon Malcolm's buttocks all the way into the next week, whereupon it would be almost instantaneously replaced with the fine perforations of his future days.

'Dammit,' Mr Orange muttered, as the Oranges rolled into Portland, Oregon, 'I've just about had it with the lot of you. Eating me out of house and home, fighting, causing consternation every town we stop in, never content with what you got. I've a good mind to leave you all to fend for yourselves. See how you like it on your own.'

Twenty-four hours later, the idea having germinated thickly under his baseball cap, Jimmy Orange slipped out the door of their motel room, filled the Volvo's tank with gas and left town with Mexican intentions.

In a fit of never-before-witnessed generosity, he stopped to pay the week's motel bill in advance.

This, Martha Orange would later recount to her only remaining relative – a Boston-based stepsister – was the nicest thing her husband had ever done for her.

– Chapter Three –

Jesus God

There are worse places to be abandoned than Portland, Oregon: Oklahoma City, for one, Arkansas for another.

Later, when the guilt finally caught up with him, creeping up the neck of his fifteenth Corona, Jimmy Orange turned to the Mexican barman who had lately become his sole confidant and muttered self-righteously, 'There's worse places to leave your woman than Oregon: Oklahoma City for one. I thought long and hard about leaving Martha in Portland. She should thank her lucky stars I didn't dump her in Idaho.'

And the Mexican barman, blessed as he was with little more than game show American, caught only the barest hint of sentiment and slid the white man a sixteenth Corona, transferring the lime slice from one bottle to the next. Jimmy Orange was long past appreciating aesthetics.

'*Sí*, sir,' he nodded, all the time noting the sixteenth drink on the tab, and automatically adding a seventeenth bottle for himself. 'Portland, Oregon . . . Very rainy. Much, much rains.'

In the year nineteen hundred and ninety five the rain in Portland fell mostly in the winter months, occasionally beginning on the first day of fall and stretching willfully into spring. The seasons split the city in half. For eight calendar months, seven on a leap year, the rain rained incessantly, stirring the Willamette to a seething mass of piss and mud and sin. The streets were streams and aspiring rivers, nursing impossible ambitions of Venice, of Oxford and Egyptian canals.

All infants born during the rainy season swam long before they found their standing feet. The older residents grew flippers, plundering thickly through the sweaty streets. They congregated on the buses, emanating the deep stench of damp wool and just-drowned dog. The smell was their own local peculiarity, deeply comforting to the homegrown and offensive to the few tourists who visited Portland during monsoon season. These peculiar locals stalwartly refused the comfort of an umbrella, choosing to wear their hair short and frizzy, long in the summer months. They hid their smiles behind enormous beards, all their fickle joys hibernating through the watery season. They ran on tar, dark coffee and good intentions. Their pant legs decayed slowly, turning moist and mushy; moldering from the ankle up. They relished the growing potential of damp living. Most Portlanders believed themselves capable of sprouting an extra inch every winter and consequently spent the summer months receding into their own skin. They did their sinning in secret, hiding behind the daily shower curtain.

All the city's darker elements – the cross-dressing kids on the late-night bus, the crusty bums beneath the Burnside bridge, the meth labs flaming and strip bars belching elderly men into the early evening fog, the churches crumbling into cocktail bars and under-age punk clubs – all were ritually drenched, baptized beneath a sheath of never-ending sky sulk. Terrible things took place in the rain and blurred, as beneath a sheaf of greaseproof paper, no one seemed to notice.

When the summer months finally freckled their way up the

Willamette, peaking wistfully over the Steel Bridge, it was a future city they found already blooming in anticipation. Every second street boasted a green grass park. The squirrels, recently released from their storm drains, oscillated up and down the telephone wires, humping and fuzzing like greased electricity. The trees shook their spindly fingers – once, twice, for miracle luck – and gave birth to wild, broccoli babies until all the streets ran thick with cloudy greens. The local children sped bare-chested through the downtown sprinklers. The crusty bums emerged from beneath the Burnside Bridge, peeling back their plaid shirts to reveal chests, backs and lumberjack necks already tanned the sweet-talking color of beef jerky. The entire city sprouted wheels and cycled madly up and down Hawthorne Boulevard, running stop lights until all the little last drops of winter dew drained from their heels. No serious Portlander spent a single ounce of summer time indoors.

The best and most blessed thing about Portland, Oregon – twin, spliced city of the Pacific Northwest – was the taste; the taste of youth and hope and bottled water, which lingered long into the summer, eclipsing the thought of October showers and those dank, beery days ahead. And this taste was tart, sharp and toothpaste-clean; the freshly scent of an entire city just laundered.

There were worse places to leave your woman than Portland, Oregon in late summer. It would be many, many years before Malcolm's mother came to appreciate this fact.

On the morning after the grand departure, Martha Orange woke early, turned her underwear inside-out – for it had been almost a week since she'd last had the opportunity to launder – and prepared to face the weekend alone. Whilst Malcolm dozed on the other side of the queen-size, his mother rescued Ross from the trouser drawer where she'd managed to wedge him for the evening and fed him half a lukewarm bottle, briefly heated beneath the bathroom faucet. Once finished, she burped the baby over the crook of her elbow, returned him to his sports bag and set about fixing breakfast for Malcolm and herself. First she split a fresh bottle of Mountain Dew evenly between two Dixie Cups. Then she opened a pack of miniature Oreos, arranged six cookies each on two squares of toilet paper and, for nutritional value, emptied a box of raisins on top of each makeshift plate. Breakfast preparations complete, Martha Orange switched the bedroom's grainy television set to the Mexican channel, pumped up the volume and waited for her son to rouse.

Malcolm Orange, who had been wrenched from yet another dinosaur dream, took almost two minutes to work out where he was. It was a relatively exotic experience to find himself sleeping in an actual bed. To wake as sole occupant of a bed too large by far, both forwards and sideways, was a luxury beyond Malcolm's wildest imagination. For a brief and beautiful moment he imagined himself finally adopted into a normal family. The reality hit him like a midlife crisis.

'Your dad's not coming back, Malcolm,' his mother announced, sliding his toilet paper breakfast across the bedspread. 'Better enjoy these Oreos. They might be the last cookies we can afford for a good long while.'

Worse things had happened in Texas.

Malcolm Orange chose to ignore the disappearance of his long-loathed father, an occurrence he'd been petitioning the Almighty for, for the better part of three years (occasionally turning to Allah when the Jesus God fell silent). Instead of rising to meet his mother's mounting panic, he yawned deeply, lay back on two fat blue pillows and relished the sensation of eating breakfast cookies in a giant bed.

Martha Orange perched her backside on the edge of the bed, naked feet wedged against the radiator, and fed herself Oreos absentmindedly, all the time staring at the Mexican couple arguing on the television screen.

From his vantage point at the stern of their bed, Malcolm Orange scrutinized the back of his mother's head. Five feet removed, with her neck obscured by a generous sheath of auburn hair, his mother could easily pass for any age or race. In the right shirt or the wrong pants she might even be mistaken for a girlish boy. Only her shoulder blades, straining beneath the faded soccer shirt she wore at night, revealed anything concrete about the stranger sharing Malcolm's bed. Martha Orange was struggling to climb out of her own skin.

Malcolm's mother had not always been this strained. He remembered her enormously in his preschool days. During those early years when the road had seemed golden, temporary and paved with twenty-five different Oklahoma exits, Martha Orange had lived loud and footloose from one state to the next. She was young and beautiful and paraded her youth in catalogue dresses and six-inch shorts, slashed from the remnants of old Levis. Malcolm Orange knew his mother was beautiful beyond ordinary mothers. Strange men offered her cigarettes and soda pop on the gas station forecourt. Upon noticing Martha, even from behind, other mothers automatically paused to fix their hair, settling their skirt tails self-consciously. Elderly gentlemen slobbered into their summer vests when she walked past. And in Arkansas, once on a cloudy afternoon, two older boys had arrested Malcolm atop the play structure outside McDonald's, eager to discuss his mother. The larger of the two was wearing a Mötley Crüe T-shirt. Malcolm Orange did not know what Mötley Crüe was but was nonetheless awed.

'Is that your mama, kid?' the second boy asked. (He was larger and wearing a white shirt with the sleeves pulled off at the shoulder. Tiny shards of cotton thread and shirt fabric were beginning to unravel around his upper arms.)

Malcolm Orange nodded. He was barely five years old and not yet wary of teenage boys.

'She's smokin' hot,' the Mötley Crüe boy said, accompanying his observation with a long, low whistle, reminiscent of a just-boiled kettle.

'I'd give her one,' the second boy added and though Malcolm Orange wasn't entirely sure what the boy wanted to give her, he knew it wasn't something worth discussing with his mother and took the opportunity to shove the boy, elbow first, off the play structure. The resulting injury and subsequent howling forced the Oranges to make yet another of their infamous speedy getaways. Five-year-old Malcolm was thrust violently into the backseat of the Volvo, landing unceremoniously in his grandmother's lap with both feet wedged under his Step Nana's enormous thighs. He had barely enough time to turn himself right side up before the interrogation began.

'What the hell was that about Malcolm?' his father yelled, face fuming in the rearview mirror.

'You can't go pushing older kids around, Malcolm!' his mother continued. 'You'll get your ass kicked if you do.'

'They said mean things,' whispered Malcolm.

'You've got to rise above it, Malcolm,' said his father, 'you can't go punching every no-good Johnny who calls you names.'

'What sort of mean things?' his mother asked, already beginning to display a righteous tendency towards ignoring her husband.

'Don't want to say . . .' replied Malcolm, remaining tight-lipped in the backseat.

'Malcolm, you can tell me. I'm your mama, you can tell me anything.'

'I can't tell you this, mama. You'll just get mad with me.'

'We're already mad with you, Malcolm. Tell us now,' his father fumed, 'or so help me, I will leave you at the next Greyhound station.'

And, because he could not bring himself to hurt his mother, who was beautiful in his eyes, like a Christmas tree angel, or Jesus' own mama, Malcolm decided to crucify his father instead, 'They said you were ugly Papa, like a gorilla, and that you smelled like fried onions.' (Malcolm Orange, not yet officially schooled, awarded himself two proud points for ingenuity. Both these insults were for the most part true, though the onion thing was seasonal and seemed markedly worse during summer months.)

In the rearview mirror, with his sunglasses shoved, *Miami Vice* style, high on his forehead, Malcolm's father turned the color of pickled beetroot and thumped the inside section of his steering wheel so it emitted a tiny, strangled parp.

'Punk ass kids!' he yelled. 'I'm going to turn this car around and teach them a thing or two about respect.'

'Rise above it, Jimmy,' his wife replied, sharp as polished piss. She turned to stare out the passenger window. In the wing mirror Malcolm could see a bent back reflection of his mother's naked face. She was grinning wildly with one hand covering her jaw. Aged just five years old, with only five states to compare, Malcolm Orange suddenly realized that his was the most beautiful and best mother in the whole of the United States.

As the years rolled the Oranges all across America with an ever-depleting cargo of elderly relatives, Malcolm began to better understand the fragile wonder of the woman who had given birth to him in the dugout of a Detroit baseball field. Her highs were loud and cloudless, her lows parchment thin and each year more frequent than the last. As he progressed from childhood towards the possibility of something equating to puberty Malcolm Orange kept a tally of his mother's ups and downs. These findings were recorded, collated and eventually analyzed in the same dime store notepad which held his 'Lamp Posts of America' and 'Miles between Dairy Queens' research projects; two important pieces of scientific investigative research he one day hoped to present to the President of the United States.

Observing his mother now on this, the first morning of her enforced widowhood, Malcolm Orange struggled to recall a single skyscraper day in the last eighteen months of road raging. (He made a mental note to check his research notes later when his mother wasn't in the room.) Terrified that he might, for the first time in two years, cry without the believable excuse of chicken pox or funerals, Malcolm dug his heels further into the folded sheets and forced his head to remember the way his mother had once been, many years ago when she was oftentimes hilarious and ill-inclined to daytime television.

He remembered her twirling down the aisles of Walmart dancing arm in arm with her own elderly – but not yet crazy – mother whilst the overhead speakers pumped Kenny Rogers into the shampoo section. He remembered her rhinestone heels, stolen from the shoe department of the Goodwill; left foot stuffed down the back of his pushchair, right foot concealed inside his sweater vest. Malcolm, who was young enough to escape jail and old enough to know better, had held his tongue, relishing the thrill of illegal, complicit adventuring. He remembered her ordering ice cream for breakfast on at least fifteen separate occasions, most often going for pistachio over any of the more obvious flavors.

Malcolm Orange remembered her singing; holy smokes, there had also been fabulous singing.

Malcolm's mother kept a shoebox of country and western cassettes under the Volvo's passenger seat, insisting upon their ongoing presence, even as perfectly good toaster ovens and umbrellas fell victim to the packing whims of Jimmy Orange. With the windows fully recoiled she liked to pass the miles singing lustily along with Dolly Parton and Tammy Wynette while the mid-western winds whipped her hair into a wild nest of earthy tendrils. Approaching this diner or that interstate motel she'd quit her singing to roll the windows up and, with a single, fluid motion, well-rehearsed, whisk her hair north, south, east and west, securing the nestled mountain neatly with an old shoelace. Seated directly behind his mother, Malcolm Orange soon learnt to draw breath and close his eyes when the hairspray emerged from the glove compartment, ready to coat his mother's hair – and, by proxy, the occupants of the Volvo's cramped backseat – in a sticky layer of breath-quenching hair glue.

Finally, there was the knitting; yards and yards of blue and white striped scarf which filled the front seat of the Volvo and threatened to spill into the backseat, strangling the occupants in a mile or more of wool mix yarn. This same scarf had been knitting for longer than Malcolm had existed and ran like a constant, stripy seam through all his childhood memories. Having reached saturation point in the year nineteen hundred and eighty eight, Martha Orange had simply begun to unravel the earliest sections of the scarf and proceeded to knit on, using the raveled thread; a stroke of knitting genius which had eventually formed a colossal, nautical-themed Möbius strip.

Malcolm was not to know the origin of this never-ending scarf but he soon became familiar with the aura of deep, tantric peace which came over his mother each time she picked up her needles. Watching her fingers flying from the backseat, Malcolm thought of the ancient Mexican ladies who populated the doorways of most every city he'd ever lived in, knotty fingers feeding rosary beads left to right in an endless parody of activity.

(Martha Orange's knitting was conceived in youthful hope and yet had, over the years, slowly pickled to become a form of quiet, costless therapy; an adult attempt at thumb sucking. The scarf had begun on the first morning of Martha Orange's honeymoon. Having loved her long into the night in a fashion rarely seen or sampled in rural Oklahoma, having offered up his grandma's antique ring for a wedding band, and ponyed up for a proper hotel – one of the cheaper rooms in one of the cheaper hotels advertised on the Vegas strip – Jimmy Orange had been slowly rising in the estimation of the freshly-baked Mrs Orange.

Rolling over to meet his eye, she'd smiled silently, bit her lip to avoid inhaling last night's whiskey breath and audibly wondered what the future might hold for the Oranges.

'Baby,' he'd whispered, as he ran his fingers up and down her perfect legs, rubbing the stench of stale sex and motor oil deep into her shins, 'one year from now I'll have you knocked up and rocking in a little cabin somewhere in Alaska, just you and me and a hound dog. I'll keep you fat and naked and you can knit me scarves and sweaters to keep the frostbite out.'

Thereafter, Malcolm's mother had crept out of bed, grinning ear to ear with the bed sheets wrapped modestly round her chest and silently thanked the Lord for a man who did not smell like manure, who was more than moderately handsome and, most importantly, going places fast. She'd showered quickly with the bathroom door open, still scared her new husband might slip off without her and, whilst Malcolm's father completed his bathroom ablutions, cast off and commenced the scarf which would keep her fingers in constant anticipation of Alaska for the next thirteen years.)

Malcolm Orange loved his mother. She was beautiful to him like a TV chef or a first grade teacher, but he no longer knew what to say to her. She was unraveling before his eyes, a forty-foot scarf left one decade too long in the damp.

'Now your dad's gone,' she muttered, raising her voice in competition with the angry Hispanic sentiments now flooding the bedroom, 'I should get some kind of skill. I'm only good for cooking and cleaning. Maybe I could learn computers or Spanish. A bit of Spanish would come in handy round here. There's Mexicans everywhere.'

'Sure, mama,' Malcolm Orange answered. 'Learn Spanish. Maybe you can get a job in Taco Bell.'

'You don't need Spanish in Taco Bell, Malcolm. They have those little pictures on cards to point at when you order.'

'We could move to Mexico if you learned Spanish, mama.'

Preoccupied with the notion of learning a second language, Martha Orange ignored her eldest son, pumped up the volume on the TV set and administered her first of many, many thousands of impromptu kisses to the crummy remote which lived on the nightstand.

Portland, Oregon was wasted on Martha Orange. It would take her almost three days to gather enough energy to leave the motel room. During the interim she would survive on gas station candy and soda, fetched by Malcolm three times daily from the Texaco across the road. Eventually the motel owner – a slack-faced Asian man in an Adidas tracksuit – appeared at their door, cordless telephone in hand, and threatened to call the cops if they did not check out immediately. The remaining Oranges packed their belongings, Ross included, into two sports bags and a garbage sack, left the room ankle deep in candy wrappers and stumbled, bleary-eyed, into the city which was to become their home.

(Martha Orange, finally convinced that Alaska would never come to pass, abandoned her scarf beneath the queen-size bed. It hibernated there for several months, unnoticed by a series of incompetent housekeepers until the autumn damp caused its well-fluffed fibers to swell further, forcing the lower left side of the bed two inches off the carpet. Surrendering her scarf, Martha Orange would later come to realize, had left her sadder and somehow more perturbed than the loss of a full-grown husband.)

Sitting on the curb of the motel's parking lot, Malcolm and his mother considered their options.

'You could do waitressing again, mama,' Malcolm suggested.

'What would I do with Ross?' she replied.

'I could mind him.'

'Don't be ridiculous, Malcolm. You're only eleven. You're supposed to be in school.'

Malcolm Orange held his tongue. This, he realized, was not the moment to defend his twelfth birthday or point out that most of Ross's practical care already fell at his feet.

'We could go to a church and ask God for help. Maybe he'd let us sleep there for a while.'

Malcolm's mother said nothing. She crossed her legs at the ankle and stared plaintively upwards. Malcolm assumed her preoccupied with the act of fervent prayer.

'I could sell lemonade,' he continued. 'Though I don't think we have a jug for making it in . . . you could do laundry for rich folks . . . we could live in a tent at least 'til the rain starts . . . you could take your clothes off for money. I saw it on TV. It pays really well.'

Malcolm Orange had spent most of his formative years moving forwards at a rate of some sixty-five miles per hour and with the disappearance of his father had been suddenly and unceremoniously thrust into the possibility of a permanent zip code. The hope of normal American living filled him with a terrible, excruciating excitement, pinching, as excitement often did, at the neck of his bladder. Malcolm could not see anything beyond a semi-permanent silver lining to all the Oranges' troubles. He bounced around on the curb, itching like a kid caught short, and waited for his mother to join in with his enthusiasm.

Conversely, Portland, Oregon was wasted on Martha Orange for she could not see past the Volvo-shaped hole in the parking lot. She drew both knees to her chin, clasping her hands across her shins like a belt buckle, and began to rock slowly, coaxing the sadness out of her fingernails. A single tear peaked out of her left eye and rolled down her cheek, losing momentum and disappearing into the skin around her nose. She wiped her face with the back of her hand and felt fifty-eight years old at least.

'I'll learn Spanish,' she said, 'I'll learn Spanish. There's a lot you can do with Spanish.'

'And in the meantime what will we do for food?' Malcolm asked, genuinely concerned by the tremulous hunger which was already beginning to gnaw at the inside of his lungs. 'We need to make enough money for eating. It shouldn't be too hard to find a job of some sorts. You've got a lot of options, mama. You could do the laundry thing again, though we didn't make a lot off that in Idaho, or take your clothes off for strangers, or ask God to help us out.'

And because she had no money for tents and knew in her darkest heart that no one in Portland, Oregon would pay to see a thirty-seven-year-old stripper with deep-veined nursing breasts,

Martha Orange reluctantly agreed to ask God for help.

It was a significant stretch, for neither Malcolm Orange nor his mother entirely believed in a benevolent God.

Martha Orange had been brought up Presbyterian with a new church hat and frock twice yearly. Even after almost fifteen years of practiced religiosity she had never admitted, even to herself, that it was the promise of a new dress, combined with the ominous threat of her father's belt buckle, which kept her regularly attending the meeting house long past her thirteenth birthday. God himself seemed many million miles beyond Oklahoma, hovering on the edge of some ancient nursery rhyme, mythical, bearded and seasonal as Santa Claus

Martha Orange was not a believer in the strictest sense of belief.

Her own father had died of the cancer six weeks before her fifteenth birthday, shriveling slowly into a small, raisin-skinned man who took his liquids from a baby bottle and spent two hours straining to expel his daily shit. Martha, as the oldest child, had been contracted to lead the nightly prayer shift, reading aloud from the ancient leather-bound King James and endlessly repeating the Lord's Prayer (for it was the only prayer she felt confident to deliver convincingly). During this evening ritual a thin, peaceful veil habitually descended over her father's face. And though Martha wrestled against the peace that passes all understanding, cherry-picking passages of bloody wrath and Revelation and reading them with mounting anger over his wasted frame, her father smiled on, beaming beatifically at the ceiling fan.

'The Lord giveth,' he would whisper as each nightly reading came to a close, 'and the Lord taketh away. Blessed be the name of the Lord.' Though the drugs were by this stage turning his mind to mush, he'd still sounded believably contrite.

Young Martha, deep-filled with righteous anger, could not bear his faith. It slid around her like a constricting hunger, ridiculous and yet perversely insatiable. Eventually, when the evening drove her to breaking point she'd quit her father's bedside and carry her consternation to the back barn where she smoked contraband packs of Lucky Strikes and raged against the Almighty for his bloody-minded ability to favor the fine art of taking away.

God, she'd finally concluded at fifteen years old, flat on her back beneath her father's freshly-promoted foreman, was for halfwits and folks who couldn't sort themselves out.

By the age of ten, with a dozen or more funerals under his belt, Malcolm Orange was all but ready to agree with his mother. If God was good and God was love Malcolm could not help but wonder why he seemed to throw himself with such great gusto into so many acts of willful destruction and suffering; floods and famines and plagues and elderly grandparents whisked into the next world halfway through *Ghostbusters*. Furthermore, the Almighty, until very recently, had not seen fit to answer a single one of Malcolm's prayers.

Malcolm Orange knew exactly how many prayers God had yet to answer. He was keeping a list.

Over the course of the last decade Malcolm Orange had daily prayed a series of humble, selfless prayers, which in his small opinion, were absolutely achievable by a God who claimed (with little significant evidence) to have created the entire universe in less than a week, to have walked barefoot on the sea and, on one notable occasion, brought himself back from the dead, bursting from an underground tomb in a move ripped right out of an X-Men strip. On paper, God was someone worth believing in. In reality he had yet to deliver on the dogs, the bunk beds, the death rays or kick-ass siblings Malcolm Orange had asked for over the last ten years. Malcolm Orange felt entirely justified in distrusting God, for God had purposefully stricken him with chicken pox on three separate occasions, bounced him round America like a five-foot ping pong ball and added insult to injury with the arrival of the mild-mannered Ross, who in Malcolm's opinion was simply another example of the Almighty taking the piss from on high.

However, in light of his father's untimely exit, Malcolm Orange was now prepared to give God a second chance, considering all those smaller unanswered demands a mere preamble of faith to this, the ultimate answer to prayer.

'I think we should ask God for help, mama,' Malcolm said. 'I have a feeling he'll listen this time.'

'OK,' his mother replied. She sounded like a birthday balloon deflating.

'Which God should we ask?'

'Our God, Malcolm. You get born with one God and you're kind of stuck with that one . . . unless you marry someone foreign. Then you're allowed to change your God for a different one. That's the way religion works.'

'So, you didn't get to change Gods when you married Papa?'

'Well,' she said, smiling sadly, 'that's a fine question to be asking, sweetheart. I didn't get a different God from your dad. I ended up giving up the only God I got. Your daddy wasn't a big one for religion.'

'No ma'am, Papa didn't believe in any God at all,' Malcolm replied, nodding fervently. 'Sure, once I asked him for a Bible and he gave me a book of *Charlie and the Chocolate Factory* instead and said there was more sense in going to the movies than reading the G-D Bible. And I never even bothered reading *Charlie and the Chocolate Factory* because I didn't want to make God mad, but I didn't want to make Papa mad either, so I pretended real good that I was reading it for miles and miles in the backseat of the car.'

Malcolm Orange's mother laughed, leaning back on the curb to let the noise out. Malcolm laughed too. He wasn't sure why they were laughing but it made a welcome change from melancholy Spanish.

'Mama,' he asked cautiously, when he was almost sure the laughter had run its course. 'Is it the Jesus God that belongs to us?'

'Yes,' she said, scuffing his sneaker affectionately with the toe of her sandal, 'ours is the Jesus God.'

'Good,' replied Malcolm, 'he's the one who made the world so we should be alright.'

After which the remaining Oranges shared a Snickers bar, gathered their resolve and wandered across 82nd street into the residential part of town. They'd barely gone five blocks before they stumbled across their first church.

'Evangel Baptist Church,' Malcolm read aloud from the streetside sign. 'Is this the kind of church where our God lives, mama?'

'Baptist,' murmured his mother, rolling the words round the inside of her mouth like a brave new taste, as yet undecided. 'Yeah, Malcolm, I think Baptist will be just fine. There were good Baptist folks at the end of our road in Oklahoma. The day after he passed they brought us a whole suckling pig for my pa's funeral. I think Baptist might be just the ticket today.'

They climbed the four steps to the church door. A homeless person of indeterminate gender was dozing noisily under the porch, the greater part of his or her body covered by a mossy green tarp. One arm emerged from beneath the tarpaulin's edge, sporting, at the furthermost end, a salami pink hand hooked round a shopping cart. Malcolm's mother stepped carefully over the homeless person, motioning with a finger for Malcolm to be quiet. She tried the church door and upon finding it open stepped inside, deposited her possessions on the foyer floor and assisted her son as he swung himself clumsily over the homeless doorstop.

Malcolm Orange had never before been inside a proper church. All Orange funerals had, for financial reasons, been conducted in funeral crematoriums and Dairy Queen parking lots. He hesitated on the threshold of the sanctuary, adjusted his tube socks and considered the possibility of what might lie behind the enormous mahogany doors.

The better part of Malcolm Orange trilled with a curious longing to see where the Jesus God lived. However, he was also reasonably terrified, having read enough comic books to acknowledge the possibility of winged beings: angels, saints and ill-imagined demons hanging from the interior roof beams. Furthermore, Malcolm Orange remained convinced that God – who knew everything, even invisible nighttime indiscretions – was still pissed about Malcolm's bigger sins: the naked lady programs and cancer lies, the tail ends of umpteen cigarettes smoked to the nub and the many, many booger balls, surreptitiously rolled and wedged down the inside of the Volvo's seatbelt holders. Malcolm's bowels began to churn in the customary manner. In such circumstances a bout of nerve-induced diarrhea seemed all but inevitable.

All things considered, Malcolm Orange thought it best to go second. If someone was to be struck down upon entry, he preferred it not to be him.

With one hand on the small of his mother's back he wedged the sanctuary doors open and ushered her inside. She shuffled forward and disappeared into deep, all-encompassing darkness. The doors closed behind her backside with a moist, snowy whoosh. Malcolm Orange stood on his heels, rocking forwards and slowly backwards in time to his own breath. He felt eleven years old – closer to ten than twelve – and terribly far from home. Thirty seconds later, realizing that his pilgrim mother had left him standing solo in the church's darkly lit foyer, he gathered his guts and slipped into the darkness behind her.

(Whilst Malcolm Orange and his mother investigated the inner sanctum of Evangel Baptist, Ross, who even for a young infant, prematurely born, seemed above-averagely fond of sleeping, dozed lazily in his sports bag under the welcome table. Ten minutes into the escapade he would be discovered by an elderly cleaning lady who, in an early morning attempt to make the 7:43 bus, had rushed out of her house at 7:38, leaving her seeing glasses marooned on the nightstand. Ill-equipped to differentiate between babies and sports clothes, she would unsuspectingly throw Ross into the lost property cupboard, the final straw in a morning of visual faux pas which had included mixing the pew Bibles with the hymnbooks, polishing the pulpit with toilet cleaner, and, perhaps most worryingly, mistaking the pastor's wife for the enormous lady who came to do the flowers on Friday afternoons.

'You just don't think to check for babies,' she would later confess, mortified. 'You just assume a sports bag's gonna be full of gym clothes or sneakers, not babies.'

'Not to worry,' Mrs Orange would reply, fishing her youngest son out of the lost property cupboard where he had become entangled in a pair of long-abandoned swim goggles, 'there's not a day goes by when I don't forget about Ross.'

'He's a very forgettable baby,' Malcolm would automatically

add, receiving a bitter clip around the ears for his impertinence.)

Inside the sanctuary the blackout blinds had been drawn as they most often were on weekdays; a church-wide policy designed to preserve the royal blue carpet from the sort of daily fading which had sent the last two royal blue carpets to their early graves. Mrs Orange had progressed a mere two feet up the aisle and, not yet adjusted to the darkness, Malcolm found himself banging into her back.

In the pitch black with the Jesus God watching, Malcolm Orange felt incredibly protective of his mother. He slipped his arms round her waist and stood on his uppermost tiptoes, attempting to rest his chin reassuringly on her shoulder. Through her shirt he could feel the outline of her shoulder bones, curving like a pair of polished doorknobs atop each arm. They were moving up and down slowly, independent of her elbows. Without looking he could tell she was crying.

'Mama,' he asked, whispering into her left ear, though he knew it was pointless to try and conceal even the slightest secret from God, 'shall I talk to him for both of us?'

'Yes,' she replied and the sound of tears was unmistakable, a choked catch at the back of her throat, clasping like the moment before a truly satisfying sniff.

'Should we kneel?'

'It's dark in here. I don't think it really matters.'

'God sees everything, mama, even things that happen underground. He has special eyes for seeing everything.'

So they kneeled, bare, naked knees burrowing into the royal blue carpet. Twenty seconds into the prayer Malcolm's thighs began to ache from the pressure. Thirty seconds in his shins followed suit, throbbing from underuse. (Reliable though it had been, the Volvo had offered little opportunity for exercise;

consequently all the Oranges – Ross excepted – were hideously unfit and prone to breathless huffing at the merest hint of an incline.) To his left Martha Orange was similarly preoccupied with the muscle burn creeping up and down the back of her perfectly tanned thighs.

'Make it quick, Malcolm,' she whispered, adjusting her weight from one leg to another.

Malcolm was a mere two lines into the Lord's Prayer, feeling the need to begin with something familiar. He was taking his time, relishing a captive audience and pronouncing each word with showy, theatrical intent.

'Our Father,' he proclaimed, rolling his eyes towards the ceiling, 'Who ART in Heaven. Hallowed be THY name . . . and also Jesus be THY name,' he quickly added to avoid confusion with other, lesser-known Gods who might be listening in on their conversation.

'Malcolm!' his mother hissed, poking him viciously in the rib cage, 'get to the important bit.'

Exasperated by his own mother, who did not seem to understand the etiquette associated with prayer, Malcolm Orange prematurely abandoned the Lord's Prayer, raised his hands like a deep south Revivalist and addressed God in the very voice his father usually reserved for parking attendants and persnickety authorities of all ilk and persuasion.

('If you want something done, Malcolm,' Jimmy Orange had explained on several occasions, 'speak up like a man. Shout if you can and if you got yourself a gun, it never hurts to let folks know. Folks won't give you nothing if you go round talking like a pussy. Find yourself a man voice and get used to it.'

Thereafter, Malcolm had been keen to find his own man voice

and had eventually trained himself to speak in a fashion which he felt most keenly resembled Wolverine, the most masculine man he had yet to discover. He practiced his man voice on fence posts across America and, when his confidence had finally peaked, made a failed attempt at intimidating the Dairy Queen checkout girl into giving him a free ice cream.

'Dammit, woman, get your fat ass over here and take my order,' he'd barked over the countertop. 'Two small fries, a chicken strips basket, three Diet Cokes and throw in a G-D Blizzard for free. I been freezin' my butt off out here for the last two hours, waitin' for you to get your act together.'

Satisfied by his delivery, Malcolm Orange had risen up on tiptoes to clock the woman's reaction. Two feet from his nose, safely ensconced behind a large slab of security glass, a well-built African American lady was giving him the kind of look oft-delivered by his mother, mere seconds before a good slapping.

'Young man,' she'd said, depressing the intercom button so the four people in the line behind Malcolm could also hear her comeback, 'you better thank the good Lord that I ain't your mama. I'd tan your hide for that speech if you were one of mine.'

Not to be outdone, Malcolm Orange had held his ground and continued in his best man voice, 'Woman, you don't want to be messing with me. My papa's got a gun in the car and he probably won't let me use it myself but I might ask him to shoot you for me.'

Thereafter, the possibility of a Butterfinger Blizzard, even at full retail price, slid swiftly out of the picture and Malcolm Orange had found himself making a desperate run for the Volvo's backseat, anxious to avoid the imminent arrival of the cops.

'Sorry Papa,' he'd muttered from the safety of the backseat, 'they're all out of chicken strips, soda and fries. Worst Dairy

Queen I've ever been to. We'll have to go somewhere else I guess. We should probably go pretty quick.'

During the short drive from Dairy Queen to Burger King, Malcolm Orange had peered out the Volvo's back window, scanning the road for cop cars and surreptitiously practicing his man voice.

'What in blue hell are you doing with your voice, Malcolm?' his father had asked. 'You sound like Pee-wee Herman.'

Having ascertained that this mumbled squeak was Malcolm's attempt at a man voice, the adults in the car had mocked him at intervals for the next two days, performing progressively hysterical Malcolm impressions every time the car fell silent.

Malcolm Orange refused to be dissuaded. He ignored their mockery and placed his man voice on the back burner, secretly hoping the opportunity for intimidation might arise sooner rather than later.)

'Hello God,' Malcolm Orange yelled, raising his voice against the possibility that God might be otherwise occupied with some other urgent conversation. 'Hallowed be thy name. We need a place to stay and my mom needs a job so we can eat. Can we stay here in your house, please?'

'You can't stay here, son,' God replied. He sounded an awful lot more Southern than Malcolm Orange had expected.

'God Almighty,' whispered Mrs Orange, immediately realizing her own profanity and clamping a muffled hand over her mouth. 'I wasn't expecting an actual answer.'

Malcolm, on the other hand, had secretly suspected that today might be the very day on which God redeemed himself and, thus convinced, proceeded boldly.

'Bullshit,' he said. 'You've got more than enough room here for the three of us. Why can't we stay just for a couple of nights?'

'No swearing in the house of the Lord,' God replied. He seemed to be moving closer in the dark.

'Sorry,' said Malcolm Orange.

'Sorry,' said Martha Orange.

'No harm done,' said God. 'Seems y'all are in a bit of a pickle. Hard times makes good folks forget their manners. Listen, I'll just put the lights on and maybe we can wander over to Dunkin' Donuts and see what I can do to help you out.'

'Awesome,' said Malcolm Orange, who had already in his secret heart forgiven God for the chicken pox and the lack of death rays and was beginning to consider the possibility of forgetting the entire Ross mix-up.

'Cover your eyes, Malcolm,' shouted his mother, who had enough Old Testament knowledge to know that looking God in the eye, be it accidental or self-initiated over a large cappuccino, never ended well.

And with a wry little disclaimer of 'Let there be light', God flicked the light switch and flooded the sanctuary with a raw, halogen glow.

God was an African American man – five foot eight at a generous estimate – dressed head to toe in a sinless white suit.

For the first time in over three years, Malcolm Orange was speechless. Real life God, he suddenly realized, was just as disappointing as all the real life people he claimed to have magicked into existence.

Martha Orange, raised on a diet of conservatively illustrated Ladybird books, knew full well that God was old and olive-colored and particularly well-bearded and as the man standing in front of her was none of the above, nor even trying, was reasonably relieved to discover the Oranges had not accidentally rolled into the unveiled presence of the Almighty.

'You're not God, are you?' she asked somewhat hesitantly. It was not the kind of question she was accustomed to asking strangers.

'Goodness, no. Never claimed to be,' the man replied, laughing hard and loose like a plate of barely set Jell-O. 'I'm just Steve.'

'Steve who?' asked Malcolm who always preferred full and formal names over half-assed first names.

'Steve Marten,' Steve replied.

'Like the actor?' asked Mrs Orange.

'Bingo ma'am. But mine's spelt with an e instead of an i.'

'Sounds the same to me,' muttered Malcolm, who'd never heard of Steve Martin, either with or without an i. 'What were you doing hanging out in the dark pretending to be God?'

Steve Marten let out another belly laugh and, bending his skinny legs, lowered himself down to Malcolm's level, a move which Malcolm Orange never ceased to find infinitely patronizing. 'I never claimed to be God, young sir. I was just taking a nap on the front pew after I got the hall floors polished.'

'So, if you're not God and you're just Steve Marten, you won't be able to help us much will you?'

'Depends on what you're looking for in the way of help. The offer of a coffee still stands. There's a Dunkin' Donuts three blocks from here. I'd be more than happy to buy you good folks a snack, looks like you could both do with a bit of sustenance.'

'And what about after that?' Malcolm Orange asked, dredging the pit of his swagger for the last remnants of a man voice. 'Seems to me we're still screwed whether you buy us a coffee or not.'

'Malcolm!' his mother exclaimed, stretching to deliver a swift, admonishing clip to her son's right ear. 'Don't be so rude. Mr

Marten is terribly kind to offer us a coffee. Apologize now before I skin you alive.'

Malcolm Orange mumbled a half-hearted apology while Steve Marten belly laughed his way out of the sanctuary and all the way down to Dunkin' Donuts, where he bought them drinks and pastries and offered to put a good word in at the Baptist Retirement Village on the edge of town.

'My youngest sister's been working there for three years now,' Steve Marten explained over his caramel macchiato, milk foam clinging to his upper lip. 'It's not so bad, if you don't mind wiping old folks' butts and smelling like porridge. They're always looking for new starts. I'll get our Marge to put in a good word for you.'

And true to his word, for Steve Marten was a born-again Christian and struggled to lie, even on his tax returns, Malcolm's mother found herself starting in the retirement community just two days later. Less than a week thereafter, the Oranges were offered an empty retirement chalet in return for an extra night shift and a thirty percent cut of Mrs Orange's pay packet. Malcolm Orange duly located his tennis racquet, packed his extra pants into a carrier bag and moved into his first permanent home of the last five years.

'Mama,' Malcolm Orange said, as they ate their first meal at the new kitchen table; a meager mishmash of Kentucky Fried Chicken and ramen noodles, picked straight from the packets, 'I think God kind of did help us out, don't you?'

'Definitely,' agreed his mother, though she knew it had all been the doing of Steve Marten, the floor polisher, who had for his excessive Christian charity demanded, and been duly awarded, fifteen sweaty minutes in the broom cupboard, alone with Martha Orange.

'The Lord works in mysterious ways, his wonders to perform,' she mumbled through a mouthful of fried chicken, and could not help but wonder when she'd first begun to sound exactly like her own, long-gone father.

– Chapter Four –

Soren James Blue

On the first full morning of his disappearance, Malcolm Orange woke to the sound of labored lovemaking creeping through his open window. During the night his curtains – whipped senseless by the chalet's overzealous air conditioning – had parted company, permitting all manner of unwanted sounds and sights to enter his bedroom.

Having recently emerged from his fifth dinosaur dream of the week, Malcolm was too exhausted to contemplate closing the window himself, so he shoved last night's Kleenex wad further into his head and crawled back beneath the blankets. Thus cocooned, he hoped to slip back into sleep, recommencing the dream exactly where he'd left off. However, the noises persisted, tunneling their way through four inches of duvet, X-Men-themed. After several minutes of feigned indifference Malcolm poked his head out to glance at the wall clock; a gaudy Coca-Cola number purchased with tokens from Texacos all across America. Un-muffled, the noises were ten times louder and undeniably sexual. Somewhere on the cul-de-sac, someone was having themselves a really great time, and it hadn't even turned seven yet.

Malcolm Orange was not the sort of child driven by sexual curiosity. He knew how babies got born, both accidentally and on purpose and, due in part to his beauty parlor education, was more than familiar with all the insertions and extractions involved in the process. Having spent most of his formative years dozing on the dirty floors of midwestern motels, he was also preternaturally well-accustomed to the odd noises people made in bed together. Malcolm had little interest in what was going on under his nose, but it irked him slightly to be incapable of putting a name to the grunts.

Malcolm, still overly enamored with the acquisition of a permanent neighborhood, prided himself on knowing everyone and everything that happened on his cul-de-sac. After six short weeks in the Baptist Retirement Village, he could now differentiate between each of the individual noises which kept the community ticking arthritically towards its next meal.

In the distance he could hear the faint whirr of Miss Pamela Richardson's electric wheelchair making its umpteenth circuit of the block. He pictured her crisscrossing the streets in a tartan picnic blanket, gunning her Zippy Wheel 2000 as she attempted to outrun the Grim Reaper. Beneath Malcolm's window the morning sprinklers were already sizzling, drowning his mother's long-parched lawn in a fine aquatic mist. Bill and Irene, in the second chalet down, were practicing their daily hymns, grating painfully on a substandard duet of 'The Old Rugged Cross'. Irene had forgotten all but the hymn's refrain and was substituting lyrics from the *Lion King* soundtrack in a futile attempt to keep up with her husband, who, at five years her junior, was now three times sharper in the head. Their early morning sing-songs had become a regular feature since the Director announced his music ban. The parking lot gravel crunched and grumbled as the staff exited and entered the Center; two dozen beginning and two dozen ending their daily dose of butt wiping and pill counting.

Four blocks over, the inevitable sirens – police, ambulance and the occasional fire truck – simmered up and down 82nd, forming a shrill city soundtrack as they shuffled homeless men and prostitutes from one street corner to another in an endless parody of human chess.

The Baptist Retirement Village ran like a cheap opera with every sound, every conversation and elderly cough a carefully choreographed part of the whole. Malcolm Orange knew each of these sounds by ear. He recorded his findings neatly in a brand-new dime store notebook, eventually hoping to determine patterns, progressions and mysterious anomalies peppering this, the most comprehensive research project of his short career.

The Baptist Retirement Village was comprised of two distinct sections. The Oranges lived on the cul-de-sac, a sweeping, circular street of some twenty-odd chalets each housing an elderly person, sometimes single, oftentimes doubled up for marital or budgetary reasons. Mrs Orange, having presented her family as a particularly needy case before the Baptist council who ran the Village, had been given the keys to Chalet 13; a two bedroom matchbox situated at the snake head of the cul-de-sac.

The Oranges were Chalet 13's fourteenth set of occupants.

All but two of the previous occupants had since passed away. Occupant number eleven had been lingering stoically, exploiting the dull end of a diabetic coma for the past eight years, whilst occupant number three, having used an orthopedic cushion to smother occupant number four in her sleep, had last been seen hailing an airport taxi outside the local Rite Aid.

One month previously Chalet 13 had been occupied by Denise DeWitt; a buxom blonde lady of eighty-five who grew tomato plants in the spare room. The metallic scent of tomatoes would linger in Malcolm Orange's bedroom for the next two years, infusing all his underwear with the faintest hint of greenhouse gases. Every so often, in the darker corners of the closet, he would stumble upon a particularly wily tomato shoot attempting to sprout, uninvited, from the shag pile carpet. Unaware of Chalet 13's previous occupants, the tomato plants both fascinated and perplexed Malcolm Orange. They were one of the many conundrums he'd come to associate with retirement living.

Denise DeWitt had been something of a legend on the cul-de-sac. Having worked her way through four husbands and a subsequent seven live-in lovers she had finally, in the fall of her eighty-fourth year, pronounced herself done with men.

'Damn men,' she'd confessed to the Meals on Wheels lady, 'are like damn buses . . . when you're my age, you get a back ache every time you ride one.'

Within days she'd swapped her spandex pantsuits for a series of figure-defying smocks and taken to wearing a sloppy knit cap to conceal her purple-blue hair which was beginning to dreadlock. Shortly thereafter she'd unceremoniously evicted the forty-five-year-old Nigerian man who'd been squatting in her spare room for the past six weeks. (It had been common cul-de-sac knowledge that Denise DeWitt – who had on several occasions returned from the Rite Aid on 82nd with both her diabetes medication and a virile-looking homeless man – had every intention of seducing her lodger just as soon as the opportunity arose.) With no excuse for flirtation, no shirts to iron or sandwiches to fix, Denise DeWitt soon found her days dragging tediously towards the weekend.

'I'm too old to get laid now,' she'd announced at the weekly potluck supper. 'Is there an alternative to sitting on my ass waiting to clock out?'

After she'd pronounced the normal distractions – bingo, daytime television and membership of Bill and Irene's recently formed People's Committee for Remembering Songs – substandard uses of her time, Denise DeWitt had landed upon gardening, specifically the cultivation and manipulation of tomato plants.

'I'll grow them in my spare room,' she'd explained, 'that way there won't be room for a man, should I ever get tempted.'

Thereafter, the residents of the cul-de-sac had found themselves well-supplied with tomato chutneys and pickles, soups and fresh salsa for all their chip-dipping needs. Denise DeWitt had found in her tomato plants the kind of stalwart stickability she'd been missing in every one of her eleven lovers. Her spare room ran thick with vines and creepers. Her fingers turned green and calloused almost overnight. Her dreadlocks, daily drenched in a fine mist of organic plant food, sprouted from her hat and ran wild as mermaid tendrils down her flabby back.

Denise DeWitt was eighty-five years old, enjoying the finest few months of her life, when she suddenly and unceremoniously died, bolt upright in the bath with a jar of tomato chutney in her left hand. The Meals on Wheels lady stumbled upon her almost twelve hours later. The tomato chutney had slipped from Denise's hand, turning the bathwater blood red and consequently leading to some six hours of confused gossip concerning the cause of death. Having served the retirement community for the better part of thirty years, the Meals on Wheels lady was well-accustomed to finding the odd corpse. With little or no thought for ceremony, she phoned the relevant authorities, pulled the plug out and threw the bath mat over Denise to preserve her now wizened dignity. Whilst she waited for the coroner to arrive, she sat on the toilet seat and polished off Denise DeWitt's morning porridge. 'It's not that I'm not sad or anything,' she explained to the coroner when he finally arrived, 'but there's no point letting a good breakfast go to waste.'

Less than a week later, the bathtub had been thoroughly disinfected and a regular wilderness of tomato plants relocated to the compost heap behind the Center. The Director, horrified by the state of Chalet 13, had successfully billed Denise's relatives for the kind of deep clean normally associated with a violent crime scene, but the stench of tomatoes lingered on, making it almost impossible to rent the chalet to a proper resident for proper money. Martha Orange's arrival had been extremely timely for the Baptist council. When the worst of the death smell had dissipated, they'd shuffled Martha and her kids into Chalet 13 and docked a significant slice off her pay for the privilege.

Malcolm barely noticed the smell. He felt more at home in Chalet 13 than any of the two dozen shops, shacks or stucco bungalows he'd previously lived in. The chalets had been erected in 1978, with good intentions and vast amounts of concrete. Seventeen years of incessant drizzle had yet to erode even the upper epidermis. Malcolm was a big fan of concrete. It reeked of permanence. He fully intended to spend the rest of his waking life on the cul-de-sac, sliding from youth to manhood and eventually the kind of tremendously ancient state which could only add credibility to his claim for permanence.

However, the Baptist Retirement Village was a game of two halves and the second kingdom hovered like a Death Star over even this, his simplest hope. The Center was more than a building; it was, to Malcolm, evil incarnate. Some of life's larger travesties, he was coming to realize, were just too monumental to ignore.

Malcolm Orange lived in constant denial. 'It's only a building,' he told himself. 'It's just a building like our house, or next door's house or the house we lived in for six months when I had the chicken pox. Buildings can't really hurt anyone.' Malcolm's sensible head – the section capable of arithmetic and evaluating his mother's increasingly outlandish behavior in a reasonably objective fashion – continued to reassure him that buildings were unworthy objects of fear. The more prominent part of Malcolm's head – the section devoted to dinosaurs, to X-Men and outbreaks of perforated hysteria – was incapable of shirking the sensation that something truly horrible was taking place in full view of his bedroom window.

At the far end of the cul-de-sac, masked by a suspiciously large privet hedge, stood the Center, a four-story brick and metal cage, puckered with occasional screen-sized windows. A single double door opened on to the front of the building permitting assisted entry, one patient at a time, to the Center's foyer. A second door protruded from the building's backside, expelling food waste, laundry and the occasional chain-smoking employee.

The Center received elderly people on an almost daily basis.

Malcolm, on the days when he wished to remind himself that God, despite his recent benevolence, could not be trusted, hid out behind the privet hedge and watched the Center swallow a series of rickety old folk. It was hard to tell from ten feet, but each of these individuals appeared extremely reluctant to enter the building. Though most were beyond the ability to resist with violence, several offered mouthfuls of prehistoric expletives, whilst the most mobile swung canes and walking devices, kicking the porters pointedly in the shins.

It was common cul-de-sac knowledge that the Center had been significantly placed at the end of the road. Malcolm had yet to see or hear of an elderly person emerging from the Center's doors, either front or back. Those who left the cul-de-sac for the Center did not return. Those unfortunate to arrive at the Center in ambulances and relatives' hatchbacks were destined to disappear before any of the regular residents could even catch a Christian name.

Malcolm's mother worked in the Center. She washed old people and fed them turkey dinners liquidized in a blender. She changed their monster-sized diapers, injected them with habit-forming drugs and twice a week rotated the elderly men out of Monday's pajamas and into Thursday's. Malcolm's mother hadn't a good word to say about the Center or the Director who ran the outfit, somewhat anonymously, from the big bungalow on the hill. Martha Orange knew a shitty operation when she saw one, but for the sake of sustenance and a quiet life, held her tongue on the subject. Malcolm himself lived in constant fear of the Center, suspecting the building capable of fast-tracking even the healthiest individual towards the crematorium. It was all he could bear to permit his mother to slip into her powder-pink scrubs and enter the Center each morning.

'If you feel sick while you're in there, mama,' he exclaimed adamantly, 'even normal sick, like a headache or an upset belly, you need to get out right away. Call me if you need me to break in and save you. You'll just get sicker and sicker if you stay in the Center. People die in there you know.'

'Yes, Malcolm,' his mother explained for the umpteenth time that week, 'people do die in the Center. They die because they're old and they're done with not being dead. It's a perfectly natural process, nothing to be afraid of. I'm not going to die in there.'

'Promise.'

But Mrs Orange no longer believed in promises. The Volvo-shaped space in her driveway served as a constant reminder to the fact that all promises, even the eternal kind, bound together with antique wedding bands, tended to disintegrate in the end.

'I can't promise, Malcolm,' she said. 'It's unlikely that I'll die in there but who knows? I may have an accident in the kitchen, stranger things have happened. I'm pretty sure I won't die in the Center though.'

'How sure, mama?'

'Pretty damn sure, Malcolm.'

'Like ninety-five percent?'

'I don't want to measure it in a percentage.'

'Seventy-five percent?'

'Drop it, Malcolm. This conversation is getting ridiculous.'

And, because his mother had refused to be drawn into percentages, Malcolm Orange nurtured the morbid fear that some morning, most likely a morning least expected – a birthday for example, or Thanksgiving – his mother would leave for work and simply never come back.

Malcolm Orange did not trust the Center, but he could not keep himself away from its ominous front door.

He spent long afternoons buried in the privet hedge with Ross's sports bag wedged at his feet, while he watched the front of the building through a pair of binoculars lately stolen from Roger Heinz's shed. Malcolm kept a careful tally in his notebook. Over the past three weeks, some sixteen elderly people had entered the Center. Only one had escaped, slipping bare-assed through the laundry window to run loud and naked round the cul-de-sac. The entire street had come out to cheer him on and mock the orderlies as they attempted to curtail him by the turn circle. After less than five minutes of liberation the poor man had found himself swaddled in a baby-blue hospital blanket and dragged, against his will, back into the Center. The cut of his naked buttocks, slapping like a pair of shrink-wrapped fillets, had been the last visible sighting of the Center's only known escaped prisoner. Just two weeks later Malcolm Orange feared that the bare-assed man no longer existed.

Malcolm Orange knew every inch and angle of the Baptist Retirement Village. Only the space beyond the Center's electric doors evaded his scrutiny. He kept detailed notes, priding himself on omniscience. Malcolm could not permit anything, even the smallest cul-de-sac incident, to occur without his knowledge. Secrets offended his attention to detail.

This morning, above all ordinary noises, Malcolm Orange found himself preoccupied with the sexual grunts and wallows floating through his bedroom window. Here was an anomaly: a not yet recorded piece of data happening right beneath his nose. Scientific Investigative Research demanded he look further into the matter. Sheer laziness kept him flat on his back, surreptitiously picking his nose and wiping it on the duvet cover.

Malcolm Orange lay in bed for a few moments, arms folded behind his neck, trying to concentrate on other more pressing concerns: absent fathers, halfwit mothers, and his own disappearing parts which had, no doubt, multiplied during the night. He inspected the inside section of his left wrist, removing his watch to aid investigation. Beneath the plastic strap, in the space normally occupied by a series of raised dots, he found a missing section roughly the size of a nickel. Holding his arm to the light so it formed a kind of telescope, he was able to read the Coca-Cola clock right through his own wrist. It was five past seven now, almost ten past. If he angled his arm right Malcolm could frame the entire clock face so it looked like an actual wristwatch. He played around with his arm for a few seconds, closing one eye and squinting at the window, at the dresser – one drawer wedged open to reveal a still-sleeping Ross – and at the poster of Wolverine which he'd recently tacked to the bedroom wall. Watching the world through your own arm, Malcolm Orange concluded, was really friggin' weird.

In the kitchen he could hear his mother muttering in Spanish as she fixed a full day's worth of meals to leave for her children. Milk bottles for the baby would be left in the fridge, 'morning', 'afternoon', 'evening', and 'emergency' scrawled in eyeliner pencil on the side. It was Malcolm Orange's duty to stick the correct bottle into Ross at the right time of day. He performed this task with the utmost insincerity, occasionally missing a bottle or emptying all four in one go. Ross did not seem to mind and continued to grow at the acceptable rate for a small infant, prematurely born. Malcolm Orange had eventually come to conclude that it mattered not one jot what he fed the baby and had lately taken to spoon-feeding his younger brother Campbell's condensed cream of chicken soup, unheated, straight from the can. He had yet to mention this experiment to his mother but justified it under the disclaimer that milk was all very well and good but most likely somewhat bland after the third month's straight consumption.

Malcolm's own meals – sandwiches, ramen noodles and microwaveable macaroni dinners – were left in a stack by the cookie jar; a silent nod to the fact that should all else fail, cookies could always be relied upon to keep him coasting towards the next square meal.

Most weekends, Mrs Orange was released from her duties in the Retirement Village, and the Oranges ate like kings and tiny princes, rotating their dining adventures between Red Robin, IHOP, Denny's and Shari's, where they often bumped into the more mobile members of the Retirement Village treating their elderly dates and spouses to a Seniors Special for two.

Malcolm Orange dozed on until the Spanish sentiments petered out. Five seconds later the swooshing front door heralded his mother's exit. He counted to one hundred the old fashioned way – using thousands to measure the seconds – and, when he was all but certain that his mother had safely made it across the parking lot, pulled back the covers and slipped out of bed.

Standing in the early morning sunlight he inspected his naked chest for perforations. It was difficult to say with any certainty, for his investigations had yet to officially begin, but Malcolm Orange appeared to be a great deal holier than the previous evening. There was a fresh constellation of tiny pinpricks clustered around his right nipple, whilst in the centre of his torso, congregating around his belly button, a number of larger holes had merged, forming a sort of doughnut-like tunnel right through his intestines. Unaware of any biblical undertones, Malcolm Orange unfurled a single doubting finger and pressed it deep into his belly. It disappeared up to the knuckle and upon withdrawal came away cleanly with not so much as a hint of blood, bile or anything more sinister.

Malcolm repeated the finger experiment several times, applying increasing amounts of pressure as he delved deeper into the dark cavern of his own innards. Each time his finger came away smooth and clean as a well-oiled earthworm. For a brief moment, temporarily distracted by the unholy coolness of being able to stick his hand right through his own belly, Malcolm Orange forgot about the fact that he was disappearing, forgot about his Mexico-bound father and his Spanish-speaking mother, forgot about the very fact that he now lived in a Retirement Village, surrounded on all sides by the old, the odd and the mentally unbalanced. Malcolm Orange, who was – despite fervent prayer and supplication – still his father's son, stood in the middle of his own bedroom, naked from the waist up, poking himself repeatedly and trying to work out whether this was something he could do on television, for money.

The unmistakable sound of sexual climax, louder now that he'd crawled out from beneath his X-Men duvet, brought Malcolm Orange back to reality with an undignified thump. It was time for a spot of undercover investigation.

He slipped a T-shirt over his pajama shorts, located one flip-flop under the bed and the second beneath a pile of pre-worn pants and socks which were evolving, Everest-like, from the foot of his bed. As an afterthought he carefully placed the *Oxford English Dictionary* on top of Ross's sleeping chest. 'Try wriggling your way out of that one,' he muttered, but Ross said nothing. Ross, aged almost three months, possessed the lackluster ability to sleep, undisturbed, through natural disasters, marital implosion and all but the top three volume notches on the remote control. Malcolm Orange observed his brother for a few seconds, watching his bottom lip furble and flop over each baby breath whilst the dictionary rose and fell unencumbered. Satisfied that Ross would not escape the underwear drawer this morning, Malcolm Orange grabbed a notebook and pen, lowered himself through the bedroom window and landed, unobserved, in his mother's flowerbed.

(There was no need for Malcolm to be endlessly entering and exiting the chalet via the bedroom window. The Oranges' new home was perfectly well equipped with not one but two external doors, each of which was capable of opening and closing as doors should. 'Yes,' Malcolm would later admit to his mother as she complained for the millionth time about her dead and dying flowerbed – the only six-foot scrap of her garden which refused to submit to the lush growing conditions of a Portland summer, 'technically I could use the door but the window just seems more like an adventure.'

Thereafter, Mrs Orange, who could no longer bear the physical intimacy associated with an actual thrashing, threw all six sofa cushions at her son, angrily and with vicious accuracy. 'Dammit, Malcolm!' she screamed. 'Use the door like a normal kid or so help me, I'll make you sleep in the broom closet again.'

The broom closet was a legitimate threat, visited upon Malcolm on various occasions in various motel rooms when conjugal rights required a spot of privacy for the older Oranges. Aged three to seven, Malcolm had barely made it through a single broom cupboard night before the sheer, unrelenting blackness had triggered an unfortunate outbreak of diarrhea. Between the ages of eight and eleven, finally wise to the ugly drama unfurling on the far side of the door, Malcolm had manipulated the moment, bartering his way into candy bars, five-dollar bills and, on one notable occasion, an entire pack of Lucky Strikes, unsmoked.)

Standing up to his ankles in dead begonias he raised a single hand to his ear and cupped it firmly, forming a half-assed funnel. Most all of the cul-de-sac's subtler sounds were lost on Malcolm, who could barely hear Christmas through the well-waxed remnants of Kleenex which kept his inner ear canals permanently congested. He held his breath, ignoring the bloody thump of his own pulse, and, above the perpetual hum of traffic stop-starting its way along 82nd, the hymns from two doors down and the telephone trilling faintly on the Center's reception desk, Malcolm could just about distinguish the sound of bedsprings creaking in obvious relief.

He followed his suspicions two chalets down and one across, all the time holding his ear like a tracking device. Eventually the sounds led him to Chalet 7. He paused by the gate and made a tremendous show of tying his shoelace, hoping no one would notice the obvious lack of lace on his drugstore flip-flops. As he crouched on the edge of trespass, Malcolm continued to listen to the drama unfolding inside Chalet 7.

Even from this distance Malcolm could make out every word of the post-coital conversation, for Mr Roger Heinz – the current occupant of Chalet 7 – was one of the many screamers who lived on the cul-de-sac. Having lost the hearing in one ear, every utterance, even of the most intimate nature, was delivered with all the delicacy of an amplified juggernaut.

'Just leave the plate in the microwave, pumpkin, I'll heat it up later and you can pick it up when you come back for round two. If I get the chance I think I'll change the bed sheets before this evening. They're starting to stick together!' he yelled. 'Or maybe we could do it on the sofa for a change tonight.'

The response was lost on Malcolm, for Mr Heinz's lover had none of his hearing problems and was able to execute conversation at a discreet level. Bent forward like an upturned paperback, Malcolm could see nothing beyond his own toes and the tiny clumps of gum and dog shit which littered the asphalt sidewalk, but he could well picture what was going on in the living room of Chalet 7. In such circumstances the polite, and unarguably American thing to do, would be to walk away, imagination intact. Malcolm Orange was neither polite, nor particularly American in his outlook. In Malcolm's world, manners took a backseat to Scientific Investigative Research and so he ventured surreptitiously forth on an impromptu reconnaissance mission. Rising to his full height he made a showy attempt at stretching, checked the cul-de-sac for casual observers, and slipped unnoticed down the side of Mr Heinz's aging Chrysler. In the alleyway between Chalet 7 and 8 Malcolm crouched behind the recycling bin and peeked over the windowsill.

Chalet 7 reeked of masculine occupancy. A single La-Z-Boy armchair, already reclined, dominated the floor space. To the right, at arm's length, a number of empty beer cans and a well-stuffed ashtray bore witness to the chair's integral role in Mr Heinz's day-to-day existence. On the wall, directly opposite the window, an enormous television was showing footage of a recent golf tournament with the volume set to mute. A stack of filthy plates and dishes almost two foot high was threatening to topple off the edge of the coffee table. Malcolm Orange swiveled on his heels, taking in the open-plan kitchen unit, encrusted as it was in a thick layer of oily grime. Dust motes danced frantically in the single sunbeam peaking beneath the kitchen blinds. A solitary pair of sap-gray briefs, probably male, hung impotently from the kitchen chair.

It was an undeniably masculine room – ageless in a sense, for the occupants could easily have been early-twenties slackers, middle-aged divorcees or elderly men in sweatpants. The thinnest smell of stale fart and tube sock was slowly leaking through the living room window. For Malcolm, who had grown up on hand-me-down army fatigues and the gummy dregs of his father's Budweiser cans, there was something familiar and faintly reassuring about the sheer manliness of this squalor. 'When I grow up,' Malcolm Orange thought to himself, 'I will have a room in my house just like this room. The rest of the house will be normal but one room will be exactly like this.' The thought pleased him immensely. He planned to make a note of it as soon as an appropriate notebook became available.

Mr Heinz and his mysterious lover were just offstage, most likely concluding business in the bedroom or washing up in the bathroom. Malcolm knew from the naked lady programs that most people liked to brush their teeth after sex. He was, as yet, unsure as to how intercourse directly affected one's teeth but suspected it was something to do with the kissing, which, in his eleven-year-old opinion, seemed like a most unhygienic use of the mouth and tongue.

Malcolm Orange perched himself on an upturned bucket and angled around for a better view. Inclined at a ninety degree angle, with one foot raised for balance, he could just about discern a set of female heels struggling to wedge themselves back into their ancient Reeboks. They were olive, white and cracked as a pair of sun-bleached pebbles. The left ankle bore the mark of the cross in faint indelible ink. It had stretched out over at least three decades' hard labor, becoming blurred around the edges like a well-worn photocopy. Based on the back of her legs, Malcolm Orange placed Mr Heinz's lover at approximately fifty-five or sixty: not quite old enough to be officially resident on the cul-de-sac. Malcolm leaned further forwards, risking chronic imbalance, for further clues as to the woman's identity. He could see nothing more than a solitary varicose vein snaking up the inside of her calf.

After a substantial pause, during which the sound of tired elastic and frantic zippering suggested post-coital redressing, Mr Heinz broke the silence. 'You're right, Sonja,' he yelled, 'I should be thinking of my back. Best to stick to the bedroom. Great idea keeping your dress on this morning. Probably for the best, my love, the porridge goes cold if we take more than ten minutes and I don't want to get you in trouble again.'

'Sonja,' Malcolm made a mental note of the name, fully

intending to start a new page in his research notebook as soon as he returned to Chalet 13. As far as he knew, there was only one Sonja who frequented the cul-de-sac (though he would, for the sake of scientific accuracy, interrogate his mother discreetly over tonight's evening meal). Mr Roger Heinz, the elderly man who occupied Chalet 7, and had in his pre-retirement days been a semi-successful salesman of used cars and trucks, was having a secret affair with the Meals on Wheels lady.

Though Malcolm was yet to realize it, most everyone on the cul-de-sac had been aware of this setup for the better part of two months. Rising early, as most elderly folk do, they'd been treated to the same open-window talk show Malcolm was now party to, most every morning for the entire summer. Roger and Sonja – who was Portuguese, substantially hipped and twenty-three years his junior – did it twice daily; once at 7am, mere moments after she'd trundled her heated trolley up his garden path, delivering porridge and reconstituted eggs to the elderly residents of the cul-de-sac, and once again at 6pm whilst his evening meal slowly cooled in its microwaveable dish. In the evenings they kept the windows closed, guarding against the mosquito epidemic which was currently plaguing Portland.

'Lord Almighty,' Malcolm Orange whispered and almost toppled off his bucket with the shock. Mr Heinz was at least eighty-three years old. Malcolm had previously imagined that the necessary mechanics quit after one's sixtieth birthday.

Just as this thought had begun to settle into the soft space between reality and fiction, the Meals on Wheels lady emerged from the bedroom, patting her well-lacquered hair into place as she walked. Mr Heinz appeared two steps behind, rubbing her backside affectionately as she fished her purse out from under the coffee table. Suddenly disturbed, a generous stack of magazines toppled and fluttered to the ground, coating the living room carpet in a maelstrom of unfortunate images: gardening aids, fly-fishing shots, incontinence adverts and glossy photos of foreign ladies, all-over naked in outlandish positions.

The noise caused Malcolm Orange to start suddenly, readjusting his position in a maneuver which made the bucket rush suddenly left, then right, forwards and back, before finally coming to rest in its original position, emitting the sound of two dozen plastic-hooved horses stampeding down the alleyway.

Mr Heinz, who was naked from the waist up, exposing a foot-long bypass scar, quit feeling up the Meals on Wheels lady and made an arthritic dart for the living room window.

'Who's out there?' he yelled, his lack of aural discernment causing the very windowpanes to reverberate in protest. 'Come out and show yourself you old pervert.'

Malcolm Orange sensed that this was the appropriate moment for yet another of the Oranges' infamous speedy getaways. Without thinking he jumped backwards from the bucket. It was his intention to crouch upon impact with the ground and thereafter crawl, commando style, all the way back to Chalet 13.

Malcolm Orange had not figured Chalet 8 into his plan.

Propelling himself backwards from Chalet 7 at a rate of some thirty miles per hour, the back of Malcolm's skull collided with the gable wall of Chalet 8 approximately four feet and seven inches into midair. Before he could even register the stupidity of his own plan, Malcolm passed out, plummeting to the ground where he lay, comatose, for anything up to three minutes. During the interim his presence went undetected by Mr Heinz, whose eyesight was only slightly better than his hearing, and Sonja, the

Meals on Wheels lady, who kind of liked the idea of someone watching at the window.

Anything up to three minutes later Malcolm Orange came to. He was no longer lying in the alleyway between Chalet 7 and Chalet 8.

Turning his head slowly from side to side, a movement which required gritted teeth and superhuman levels of concentration, Malcolm managed to ascertain his location. If his calculations were correct, he'd managed to walk, or perhaps crawl, unconscious from Chalet 7 to the privet hedge which bordered the Center on three out of four sides. For a few seconds he lay quietly under the hedge, eyes wedged shut, trying to work out how long he'd been unconscious for – weeks perhaps, or even years. He lifted his hands to his face. They were still the hands of a prepubescent boy. 'Thank God,' Malcolm Orange thought, 'I can't have been out for more than a couple of years.'

'What are you doing with your hands, pervert?' a voice asked from many miles above Malcolm's head. It was a girl's voice; shrill, sharp, incessant as tinfoil wedged between teeth.

Malcolm tried to open his eyes; left first, then right. The sunlight swaggering through the privet hedge punctured his head in fourteen million separate spots.

'I saw you,' she continued. 'You were watching those old folks doing it through the window. You're such a pervert.'

'I was not,' said Malcolm, not yet sure who he was arguing with.

'Were too. We saw you.'

'Who's we?'

'Mr Fluff and me.'

'Mr Fluff doesn't sound like a real person.'

'You can argue that out with her yourself,' the voice continued, upon which a particularly angry, orange puffball of a cat was deposited suddenly and with great force upon Malcolm's middle.

'There you go. Now you can see she's real and she says you're a pervert too.'

'She's a cat. She can't say anything.'

'She's a talking cat but she only talks to me. See, we have this special bond. It was me that rescued her. Anyway, all that's beside the point. What were you doing watching those old people screwing?'

'I wasn't!' Malcolm shouted. He felt weary beyond his almost twelve years.

'Were too. We saw you.'

'Look,' replied Malcolm, realizing the circular nature of the conversation. 'You're right. I was trying to watch Mr Heinz and the Meals on Wheels lady, but I couldn't see anything and it was for my Scientific Investigative Research. Anything's OK if you do it for scientific research.'

'Well, we were doing research too. We've been following you for the last few days. Bet you didn't even notice.'

Malcolm Orange felt himself all of a sudden ready to faint for a second time. The need to fall over, though technically impossible from a prostrate position, came over him in undulating waves like five thousand nauseated butterflies flittering round his brain.

'You're lying,' he whispered. 'I'd have noticed you. I'm incredibly observant for an eleven-year-old.'

'Nope,' she said, 'you're the only kid in the Village and we've been following you since we moved in.'

'Prove it.'

'Easy peasy. Porridge for breakfast, every morning, PB and J for lunch yesterday, X-Men duvet on your bed, small baby – a brother I assume – in your underwear drawer AND you spend an awful lot of time looking at yourself naked in the mirror.'

Malcolm Orange struggled not to swallow his own tongue.

'Who are you?' he asked when the gagging fit had finally subsided.

'Soren James Blue,' she replied. 'You can call me Sorry. My father says it suits me.'

Raising himself up on one elbow Malcolm Orange forced both eyelids open at once. When his eyes had finally focused he found himself staring into the pug-nosed face of a furious demon girl. Two thick black braids framed her face. A tight black T-shirt, puckering around the section where her breasts would soon be, clung to her chest, riding high to reveal a thick slice of milk-white belly. Her ears were pierced three times individually on one ear, five times on the other. Her teeth were still fenced off in a set of junior high retainers. She couldn't have been any more than thirteen, fourteen at very most.

Malcolm Orange smiled up at her, squinting into the sunbeams which were busy forming an ironic halo around her head. Aside from his mother, she was the most beautiful lady Malcolm had ever seen with clothes on.

– Chapter Five –

Scientific Investigative Research

On normal days in normal circumstances, Malcolm Orange struggled to see the point in having a younger brother. Ross was little more than a ten-pound earthworm, passing food from one end of his fat, pink body to the other with little concern for the noxious odors this process produced.

The older ladies on the cul-de-sac (halfwit Irene and Emily Fox who liked to suffocate Malcolm daily, pressing him against her papery bosom so he smelt for weeks of lilac water and Johnson's Baby Powder) were very fond of Ross. 'What a cutie,' they'd say, tugging on his lardy little cheeks. 'Can we keep him, Malcolm?' And Malcolm Orange would inevitably feel his hopes rise, buoyed by the possibility of finally being rid of both his father and Ross, the vulgar fruit of his father's loins. Adopting his most convincing smile – the very same smile which had kept the pastrami sandwiches rolling throughout his exile in Idaho – Malcolm would reply, 'Of course you can keep him, ladies. He's all yours. Will I get his diaper bag?' Both ladies would laugh long and hard, as if party to some tremendous joke. Malcolm automatically felt the need to run away, rather quickly in the opposite direction, for halfwit Irene looked a lot like the Joker from Batman when she laughed.

Neither lady had ever taken him up on the offer, so Malcolm Orange had begun to explore alternative options for the disposal of his unwanted sibling. On several occasions since the advent of Ross, Malcolm had seriously considered listing his brother in the classifieds section of the *Oregonian*.

'We should charge a little for him, mama, maybe five or ten bucks,' he'd explained to his mother, who was busy at the time, feverishly kissing the back of a wooden spoon. 'People are suspicious of free things. We're much less likely to get rid of Ross if we offer him for free.'

After which, in a rare display of physical affection, Martha Orange had removed the wooden spoon from her lips and administered five quick clips to the back of her son's thighs. Malcolm Orange remained confused. Fully aware of his own gifts and abilities, he could only assume his mother perpetually disappointed by this second, substandard child. Stranded in Portland, Oregon with no friends or living relatives to tell tales, every day offered her a fresh opportunity to abandon the baby and return to a simpler, Ross-free set up.

On normal days in normal circumstances Malcolm Orange would have paid the gypsies half his annual allowance to take Ross away. This morning, with his head rolling round the underside of the privet hedge and his outer extremities disappearing at a righteous clip, Malcolm Orange felt something equating to affection for his long-lost brother.

'You should check on Ross,' he whispered, struggling to raise himself up on one elbow. 'I don't think I can move yet but you could climb in through my window. It's the front one with the blue curtains.'

'I know which bedroom you sleep in,' Soren James Blue replied, balancing her hands adamantly on her hip bones. 'But

I'm not going. Go yourself if you're that worried.'

'I'll faint again!'

'Bullshit!' she replied and dragged him into a standing position, digging her heels into the bark dust for leverage. She was surprisingly strong for a girl.

Upright now, Malcolm Orange observed Soren James Blue from a vertical perspective. Her proximity was unsettling. He could smell the breakfast bacon still lingering on her breath. He could see that the fourth earring on one side was actually an unfortunately placed mole.

'You have a mole on your ear,' he said. (This was Malcolm Orange's first experience of talking to an actual, real-life girl. It was like learning Spanish. He could understand small sections of what she said, but hadn't a clue how to respond.)

'I've got moles all over me,' Sorry replied. 'Do you want to see? It's only fair. I've seen you naked already.'

Malcolm Orange took his second funny turn of the day, this time slowly and with all the grace of a wilting tulip. Sorry caught him before he hit the ground. The feeling of girl hands snaking under his armpits was both pleasant and slightly nauseating. Malcolm hung there limply for half a minute trying to make sense of this, the latest in a number of unsettling new experiences.

'Right,' Sorry said, forcing him once more upwards, 'quit feeling me up and let's go check on Ross. I'm assuming Ross is your kid brother . . . the baby in the dresser?'

'Uh-huh,' Malcolm replied and, for the first time ever, wondered if it was normal practice to keep a baby in the underwear drawer. Had he been better balanced he would have run ahead of Sorry to remove the *Oxford English Dictionary* before she had the opportunity to further judge his parenting skills. No such opportunity arose, for Sorry was already off, half-stomping, half-running in the direction of Chalet 13. Mr Fluff followed at a safe distance, pausing every quarter block to sniff eagerly every suspicious looking stain on the sidewalk. As they proceeded from one end of the cul-de-sac to the other, Malcolm Orange found himself giving an impromptu guided tour of his new neighborhood.

'Bill and Irene live in there,' he said, indicating their front door with one extended finger. 'They run the People's Committee for Remembering Songs. Irene's not all there but Bill's a decent enough guy. Sometimes we play tennis over his hedge. I let him win because he's really old.

'Here's the mailbox,' he continued, instantly regretting his decision to state the glaringly obvious. 'And the public telephone if you need to make a call.

'Emily Fox lives in the house with the pink door. She's really, really fat. She sleeps sitting up on her sofa because if she lay down she'd never be able to sit up again and she'd die and she can't fit in the bathroom any more so a lady comes to wash her and empty her pee once a week. They pour water over her with a hose. I've never seen because they close the curtains first, but my mama told me all about it. Emily Fox is probably going to die soon because she's too fat for her heart. You want to stay away from her until she dies because she always hugs children and it hurts a lot and smells funny.'

Sorry said nothing. She stared at Emily Fox's chalet. The living room curtains were tightly closed. Emily Fox was in Minnesota visiting her nephew, Francis.

(This visit had been the talk of the cul-de-sac for almost a month. Since her departure, residents had taken to stopping each other on the street corner to speculate on the logistics of long-distance travel for the morbidly obese.

'I heard she'd booked a mini-van and driver all to herself,' Bill had suggested at the penultimate meeting of the People's Committee for Remembering Songs, cutting himself off quick sharp when the sound of a creaking access ramp heralded Emily Fox's imminent arrival.

'Bullshit,' Roger Heinz had continued. He had quit wearing his hearing aid and was chronically unaware of anything less subtle than an earthquake. 'That woman's so fat she'd need a flatbed truck just for herself.'

Emily Fox had, by this stage, lowered her legendary backside on to the three seats immediately to Mr Heinz's left, and was busy repositioning both of her enormous legs. They quivered in protest like two Jell-O tree trunks, sweatpant sheathed. 'I,' she'd stated adamantly, addressing the entire room, 'am flying United, Portland to Minneapolis. I've two seats booked for myself, just in case one's a little too cozy.'

'Damn, girl,' Roger Heinz had interjected and slapped her thigh complicitly, setting off a series of deep, undulating ripples which moved simultaneously downwards and upwards, threatening to instigate an avalanche across her massive belly. 'You want to give United a call and make sure they don't put you in the tail or they'll never get the G-D plane off the runway.'

Emily Fox had taken Roger Heinz's comments in good humor. She was old enough and fat enough to view her three hundred and something pounds as a battering ram rather than a dead weight.

Thereafter, Malcolm Orange had spent the week watching the news eager-eyed but had yet to hear of any plane crashes between Portland and Minneapolis. He could only assume Emily Fox safely absconded to Minnesota, eating her unsuspecting nephew out of house and home.)

'They're probably hosing her down now,' he whispered to

Sorry, hoping to impress her with yet another small-town lie. 'They only close the curtains when they're washing her.'

Soren James Blue remained frustratingly unresponsive. Malcolm Orange began to wonder if she might be made from the same mould as Ross: another of life's crippling disappointments. It had, however, only been fifteen minutes since their first acquaintance, so Malcolm swallowed his skepticism and proceeded with the tour.

'And that,' he whispered, pointing out a particularly innocuous-looking section of the sidewalk, 'is where Ronnie threw up after the July Fourth barbeque. You can still see the puke stains on the ground. The day after he was too sick to stand up so they took him to the Center and we never heard from him again.'

Malcolm Orange delivered the last line of this soliloquy with sober intensity, hoping to instill in Soren James Blue his own healthy fear of the Center. Sorry popped a bubblegum bubble loudly and itched her naked midriff. She appeared overwhelmingly unconcerned. Malcolm Orange was a muddle. He found himself trapped between the desire to punch Sorry hard on her insolent little nose and the urgent need to possess the half-chewed gum protruding from between her lips. Resentment he could handle, out-and-out violence seemed bearable, but after eleven years of seasonal friendships, of halfwit mothers and senile conversations, Malcolm Orange could not cope with yet another disinterested player.

Driving a reaction out of Soren James Blue was absolutely imperative now. Malcolm Orange stood tall in his drugstore flip-flops and shouldered the challenge like a full-grown man. Staring Sorry straight in the eye he leaned against the door of Chalet 13 and said the most shocking thing he could think of.

'I live here,' he confessed with a carefully affected nonchalance. 'Not for long though. I'm starting to disappear. By next week there probably won't be anything left of me.' He folded his arms and waited for a reaction.

Soren James Blue laughed in his face. She sounded like fireworks going off, indoors and underwater. It was a thick and wonderful noise to stand under. Though it was hard to tell with cats, Malcolm Orange could have sworn Mr Fluff was laughing too. Her marmalade belly expanded and contracted several dozen times in quick succession until, with a noise like a dying hairdryer, she hacked an enormous hairball onto the Orange doorstep. Forgetting for the moment that he was in the presence of a lady, Malcolm instinctively went through the vomit with the toe of his flip flop. He was fascinated by the chocolatey mess and wondered how on earth an all-over-orange cat could cough up mud-brown fur. 'Perhaps,' he concluded, keeping his thoughts to himself, 'Mr Fluff has been licking other cats or eating the trimmings from the hairdresser's floor.' Far from disgusted, he deeply respected Mr Fluff for her chocolate-colored vomit.

Whilst Malcolm poked around in the cat sick, lamenting his lack of a magnifying glass, Soren James Blue continued to laugh over his shoulder. 'You're a weird kid, Malcolm,' she muttered between huge, choking gulps of laughter. 'I like you. Here's hoping you don't disappear before I get to know you.'

Malcolm blushed all over. It was a new experience for him. He wiped the vomit off his toes and fished the front door key out from beneath the welcome mat.

'Do you want to come in?' he asked, hesitant and half-inclined to leave the strange girl and her cat standing on his front doorstep.

'Sure,' she replied, 'but we don't, as a rule, do doors. We'll meet you inside.'

By the time Malcolm had made it through the front door and

down the hall to his bedroom, Mr Fluff was fast asleep on his X-Men duvet, sweating ginger fur all over the pillow. Sorry was still entangled in her entrance, wriggling the last few inches of foot and ankle through the open window. Malcolm stood in the doorway watching her flop around, belly flat on his bedroom carpet as she extricated her left bootlace from the window latch. She looked like a drowning trout. It was hard to feel intimidated by her, tangled as she was becoming in the bedroom curtains.

'Do you need some help, Sorry?' Malcolm asked.

'Piss off,' she snapped back, and in her panic tore the curtains right off their hooks.

Soren James Blue was not the kind of girl given to apologies. She snatched the broken curtains from the floor, bundled them into a large gingham bushel and stuffed the evidence under the bed. Malcolm said nothing, but made a mental note to blame halfwit Irene, who was occasionally prone to stealing soft furnishings – flannels, scatter cushions and the odd electric blanket – when the opportunity presented itself. Shot of the incriminating curtains, Sorry wiped both hands on the back of her pants and strode purposefully towards the open dresser drawer. Malcolm Orange, overcome with embarrassment, made a kind of lurching dash for the drawer and managed to make it there at exactly the same instant as Sorry. The *Oxford English Dictionary* had come undone and fallen to the floor, landing open on the page outlining Fr words. Grabbing the book from the floor, Sorry read aloud, 'Freak: a thing or occurrence that is markedly unusual or irregular.' Malcolm blushed again. This time he could feel the hotness in his throat leaking, like spilt soup, down the neck of his T-shirt.

Ross was still sleeping. He'd shifted slightly over the course of the morning and his head was now in the place previously occupied by his elbow. Malcolm's socks had parted to make a nest for the dozing baby so Ross was now buried up to his chin in off-white cotton-polyester mix. He was not dissimilar to Baby Jesus in the manger. Soren James Blue stood over the baby, staring intently and pressing the *Oxford English Dictionary* against her chest. Malcolm feared she might drop it on his brother's head. Eventually, when the silence had become an ever-expanding cloud sucking the room dry, Sorry spoke. 'He's a funny-looking baby,' she said. It was a sentiment Malcolm Orange could easily agree with.

'I think it's because he has no hair,' he speculated. 'It makes his head look out of proportion.'

'Like an alien.'

'Or a turtle. I think he looks really like a turtle most days.'

'Do you like having a brother who looks like an alien turtle?'

'I don't like having a brother at all. I asked my mom to get us an alligator and she got herself knocked up with Ross instead. What about you, do you like having a brother?'

'Oh, there's just me – no brothers, no sisters – just me and dad.'

'Where's your mom?'

'Where's your dad?' Soren James Blue fired back defensively. Her chin had begun to wobble slightly. Having no previous experience with girls, Malcolm Orange was unsure as to whether she was about to cry or punch him. He answered her question truthfully. (Sometimes, Malcolm had discovered, telling the truth in an offensive manner could be just as effective as a well-placed lie.)

'My father's run off to Mexico by himself in the car,' he confessed. 'That's how we got stuck here in Portland. It's just me and mom and Ross now. I don't mind it too bad. It's much worse to lose a mother than a father.'

Soren James Blue reached across the open drawer and punched him succinctly and with surprising force, square on the tip of the nose. Malcolm Orange, unused to the pleasure of being punched in the face, leaned forward and thus caught the full force of the blow somewhere approximately two inches north of his open mouth. His nose made a noise like a plastic ruler snapping. Two thousand outdoor fireworks exploded simultaneously, cascading round the inner sanctum of his head and, with a noise like the Willamette in full flood, a river of blood burst forth from his left nostril. Without further ado Malcolm Orange lay down on his bed and succumbed to his third funny turn of the day.

Several seconds later he woke to the now familiar sight of Soren James Blue towering over him. In her right hand she held one of his mother's recently laundered dishcloths, in her left, force of habit had her clinging to the *Oxford English Dictionary* for comfort.

'Take your shirt off,' she commanded. 'It's covered in blood.' And before Malcolm had a chance to protest, she'd yanked his arms out of their sleeves and was dragging the shirt free of his head, splattering the walls with a generous constellation of fresh, red nose blood. Malcolm was mortified but too dizzy to protest. He lay there, semi-naked on his X-Men duvet, and attempted to cover his perforations, first with his hands, and then as good sense slowly crept back into his temporal lobe, with an X-Men pillow hastily located from behind his head.

Soren James Blue, seemingly undeterred, slammed her butt onto the bed beside Malcolm and, in the process, budged him several inches closer to the edge. Her breath was audible, whistling through the stained tracks of her braces. One sneaker slid loose at the heel and dangled delicately from the end of her big toe. Her thumbs brushed, intentionally he assumed, against

Malcolm's thigh as she scrambled to drag Mr Fluff on to her lap. It was almost too much for Malcolm Orange. He hugged the X-Men pillow tight to his chest, relishing the damp comfort of his own breath, breathing back, and contemplated the possibility of an enormous panic attack, right here in his very own bed.

(Malcolm Orange had been suffering for years from the possibility of panic attacks. Though he had yet to experience an actual outbreak of anxiety, many, many situations had had him almost hyperventilating. Diarrhea was also a constant, worrying possibility. Guarding against the potential of being caught short or breathless he had, for years, kept an empty popcorn sack folded in the seatback pocket of the Volvo. However, after the untimely death of his Step-Nana – bolt upright in a *Ghostbusters* matinee – the very thought of popcorn was enough to instigate the possibility of a panic attack and thus the empty sack found itself unceremoniously tossed from the rear window of a speeding station wagon, somewhere south of the Illinois border.

Malcolm Orange had a number of odd and oftentimes inexplicable phobias. These included bathroom hand driers, movie rental stores, unnaturally colored candies and, for a brief and torturous period in Kentucky, an intense horror of stoplights which had him digging his heels deeply into the driver's seat each time his father paused at a red. Though incapable, at the tender age of eight, of expressing a logical reason for his stoplight fear, Malcolm later came to realize it had everything to do with a particularly adult zombie movie he'd once been positioned in front of whilst his parents indulged their carnal needs in a motel bathroom.

It would be many weeks and months before Malcolm fully recovered from the fear of stoplights. During the interim he traveled exclusively on the right side of the car, hanging from the passenger window and calling red lights from half a mile out in the hope that his father might show a rare benevolent streak and slow his pace in anticipation of the green. His mother – an Orange by marriage rather than blood – might have indulged Malcolm's lesser oddities. However, she'd never progressed beyond tractor-handling, and so the family's driving responsibilities fell solely at Jimmy Orange's feet. Jimmy Orange rarely, if ever, indulged anyone who wasn't in the market for second-hand tires, so Malcolm Orange was forced to go cold turkey on his stoplight fear.

Throughout his youth and early childhood Malcolm remained chronically incapable of conquering the possibility of panic attacks. The fear of hyperventilating, or indeed succumbing to bowel thunder, kept him safely buckled to the Volvo's ample backseat whilst any number of small-town adventures passed him by, unsampled.

'No, mama,' he'd invariably whisper, when offered a sample of some zany new ice cream flavor, a rare family outing to one of the midwest's many hokey amusement parks or a new cassette tape for his Walkman, 'I think I'll just stick with what I know best. I can't be sure it won't give me a panic attack.'

Though his father attempted to scare the fear right out of his son – employing elaborate horror stories, cold, hard facts and, when all else failed, the mean side of his belt buckle – Malcolm continued to suffer from the crippling possibility of panic attacks. 'Let him be, Jimmy,' his mother would eventually mutter, coming a little too late to her son's defense, 'there's no harm in it and he always grows out of it in the end.'

And for the most part when the end came, five days, four months, or – in the case of adults in fancy dress – six years into the problem, Malcolm Orange almost always got over his fear and moved on to nurture a brand-new hysteria.)

Soren James Blue shuffled her butt several inches closer to Malcolm's and made a feeble attempt at an apology.

'So,' she said, rolling up the left leg of her pants to pick at a weeklong scab, 'I'm sorry I hit you, but you deserved it.'

Malcolm Orange said nothing. He was unsure whether the blow had been deserved or not. Teenage girls and the terrible reasonings of their teenage minds were an absolute mystery to him. He continued to breathe damply into the edge of his pillow, counting each individual exhalation in a dumb attempt to slow his racing pulse.

'I don't like people bitching about my mom,' Sorry continued, flicking the crusty edge of her knee scab towards the open window. 'It makes me mad and when I get mad I usually punch people, or throw up. I throw up a lot when I get angry.'

'I have diarrhea,' Malcolm confessed. 'But mostly when I'm nervous.'

'Gross,' Sorry replied, screwing her mouth up like a grimacing gargoyle. 'You're disgusting.' But Malcolm could tell she was secretly impressed. The curiosity got the better of his fear. He continued with his interrogation.

'Did your mom leave?' he asked, raising the X-Men pillow to protect his nose against a second onslaught.

'Kind of . . . but not really. It was sort of my fault. Look Malcolm, it's a personal story and I barely know you. I'm not sure I want to tell you any of it.'

'You've seen me naked,' he said, smirking. It was an uncharacteristically bold move on his part; a little strand of his father's malignant DNA finally clicked into place even as he formed the sentence, 'We're pretty much bonded for life, Sorry.'

She laughed awkwardly – like a garden sprinkler struggling to force the water out – and ran one hand through the front of her hair. It rose obtusely and stayed risen long after she'd removed her hand. Sensing the onslaught of a story, Mr Fluff stood up, shifted her furry hindquarters one hundred and eighty degrees clockwise, and settled in for the duration.

'So,' she said, for most of her stories, it would transpire, began with a deep-stacked 'so'. 'My parents got a divorce when I was seven years old.'

(She pronounced the word 'divorce' with a long emphasis on the first syllable, stretching it sixteen shades of southern so it emerged sounding like 'deevorce'. Malcolm Orange enjoyed the way she said it. Under her tongue it sounded less like cruelty and more like an actual possession, most probably a small, domesticated animal or kitchen appliance.)

'The divorce was no big deal. My mom didn't like my dad. Neither did I. He smelt too strong of cologne, even first thing in the morning. He smelt like he was trying to cover up something terrible. I think he had an affair with a hairdresser or a real estate lady, maybe both. My mom never talked about it but my grandma filled me in over Thanksgiving dinner. My grandma's dead now, but she was a great lady, a little crazy sometimes but pretty awesome for an old person. Towards the end she got a bit muddled and mixed me up with mom a lot. She bought me a rape alarm for my first day at kindergarten and taught all the kids how to top a beer bottle at my tenth birthday party. She swore like a trooper and boy did she hate my dad. I couldn't repeat some of the things she said about him when she thought my mom wasn't listening. She decided that I should know the facts about him, even though I was only seven years old. Turns out my dad had a second apartment on the other side of town just for screwing around. My mom only found out about it six months before the divorce. For a smart lady, my mom can be pretty dumb about certain things.

'Even when he wasn't screwing around dad would still go round there a lot so he could get wasted and play video games without my mom seeing. My mom disapproves of video games. She doesn't let me play them, even at the arcade. "They stunt your growth," she says. Complete bullshit! My dad's the tallest guy I know.

'After dad left we rented out the California house and moved to Chicago for the summer. It was only meant to be a temporary deal but my mom got offered a job in the university so we stayed for a year and then a second year. When I got to junior high I started asking how long we'd have to stay in Chicago for. It turned out the answer was permanently. The California house had been sold years ago and no one had bothered to tell me. I was pretty mad about that. I kept thinking about the other kids who were living in my house now. They were probably sleeping in my bedroom and coasting down the sidewalks on my skateboard. Well, eventually I got so mad at those dumb kids I made myself physically sick. I spent an entire week continuously throwing up about the California house and ended up in the emergency room with dehydration. I was pretty proud of my own persistence. It's not everyone that can keep vomiting regularly for more than two days. I'm a master at the art of puking.'

(As if to prove a point, Sorry stuck two fingers down her throat and made a convincing attempt at simulating a gagging fit. Mr Fluff, having previous experience of Sorry's gastric acrobatics, leapt from her lap and took cover under the bed. Malcolm quickly moved the X-Men pillow from his face to his lap, ready to protect his only clean pair of shorts, but the whole exhibition proved a mere preview of expulsions to come.)

'Eventually I stopped vomiting and the hospital told me I was better and could go home. But I didn't stop. I kept right on throwing up after every meal. I always left the bathroom door open so mom could hear. I made a real big deal of the puking. I wanted my mom to freak out and she did. I was thinner than any kid on our street, even the foreign kids, and my eyelids started to turn gray from not getting enough food. Plus, I sort of stopped talking to my mom, unless there was something I really needed; you know, like toothpaste or clean underwear or cigarettes. The silence thing really freaked her out. She tried to send me to a shrink to get me talking but I wouldn't speak to the shrink either. I could tell I was getting to my mom. By the third week of throwing up she'd started staying home from class to watch me. By the fourth week she'd upped my allowance to fifty bucks and I caught her crying in bed with the television turned up. I figured that by Christmas, if I kept quiet and continued throwing up, she'd give in and move us back to California.

'But my mom is almost as pig-headed as me. She's always hated the west coast. God only knows why, but she was pretty happy in Chicago. She was doing well at the university and dating this guy, Mike Pacchione, from the architect's firm on the corner. He was fake Italian and his eyes crinkled like stewed prunes when he smiled. Secretly, I liked him better than dad, but I'd never give her the pleasure of admitting that. My mom refused to move west. She thought if we stayed in Chicago, Mike Pacchione would marry her and we could be a kind of normal family again. No matter how many times I threw up on the living room carpet she refused to even consider California.

'I was starting to look really ill by this stage. People in the grocery store thought I was a heroin addict and wouldn't stand beside me in line. I could see my teeth through my cheeks when I breathed in. I dropped two dress sizes in less than six weeks and I wasn't fat to start with. My mom got so worried she called my dad in Portland. I knew things were getting really serious then. It was years since mom had asked for my dad's input on anything aside from the divorce. But my dad is a doctor and she figured this was a medical matter. I guess she wanted to get me fixed before I faded away to nothing. Two days later, I was standing at the departure lounge with my mom sniveling all over my jean jacket as she packed me off to Portland, Oregon for the summer.

'Last time I saw my dad he was a big time surgeon down in LA. He did operations for rich people; mostly famous actors and politicians. No one in LA trusted him but they kept paying him money to fix them up anyway. LA's kind of weird like that. Later I found out that he used to go to the papers with all the gossip on his patients. Even when I was really young I knew my dad was not a good guy. People glared at him across the room in restaurants. "Your dad's a great doctor, Sorry, but a lousy excuse for a human being," my grandma once told me. That pretty much sums him up. My parents were stinking rich and really miserable. I was too young to really understand why.

'So, when I got to Portland airport last month, there he was, waiting by the baggage claim, not one day older than 1989 and wearing the same big-shot business suit and shiny shoes. For the first ten minutes he made a massive deal of pretending to be glad I was here, hugged me and everything. In seven years of living in the same house, my dad had never once touched me. The airport was pretty damn awkward. I'm not a big hugger. Being touched makes me angry, so I threw up on his shiny shoes. I could tell my dad was really mad – his eyes went crazy and kind of joined up in the middle – but he didn't want to cause a scene in the baggage claim so he wiped the worst of it off with a napkin and yelled at me in the car later.

'"Things are going to be different around here, Soren," he said, and punched the steering wheel while he was driving. "Your mother's spoiled you. I can tell you've been a real brat for her but you won't get away with it here. You'll eat properly. You'll speak when you're spoken to. You'll do exactly as I tell you. And if you don't, you'll find I'm quite capable of making your life a living hell."

'I said nothing. It was part of my shtick to say nothing but even if I'd been in a talking phase, I wouldn't have known what to say to my dad. Twenty minutes later we arrived in this shithole and I realized that this was going to be the worst summer since the one before the divorce. I worked out real quick that my dad's not the big-shot doctor he was when I left California. Now he's stuck here managing this crumbly old folks home in the dampest city known to man. I've been here for weeks now, "getting better" and doing my damndest to bug the life out of my dear old dad. I figure, eventually he'll crack up and send me home. Even Chicago would be an improvement on this dump.'

Soren James Blue paused and folded her hands dramatically across her middle. Malcolm Orange lay back on his second X-Men pillow and began prioritizing the barrage of questions which had been buzzing round the inside of his brain. 'Hold on,' he said, somewhat confused, 'if you've been here all summer, and I've been here all summer, how come I've never seen you before? I've never even heard of you until this morning. I can't believe you managed to avoid everyone on the cul-de-sac, all summer.'

'I wasn't living on the cul-de-sac,' Soren James Blue stated bluntly. 'I was in the Center.'

'No way!' said Malcolm. It was a dumb kid thing to say and Malcolm rarely permitted himself the luxury of platitudes but the enormity of Soren's confession had struck him like a dive-bar roundhouse.

'Yeah,' Sorry replied, 'I've been in the Center for nearly two months. Dullest summer of my life, for sure. But, look,' she raised her shirt further to pinch a generous inch of white belly flesh, 'I got better. I'm sort of fat now.'

Malcolm Orange was dumbfounded. He looked at Soren James Blue's naked middle. She was very much alive, and reasonably angry. Perhaps the Center wasn't the death curse he'd always imagined. He had approximately two hundred thousand questions to ask Sorry, beginning at the Center's front door and progressing logically to her ultimate escape, several days previous. His fingers itched for a notepad in which to record this, the most important research project of his life.

'I have a lot of questions,' he said, almost choking on his own teeth with enthusiasm.

Soren James Blue yawned deeply, exposing an entire mouthful of polished metal. 'I'm bored talking about me,' she replied.

'But I need to know about the Center for my research project. I need to know what goes on in there and how you managed to escape. Are you like a fugitive now? Do you need a place to hide out? You can trust me and I'll talk to my mom, she'll understand. You can sleep under the kitchen table so no one sees you through the window.'

Sorry laughed, the very same sprinkler laugh that made him feel suddenly young and thin and incapable of being taken seriously.

'Hold on kid,' she giggled, tugging the X-Men pillow free from his grasp, 'let's get our priorities right. I heard you were disappearing. I don't want you to vanish before I've had a chance to get to know you properly.'

Without further comment she slid off the bed and rescued Mr Fluff from the cavernous pit under Malcolm's bed. Mr Fluff, it appeared, was well used to being hauled around town and immediately settled into position across Sorry's neck, forelegs flopping over one shoulder and hind legs over the other, like a lost lamb straddling the Good Shepherd. Wearing her cat like a mink stole, Sorry scooped Ross, still sleeping, into her arms and strode out of the bedroom, heading for the kitchen.

'I'm thirsty,' she shouted over her disappearing shoulder, 'too much talking. My tongue's gone dry. I need a drink. Do you have any beer, Malcolm?'

Close inspection of the fridge revealed nothing runnier than a bottle of ketchup, two months out of date, and so Malcolm, ever the initiative-taker, screwed the top off Ross's milk bottles and he and Sorry drank 2% straight from the bottle. They drank without speaking, polishing off an entire packet of Chips Ahoy whilst they stared at each other over the kitchen table. Ross, still sleeping, as only Ross could, had been abandoned in the laundry basket by the washing machine with an unwrapped Snickers bar by his head in case he woke hungry.

Soren James Blue had never encountered a baby as small or unresponsive as Ross Orange and, uneducated in all matters infantile, displayed an inappropriateness unrivalled even by Malcolm himself. It had been her original suggestion to strip Ross naked and leave him submerged for the afternoon in a bathtub of lukewarm water. 'Babies poop a lot,' she reminded Malcolm. 'And I'm sure as hell not wiping it up. If we leave him in the bath he'll kind of clean himself off and we can just drain the water before your mom gets home.'

Thankfully the bathtub's only plug had been long since removed; a cautionary move, instigated after Denise DeWitt's untimely death. Malcolm was thus saved the annoyance of explaining to Sorry why a three-month-old baby, unwanted as he was, could not be left free-floating for the afternoon in a bath of lukewarm water. Instead he simply mumbled something about a missing bath plug and left the matter unresolved.

In his own kitchen with a belly full of Chips Ahoy, Malcolm Orange felt his confidence returning. Granted, he was still disappearing and burdened with Ross for the foreseeable future, but he was almost certain he'd found in Soren James Blue an unlikely ally, a friend even, capable perhaps of making some sense of his perforated existence. Thus reassured he licked the crumbs from his fingers, individually, with precocious attention to detail, and stood to address his new friend.

'Sorry,' he said, 'I'd like you to look at my back and tell me how bad it is. My head won't turn far enough to check for myself. I have a flashlight if you need one.'

Soren James Blue had lived through enough serious situations – divorces, hospital wards and psychiatrists – to recognize the need for gravity. She popped the tail end of a final cookie into her mouth, shuffled the crumbs from her lap and turned to face Malcolm.

'Right,' she said, invoking the spirit of some other, dreadfully grave little girl, 'if we're going to do this, we should do it right. I'm a big believer in scientific research Malcolm, so we should probably record the information somewhere.'

'Hold on,' cried Malcolm and dashed from the kitchen, returning momentarily with a brand-new notepad, un-noted. 'I was saving this for a big project but I don't think they come much bigger than this. Take as many notes as you like.'

Soren James Blue opened the notebook at the first blank page and, with scientific precision, in royal blue ink, printed the words 'MALCOLM ORANGE DISAPPEARS' in block capitals. Dampening her pointer finger with spit, she turned the pages by their corners until, having arrived at the third blank page, she prepared to begin her investigation proper.

'Malcolm,' she said, taking notes in a furious hybrid form of shorthand which most closely resembled Morse code indentations, 'when did you first notice yourself disappearing?'

'Yesterday,' he replied, 'in the evening, just before dinner.'

'How do you know you're disappearing?'

'I'm covered in little holes and some of them are pretty big.'

'I see! Are you bleeding from any of these holes? Do you leak when you drink water?'

'Not yet. I mean, you just saw me drink a whole bottle of milk and none of it came out. But I am worried about leaking, or letting water in in the shower. I've put Band-Aids on the biggest holes, but I'm not sure that's going to make much difference in the shower.'

Soren James Blue continued to scribble furiously in the notepad. Malcolm was not sure what she was writing as he'd long since quit speaking. Perhaps she was dyslexic. Dyslexic people took almost three times as long to write down even the simplest sentence and, even then, they usually got their spellings wrong. His father had claimed to be dyslexic, though Malcolm's mother remained militant that this was not real dyslexia, but rather another example of her husband's chronic laziness and bullet dodging. Finally, Sorry looked up from her notes and continued with the interview.

'Is there a history of disappearing in your family?'

'Well, my father disappeared to Mexico with the car and all my grandparents are dead, but it's not really the same kind of disappearing, is it? Mine's more holey.'

'What about drugs? Do you take any drugs, even the medicine kind?'

'Nope.'

'Not even for the diarrhea?'

'Quit bringing up the diarrhea, Sorry. I wish I'd never told you about it. It hardly ever comes out any more. Mostly I just think I'm going to have diarrhea but it doesn't actually happen.'

'Allergies?'

'Well, I don't like bathroom hand driers, or red stoplights, or Kentucky and I once got stuck by the shoelace on a department store elevator, so I'm not that fond of those either, but I wouldn't exactly say I'm allergic.'

'No, you're just chicken shit nervous as far as I can see.'

A further scientific silence ensued.

'It might be dreams,' Malcolm shared, hoping to pique Sorry's interest further. 'I've done a lot of research into dreams. You can really easily dream things true if you're not careful.'

'Balls,' she replied. 'No real scientist would seriously consider dreams. There's a perfectly good explanation for why you're disappearing, Malcolm and I'm going to help you find it.'

'And then will you help me stop it?'

'Maybe. It all depends on how serious the problem is. Look, kid, it's all speculation until I actually have a look at you. Take your clothes off and stand on the table.'

'No way! I'm not getting naked in front of you. You're a girl and you're not even my mom.'

'I've seen it all before,' Sorry replied, chewing the tip of her pen disconcertingly. But Malcolm Orange dug his toes into the kitchen table and stalwartly refused to get naked for her. Stalemate raged for twenty full minutes as science waged war on modesty, locking horns angrily somewhere over the condiments. Eventually a compromise was reached; all clothes would be removed, with the exception of a modesty-concealing pair of underwear. (Horrified by the prospect of an intimate examination by a girl, even if tempered by the security of underwear, Malcolm slipped into his bedroom, removed last night's slightly stained boxers and replaced them with not one, but two pairs of tight white Y-fronts, straight out of the pack. Malcolm Orange was taking no chances when it came to medical research.)

The examination itself was relatively painless. Soren James Blue made a quick outline sketch of a young boy in her notebook and, when complete, bade Malcolm mount the table and disrobe.

'I'm ready,' she said. 'Get up there and take your clothes off. I'm going to mark the disappearing parts in my notepad so we can analyze the data afterwards.'

'Good idea,' replied Malcolm. 'And you should also mark the holes on me with a Magic Marker. That way we can monitor how much bigger they are tomorrow. I saw it on a medical drama. It's how real doctors keep track of infections. If you look in the drawer under the microwave you should find a pack of Magic Markers you can use.'

Soren James Blue went rifling through the drawer and returned with a luminous orange marker, and a pair of his late grandma's reading glasses. 'Score,' she yelled, holding one lens up to her right eye. 'These bad boys are stronger than a friggin' microscope. I'm not going to miss any of your disappearing bits now.'

Malcolm Orange scrambled onto the kitchen table and

removed his shirt and shorts, flinging them across the kitchen where they came to rest half in, half out of the sink. His feet straddled the salt and pepper cellars. His head came within inches of the ceiling fan. The thrash of it, rotating mere fingers from his crown, caused his hair to rise and fall in a well-fluffed parody of flight. He looked at the dripping faucet and tried to conceal his embarrassment.

Soren James Blue began at his ankles and, swapping the flashlight and spectacles from hand to hand, moved ever upwards, taking occasional notes in her notebook. She worked silently, placing a firm, directorial hand on Malcolm's ankle when she wished him to pivot left or right. At first she was bent double, folded like a paperback novel, as she approached his crotch she straightened up and by the beginning of his shoulders was forced to employ a kitchen stool for a proper view. For a girl, inclined to excessive outbursts of anger and vomit, she made a meticulous researcher. Arriving finally at Malcolm's face she explored, with an upturned teaspoon, the inside of his mouth, ruffled through his hair and eyebrows and even made a cautious exploration of his eardrums. Somewhere about the kneecaps, Malcolm Orange began to relax and by the time Sorry was approaching his midriff, had settled right into the idea of being investigated by a girl, if only for scientific research.

Approximately fifteen minutes later, Soren James Blue recapped her Magic Marker and jumped down from the kitchen stool. The investigation was over. Malcolm looked down at his naked torso, expecting to be peppered in dots and circles. Sorry's fingers, frantically poking and prodding across the landscape of his naked flesh, had left him convinced that the perforations were worse than even he had anticipated. However, only a single orange circle, navigating the edge of his bellybutton, blared beacon-like from his middle. Malcolm was confused. He ran a finger round the circumference of his bellybutton, following the outline of the Magic Marker, and looked to Sorry for guidance.

'That's the only hole I could find,' she said. 'And it looks perfectly normal to me. It's just an ordinary bellybutton. Congratulations, Malcolm. It turns out you're not disappearing after all.'

This was a mystery to Malcolm. Even now, with an audience, he could clearly make out the holes all over his naked arms and torso. His knees were almost entirely missing. Even the microwave door supported his worst suspicions. The backs of his shins were pickled with reflected perforations. His heels were holes, grasping at the base of his ankles. Malcolm Orange was disappearing, this much was obvious, and Soren James Blue simply wasn't willing to admit it.

'Dammit, Sorry,' he said, raising his voice to outdo the ceiling fan, 'I AM disappearing. Why won't you admit it?'

But before Sorry could rise to her own defense the back door flew open (having been long in need of a good oiling, the doors of Chalet 13 willfully resisted all ordinary openings and closings and could only be forced into acquiescence with the kind of brute force which rendered all movements sudden and somewhat dramatic).

The clip of the door slamming into the kitchen wall caused Mr Fluff to rise from her sleeping spot atop the microwave oven and land, vitriolic and spitting, upon Sorry's shoulders. Thereafter Sorry, suddenly unbalanced, fell forwards on to the kitchen table, dislodging Malcolm, who tumbled naked and sprawling across the kitchen floor, forming a squirming roadblock for the kitchen's latest occupant.

The door swung back on its hinges and before Sorry and Malcolm could untangle themselves, opened again, admitting a somewhat frail and tweedy man fumbling forwards with two garden canes. The inevitable proceeded in slow motion. The old man, with a hearty cry of, 'Malcolm, I've come to get you for the People's Committee,' took two tentative steps forward and made untimely contact with Malcolm's naked heel. One garden cane ventured due south, whilst the other headed north, and the elderly man, like a tin can pyramid, toppled forwards, sandwiching Malcolm Orange between his own skinny belly and Soren James Blue, who was now pinioned chin first to the kitchen floor. After the impact and the inevitable round of mutters and arthritic groans, Sorry raised herself up on one elbow, allowing Mr Fluff free passage to extricate her tail and left paw, which had become trapped at the base of the pile. 'Holy Crap,' she thought, fully aware of her father's fury and the compromising nature of her current position, pinned to the floor by a semi-naked stranger, 'this looks bad. Really, really bad.'

Speaking from the side of her mouth, utilizing to the best of her ability the limited movement afforded by the full weight of Malcolm Orange's shoulder, she addressed the elderly man, wriggling atop her, 'This isn't what it looks like, sir. There's a really good explanation for all of this.'

Soren James Blue need not have worried, for Cunningham Holt had been blind as a bat since the age of six, when an unfortunate incident with a Fourth of July firework left him with two painted marbles in lieu of real eyes.

– Chapter Six –

Cunningham Holt

Cunningham Holt was just getting used to his eyes when they upped and left him; right first, followed, some three violent seconds later, by the left.

The left eye was never found. The right eye popped clean out of the socket – removing a small section of eyelid in the process – and was located hanging by the thinnest wire of nerve from the tip of his nose. Mr Holt, who'd seen more than his fair share of farmyard horrors – severed limbs, bull-gored boys and two-headed lambs – calmly scooped the errant eyeball into an egg cup and commanded his son to hold his own eye, 'steady as you can', all the way to the local doctor's house.

Though it was rare for the Holts to agree on anything more complex than the day after Christmas, the whole family worked together to save young Cunningham's sight. Mr Holt drove like the devil himself, making town in less than half an hour. Mrs Holt – a strong believer in the preserving power of saline – salted the eyeball until it looked like a piece of boiled candy, while Cunningham's older sisters, Valentine and Sharon, did their part by staying home to lead a torch-lit, and ultimately futile, search for the absent left.

Despite the best efforts of the entire Holt family it was

immediately apparent that the remaining eye could not be saved. By the time Cunningham arrived at the doctor's door the right eye was already beginning to turn green around the edges.

The town doctor, a kindly-faced man who peddled home brew and butterscotch from the back door of his surgery, was far from encouraging. 'Take young Cunningham to the tent revivalists,' he suggested, washing his hands as he passed the buck back to God. 'That's my best advice, folks. Take him to the charismatics and get them to pray for a miracle. There's no medical hope for the child, but those colored folk can do strange things with the Holy Ghost. I'll tidy him up of course, pop some marbles in so he don't look so misshapen and give him a dose of something for the pain, but he won't ever see again in this life.'

For many weeks thereafter Cunningham Holt, swathed nose to crown like a shrunken Punjabi, was transported to every tent revival within a three county radius. Accompanied by either his mother or one of her three formidable sisters, he found himself unceremoniously hauled up for healing at the end of every meeting. Oftentimes the offer of a Holy Ghost miracle was only made available to born again believers and so young Cunningham was coerced into getting saved on half a dozen separate occasions, only narrowly avoiding the possibility of baptism by claiming an extreme allergy to river water.

During these unfortunate outings all manner of righteous humiliation was visited upon the boy, most often in full view of the entire cackling congregation. Twice he found himself anointed with a stinking paste of spit and mud, twice he was knocked to his knees, once there were snakes and, on each and every occasion, manifold hysterics and hollering. Though his body shook, responding to a bipartisan mix of divine intervention and human prodding, though his heart raced and the Holy

Ghost was said to be shimmering like a pillar of fire over his head so he pissed himself from sheer, undiluted fear of the Lord, Cunningham's marble eyes remained stubbornly unchanged.

Eventually, when every two-bit revivalist had been proven incapable and even the preacher who claimed to raise the dead had refused contact for fear of his reputation, Mrs Holt put her foot down and pronounced her son an agnostic.

'The Lord giveth and the Lord taketh away,' she announced to the entire Holt family, 'and if the Lord don't see fit to giving back a six-year-old child's eyes then I figure I'm just about done with religion, and Cunningham too and all the littl'uns. Papa, you can make your own mind up about all that Jesus stuff. You're big enough and dumb enough to decide for yourself, but don't be expecting us to go to no church services with you.'

The matter was closed. Cunningham Holt would be blind for the rest of his mortal days. God was to be blamed in part. His own father confessed his partiality, having been directly responsible for the explosion; whilst the remaining portion of blame was delegated to an unnamed Mexican lad who had, on the third of July, unwittingly swapped a crate-load of faulty fireworks for a bag of the Holts' finest potatoes and a small side of salted beef.

In place of eyes the six-year-old Cunningham found himself ill-blessed with a pair of meaty gashes. For one full year his eye sockets were tender to the touch and prone to inopportune weeping, bursting forth like a Holy Mary statue at the first mention of beauty. Later the sockets were stretched to host a seasonal rotation of hand-painted marbles. Cunningham Holt was suddenly afforded the pleasure of changing his eye color daily; matching his pupils to his ankle socks, to the kaleidoscopic spectrum of the Kentucky skyline or the smallest whims of his imagination. Though the very idea of color was fast slipping from his memory, he almost always favored the original blues. On somber occasions and the Fourth of July, however, he was known to insist upon gray eyes. 'I want people to know I'm feeling serious inside,' he confessed. 'And also a little bit sad.'

His older sister, Valentine, whose job it was to place the correct marbles in his hand each morning, turned slowly mean on the guilt of her own perfect vision. Taking her resentment out on Cunningham she would, from time to time, slip him a blue and a brown marble, a pair of cat's eye or a milk-white gaming marble just for the delight of making him look like a moron (As a grown-up lady she would deeply regret her own actions and make several stilted attempts at confession before leaving a deathbed letter outlining these and other childhood indiscretions, long-forgotten.)

Cunningham Holt grew thin on the absence of pictures. He grew upwards and inwards – taller at twelve than any kid in the county – but failed to fatten up. By the age of sixteen he was six feet and eight inches high, yet painfully slight and capable of squeezing himself, with little effort, through the inside of an unstrung tennis racquet. Cunningham's mother, an intuitive lady who boasted quarter-strength Sioux blood, assumed her son absolutely empty inside. 'It's not your fault,' she whispered to Cunningham as he fussed over his protruding ribs. 'You've nothing to thicken yourself up with. It's memories and thoughts that mark the difference between a man and a skeleton, and you've only got six years' worth of things to consider.'

Her musings proved cold comfort to Cunningham Holt who, just one decade after July Fourth, was already running out of things to consider.

He passed most of his teenage years in a purpose-built shed, reclining in pitch darkness. 'For what,' he argued adamantly, 'was the point in wasting electric light on a blind man?' Close friends and family, friends of the family, and sometimes neighbors, were permitted to enter each day between the hours of two and five. They traveled many miles, often on foot, to visit with Cunningham. Most counted it Christian duty to do their bit for the tragic. Having exhausted the usual round of orphans and widows they'd finally arrive, well-intentioned, on the Holts' doorstep. They brought with them small jars, scrapbooks, shoeboxes and occasional crates containing sights for Cunningham's collection. Venturing into the shed, Magi-like, they presented their gifts to the boy and took great pains to describe, with collared accuracy, the peculiar attributes of each sight.

Some sights had been collected for their beauty. Thus, sea shells, oil paintings and porcelain dolls found their way on to the racks of Cunningham's shed where they shared precious shelf space with jars of dog shit, broken bottles and formaldehyde mice, each selected for the offensive nature of its appearance. Cunningham Holt, painfully aware that his own library of visual memories was extremely limited, relied upon this ragtag collection of other people's sights to keep his senses sharp and excited.

Each evening, before bed, he would ask his mother not for a bedtime story or blessing but rather a lengthy description of one of these specimens. By the time he arrived at his eighteenth birthday the collection had expanded to fill two subsequent sheds and was now rife with sights Cunningham could no longer stretch to imagine. Having never had the opportunity to experience for himself a toaster oven, a sticking plaster or, perhaps most pertinently, a television set, Cunningham was forced to rely on his six short years of memory to conjure up appropriate comparisons. Thus a toaster oven, though painstakingly and repeatedly described by Cousin Herb from South Dakota, was filed away in the recesses of Cunningham's mind as an object roughly comparable to a self-heating mailbox. Meanwhile, a sticking plaster appeared to be a cross between envelope glue and a pair of his mother's nylons.

The television set proved impossible for Cunningham to imagine, even when parked in front of its screen with the volume set to high.

Had he been given prior warning Cunningham Holt might have taken the trouble to catalogue a range of suitable visual memories; the sort of sights which would keep him smiling through the proceeding seven decades. Naked ladies, technological advances and the cut of his own face, adult now and peppered with coarse stubble, were right at the top of this wish list. However, Cunningham's final seeing memory remained, for now and all time, the somewhat disappointing sight of his father's backside, exploding glutinously from his weekend britches as he bent to light firework fuses. Other memories were childish in the extreme: scarecrows, candy apples and the back of his mother's meeting hat, bobbing along to the Sunday hymns.

Cunningham Holt struggled to contemplate the rest of his life with only six short years' worth of references to play with. (Two of these years, he noted with grim realism, had been wasted in a state of blank infancy.)

On the Fourth of July, 1938, Cunningham was nineteen years old and purposefully ignorant of the situation simmering in mainland Europe. Closer to home, cataclysmic change was also about to descend upon the Holt household. Blissfully unaware of how the day would progress, Cunningham woke at the normal hour, consumed for breakfast his usual bowl of porridge and prunes, sat for three hours in one chair and two in another, before proceeding to shed number three where he planned to greet the day's visitors. (July Fourth had for the previous thirteen years gone uncelebrated in the Holt household. The only indicator that this particular Monday was to be marked beyond all ordinary Mondays was Cunningham's choice of dove gray marbles.)

At 2pm on the dot Cunningham Holt lowered his backside into his normal seat and shoved the shed door open with the toe of his boot. Knowing full well the ridiculous regard with which most Americans held July Fourth and the celebrations currently unfolding in backyards and picnic fields all across Kentucky, Cunningham was fully prepared to receive no visitors beyond his immediate family.

However, the open door revealed a single visitor waiting with eager intent on the steps of his shed. After clearing her throat somewhat theatrically, announcing her presence not only to Cunningham but also two curious chickens and the sheepdogs who lived between the sheds, she stepped inside and stood on the little red rug immediately in front of his feet.

'Hey,' she said. Her voice was uppity, east coast: Boston or New York perhaps. Cunningham flipped through his back catalogue of radio memories and struggled to place her geographically. He was absolutely certain they'd never met before.

'Hey,' he said. 'What's your name?'

'Claire,' she said, and in the thirty-six months of their mutual existence Cunningham Holt was never to find out her second name.

'What did you bring me?' he asked.

'Myself,' she replied, and kicked the shed door closed with the back of her heel.

Four hours later the couple emerged, glowing red and ravenous hungry. They devoured an entire batch of Mrs Holt's home-baked scones fresh from the stove and were married within the week. Two months later Claire was great with child and fast expanding to fill the guest room bed where the newly-wed couple had taken up residence.

Though speculation raged loud around the Holt farm, the details of Cunningham's seduction went no further than the walls of shed number three. When asked by his father, who'd retained, alongside his agricultural skills, a particularly Lutheran notion of morality, exactly what they'd been doing in a garden shed for four hours with the door closed, Cunningham simply smiled wistfully and said, 'Using our imaginations.' In reality Claire had opened his eyes to a world much bigger than specimen jars and shoeboxes. Cunningham Holt was never the same again. His thoughts were no longer limited to six small years and sliding. His empty head quickly became a cavernous frame for crazy pictures and fresh, imagined sights not yet existent in the actual world.

Cunningham Holt, newly inspired by his young bride, became God of a universe where colors, shapes, tones and textures were just waiting to be invented. Within hours his nineteen-year-old mind had made the monumental leap from lamenting his lack of sight to rejoicing in the possibilities offered by an imagination undiluted by the limitations of reality.

Each morning Claire was a brand-new lady, ripe for discovery. 'Who are you today?' he would ask as soon as he awoke, rolling towards the sound of her voice.

'I am a Chinese lady with sin-black hair,' she would say on Monday.

'I am a freckle-faced redhead,' on Tuesday.

'I'm old enough to be your mother,' on Wednesday and perversely, on Thursday, 'I'm fourteen years old and recently run away from home.'

Cunningham Holt's imagination ran loose and free all over her body, picturing patterns and colors and features stolen from God himself. When she finally claimed, two weeks into their marriage, to be striped all over like a human zebra, he had no problem summoning up the cut of her naked shoulders, criss-crossed black and white.

The remaining members of the Holt family held their tongues for fear of upsetting the delicate balance of Cunningham's imagination. Though he begged nightly and bargained for an accurate description of his new wife, his mother stalwartly refused to oblige. It was thirteen years since she'd last seen her son so fat or happy. She was wise enough to admit that the image he'd created was ten times more inspiring than the lazy eye and mousy hair which kept Claire plain as a paper plate and, no doubt, hankering after a blind husband.

By the time Claire's belly had swollen to a point where Cunningham could feel his unborn son beating frantically just below the skin, she was beginning to get itchy feet. Claire was a canny young thing and fully aware that Cunningham's future devotion depended entirely on the preservation of an illusion. She kept her past – a desperately mediocre tale of middle-class parents and secretarial school – a well-guarded secret and militantly refused to give any clues to her origins. Cunningham correctly suspected his wife to hail from the East and so it came as no big surprise when she suggested they pack their bags and move to Brooklyn, New York.

'Lord Almighty, woman,' Cunningham retorted, instigating the first proper argument of their five-month marriage. 'What on earth will I do in Brooklyn? I'll be run over by a streetcar. I'll be mown down in my prime.'

'Nonsense,' Claire replied, 'we'll get you a seeing eye dog, and a cane.'

'What will my parents do without me on the farm?'

'I'd say they'll manage just fine. You don't do anything round here except eat and move from one chair to the other all day.'

'I can't leave my sheds,' he said at last, desperate for an excuse to stay somewhere close to the familiar. 'It's taken me years to build up the collection. I can't leave it now.'

And so Claire, who knew a roadblock when she saw one, bribed her in-laws with an antique watch, property of her late grandfather, and the sure-fire promise that Cunningham would be happier and closer to a normal nineteen-year-old if he was finally encouraged to leave the family homestead. Armored then with the unequivocal backing and finances of all four Holts, she crossed her fingers and woke Cunningham early on the very next Sunday.

'Wake up, sweetheart,' she cried, shaking him violently by the shoulder so one of his marble eyes came loose and rolled across the bedspread. 'Wake up now. I have something to tell you.'

Bleary-headed, Cunningham Holt rolled towards her voice and caught the faintest whiff of coffee breath. 'Who are you today, Claire?' he asked, assuming the dramatics were all part of her daily service. 'You know it really gets me going when you do the hysterics.'

'I'm serious, Cunningham. I have terrible news.'

'Is it the baby?'

'No it's not the baby, and before you ask, it's not your folks. No one's sick. No one's died but it is bad news.'

'Look, honey, just tell me quick. Bad news should be told quick or it just hurts more.'

'The sheds have sunk.'

'What?'

'The sheds have sunk.'

'It's not possible. Sheds don't sink. They catch fire or blow away in tornadoes. They don't sink.'

'Believe me Cunningham, the sheds have sunk overnight. It must be more marshy out there than we thought.'

'All three of them?'

'Gone.'

'And my collection?'

'Gone. I'm so sorry, Cunningham. I wish there was something I could do to bring them back.'

Cunningham Holt, devastated by the realization that the earth would choose to conspire against him in such dramatic fashion – suddenly, overnight, and with no previous warning, not even a slightly mushy patch of field – pressed his face into the pillow and howled like a newborn baby. Thirteen years of his life had been swallowed up without permission. It felt just like Fourth of July all over again.

No one ever told Cunningham Holt the terrible truth behind his sinking sheds. His elder sister Valentine, who had always been the meaner of the two, confessed all in a posthumous letter but as this letter, for necessity's sake, had been read aloud to Cunningham by his youngest sister, Sharon, who could not help but see the best in everyone, all mention of the conspiracy was intentionally censored out.

Truth be told Mr Holt, under his daughter-in-law's direction, had dismantled all three sheds during the night and dispatched both the structures themselves and their contents to the back field where they'd formed the basis of an enormous fifteen-foot bonfire. Folks two counties over, intrigued by the ungodly orange glow now illuminating the Kentucky horizon, presumed yet another incident at the state asylum. Double-barring their backdoors against the possibility of an escapee, they fell asleep with loaded shotguns and pickaxes tucked beneath their bed frames.

After two days the bonfire burnt itself out and though Cunningham queried after the prevailing smoky scent and the fine flecks of ash which coated everything, even his morning coffee, in a sulphuric powder, he was never to know the truth behind the bonfire. 'It was a tree,' his father explained, adding his own particular thread to the fine web of lies Claire had already begun. 'You know, the big oak in the corner of the back field? It got struck by lightning last night and there was nothing to do but let it burn.' Cunningham Holt was suspicious, knowing full well that this particular oak had been sacrificed for last Christmas's firewood, but said nothing, for he'd had no reason to doubt his father.

By the beginning of the following week all that remained of Cunningham's collection was a charred spot in the cornfield, approximately the size and shape of a family sedan. Though Mr Holt continued to till the corner of his cornfield annually, to water it and spread liberal amounts of the purest fertilizer, thick as frosting, over its topsoil, nothing ever grew in this particular corner of the field again. Each subsequent year of ungrowth added to the weight of guilt Mr Holt was already shouldering. He was an honest man, Lutheran to the back teeth, and this was the only intentional lie he could recall telling. Though he repented nightly, asking God to forgive his trespasses, particularly the one about the sheds, the stress of it drove him to a premature death at the age of forty-six, from complications attached to the removal of an ingrown toenail. On his deathbed, turned crazy by almost ten years of guilt, he asked to be buried upside down in the corner of the back field. Thereafter, the charred patch suddenly burst into life, sprouting grass and corn and all manner of unctuous, creeping wildflowers.

On the day of the sinking Cunningham Holt lingered under the bed sheets for the entire morning, allowing the disconcerting news to settle into the spare room wallpaper. He rose around lunchtime and, still wearing carpet slippers and bathrobe, demanded a tour of the empty space recently occupied by his sheds. Claire guided him down the steps and then watched from the front porch as her husband, on hands and knees, meticulously poked and prodded his way round fifty square foot of field. Not once during the four and a half hours which it took for Cunningham to reassure his own sense of loss did Claire experience even the smallest sliver of regret. Duplicity was a necessary evil when it came to keeping blind husbands keen and Claire was capable of duplicity on a scale seldom seen in rural Kentucky.

'Darling,' she yelled when the rest of the family assembled for their nightly helping of fried chicken and corn, 'it's getting dark out. Why don't you come in for dinner?'

Her words went unacknowledged by Cunningham Holt who, flat on his face in the starchy grass, was rediscovering a religion long lost. All through the night he pressed his cheek to the ground and prayed earnestly for a genuine miracle.

'Heavenly Father, Lord God Jesus,' he muttered, ill-equipped with the rhetoric of religion, 'if thou hast raised from the dead, on several occasions and counting, couldst thou also see fit to raise from the miry clay one of my sheds, or two if it's not too much bother?

'And if thou shouldst see fit to raise from the miry clay one of my sheds,' he continued late into the night, when the rest of the family were long gone to bed and dreaming, 'couldst thou see fit to raise the second shed particularly? You know, the one with the stuffed animals?'

The Lord God kept frustratingly quiet, holding both his tongue and his resurrection hand all the way through the early hours until Cunningham Holt, almost spent with yearning, finally cried out, 'Lord God, Holy Jesus, I have hast enough of thee all over again. First thou taketh away my eyes, then thou cometh back for the sheds. Thou really ought to go ahead and give me something for a change. Amen.'

That afternoon Cunningham Holt gathered his collection of painted marbles in the toe of an old wool sock, took his wife in hand and set out for Brooklyn, New York. For the second time in twenty years he spurned the Lord's advances and converted to agnosticism. Though he didn't know it at the time, he was never to set foot on Kentucky soil again.

New York swallowed Cunningham whole. As he made his daily, nicotine-charged pilgrimage from the front stoop to the bodega on the corner he felt like Jonah searching for an emergency exit. He walked deliberately, counting the individual sidewalk tiles – one to seventy, there and back – all the time struggling against the walls of pressure which seemed to rush against his rib cage, viciously and with preternatural force. The city was an ever-constricting vice and Cunningham Holt struggled not to suffocate every time he stepped outside.

The Kentucky of his childhood had been an enormous kingdom strung together with empty, unambiguous fields and the vague hope of an occasional tree. Prior to the advent of July Fourth, 1919, Cunningham Holt had known by name only a half dozen individuals outside his own immediate family. He prided himself on small-time living, relishing the detail afforded by a limited number of human variables. The Sunday school picnic, organized annually by the local Baptist congregation, remained the largest gathering he'd ever been party to. Even then, with the possibility of some two hundred individuals to play with, the five-year-old Cunningham had favored, over new friends and neighbors, the company of an elderly Jack Russell and a platter of homemade deviled eggs. With no composite memory to fall back on, he struggled to believe in something as large and loud as New York City.

Cunningham Holt began to picture himself buried alive in an underground city. His New York was a tunneled kingdom; a moleish world of condensed living where rich and poor, old and creeping young were thrown one upon the other like sweet onions peering from a pickle jar. While the city thrilled like a liquored kid and the tower blocks rose to clasp hands sixteen storys above his head, while the tall buildings shook and the sidewalks trembled with the chumbling surge of each passing streetcar, he felt only blind isolation and the absence of sunlight like an old friend, recently deceased.

Each day the noise wore Cunningham a little thinner round the edges until he began to see himself as a slice of greaseproof paper, transparent against the light. The city waged war on his eardrums beginning with his first waking thought and stretching long past midnight when the never-ending din would finally settle as a toothache migraine in the space behind his eyes. Accidental fireworks aside, New York was the loudest thing Cunningham Holt had ever heard. The skittling thunder of city living formed walls and bridges around his every waking moment. Each raised-voice conversation, each siren, scream, screech-brake stop and unloosed hydrant, bursting forth with gassy enthusiasm, formed another brick in the thick wall which conspired to keep him claustrophobic and lonely in the third-floor apartment he refused to call home.

'What sort of a hell have you dragged us to?' he asked his new wife as they lay awake on their very first evening, clamoring between the police sirens and the impossible August heat. Cunningham stretched out stark naked on the sheets, having sweltered his way though all three of his decent undershirts. The unborn baby, which had recently swollen to the size of a clenched grapefruit, was taking liberties with his mother's innards and Claire, having grown tired of trekking down the hall to use the third floor's only working bathroom, had spent the better part of the day retching into a mop bucket beside the bed. The smell of sweat and vomit dripped from the ceiling; homely scents, mingling sickeningly with the exotic stench of spice and coconut milk emanating from the Indian family on the floor below.

As they lay side by side, glistening pink like a pair of uncooked sausages, the argument wilted on their lips, falling victim to the hour and the heat and the incessant hum of the electric light bulb. They made lackluster love on the bedroom floor – for the summer had sapped them of all but the last remaining ounce of energy – and fell asleep with the ice box open. It was the first of many east coast arguments, all of which struggled to arrive at a satisfactory conclusion.

Cunningham Holt daily proposed an absolute and immediate move to a more temperate home and yet would find himself, fifty-two years later, unfulfilled and still making the very same argument.

Claire bloomed through the honeymoon years. Her teeth turned fast and tight, flashing their way through a smorgasbord of newborn experiences: foreign folks and fancy foods, concert shows, conversations and the cosmopolitan rush of sidewalk fashion. Her belly grew fat and burst suddenly, shoving an urgent red boy child onto the end of their bed. Without consulting her husband, who had never seen a movie, silent or otherwise, she named their child Chaplin and the boy became as much of a mystery to Cunningham as his mustachioed namesake. Within the year Claire's head had grown a half inch wider in circumference, swelling to store a hundred sheds worth of grim and glorious sights. (Having hooked a husband incapable of leaving her, Claire quit bothering to indulge him and refused to describe these New York experiences. 'Use your imagination,' she snapped when he asked for a blow by blow retelling of the Empire State Building. Cunningham cried a little, discreetly into his sweater sleeve, and pictured a knitting needle, steel grey and tall enough to puncture the cloud line. Later, with guilt and righteous hope, he dreamt of pushing his wife from the topmost pinnacle.)

Claire took a job in the downtown offices of a fashion magazine and in less than a year had wheedled her way upwards from intern to junior clerk and, finally, assistant editor; a role which came with a desk, a chair and the opportunity to screw the editor proper twice a week during lunch breaks. It was partly her editorial skills, perfected many years previously at the Boston Secretarial School for Young Ladies, and partly her ability to keep the editor proper grinning for the entire fifty-minute duration of lunch break, which landed Claire the opportunity to edit a sister magazine in Chicago. Preoccupied at first by the paycheck and the promise of an office window, south-facing, she sunk her fingernails into his naked back and accepted the offer before the editor proper had a chance to withdraw. Only later, as she fixed her make-up in the bathroom mirror, did she consider the deadweight reality of Cunningham and Chaplin, waiting on her nightly return.

Claire was an ambitious young lady, and having taken the Holt family for the cost of a single to Penn Station and a year's worth of rent, she had no further use for a dumb hick husband, too blind to bring in a wage. Chicago, she'd heard, was bubbling over with nightclubs and restaurants and elderly men, rich and discerning enough to ignore her plain horse face in favor of the fancy hairdos and frocks she'd been spending her pay packet on. Before the afternoon was out Claire had already decided to leave her husband.

While his wife went out to work, Cunningham Holt stayed home and watched the baby who, for safety's sake, spent working hours encased in a purpose-built baby cage and was only removed for the occasional diaper change or feed; maneuvers which had taken Cunningham some three unpleasant months to perfect. During the early days of Chaplin's existence his mother would often come home to find him placidly cooing from his orange box crib, smeared in part in his own shit or milky vomit. 'For the love of God, Cunningham,' Claire had yelled at her husband on several occasions, 'if you're not sure whether the kid's clean, stick him in the bath tub for ten minutes. Don't leave him to rot in his own puke.'

Ultimately it was Cunningham Holt's fear of neglecting the child which gave Claire an opportunity to put her escape plan into action. Coming home early on a Friday evening in late November she stumbled upon Cunningham perched on the edge of their bed, watching blindly as his son lay, back flat in the bottom of the tin bathtub. Chaplin Holt, well used to the bitter boredom of being ignored, had fallen asleep in the tub, his little chest rising and falling as it broke the surface of the graying bathwater. It was impossible to tell how long he'd been there, minutes perhaps, hours even. Claire leaned over the edge of the tub and tested the temperature of the water. It was lukewarm to the touch. Momentarily possessed by the Devil and all his devilish subplots she stood up, opened her mouth and shrieked like a wildcat.

'My baby!' she yelled. 'My poor baby!' She pitched her voice loud enough to register intent but was, at the same time, careful not to wake the sleeping baby.

'What's wrong?' cried Cunningham Holt who was also dozing, upright on the edge of the bed. (It was often hard for Claire to tell whether her husband was awake or asleep as his eyelids, missing a substantial chunk on the right side, closed only when manually pinched shut.)

'Chaplin's gone.'

'No, he's not. He's right there in the bathtub. He was covered in crap so I gave him a wash.'

'He's sunk.'

'Impossible. There's only half a foot of water in there.'

'The baby's sunk. He's drowned dead, Cunningham, what will we do?'

'Call for the doctor Claire. The doctor'll be able to fix him!'

'It's too late for the doctor, Cunningham. You let our baby sink.'

While Cunningham Holt sobbed mercilessly into his pillow, cursing the Almighty for yet another untimely sinking, Claire lifted her baby, still sleeping, from the bathtub and wrapped him in one of Cunningham's old sweaters which had begun to unravel at the elbow.

'I'm running down to the drugstore to phone the undertaker,' Claire shouted as she left the apartment, 'You have to tell them when someone dies or the police get involved.'

Thereafter, she slipped undetected down the back stairs and

without a second thought left her six-month-old baby, haphazardly bundled against the November chill, on the steps of the Catholic Mission. (Chaplin Holt would be found half an hour later by a gaggle of middle-aged nuns on their way to early evening Mass. When local enquiries had surfaced no clues as to the little boy's identity, he was to be renamed Patrick – for several of the nuns were of an Irish disposition – and ushered into the first of three subsequent Catholic orphanages before being placed, quite happily, with a childless couple in the Hamptons who would rechristen him Michael and bring him up as their very own. For the rest of his life Michael would nurture an inexplicable fear of bathtubs, always preferring to shower, or, when a shower was not available, bathe in a supervised context. A series of lovers and wives would be baffled and slightly unnerved by his inability to wash without an audience, assuming latent voyeuristic tendencies. Swimming pools and Jacuzzis would also prove problematic.)

It was with a sinking feeling, akin to a six-month-old baby or garden shed, that Cunningham Holt contemplated the coming years in Brooklyn, New York. With all the darkly yearning of an Old Testament prophet he predicted a future full of loss and solemn sinkings. For God so favored all men aside from Cunningham Holt, it seemed inevitable that everything and everyone he'd ever loved would be snatched from him and drawn into that dark place just below the mortal grasp. The city, he felt sure, would remain, for he hated New York with a devotion rarely seen or settled in the irreligious. Whilst friends and family and all good things were peeled from his possession, New York would prosper on: bridges and buildings and telephone wires stretching Babel-like towards the future sky. On the eve of his twenty-first birthday, with not so much as a cake to mark the passing, Cunningham Holt sat down on his sofa and resigned himself to loss; past, present and apocalyptic.

'At the current rate of sinking,' he remarked to himself, one-third of the way down his birthday bottle of Jack, 'Kentucky state'll be underwater before my twenty-fifth.'

The loss of his wife came therefore as less of a surprise, than a prophecy fulfilled.

Driven by a rare streak of benevolence, Claire had decided to give Cunningham Holt a month to recover from the death of his son before absconding to Chicago with the remaining two hundred dollars of his family's money. 'It would be a sin,' she told the editor proper, who was eager to have her installed before the New Year, 'to leave anyone just before Christmas. I'll stay 'til the twenty-sixth and buy him something nice for Christmas – a new sweater or some carpet slippers – it'll soften the blow.'

'Whatever you say, sugar pie,' replied the editor proper, and presented her with the very same pair of diamond earrings he had already purchased for his wife. 'An early Christmas present,' he whispered as he pinned them to her earlobes. 'Let me take you out on the town to show them off.'

That night, driven by a dark, city lust, Claire offered her husband the excuse of an office Christmas party. She fixed his dinner at the ungodly hour of 4pm, washed and curled her hair and prepared to sneak out of the apartment in a borrowed gown worth almost half a year's rent. 'Don't wait up, honey,' she sang over her retreating shoulder, 'it'll be a late one. The girls from the accounts department sure do know how to party.' The smell of expensive perfume lingered in her wake like an exotic antidote to the apartment's usual kitchen scents.

Struck by a wave of nostalgia, Cunningham Holt reached to

grab at his wife's fleeting elbow, capturing instead a handful of thick cashmere coat. 'Who are you tonight, Claire?' he asked. She laughed like a birthday balloon recently punctured and said, 'Salome, off to dance in a borrowed dress.' Cunningham Holt held his tongue and smiled, still wary of admitting ignorance in front of his new wife.

(Much later, after the sinking and the funeral, when the thought of Claire had been surrendered to the soil in a plywood coffin weighted with bricks, Cunningham Holt would turn to the itinerant preacher conducting the service and ask, 'Sir, is there a lady named Salome in history or the Bible?'

'Shoosh,' the itinerant preacher would hiss somewhat hysterically, being of the short-sighted belief that the blind were almost inevitably also hard of hearing. 'I don't care if your wife was Jezebel herself. It's wrong to speak ill of the dead, Mr Holt.'

Though he'd never heard of Jezebel either, Cunningham Holt would gather it was neither the time nor the place to pursue his ignorance. 'God rest her pretty soul,' he'd cry, eye sockets sopping with treacherous intent. 'The Lord giveth and the Lord taketh away,' he'd say as the itinerant preacher raised a loud 'Amen.' 'Blessed be the name of the Lord,' he would mumble into the advent rain and curse his own dumb luck, and curse the Lord of luck and also loss, and finally curse his Jezebel bride to the very bottom of the Atlantic Ocean.)

Once the apartment door had swooshed closed behind her, Claire became a different person. Leaving all memory of Cunningham dozing dully on the Chesterfied suite, she swept her skirt tails up in one hand and ran down all three flights of stairs, giggling like a prom-bound teenager. Outside she walked two brisk blocks and hailed a cab to downtown Manhattan. The night proceeded along lines long established by all those adulterers who'd passed before them, lustering down Fifth Avenue and skirting Central Park in rented buggies. The editor proper dined Claire first and subsequently wined her in a series of exclusive bars and nightclubs. As the night progressed towards its inevitable conclusion the editor proper became less proper and more adept in his exploration of her undergarments. 'Perhaps we should slip away from here,' he suggested, yelling across the third of four empty Martini glasses, which littered their section of the bar. 'Let's find somewhere a little quieter.'

And thus it came to pass that Claire Holt found herself supine in a sailboat, fumble-minded and hitching her fifty-dollar skirts for a balding man from North Carolina. Overhead, on the pier, other courting couples kissed and conversed and admired the November night sky, whilst in a small dinghy fifty feet below the pier Claire closed her eyes and hoped to high Heaven that all this sweaty unpleasantness would definitely lead to a corner office, south facing. However, it was not the thrashing, crashing act of adultery exercised in a floating vessel which led to Claire's untimely death, but rather the combination of six gin and tonics (which caught her on disembarkation, fuzzy-footed and toppling into the ice cold river), and the cashmere coat (which was a lead weight when damp, dragging her quickly to the bottom of the river).

The editor proper, who was an honest man at heart – a non-practicing Catholic with guilty feet – did the honorable thing and offered to break the news himself.

'I'm afraid I have some bad news about your wife,' he announced to Cunningham, standing in the living room of the apartment, somewhat reluctant to commit himself to the Chesterfield suite.

'She's sunk, hasn't she?' replied Cunningham Holt and plucked out his painted eyeballs, left first, followed by right, for they tended to slip out when he wept.

The editor proper, removing his hat in a gesture of sympathetic guilt, backed quickly out of the apartment and fled home to his own wife who, despite her similarity to an aging sheep, was very much alive and unsunk. Later, when the shock had finally abated and the sleeves of his overcoat were beginning to dry out, the editor proper would wonder how Cunningham Holt could possibly have known.

Trapped by the unknown jungle outside his front door, Cunningham Holt wasted fifty-two years in Brooklyn, New York. He braced himself nightly for the earthquake he knew was coming. 'No man knoweth the hour nor the day,' he muttered under his breath as he lumbered up and down the sidewalk on his daily pilgrimage from the front stoop to the bodega on the corner. The world, he knew, would not end in fire or flood but in a sinking to end all sinkings. Cunningham Holt woke each morning surprised to find his tenement had made it through another night without succumbing to the sidewalk.

Over the years he developed a fine ear for a good, sure thing and survived on five full decades of bets and wagers. In the early days he confined himself to the horses, multiplying his wife's life insurance policy to twice, thrice and finally four times its original value before the first anniversary of her death. Later he moved on to football (both American and European), to baseball and basketball games and to Nascar (of which he had no visual notion and consequently could not understand the appeal). Having exhausted the sporting realms he ventured into politics, beauty pageants, the popular music charts and even the weather, which, whilst all else kept to seasons and fixtures, offered a constant opportunity for a sly wager.

Cunningham Holt was remarkably adept at predicting the

future. Whilst he remained preoccupied by the surefire knowledge of an apocalyptic sinking, he was equally capable of short-term prophetics. Ordinary folks and small-time gangsters came from five blocks out to pick his tipping brain. He charged two bucks a premonition, later upping his rate to five bucks, tracking the rise of inflation in the late seventies. He grew moderately rich on his winnings but refused to spend a solitary cent beyond the necessary. As the fifties and sixties rolled slowly across America, trumpeting in the protest movement, Cunningham Holt began to fear for the safety of his fortune. Riots on the wireless soon erupted into riots in the street outside his window and so Cunningham collected his lifelong earnings in an old suitcase and shuffled down to Wells Fargo where he opened the very first and only bank account of his existence.

Cunningham Holt lived a simple life, eating meager meals – bread, cheese and shop-sliced pastrami – at the card table in his kitchen. He refused to redecorate the apartment or purchase soft-furnishings more in line with the current trends. 'What,' he joked to the various friends and business associates who kept his days trundling slowly forwards, 'is the point in a blind fella wasting money on fancy wallpaper?' He purchased a solitary pair of new pants and a V-neck sweater once every other year on rotation and never, not once in all his fifty-two New York years, considered for a moment the possibility of a vacation.

In the February of his seventy-first year, approximately halfway between his front stoop and the cigarette counter, Cunningham Holt slipped in a patch of frozen dog shit and fractured his left leg in two separate places. It was the final blow in a half-century war. Cunningham Holt cursed New York for the very last time and moved as far from the east coast as his absent passport would allow.

And thus the Baptist Retirement Village of Portland, Oregon, for no better reason than distance, had found itself blessed to admit Cunningham Holt, complete with seventy-one years of accumulated wisdom, a sock full of marble eyes and a stinking, bad attitude. The Board of Directors – after much negotiating and haggling over the cost of customizing a chalet to meet the needs of the visually impaired – decided to place Mr Holt in Chalet 6. In strict compliance with health and safety legislation, buzzers, handles, bells and whistles were duly fitted throughout the chalet. The Board of Directors, as was their normal custom, were one-third motivated by Christian benevolence and two-thirds driven by the fear of a lawsuit.

Cunningham Holt took one tour round his brand new chalet home and swiftly asked to purchase an RV.

'Mr Holt,' the appointed delegate from the Board of Directors asked, 'with respect, can you tell me what use a "visually impaired" gentleman such as yourself should hope to get out of such a large motor vehicle?'

'I shall park it in my drive and sleep there nightly,' replied Cunningham. 'I'm old and cranky and blind in both eyes. It's my prerogative to do exactly as I want and I want to sleep in an RV.'

No amount of arguing or bribery could change Cunningham Holt's mind. An enormous beige and brown RV was purchased and parked semi-permanently in the drive beside Chalet 6. To the great surprise of all those who'd known him in his early days (one remaining sister and a small-time crook, Brooklyn-based, who kept in touch for occasional tips), Cunningham Holt cast aside his grumpy demeanor and quickly became the life and soul of the cul-de-sac: feeling up the cleaning ladies, coordinating the Annual Thanksgiving Turkey and Tipples Tea Dance and, with the eager help of Bill and Irene, volunteering as a founding member of the People's Committee for Remembering Songs.

Five thousand miles from New York City and suddenly unwalled, Cunningham Holt made a late return to the Kentucky kid of his first six years. He laughed hard at every given opportunity. He stood for hours in his pocket-sized back yard savoring the seasons in all their harsh splendor. He struck up a friendship with anyone who spoke American and made valiant attempts with the many Mexican speakers who kept the cul-de-sac clean and well-fed. He spent every night dreaming deeply inside the RV, fast asleep on the kitchen table which had been specially designed to transform into a bed. 'I like it here,' he lied to anyone who questioned his logic. 'Makes me feel like I'm on a permanent road trip.'

The residents took to calling him 'Easy Rider' as a joke. The joke was wasted on Cunningham Holt, who had cruised through the entire twentieth century without glimpsing so much as a five-second reel of movie footage. When the residents ribbed him, regularly and with great affection, he simply smiled and confessed his ongoing love for the traveling life.

In truth, Cunningham Holt could not bring himself to spend an entire night inside Chalet 6. The sinking was coming and on the day of the Lord's reckoning he wished to be found inside a building unhindered by bricks, sticks or any such heavy, dragging things. Like Noah before him and many big-time saints, Cunningham Holt ignored the mockery of the ignorant. He stuck with his RV bed, sleeping in fully laced boots and socks, mentally rehearsing his escape plan; up the curtains and through the skylight, unto the roof and down the fire escape, as soon as gravity started to steal the floor.

– Chapter Seven –

The People's Committee for Remembering Songs

Using the sideboard for leverage, Cunningham Holt maneuvered himself to his feet and brushed a piece of imaginary lint from the front of his meeting suit. At seventy-six years old and advancing, every knock and bump contained the sly potential to be his last. He steadied himself slowly, cleared his throat and, slightly disorientated by the tumble, addressed Mrs Orange's refrigerator like an old friend.

'Young lady,' he said, extending a solitary hand as if shoving the words out to greet her, 'I don't believe I've had the pleasure of your acquaintance. Cunningham Holt, Chalet 6, delighted to meet you.'

His hand met with eight square foot of bowed refrigerator belly. He withdrew it sharply and turned one hundred and eighty degrees to face Sorry. Cunningham Holt was an imposing man, almost six and a half feet tall in his brogues. He carried himself like the Washington Monument. Despite the cramped implications of RV life and other more obvious disabilities he kept himself fastidiously neat and well-dressed in the fashion favored by television detectives of a certain era. This morning he was wearing the latest of two dozen business suits; a gun-metal gray affair with open-necked shirt – sinless white as was his usual custom – unbuttoned to reveal several inches of leathered salami neck.

Soren James Blue was not accustomed to handshakes. She stretched her right arm across the divide and caught Cunningham's hand up in an awkward, swooping high five.

'Sorry,' she said, and this passed for both introduction and apology.

'Her name's Soren James Blue,' Malcolm quickly explained. 'She's the Director's kid. She's been here all summer because she throws up too much. No one's seen her because they kept her locked up in the Center.'

'I wasn't locked up,' interjected Sorry, 'I could have left any time I wanted to.'

'Whatever,' said Malcolm, affecting a disinterested drawl for Cunningham Holt's benefit. 'She's out now and she's quit throwing up so it looks like whatever they did in there actually worked. And Sorry, this here is Cunningham Holt. His is the Chalet with the RV in front. He's probably my best friend around here.'

Upon hearing this confession Cunningham Holt's face split in half horizontally, stretching upwards to meet his earlobes in a broad parody of a watermelon slice. His cheeks turned raspberry pink and the furthermost tip of his nose flushed raw in sympathy. Cunningham Holt was exceedingly fond of Malcolm Orange.

'And,' whispered Malcolm, lowering his voice to avoid embarrassing his friend, 'he's completely blind!'

'No shit?' retorted Soren James Blue, stabbing an incriminating finger in the direction of Cunningham Holt who, unaware of recent changes to the Oranges' kitchen layout, was lowering his perfectly pressed backside on to the laundry basket containing

Ross. Malcolm, exploiting the time it takes for an elderly man with rheumatoid arthritis to make the grating shift from standing to seated, dashed across the room and switched Ross for the most substantial of the kitchen chairs. Cunningham Holt sat down and rested his hands on his lap.

'What's this about you disappearing, son?' he asked gently.

'It's all bullshit,' Sorry replied on Malcolm's behalf and for her impertinence received a sharp toe poke to the shin. 'There's absolutely nothing wrong with him. I was just checking him over with a flashlight and I couldn't find a single hole . . . except for the normal ones.'

Malcolm Orange blushed furiously and ignored her. Over the last few months he'd grown exceptionally fond of Cunningham Holt. The two friends had spent many happy hours in the RV listening to the horse racing and playing marbles with the old man's spare eyes.

Malcolm was well aware of Cunningham's myriad quirks and inadequacies. He was almost seven times older than the boy and ignorant of anything more modern than a toaster oven. Blind as a bat and prone to prophetic ramblings, he'd lately pronounced the President 'a snake-tongued imbecile'; television 'an agent of the Antichrist'; and the American Constitution 'an exercise in national self-delusion.' Furthermore, the world, Malcolm had come to repeatedly learn, was due an almighty sinking, and though no man (not least Cunningham Holt) knew the day nor the hour, the end was unarguably nigh.

An ordinary boy might have grown tired of Cunningham Holt's overzealous imagination but Malcolm Orange was far from ordinary. Having spent the previous decade trawling America's back roads with a bevy of wooly-brained seniors, Malcolm Orange had come to relish the wild and oftentimes truthful revelations of the almost senile. It was not unknown for Malcolm to play the Devil's Advocate, further inciting Cunningham Holt's already frantic ramblings.

'Come quick, Cunningham,' Malcolm would often yell through the RV's open window. 'Bring your measuring tape. I think the chalet's sunk another inch overnight.'

'Listen to this, Cunningham,' he'd said on several occasions, positioning the old man in front of the latest episode of the *X-Files*, 'it's a documentary about the government's new research department.'

'Lord save us,' Cunningham Holt would cry, though he no longer believed in either the Lord or His ability to save. 'The world's gone to hell in a hand basket. It won't be long 'til the end now.'

(Towards the summer's close, when his paranoia had reached a point of no return, Cunningham Holt had grabbed Malcolm by the wrist and asked him, with heartbreaking sincerity, to bind the corners of Chalet 6 with strong ropes to something tall and stable; a telegraph pole, ideally.

'Malcolm, my boy, I have all my savings tied up in that chalet,' he'd explained, making a wrenching knot of his hands. 'God has it in for me and I know the ropes won't stop him from taking it away but they might slow him down long enough to get my furniture out.'

Moved to guilt, and small moments of repentance, Malcolm Orange had attempted to reassure the older man with increasingly elaborate lies.

'The chalet's not sinking anymore, Cunningham,' he'd confessed. 'In fact, I think it's started unsinking. I swear it's six inches taller than it was last week. I'll take a measuring tape and measure it for you myself.'

'That's very kind of you to offer, Malcolm,' Cunningham Holt had replied, unconvinced by the idea of a God suddenly capable of actual, physical resurrections, 'but sooner or later everything's going to sink. No man knoweth the day nor the hour but I'll be damned if I'm not prepared.'

'Whatever makes you feel better,' Malcolm had conceded, and spent the better part of a weekend pretending to bind an entire house to the highest heights. For this purpose he'd used imaginary ropes, imaginary wires and a swarming gaggle of expensive, helium-filled, imaginary balloons. The neighbors had appeared on their doorsteps, curious to see what Malcolm Orange was up to as he ascended and descended a borrowed stepladder, describing in loud detail this complex feat of imaginary engineering.

At first they'd mocked. Skeptic as the bastard sons of Noah, they'd patrolled the outer limits of the Holt estate, asking cryptic questions and edging ever closer to out-and-out mockery. When Malcolm had finally mounted an upturned bucket and explained to the entire cul-de-sac in hushed tones and with deliberate stealth, that all this – even the stepladder – was an elaborate exercise in reassuring Cunningham Holt, the mood changed dramatically. The residents of the retirement village were extremely fond of Cunningham, and any exercise in soothing his sinking heart seemed worthy, not only of acceptance, but also encouragement.

Bill had instantly cancelled the afternoon's meeting of the People's Committee for Remembering Songs to join Malcolm, somewhat precariously, at the top of a second borrowed stepladder. Roger Heinz, upon searching through his stash of army treasures, located a still-working megaphone and spent the weekend shouting earthquake-inducing encouragements from a deckchair on the opposite side of the street. Irene, who was crazy in the head and clearly incapable of understanding the raison d'être behind the subterfuge, had taken photos for the purpose of showing Cunningham Holt later. The remaining cul-de-sac ladies quit their usual weekend routine of primping, gossiping and *Dynasty*-watching to help out. Gathered in Emily Fox's living room, they'd spent the entire Saturday weaving imaginary ropes from the long-preserved remnants of their teenage ponytails and fixing endless cups of instant coffee, most of which were poured, still steaming, into the flowerbeds of Chalet 6, for their coffee tasted like shit roasted.

When complete, Cunningham Holt had descended from his RV for a preliminary inspection of his, now secure, house.

'Much appreciated folks,' he'd muttered as Malcolm led him by the elbow round the ramparts of Chalet 6 describing each freshly-appointed imaginary fixture in grand detail. 'Much appreciated indeed.'

Cunningham Holt had been clearly moved by the whole duplicitous enterprise, for one of his marble eyes had slipped loose and rolled to rest under a rhododendron bush.

'So you'll be moving into the chalet now it's not going under?' Roger Heinz had asked, already anticipating manifold megaphone opportunities for yelling at the removal men.

'No rush,' Cunningham Holt had answered, and three weeks later was still languishing in his cramped RV whilst Chalet 6 crouched on his doorstep, a veritable palace in comparison.)

Cunningham Holt was odd as Christmas, and kind as Christ himself. Despite the fact that Malcolm Orange had not yet arrived at his twelfth birthday, he kept a treasure drawer stacked with cigarettes, chewing tobacco and unopened cans of Coors Light, just waiting on the boy's appetite.

'Any time you fancy a long cold one, son, just help yourself,' he offered each time Malcolm came to visit.

'I'm only eleven,' Malcolm would reply. 'I'm not supposed to drink or smoke or go out by myself after nine o'clock.'

'Well, boys will be boys and if the notion ever takes you, just help yourself.'

'Maybe after my birthday I might start smoking. I'll let you know.'

Malcolm Orange had no notion of drinking or indulging in sexual intercourse for the next twenty-five years at least. He hoped, by his fortieth birthday, to have developed some sort of an appetite for the manly arts which seemed a prerequisite of adult life. At the age of eleven, Malcolm Orange found sex, cigarettes and alcoholic intoxication faintly repulsive, for they'd formed the shady outline of his father's existence. However, the fact that Cunningham Holt would encourage him in all manner of licentious adult behavior held an unholy appeal all of its own.

Besides the beer, the cigarettes and the often hinted at possibility of pornographic magazines, Cunningham Holt was careful to keep his young friend well-oiled financially. Over the last few months Malcolm had managed to save almost enough for his first ever shop-bought bicycle, on the accumulated change he'd been urged to keep each time Cunningham sent him to the store. Though Malcolm felt faintly guilty about taking advantage of a man who was blind, lonely and almost as old as the Constitution, the thought of choosing his very own bicycle kept him quietly complicit as he stashed his earnings in a tube sock beneath the bedroom dresser.

As his friendship with the old man developed he found himself more popular, more confident and less lonely than ever. Ever the scientist, Malcolm Orange plotted a graph to record and research this growing sense of well-being. Cunningham Holt was the constant running through all his happy days.

Malcolm had endless amounts of respect for Cunningham Holt. More than Sorry, his mother and all the cul-de-sac crew combined, he trusted Cunningham with the horrible truth.

'I'm disappearing, Cunningham,' he confessed from the head of the kitchen table. 'It gets worse every day.'

'What do you mean you're disappearing?' Cunningham asked, 'Sounds to me like you're right here in your mother's kitchen, just like usual.'

'I'm not leaving! I'm disappearing. There's holes all over me and they're getting bigger every day.'

And, because Cunningham Holt had seen more than his fair share of miracles in reverse he did not, even for the shortest second, doubt his young friend. He placed a limp, comforting hand on Malcolm's shoulder – hoping to avoid the worst of the holes – and nodded sympathetically.

'Don't panic, son,' he whispered stoically. 'I've no doubt you're disappearing. In my experience God's forever taking things away for no good reason. It don't surprise me one little bit to hear he's after your own flesh and blood now. Try to keep calm Malcolm. At least you're not sinking.'

'He's not disappearing,' Sorry rudely interrupted. 'He's just freaking out because his dad's left and his mom's crazy and he's stuck in this holding pen for crinklies.'

Malcolm Orange, suddenly seized by a violent, sense-defying hatred, took the first of many swings at Soren James Blue's head. Anticipating his fist, she dodged behind the kitchen door so his balled hand met several inches of unrelenting wood with a bone-crunching thud. 'Shit,' he squealed, nursing the bruised fist in the palm of his hand. It was the first time he'd ever used profanity in front of Cunningham Holt. While the old man swore like a star fighter pilot, Malcolm still felt awkward cursing in front of the elderly.

He apologized profusely all the while glaring in Sorry's direction, visually willing her to follow suit. Soren James Blue held her tongue. Her face fell into a malevolent smirk as she raised both middle fingers towards the ceiling fan and winked impishly in Malcolm's general direction.

Malcolm struggled to keep his fists sheathed. An odd tension had surfaced at the back of his throat, like two elastic bands fit to pinch and twisting. Whilst he felt the need to bend Sorry's fingers backwards until they screamed and snapped like splintered popsicle sticks, he could not help but admire the way her face folded when she was angry. When angry, Sorry's face was cute as an indoor turtle. In the jaundiced light from the open fridge she appeared a little furry round the edges. Her ears, her forehead and the outermost peaks of her paper-pale elbows smudged an indefinite, tissuey blonde against the light. Malcolm suspected she felt like unpeeled peaches. He wanted to touch her to confirm his suspicions. He didn't. Though innocent in the ways of women, he knew better than to touch a girl uninvited.

'Damn you, woman,' Malcolm whispered under his breath. 'You'll be the death of me.' (It was a phrase he'd learnt from his father, and, without fully understanding, often utilized to great melodramatic effect when his mother retreated into one of her Spanish moods.)

Soren James Blue, true to character, pretended not to hear. She was prone to inopportune outbreaks of deafness and localized hysterics. (It would take a further fifteen years of failed relationships and emotional fumblings before Malcolm Orange allowed himself to admit that these maladies were not peculiar to Sorry, but, rather, endemic to the whole female race.)

A small war was about to break out in full view of the dining room table. Seventy-odd years of blindness had developed in Cunningham Holt a preternaturally perceptive disposition. Though he remained fuzzy on the specifics, he could smell the tension reverberating round the Orange kitchen. He crossed his knotty ankles complicitly, leaned back in his chair and, utilizing all his gathered wisdom, attempted to diffuse the situation.

'Seems to me,' he said, arranging the eight remaining strands of snow-white hair across the dome of his head, 'that the problem's not going to sort itself in the next two hours and we could all do with a change of scene. Malcolm, do you think you can keep from disappearing before lunch time?'

'Sure,' Malcolm muttered, somewhat defeated. He felt betrayed. On normal days, in normal circumstances, Cunningham Holt was usually keen to join his cause.

'Young lady, do you think you can keep your tongue under control for the next few hours?'

'Yeah,' Sorry mumbled, fixing her face into the preschool pout Malcolm would soon come to recognize as her favorite expression.

'Well, in that case,' announced Cunningham Holt, rising from his foldable chair like a papal blessing, 'I suggest we go to the People's Committee as usual and discuss Malcolm's little problem afterwards.'

Malcolm and Sorry reluctantly agreed. Mr Fluff and Ross voiced no opinion either way. Cunningham Holt, having long since memorized the route from one end of the cul-de-sac to the other, led the charge at funereal pace.

The People's Committee for Remembering Songs met in Bill and Irene's living room two to three times a week. Though well-used to the young Oranges, several members were reluctant to welcome Soren James Blue. In their defense, Sorry did little to ingratiate herself, pronouncing the People's Committee 'a dumb-ass waste of time'; the ladies' coffee comparable to 'ground mud'; and Bill and Irene's living room 'absolutely stinking of potpourri'. When it transpired that she was bloodline related to the Director, who had only that week further reduced the budget for the Annual Thanksgiving Turkey and Tipples Tea Dance, there were calls for a lynching. Roger Heinz immediately fell back on combat experience and pinned her to the living room sofa with a fishing rod. Employing all manner of elderly spit and anger he accused her of being 'a skinny little spy for those Nazi bastards in the Center'. Thereafter, encouraged by Irene (who was no longer capable of differentiating between good sense and fire starting), he proposed to tie Sorry to the patio furniture with her own hair and interrogate her himself, 'for days or weeks, or as long as it takes to break her.'

It was only after Cunningham Holt had taken certain key members of the People's Committee into Bill and Irene's kitchen dinette, explaining in hushed tones how important it was for 'our Malcolm' to make friends of his own age – albeit skinny, little spy friends – that Sorry's presence was tolerated at the singing circle.

'Dammit,' muttered Roger Heinz, lifting his shirt to reveal an impressive array of BB guns and butter knives mounted on a tool belt. 'I'm still packing. I don't trust that little bitch as far as I could throw her.'

At around eleven o'clock, the People's Committee for Remembering Songs laid down their coffee mugs, shuffled their chairs into a shape roughly resembling a circle, and commenced their meeting. In the corner, by the minibar, Soren James Blue sat on both hands to keep herself anchored to the carpet and fought the twitching desire to bolt. Mr Fluff dozed furiously at her feet, emitting, as she slept, the low-level hum of a tropical fish tank.

The People's Committee for Remembering Songs grumbled thickly towards a beginning. Bill commenced proceedings with a reading of the previous meeting's minutes. Roger Heinz seconded the acceptance of the minutes and, though a third confirming voice was not, and never had been, required, Irene rose to announce that she 'thirded the acceptance of last week's minutes, although the part about the coffee being burnt was an out-and-out lie.' Objections were duly noted and the singing commenced.

Malcolm Orange, as a latecomer to the People's Committee for Remembering Songs, had found himself, somewhat against his better judgment, in charge of Elton John.

It was a big responsibility. Elton John sang a lot of songs and Malcolm wasn't even a proper resident. (The People's Committee for Remembering Songs was only open to actual residents and their lovers. However, Malcolm was both darling of the cul-de-sac and bearer of various snacks stolen, via his mother, from the Center's massive kitchen, so the residents had permitted him membership on a trial basis.) He was doing his level-headed best with his assignment but to the untrained, eleven-year-old ear most of Elton John's songs sounded exactly like most of his other songs. 'Daniel', for example, was proving particularly tricky to nail for, even after two dozen listens, it remained vaguely reminiscent of approximately thirty-five other Elton John songs.

Malcolm Orange practiced Elton John in the kitchen whilst preparing his daily meals. He spent a lot of time in the chalet's kitchen, microwaving TV dinners, heating Ross's bottles and blending household objects in the name of Scientific Investigative Research. With the blender blending and the kettle singing, the microwave pinging and the extraction fan extracting, it was hard to tell if he was hitting a single note right, but he kept practicing regardless. Malcolm Orange took his responsibilities very seriously.

Bill had lately donated a small battery-operated boom box to the cause. 'I found it at the Goodwill, son,' he'd announced, upon arriving at the door of Chalet 13 with the boom box, an industrial-sized box of Duracells and seven hand-recorded Elton John cassettes. 'You'll have to stick the play button down with a bit of Scotch tape but it only cost two bucks.' Moved to almost-tears, for it was the best gift he had ever been given and Bill wasn't even blood kin, Malcolm Orange shook the older man's hand and promised on his life, his father's life and the life of his small brother – snoring thickly in the magazine rack at his feet – to practice Elton John every day with religious attention to pitch, tone and such details as the peculiar, nasal intonations of 'Tiny Dancer'.

The People's Committee for Remembering Songs met every Monday, Thursday and alternate Saturday, at 11:30am. Every resident of the cul-de-sac, with the exception of Malcolm's mother and Simeon Klein in Chalet 8, who was deaf in both ears and chronically incapable of hearing, repeating, or even recalling any music pre-1975, was an automatic member of the People's Committee for Remembering Songs. All new residents were approached with a platter of oatmeal cookies, warmly invited and if appearing disinterested unceremoniously informed that non-participation was considered a broad highway to social exclusion. In preparation for the onslaught of elderly visitors, Bill, often aided by Malcolm, took the liberty of shoving their everyday furniture into the spare bedroom and filling the room with two dozen stackable chairs, 'permanently borrowed', one chair at a time, from the chair shed behind the Center.

Lately Malcolm Orange had been banned from bringing snacks. 'Listen son,' Mr Grubbs had said, somewhat unkindly, 'dentures are awkward enough, but folks just don't sing right with a mouthful of cookies. We appreciate the gesture, but no more snacks please.'

'Can I still be in charge of Elton John?' Malcolm had asked, humming a few bars of 'Crocodile Rock' just to convince Mr Grubbs.

'If you think you can manage. Elton John is a big responsibility and you're not even an actual resident. Just say the word and you can do Sting instead. There's no shame in Sting.'

Malcolm Orange had said nothing and stuck resolutely with Elton John. Mr Grubbs knew full well that no one, save the actually senile, wanted to do Sting. Two weeks previously the People's Committee for Remembering Songs had debated omitting Sting from the project altogether. Unfortunately, Sting had stayed put. In a project as epic and far-reaching as the People's Committee, there was no room for discrimination or personal taste.

Nate Grubbs was the self-appointed Captain of the People's Committee. Popular opinion favored Bill, for the idea had originally been his, or Cunningham Holt who had debated long and hard with both the Director and the Board to have the People's Committee for Remembering Songs elevated to the status of an official Retirement Village Organization or Club.

(The official seal of approval came with access to the Retirement Village's thermos flasks and coffee supplies, an invite to the annual Organizations and Clubs Awards Ceremony and, most importantly, a small stipend, which the People's Committee used to keep their members well-supplied in cassette tapes for the purpose of making illegal copies of the Multnomah County Library's compact disk collection.)

Nate Grubbs had been a resident for almost seven years and kept a shotgun in his wardrobe. Having long since forgotten whether the shotgun was loaded or not, just to be on the safe side Mr Grubbs had stopped opening his wardrobe door in 1989. Thereafter he had lost a whole rack of perfectly good sweaters and shoes but, as he liked to tell the other residents, 'I still got my arms. There's not a pullover on God's green earth worth losing your arms for.'

A shotgun (loaded or otherwise) opened doors on the cul-de-sac and thus Nate Grubbs had found himself Captain of the People's Committee for Remembering Songs. Responsibilities were small compared to other groups previously captained by Mr Grubbs: the Amateur Gardener's Association, a handful of male voice choirs and an ill-fated over-seventies five-a-side team.

Mr Grubbs was placed in charge of Bob Dylan, all by himself and with no assistance. He'd specifically requested this.

'Bobby sings twice as fast as ordinary folks,' Cunningham Holt had reminded him. 'That's twice as many words to remember in each song and there's a hell of a lot of songs to start with. Are you sure we shouldn't split Dylan up?' Nate Grubbs remained resolute. 'I'm doing Dylan,' he'd said, and threatened all those who objected with the possibility of a shotgun showdown. Eventually everyone, even Cunningham Holt, who recognized a suicide mission when he heard one, had backed down. 'It's your funeral, Nate,' he'd stated boldly.

Nate Grubbs could not be dissuaded. He was a stubborn man with a particularly furious way of entering and leaving a room. It was almost fifty-five years since he'd last been convinced to back down, and that particular incident had involved heavy artillery, broken bones and a handful of irate German soldiers. (It would have taken an organization bigger, louder and more viciously armed to convince Nate Grubbs to surrender Dylan. Thankfully they'd managed to talk him out of doing Bowie too.)

The People's Committee for Remembering Songs existed solely for the purpose of remembering songs. Six months previously the Director had been unduly influenced by a state-sponsored research paper highlighting the negative implications of over-excitement in the elderly. Within a week he'd taken it upon himself to ban outdoor sports, organized dancing and the annual trip to Knott's Berry Farm. Four months later the Director had also banned music. In an unprecedented fit of generosity he'd given the residents a two-month amnesty period in which to willingly dispose of their music and music playing devices. Though horrified, none of the residents had been overly surprised by the music cull. The previous week the Director had banned clocks, electric toothbrushes and satin pajamas; the week before, good-looking visitors. Later things would get worse and worse until the cul-de-sac residents couldn't so much as fart for fear of having too much fun.

The Director was not a nice man. Having failed in the face-fixing industry, he was loath to embrace the world of elderly care. The Director did not like old people and struggled to see why they could not be stacked end to end on bunk beds like overgrown library books. He kept a black tie in his blazer pocket so he could slip into funeral mode at a moment's notice. The Director enjoyed a good funeral almost as much as his daily bourbon.

At first the residents assumed the music ban was a joke. 'Ooops,' they'd said, clamping an exaggerated hand over mouth every time they caught themselves humming along to the *Dallas* theme tune, 'better not get caught singing. I might be thrown out on my ear.'

Then the pastel pink fliers had appeared under their doors.

'We, the management, regret to inform you that all residents are banned from listening to or creating music. This ban comes into effect on the first of the month at 9am. All questions and/or complaints should be addressed to the Director ASAP.' The fliers had been hastily illustrated with a picture of a smiling transistor radio, peeking over the rim of a trash can to wave a cheery goodbye. You could barely make out the radio resemblance. From a distance it could easily have been a microwave oven.

Miss Richardson, as leader of the in-house jazz ensemble, was most visibly upset. Upon discovering a flier, folded twice and stuffed under her front door, she'd locked herself in the bathroom with a box set of Carpenters records, refusing to come out for an entire afternoon.

'What about hymns?' asked Mrs Huxley and, by proxy, Mrs Kellerman, her non-speaking friend, who had in their previous lives spent a sum total of one hundred and two years married to Baptist pastors. 'How can we still be Christians and have meetings in the back yard if we aren't allowed to sing hymns, or at the very least modern choruses?'

'Bullshit,' Nate Grubbs had said and taken it upon himself to run all the fliers through the washing machine. 'You can't ban music. It's an infringement on our civil liberties. We will write to the White House and complain about this.'

It was a good plan, but no one had an envelope and the plan was quickly forgotten. Without organized leadership other attempts at mutiny soon met a similarly lackluster fate. Worn out from inventing workable solutions to a ridiculous problem, all twenty-three residents had congregated en masse outside the Director's residence. Holding aloft a ragtag collection of walking sticks, rolled-up copies of the *National Enquirer*, and, in one case, an unopened banana, they'd barged through the door and demanded answers.

'Answers!' the Director had yelled, standing on his desk to give himself that extra two feet over the residents, 'I'll give you friggin' answers. Look at these statistics.' Fishing around in his pocket, he'd produced a dog-eared sheaf of papers and begun to read aloud. '"Recent Government research suggests that music incites people to deviant behavior. A localized study into music deprivation has conclusively proven that people are less excitable, less prone to outbursts of violence, unplanned pregnancies, aggression and graffiti when they aren't exposed to music."'

Thereafter he'd unfolded the paper to reveal a supporting bar chart. 'To be specific, folks. Since my appointment here less than two years ago, I have noted, with great disappointment, the ongoing deterioration of basic moral values in this institution. There have been three unplanned pregnancies in the last month alone, one all-night drug-fuelled dance party and, of course, the incident with the inflammatory graffiti on the Center wall. I blame music. It makes all of you too excitable. Therefore we – the management – have made the difficult decision to ban all music forthwith. As you can imagine this was not an easy conclusion to reach. I myself am a big fan of music and have seen Sting live in concert on at least three separate occasions. It pains me greatly to ban music, but when you abuse a privilege you have to suffer the consequences.'

'Stuff and nonsense,' Bill had cried and pitched a stapler at the Director's head. Unfortunately it did not kill him but left staple marks, like pygmy vampire bites, on the mahogany desktop. (Two weeks later, with the matter all but melted into amnesia, Bill would receive a wildly exaggerated invoice for the cost of recovering the Director's desk.)

As a direct consequence of the uprising, Bill had been banned from the weekly potluck get-together for three Wednesdays in a row and spent four hours forcibly Scotch-taped inside the enormous cardboard box which had previously housed the Center's new fridge. It was during this extended period of solitary confinement that God had spoken directly to Bill, instructing him to form the People's Committee for Remembering Songs. Bill had emerged from the cardboard box a new and freshly determined man, having heard the voice of the Almighty and lived to tell the tale. 'You should be dead if you heard God's real voice,' reasoned Clary O'Hare. 'You're only alive because it got filtered through a cardboard box.'

That evening at 11:30 when the Director retired to his own quarters, Bill summoned all the residents to the front room of Chalet 11. Malcolm Orange, catching the whiff of mutiny mumbling over the backyard fence, had showed up with a plastic mug of deep-fried fish sticks leftover from dinner. (Snacks had not yet been banned at the People's Committee for Remembering Songs.)

'Listen here, ladies and gents,' said Bill, rising to address the entire group. 'This is a dire situation. The Director is the Devil incarnate and it looks like he's going to take our record players and radios. It's a nightmare but there's not much we can do about it. Of course we'll fight back, hit them with every stick we've got . . . and Roger if you could see fit to doing that thing where you pretend to have a stroke again? That seems like a mighty fine way to shake the buggers up a bit, but at the end of the day they're still going to take our record players. There's nothing we can do about it.'

The group visibly deflated, wheezing slightly like a cluster of elderly balloons left too long in the sun. Miss Richardson, terrified by the thought of losing a record player, began to slip her easy-listening LPs up the inside of her dress, one record at a time.

'What if we pray a bit more?' asked Mrs Huxley, and, by proxy, Mrs Kellerman, who had arrived at the meeting armed with the *Believer's Hymnbook*. 'We've already had three prayer meetings about the record players today but we could get up early and do five tomorrow if you think it's a good idea.'

'And I could use Morse code,' offered Clary O'Hare.

'Thanks ladies. Prayer is always a good back up, and yes Clary, you should definitely use Morse code as much as you can, but I think I have a slightly more practical solution. This afternoon at three thirty whilst confined inside an enormous cardboard box, God spoke to me directly and told me we should all get together and form a group to remember songs. That way, no matter how many radios and record players the Director confiscates, we can always remind each other of every song in the entire world. It's vitally important that every group has a good name, especially if they wish to be taken seriously. I think you'll agree with me when I propose that this group should be called the People's Committee for Remembering Songs.'

Everyone agreed, aside from Clary O'Hare who suggested the group should be called the Beatles. When it was explained to him that this name had already been taken, he too had to agree that the People's Committee was a more than apt name for a group such as this.

And so the People's Committee for Remembering Songs had formed and immediately broken for fish sticks and instant coffee. After the interval they made a list of every song in the entire world and split these songs up twenty-three ways. It was strange.

Malcolm Orange had been sure a comprehensive list of all the songs in the entire world would be extremely long but it turned out he was wrong. There were only two thousand, five hundred and twenty-three songs in the entire world, five hundred of which were Bob Dylan songs, seven hundred and fifty of which were hymns and the majority of the rest traditional Irish folk songs involving peasant girls falling in love and/or dying young.

Bill put all the songs into a spare bedpan and Malcolm Orange drew Elton John. Other people were not so fortunate and ended up with the Bee Gees or the soundtrack from *Riverdance*. All things considered, Malcolm was pretty happy with Elton John.

'Off you go,' Bill had said, pronouncing a quick benediction to bring this first meeting to a close. 'We only have eight and a bit weeks to remember every song in the entire world. You folks better get practicing.'

And practice they did: in their garden sheds with the lights turned out, under the bedcovers late at night, in the kitchen with their blenders set to liquidize. With headphones on and headphones off, in small groups and solitary confinement, the residents of the cul-de-sac listened and remembered and forgot and listened a little more. Music and lyrics. Lyrics and music. Music came hard to those who couldn't hold a tune but they never, for one minute, gave up. All summer long the elderly residents of the Baptist Retirement Village kept right on remembering every song in the entire world.

Every Monday and Thursday afternoon they reconvened in Chalet 11 to monitor their progress. It quickly became apparent that some members of the People's Committee for Remembering Songs were better suited to remembering songs than others.

Within one week Nate Grubbs had memorized almost four hundred and fifty Bob Dylan songs and could, at a moment's notice, perform note-perfect renditions of any one of these with all the proper Dylan drawls and affectations. It was inspiring stuff. Overawed and intimidated by the surefire possibility of his shotgun closet, ninety-five percent of the People's Committee for Remembering Songs mutinied and voted Nate Grubbs their new Captain. Confused by a multiplicity of choice Irene (of Bill and Irene fame) had voted against her own husband, mistaking Nate Grubbs for a particularly handsome young man she had once dated in high school.

Meanwhile, Mrs Huxley and by proxy Mrs Kellerman, despite drawing the collected works of Elvis, Frank Sinatra and the Pet Shop Boys, had taken it upon themselves to disregard direction and memorize the Anglican church hymnary, the Psalter and Mission Praise, Volumes One and Two, in their entirety. Called before the People's Committee for Remembering Songs, they seemed unable to offer so much as a coherent word in their own defense and instead chose to perform a rousing rendition of 'And Can It Be That I Should Gain', with Mrs Huxley taking the female lead and Mrs Kellerman, by proxy, the male.

Clary O'Hare, a long-term victim of God's humor, had drawn Aerosmith, and spent two weeks translating 'Love in an Elevator' into a series of neat tips and staccato taps which, while impressive, was of no earthly use to anyone who didn't speak Morse.

Miss Richardson, terrified of losing her own record collection, had yet to remove the box set of Carpenters LPs from the inside liner of her dress and instead of remembering songs had spent the previous fortnight seeking out increasingly obscure hiding places and depositing records as she saw fit. Abandoned Lionel Ritchie records were now beginning to turn up in the oddest places: in the closet with the bed sheets, shredded and slipped between the pages of the Holy Bible and just last week, forming the cardboardy crust of the ham and tomato quiche which she'd presented at the residents' weekly potluck dinner.

Only Bill, belligerent and sharp as a bag full of brass-backed drawing pins, seemed to be making any significant headway. Having drawn the Rolling Stones, he could soon sing his way through 'Exile on Main Street', 'Goats Head Soup' and most all of 'Sticky Fingers' in correct order with complementary dance moves. Despite widespread mockery he had taken to borrowing Irene's make-up and fixing his face in the style of Keith Richards. 'It helps me get in character,' he explained to his daughter-in-law during the Retirement Village's bi-annual visiting hour. 'When I've got my lines on I feel just like Keef. I can do all the high parts.' And, to illustrate his point, launched into a hand-jangling, caterwauling clip through 'Street Fighting Man'.

As the deadline loomed ever closer it became increasingly clear that many of the residents were incapable of remembering anything more complex than their own ankles. Despite drawing the soundtrack from *Cats* – a collection which ran to fifteen songs at most – Rose Roper struggled to recall anything aside from the Diet Coke jingle. 'Rosie,' said Nate Grubbs, addressing her directly just ten days before the deadline, 'you've got to work harder at your remembering. No more Diet Coke jingles. Alzheimer's is no excuse for laziness. Keep practicing.'

With less than a week left before the music ban came into effect, Nate Grubbs had stepped up rehearsals, calling a series of emergency meetings of the People's Committee for Remembering Songs. Seemingly things were not going well. There was talk of an ill-defined Plan B, of hunger strikes and police intervention. The residents were deeply skeptical.

Malcolm Orange had been present at every one of these emergency meetings, reeling with adolescent zeal through his Elton

John numbers whilst the other residents grew more elderly, more wizened and shortsighted, forgetful. At eleven years old, almost twelve, Malcolm struggled to shoulder their panic. His mind was sharp as a colored pencil and growing sharper by the day. Ten years of trundling had left him with a fine nose for detail. He could remember incredibly small things – buttons and perfumes and throwaway comments – which might or might not have taken place in the blurry space before his own birth. Malcolm Orange was magic in his memorizing. Scientific Investigative Research was a mere vehicle for curating his genius. Though the retirement village was the closest thing to concrete he'd ever known, Malcolm was old enough to understand there would be other homes; times and troubles beyond the entry gates; a whole lifetime of songs yet to sing and forget. It was different for his friends. Malcolm was a bucket. They were sieves. With nothing new to sing or remember they would soon leak clean.

Malcolm Orange had taken great pains to remain enthusiastic about the project.

Noticing Sorry's puzzled expression he scooched across the living room carpet and attempted to explain – in melodramatic under-breaths – what was happening.

'What the hell is going on?' Sorry mouthed, her words barely audible above the stench of Double Fruit.

'Your dad's banned music from next Friday on,' whispered Malcolm. 'All their radios and record players will be confiscated. They're trying to remember every song in the world before that happens.'

'Lord Almighty,' Sorry laughed out loud. 'They're all crazy. There must be six million songs in the world.'

'Well, two months ago there were two thousand, five hundred and twenty-three. There are only about eight hundred left now.

It's harder than you'd think trying to remember the tunes and the words at the same time.'

At Sorry's feet Mr Fluff shifted suddenly, hacking a medium-sized fur ball onto the carpet behind the sofa. Rose-pink and cream-flecked, it blended perfectly with Irene's shag pile carpet. Malcolm Orange thought it best to let the cat puke go unmentioned.

'Ladies and gents,' Nate Grubbs began, bringing the meeting to attention (sensing the gravity of the situation he had practiced this speech in his bathroom mirror, and imagined himself charismatic on a par with JFK or John the Baptist). Pausing for effect, he swiveled to look directly at his audience. Two dozen pairs of prescription bifocals glared back at him, his image reflected lazily in each lens.

'We have less than a week left. Let's get musical . . . from the top now!' he cried and his voice had all the last-ditch exuberance of a sinking ship. 'Let's hear you sing every song in the entire world!'

In the corner, by the spider plants, Roger Heinz rose arthritically and began to shuffle towards the middle of the room. Standing centre square, butt blocking the electric fire which Irene (who'd been raised, red hot, in the armpit of Texas) kept sweltering all through high summer, he cleared his mouth and prepared to begin his now famous rendition of 'King of the Road'. Legs spread, cowboy style, Mr Heinz dropped his Slavic intonation in favor of a dark drawl and angled in the direction of the three ladies resident on Irene's heavily patterned sofa.

'Trailers for sale or rent . . .'

From the void behind the sofa, a guffaw like a pitch-pinched earthquake began to gain momentum. Roger Heinz, deaf as he was, bore on regardless. Five seconds later, a half-empty pack of

Lucky Strikes came flying from behind the sofa, striking him solidly in the forehead. Though purely coincidental – the perpetrator being a lousy aim, even with a target in full view – the crumpled cardboard made contact in perfect tempo with the final syllable of the stanza. The ladies of the sofa, sensing a cold front, shuffled nervously. Well used to the threat of attack, Mr Heinz quickly abandoned Roger Millar and reached for the half dozen butter knives buckled individually, with elastic bands, about his midriff.

'Right, you little bitch,' he yelled, scrabbling to locate a knife for each hand. 'Reveal yourself. Stand up and take what's coming to you. I'll not have you mocking these good folks in their own home.'

'It's you she's taking the piss out of Roger, not me or Irene,' pointed out Bill, relishing the opportunity to make good on a grudge, three years in the grumbling.

'I'm mocking all of you,' clarified Soren James Blue, still hidden behind the sofa. 'You're all head cases as far as I'm concerned. Chuck me back my smokes. I'm out of here.'

From his vantage point behind the magazine rack Malcolm Orange watched silently as Sorry, still grinning demonically, stood up and strode confidently across the room. Observing her denim-clad butt bobbling earnestly across the shag pile and her black bangs swiping like a set of demented wiper blades, Malcolm Orange found himself once again caught between good sense and the hope of something more exciting. He reached across the rug, hooked the Lucky Strikes from where they'd landed at Roger Heinz's feet and, like a well-oiled pitch and catch duo, tossed them into her waiting hand. After which, intimidated by his own rebellion, Malcolm Orange backed into the wall and slid slowly upwards until he found himself fully upright and unsure of his next move.

In the centre of the room all hell was circling for a good spot to land. Nose to gristly chin with Roger Heinz, Soren James Blue was lighting up. Mr Heinz – fork in one hand, teaspoon in the other – was hoisting his pants up in preparation for attack. The other men had risen from their various chairs, falling into rank behind their comrade, arms full of domestic missiles: scatter cushions, sugar bowls, hearing aids, old copies of *Women and Home*. The room was bristling, thick with pre-match apprehension.

Through the fabric of his shirt Malcolm Orange shoved a skeptical finger deep into his side. It disappeared to the knuckle. He checked his wrist. It flared luminous against the electric fire. The world, he was surprisingly relieved to discover, was still a wild and overly possible place. Songs could be stolen. Small boys might disappear without so much as a weekend's warning. Grown women could, overnight, turn suddenly odd and bilingual. Anything, even a cutlery war, might happen before supper and Malcolm Orange, pre-occupied as he was with his perforations, thrilled with the possibility of a good distraction.

'What have you got to say for yourself, young lady?' spat Roger Heinz, stabbing Sorry's chest with the blunt end of a teaspoon.

Soren James Blue cocked her weight defiantly on one hip and breathed a long plume of cigarette smoke straight into his face.

'Your songs are shit,' she announced, dragging surreptitiously on her cigarette. 'You'd be doing the world a favor if you just forgot most of them.'

Roger Heinz turned the blotch-speckled color of baloney. Nate Grubbs, unsure whether to hold back or attack, pitched a scatter cushion half-heartedly at Sorry's face. It missed, crowning Rose Roper smartly so her hairpiece came asunder, sloping gently across her forehead like a clod of beached seaweed. Nate Grubbs was in dire need of a new pair of bifocals.

'You should think about doing somebody decent,' announced Soren James Blue, 'like the Beastie Boys.' Thereafter she screwed her half-sucked cigarette into Bill and Irene's living room carpet and, tossing Mr Fluff over her shoulder, exited the chalet via the open front door.

In the corner by the magazine rack, with Irene's bookcase prodding his ribs judgmentally, Malcolm Orange felt something snakish twist inside his belly. His father, though long since left for Mexico, was lingering still, singing darkly in his head; a selfish, selfish song of instant kicks, bad-news girls and no-regrets thinking. For the first time in eleven years, almost twelve, Malcolm Orange felt himself split down the middle; one half father-born, one sweet, softer half, mother. He allowed himself a quick swipe of the room. 'Old friends versus excitement?' he summarized and while his mother's voice whispered 'persevere', Malcolm went with his father, high king of the broad and easy road.

'Yeah,' Malcolm Orange found himself agreeing loudly. And though he did not understand his own betrayal and could not explain the strange, exhilarating affinity he felt towards Soren James Blue, when the moment arrived, it took mere seconds to turn his back on eight glorious weeks. 'Elton John sucks!' he yelled. 'We should be doing the Beastly Boys.'

Abandoning Ross to the magazine rack and yet another afternoon in the care of halfwit Irene, Malcolm Orange made after Sorry's disappearing back. At the door he turned to catch a last glimpse of the People's Committee for Remembering Songs. The members appeared frozen in the early afternoon sunlight like a grand-scale experiment in taxidermy. Roger Heinz was purple and prostrate on the living room carpet. Cunningham Holt was removing the marbles from his eye sockets, preparing for a fit of genuine tears and sorrow. Nate Grubbs, canny as they come, was taking the opportunity to tip his instant coffee into the fish tank.

It only took a second for Malcolm Orange to quit the People's Committee for Remembering Songs but the marbles stayed with him all afternoon, clinking like a guilty cockcrow every time he fell silent.

– Chapter Eight –

Mr Fluff

During the Fall of Soren's fifth year – the very same year in which her parents stopped talking during meals and her father began colluding with a Scandinavian dental hygienist and Sorry, incapable of verbalizing the mounting anxiety, vomited her first banana sandwich on to Mrs Blue's brand-new bedroom carpet – Mr Fluff moved into the refrigerator. Mr Fluff had not intended to move into the refrigerator. Neither had the Blues set out to acquire a cat. The Blues were not pet people. They were scientific in nature and felt that animals that could not, according to the boundaries of Western taste, be used for consumption, transportation or clothing were an unjustifiable luxury.

Magda Blue did not permit animals of any kind in her house. Once, as a small girl, she had found a lost kitten on the way home from kindergarten. 'Snoopy', as Magda had fixed to call him, relieved himself twice; once in each of her father's outdoor shoes. Consequently, Magda's father had drowned him in an empty catering-sized mayonnaise tub. After the drowning young Magda was shocked to discover just how little cat existed under all that sodden fur. 'It's no different from a rat, when the fur's gone,' she mused and fought the urge to borrow her mother's hairdryer for a pre-funeral blow dry. Two days later coyotes gave the kitten an untimely resurrection, leaving his tiny severed skull on the front porch step. A bloodied third of Snoopy was once more consigned to the trash. Burial number two seemed to satisfy the gods and Snoopy was duly forgotten. However, the experience taught Magda a valuable lesson: animals did not belong indoors.

The Blues kept the kind of angular, well-windowed house where all clutter – toilet paper and kitchen utensils included – was carefully closeted behind flush doors. They favored beige, marl and dove gray in all matters aesthetic. Consequently, a cat – particularly an obnoxiously fluffy, whirlwind of a cat like Mr Fluff – was something of an anathema. The Blues had not planned on accumulating children or pets. Soren James had been the product of an unfortunate menstrual miscalculation, a scientific slip Dr Blue held against his wife for the remainder of their marriage and mentioned repeatedly during the divorce proceedings. Mr Fluff had become theirs through a process of accidental osmosis.

Dr and Mrs Blue detested the cat in equal measure. Magda Blue took to leaving the doors of the house wide open in the unfulfilled hope that Mr Fluff might escape and be annihilated by a passing car. Trip Blue was ill-disposed to animals of any kind. As a small child he had once offered next door's horse a single Life Saver, pinched between his baby fingers. The resulting tug of war had left him with a permanent set of teeth marks around the base of his right thumb and the deeply held belief that all animals, equine or otherwise, were nothing but trouble. Trip Blue, tortured by the cat's presence, left saucers of rat poison-laced coffee creamer at strategic points around the house. Mr Fluff was too canny to partake. When she discovered the creamer plot, Magda Blue turned forty shades of furious. She feared for the well-being of Soren James, who was lately prone to downing all manner of inappropriate substances as an aid to her nightly purges. Magda Blue, freshly disgusted by her husband, instigated a sex embargo which would drive them both, at breakneck pace, towards the divorce courts.

Mr Fluff was nine animal years old when she first moved into the refrigerator.

Previous to the Blues her life had been a spastic series of starts, stops and localized abandonments. Shipped from coal shed, to shelter, to suburban duplex with little hope of a permanent address, she soon contracted a feline strain of post-traumatic stress disorder. The anxiety left her incapable of emitting even a low-level purr, suffering from sporadic bouts of constipation and insistent upon sleeping curled around permanent fixtures, tail grasped firmly in teeth like a fuzzy orange bicycle lock. The better part of Mr Fluff's tail was soon gnawed hairless, giving the distinct and troubling impression that a toilet brush had been inserted into her backside. Much as her human owners insisted, she could not bring herself to sleep in a shop-bought cat box. Cat boxes, Mr Fluff figured, could be shifted at the owner's whim. Mr Fluff required something more solid. She had neither love nor trust for the adult Blues and found Soren James alternately affectionate and pinchly mean. However, the cool permanence she discovered amidst the refrigerated condiments and margarine tubs kept Mr Fluff resident with the Blues for almost a decade.

Mr Fluff had arrived quite by chance at the Blues' front door on the Monday morning directly preceding Thanksgiving. Prior to Thanksgiving she had lived, for most of a human year, with Pete and Miranda, who occupied the house at the end of the Blues' cul-de-sac. Pete was a computer programmer and left the house, smartly suited, at ten minutes to seven each morning.

Miranda was a freelance editor and claimed to work from home. Mr Fluff soon came to realize that working from home was the human term for semi-permanent hibernation. At ten minutes to five each afternoon Miranda swapped her pajamas for proper clothes in anticipation of Pete's return. Most evenings, feigning exhaustion, she was back in her flannels before the six o'clock news had ended. She rarely ventured further than the end of the cul-de-sac and ate cereal, from the same unwashed bowl, for every meal. The stench of Miranda's unhappiness was so thick Mr Fluff could taste it, fouling on her tongue, each time she gave herself a good licking.

When both Pete and Miranda were simultaneously home, breathing and being and conversing in the same room, the apartment felt like a paper lantern, voluminous and light and inflating with each casual exchange. Minus Pete, the apartment was a coffin. Mr Fluff could barely breathe. Under pressure her bowels went whole fortnights without movement. Miranda pillowed her with affection, constantly cooing, constantly stroking; inventing odd, childish derivations of Mr Fluff's name: Flufflet, Fluffy McFluff, Fluffle Duffles. Mr Fluff felt like a toothpaste tube, pummeled for the final, hesitating drops.

Pete and Miranda could not have children. Or rather, they could have had children if they'd set their minds on it. However, the doctors insisted that these children would almost certainly turn out funny. Something about Pete's blood did not mix right with Miranda's. All this was explained to Mr Fluff, with patronizing sincerity, during her first few days at the apartment. Mr Fluff was a cat and found the situation extremely odd, having previously assumed that children – like kittens – could be selected free of charge from some sort of children shelter. Furthermore, she was surprised to hear that Pete and Miranda's blood would not mix right, for the rest of them fitted together perfectly and with irritating frequency; hands, necks, tongues and naked parts locking together at every opportunity like a set of squirming, Siamese octopuses. The sound they made together was repulsive.

Mr Fluff, the cat was told, had been Pete's idea: a stopgap to take the edge off the loneliness until a permanent solution could be agreed upon. The rest of the story was revealed to her in whispered, claustrophobic installments, crushed into Miranda's lap or bundled under the duvet whilst Pete was busy programming computers downtown. Miranda, Mr Fluff was informed, had always been the household's purchaser. Having done such a stellar job on the spare bedroom, the weekly grocery cull and the honeymoon in Antigua, she had also been given free reign over the purchasing of a pseudo-child. Secretly, fearing this might be the closest they came to acquiring an actual baby of their own, Miranda resented the freedom Pete had so readily awarded her. Just to spite him she'd picked a particularly luminous ginger cat, for she knew his penchant for tortoiseshells.

Mr Fluff had been savvy enough to note this caustic mix of spite and insecurity the moment Miranda arrived at her holding pen.

'That one's a girl,' the guy at the cat place had announced, jabbing a finger through the wire mesh to point out Mr Fluff, curl-locked round a concrete pillar.

'Shit,' Miranda had replied, shoving both hands nervously into her blazer pockets. The sleeve of her pajama shirt was just visible, protruding from the cuff. 'I really wanted a boy cat. A boy cat is what I came for. Any color's fine except tortoiseshell. My husband can't stand tortoiseshell cats. Odd, huh?'

'Fricking crazy!' the cat guy had replied with heavy sarcasm.

Mr Fluff had been resident at the cat place long enough to recognize a Type A cat lady when she saw one. Like the cat guy, she had her suspicions that Miranda, with her nervous secretary clothes and her enormous tree-frog eyes, was claiming ownership of an imaginary husband. Most cat ladies were chronically single.

'Don't you have any boy cats?' Miranda had continued, unaware her character was under scrutiny. 'I had such a lovely boy cat when I was a child. Call me sentimental but I'd really hoped for another boy cat. Ideally I'd like an orange cat, you know, to resemble Mr Fluff. I was going to name him after my old cat.'

'Sorry ma'am, it's Christmas next week. There was a rush on boy cats. People only want the males nowadays. They don't want the hassle of worrying about kittens. We only have this one orange cat left and I'm pretty sure it's a girl.' The cat guy had, without warning, uncurled Mr Fluff claw by frantic claw, turning her upside down just to verify the gender. Mr Fluff had been mortified.

'Never mind. I'll take the girl cat anyway. I'll just pretend it's a boy.'

'Hi,' she'd said as she Magic Markered the cat's name on to her collar. 'I'm your new mommy. Your name's Mr Fluff now. You're a boy cat.' And, with little consideration for personal preference, the cat previously answering to Rosie became known as Mr Fluff and found herself resigned to a lifetime of gender confusion.

As her first human year with Pete and Miranda progressed, it became increasingly clear that Miranda was more than a little unbalanced. By April she'd taken to dressing Mr Fluff in a powder-blue onesie and pushing her round the neighborhood in a second-hand stroller. Each morning she bathed the cat in a plastic baby bath, taking great pains to massage her ginger fur with a generous dollop of Johnson & Johnson's No More Tears shampoo. On several occasions Mr Fluff found herself force-fed pureed swede from a suspicious-looking glass jar. At first she'd responded with thrashing pawfuls of unsheathed claw. Later, she grew resigned to the fact that a full-grown human being, even a meager specimen like Miranda, would always win in a war with a domestic cat.

All Miranda's deviant behavior took place between the hours of seven and five, while Pete was safely closeted away, crunching numbers in his office cube. On evenings and weekends she appropriated a nervous kind of normalcy. And if Pete grew suspicious when he discovered the baby stroller stashed behind the golf clubs in his garage, if he wondered about the sickly smell of shampoo emanating from his cat, or noticed Miranda rocking Mr Fluff gently in a manner better suited to a newborn, he said nothing, for he was secretly delighted to find himself thirty-seven and not yet lumbered with a child.

In August Pete and Miranda began to think about moving. California had only ever been a temporary solution. Warm air, Miranda's grandmother had insisted, would do Pete's psoriasis the world of good. After six years of Californian living, Pete's psoriasis still looked like raw baloney. Miranda could no longer bear the thin, hairdryer heat. In September, swayed by an uncommonly cool spell, they changed their minds about moving. In October, Pete showed Miranda a picture of Vermont which he'd clipped from an in-flight travel magazine. 'Look at this darling,' he'd said, pointing out the fields, and the clapboard houses, the trees flaming menstrual red and orange. 'Isn't it the most beautiful place you've ever seen? It's cold there for six month of the year, sometimes eight.'

In late November they moved to Kansas.

As soon as the For Sale sign appeared in the front yard Miranda started thinking about Mr Fluff. Not the current, asexual Mr Fluff but rather the original, well-fluffed cat of her earliest memory. It had been over twenty years since Miranda had last seen this Mr Fluff and she had not yet forgiven Massachusetts the loss. The original Mr Fluff, Boston-based and vitriolic, had not belonged to young Miranda. An elderly neighbor owned the cat and each morning pitched him out just before breakfast, keeping the back door barred until interfering neighbors or the animal welfare people insisted Mr Fluff be readmitted. Miranda's parents had adopted a similar stance on children and so Mr Fluff and Miranda often found themselves stoic on the sidewalk, spitting and shivering and occasionally embracing, fur on frozen flesh, for an extra ounce of body heat.

Without warning, one week shy of Miranda's tenth birthday, Mr Fluff's elderly owner had upped and moved to be with a daughter in Sacramento. Mr Fluff had been dragged across the continent on an old-fashioned whim. The elderly neighbor, having lived through the Great Depression, several minor depressions and at least one world war, was of the belief that all possessions, even unwanted cats, were worth holding on to. In the future, he explained to his Sacramento daughter, he might be able to sell the cat for tobacco money, or swap it for livestock, or, if the Republican prophets were proven correct, eat it with French fries when America went to hell in a Democratic handbasket.

One morning, whilst young Miranda was shuffling through her Saturday piano lesson, the original Mr Fluff had moved, against his express will, to Sacramento in a U-Haul van. Mr Fluff never gave Sacramento a proper chance. He passed away three weeks after the move. The heat had been manageable but the cheap Mexican cat food disagreed with his delicate east coast innards. Miranda had cried herself livid on the curb for days. When the natural tears ran out she dabbed Vicks VapoRub beneath each eye and coerced an extra week out of her sadness.

Twenty years later, and reasonably married, Miranda continued to swear blind that all her adult issues (chronic anxiety, exaggeration and shoplifting, not to mention the teenage pyromania) were directly related to the fact that Mr Fluff had not bothered to say goodbye. Of course she'd grown up. She no longer blamed the cat. A cat was a cat, and capable though he'd been, the original Mr Fluff had lacked the opposable thumbs necessary to send a goodbye postcard. The blame belonged to his owner now, and to her parents who had forced her into unwanted piano lessons, and the whole sprawling, conspiratorial state of Massachusetts. The closer adult Miranda got to moving the more anxious she began to get about the cat. By the beginning of November she was drinking a quart of whiskey, distilled into her evening Nesquik, just to get to sleep.

Miranda was unhinged but seldom cruel. She was not a happy person yet devoted an unhealthy amount of time to worrying about the happiness of complete strangers. Anxiety on another's behalf seemed somehow less selfish. Lately, Miranda had been reminiscing. She'd begun to wonder if there might be some child in the neighborhood who loved her cat as much as she'd loved the original Mr Fluff; a child who'd be inconsolable if Mr Fluff left without saying goodbye; a child who'd grow up, get the hell out of California and carry this loss like a dead leg all the way to adulthood.

This was a terrible thought. It kept Miranda anxious and insomniac for weeks on end.

When she was positively wide-eyed with the worry and all her thoughts were needles and pins, she would poke Pete in the left bicep and cry, 'What are we going to do about Mr Fluff?' Very rarely did Pete respond or even acknowledge her prodding. Miranda had only acquired one husband so far but if she was fortunate enough to gain a second she planned to seek out a lighter sleeper. When her skin had turned a funereal shade of gray, and her throat a cactus, Miranda came to a decision. The only thing to do, she concluded, was to bundle Mr Fluff back into the plastic carrier from whence she had come and lug her from door to door offering a farewell to every child on the cul-de-sac.

'That's ridiculous,' Pete had insisted. 'We'll be the laughing stock of the whole neighborhood. No one needs to say goodbye to a cat.'

'Best to do these things in person,' Miranda replied, but Pete did not understand. He'd never been a lonely child propping up a sidewalk. He'd been blessed with appropriately aged siblings and two-story homes and pets chosen from actual pet stores for their good looks and character.

'Dammit, Pete,' Miranda said, surprising herself with the enormous sound which came out of her belly, 'I'm going anyway.' This statement had instigated their first, last and loudest argument.

Miranda had a face like the weather: one moment infinitely approachable, the very next, raging like a mudslide. She walked the line daily, wobbling between striking and downright ugly. She was more than used to people staring in the grocery store. Miranda took her tree-frog face into consideration every time she ventured outside. As she considered the reality of lugging Mr Fluff from door to door, it seemed sensible to accentuate the ordinary. On this occasion she wished to be the all-American neighbor; the cookies and milk woman who lives next door; the woman you might phone in an emergency and say, 'Sweetheart, I'm so, so sorry to impose but we're having an emergency here and I was wondering if you could keep an eye on the kids while John and I nip out for half an hour. I wouldn't normally leave the kids with just anyone but I know you'll do great with them. Everyone knows you're a natural.'

The situation was not unlike Halloween. Miranda was dressing up as an ordinary lady with very ordinary problems. She pulled her hair into an absolutely average ponytail. She wore a Christmas sweater even though California was sweltering and still five fat weeks from the big day. (Miranda operated under the mistaken assumption that all sweaters were inherently maternal.) She wore reading glasses to hide her too-close, tree-frog eyes. She considered bringing cookies but it would take both hands just to manage Mr Fluff and the plastic carrier. Once Miranda felt good and homely, she lifted Mr Fluff into her plastic carrier, zipped herself into the most momsy jacket she owned and pulled the apartment door behind her.

The goodbyes did not go well. The neighbors on either side were out of town for the holiday weekend. Two doors down, the mother answered the door.

'Hey,' Miranda said. 'We live two doors up with the swing set in the front yard.'

'Oh,' the mother said. 'How old are your kids?'

'We don't have kids . . . I mean, we can't have kids . . . I mean, look, it's kind of complicated. The last owners left the swing set behind. We do have a cat though.'

She side-stepped neatly to reveal Mr Fluff in her carrier. The two doors down mother looked horrified.

'Ummmm,' Miranda muttered, suddenly overcome with embarrassment. 'We're moving next week and I kind of thought maybe our cat could say goodbye to your kids so they're not sad or something when he just disappears.'

'Why would they be sad? They don't know your cat. We don't let them play outside the back yard.'

'Oh, well could I possibly see your kids anyway, just to be on the safe side?' Miranda elevated Mr Fluff's carrier, giving her an angle to peer down the hall into the kitchen.

'I don't think so,' stated the mother bluntly and slammed the door on the toe of Miranda's very ordinary shoe. She stood there mortified, considering the outside of two doors down's front door and their sign, which read, 'Happy Thanksgiving from the Mastersons'. Mr Fluff could feel Miranda's unhappiness settling down like rain.

This first front door conversation proved to be a rehearsal for a series of very similar interactions all the way down one side of the street and back up the other. By the time Mr Fluff and Miranda arrived at the Blues' home Miranda was just about ready to give up and get drunk in her pajamas.

The Blue house looked like an open invitation. Every light in the building was white, hot and beaming. The house was telling lies with its well-lit windows. It had been several months since the Blues last had a visitor and this visitor, far from slipping his work shoes off at the door, had spent an uncomfortable twenty minutes bolt upright on a dining room chair, reciting a pre-prepared liturgy of life insurance quotes.

Miranda was exhausted. She thought nothing of the lights. She stomped all over the tastefully printed welcome mat. She barely noticed the Swedish-designed doorbell. It had been a mile of a morning and she no longer expected success. 'Once more on to the breach,' she muttered and poked the doorbell twice, squarely in the eye with malice.

Behind the door Miranda heard feet, one foot first and then a second. Foot, foot, foot, faster foot, foot, gaining momentum as they approached the door. She expected another judgmental mother so she held Mr Fluff in front of her chest, half peace offering, half shield. 'God, help us both,' she thought, as she braced herself for the ridicule. 'Why am I subjecting us to this again?' The door opened into itself like a nervous smile.

A five-year-old Soren James Blue stood behind the door. She was yet to experience the growth spurt which would leave her towering over the little boys on the first day of second grade and could easily have passed for a four-year-old. She was wearing a full set of grubby-looking *Fraggle Rock* pajamas. One hand rested on the door handle while the other clutched a yellow plastic bowl which was overflowing with soggy-looking Cocoa Puffs. The milk from her cereal – already turning an over-familiar shade of brown – had formed a rivulet from Soren's open mouth, down the bridge of her chin, to the smallest Fraggle who crouched, ready for action, just above her belly button.

'What do you want, lady?' Sorry asked.

'Umm,' Miranda stalled. 'Is your mommy around?'

'Nope. She's at the office place.' Sorry took a huge, dribbly spoonful of Coco Puffs, the majority of which abandoned ship halfway to her mouth, landing like small shit mountains at her naked feet.

'What about daddy? Is he home? Or do you have an older brother or sister or someone looking after you?'

'I'm looking after me. The cleaning lady was supposed to come but she didn't,' the child replied. 'It's OK. I have a gun.' And with this Sorry fished around on the telephone table, emerging seconds later with a fully loaded plastic rifle.

'Impressive,' Miranda said. She had that creeping, fingers on her shoulder feeling she normally got when someone was watching her on closed circuit TV. 'Maybe I should come back another time,' she said hesitantly. Then she stepped over the welcome mat and into the Blues' house.

'What's in the box, lady?'

Miranda set the plastic carrier on the hall carpet, opened the lid and watched helplessly as Mr Fluff sprung out, stretched her back and planted his ample backside on the child's feet.

'Mr Fluff!' cried Sorry, bending to scratch the back of Mr Fluff's neck. Bent double and scratching, she looked happy as a pickled onion.

'How do you know his name?' Miranda asked.

'She told me.'

'You just read it off his collar. Or maybe your mommy read it for you. I'm guessing you don't read so well yet.'

'I read awesome, lady. I'm nearly six. I didn't read her name though. She told me. She tells me lots of stuff.'

'Like what?' asked Miranda, humoring the child.

'Like how you cry all day and dress her up in baby clothes,' replied Sorry indignantly.

Miranda was horrified. For the first time in her adult life she felt herself capable of strongly disliking a child.

'Also,' Sorry continued her verbal assault, 'she feels shitty cos you keep telling everybody she's a boy. How would you like it if everyone thought you were a boy?'

Sorry stopped to shovel an enormous spoonful of cereal into her open mouth, dragging the back of her hand, like a makeshift napkin, across her dripping chin.

'He is a boy cat,' mumbled Miranda defiantly.

'S'not,' Sorry continued, unceremoniously turning Mr Fluff upside down to expose her private parts, or lack thereof.

'Well I suppose you're technically right. It is a girl cat. I . . . I mean my husband and I, just decided he should be a boy cat because we liked the name Mr Fluff.'

'That's not very fair. I'm a girl and I'd be really mad if someone told me I had to be a boy and have a stupid name.'

With this Soren James Blue poked Miranda once, hard, in the ribs, with the snub end of her plastic rifle. The Cocoa Puffs, having made their escape from the bowl, had formed a muddy brown river down the leg of her pajama pants. The child had the hometown advantage. Miranda was intimidated. She had never before encountered a child so obnoxiously confident. Filthy, shock-haired and defiant as a fifty-foot pylon, Sorry cut the shadow of a wild, feral creature.

'Listen, I don't have to stand here and be lied to,' Miranda said, releasing a judgmental, waggity finger for emphasis. 'It's my cat. His name's Mr Fluff and tomorrow he's moving to Kansas. I only brought him round to say goodbye.'

'She's not moving. She doesn't like Kansas,' Sorry fired back. 'I got her a book from the library and she says it looks shit; nothing but flatness and sheep. She said she wants to stay here in California and I asked my mom and she says it's cool for Mr Fluff to move in so long as she doesn't eat the curtains again. She can live in the fridge. Mr Fluff likes it in our fridge.' The part about asking Magda Blue's permission was one hundred percent imagined. The rest, unbelievable as it sounded in the recount, was God's honest truth.

Despite herself, Miranda admired the child's bravado. Sorry exuded a confidence she had always aspired to. She liked the child and simultaneously disliked the child and was unsure where to file such a maelstrom of competing emotions. This would be a battle of good sense over emotion.

'Look here, kiddo. I don't care if the cat told you he wants to be Prime Minister of England. He's moving to Kansas in the morning so say your goodbyes and let us leave.'

Soren James Blue glared at Miranda. Miranda glared at Soren James Blue. The inside of her nose began to twitch irritatingly. Sorry glared back, unflinching as a corpse. Sorry won. Mr Fluff, bored with the standoff, uncurled himself from Sorry's shoulder, slid down her spine and wandered nonchalantly into the Blues' kitchen.

Technically the cat still belonged to Miranda and this, she assumed, gave her permission to traipse after Mr Fluff. Soren James Blue followed at a distance, dragging her plastic rifle across the terracotta floor tiles.

The entire ground floor of the Blue house was as open plan and unencumbered as architecture would allow. The living area contained two uncomfortable-looking white sofas and a mammoth entertainment system large enough to accommodate God and all his Friday night buddies. The kitchen itself appeared to be fashioned from the leftover parts of downtown skyscrapers. Most every surface was flawless, black marble. The remaining wall was windowed, the fixtures and fittings a heavily foiled chrome. Standing in the centre of the kitchen, Miranda could see herself reflected – a homely, pink blob – upside down, occasionally upright and projecting from every inch of the room.

Mr Fluff had already found the fridge.

The fridge was comparable in size and capacity to a small European car, upended. The door had been left barely open, revealing – in an intimate sliver of synthetic light – a good half inch of margarine tub and the tip end of Mr Fluff's tail, curling round the peanut butter. The rest of the house was so sleek, so very sparse and streamlined, it felt pornographic to catch a glimpse of actual, individual items – tubs and tubes and screw-top jars, brand names offered up for judgment. Miranda found herself inclining towards the fridge, curious to discover what homeowners with minimalist leanings might consume. The peanut butter sprung out at her.

'What sort of freaks keep their peanut butter in the fridge?' she wondered, but kept her thoughts politely to herself.

'You can't keep a cat in a fridge,' she observed instead, somewhat loudly, through clenched teeth.

'Mr Fluff likes it particularly in our fridge. Sometimes she stays the night in there.'

'Bullshit,' said Miranda. She was not the kind of woman prone to swearing in front of small children but the situation had unraveled her. 'Don't be ridiculous. A cat couldn't live in a fridge. It would suffocate. Besides, Mr Fluff sleeps at our house. I think we'd know if he was out all night, sleeping in strangers' fridges.'

'Bollocks,' returned Sorry, echoing a sentiment she'd heard on British television. 'Mr Fluff spends most nights in our fridge. I think she climbs out your bathroom window to escape. She breathes just fine in the fridge. I expect the air gets in through the ice cube dispenser. She doesn't mind the cold at all.'

'My cat's not staying in your fridge.'

'Yes, she is.'

'No he isn't! I'm the adult here, and I'm taking Mr Fluff home now.'

'She doesn't want to go. She likes it in the fridge, every night she draws pictures in the margarine. You don't even let her draw with crayons on ordinary paper.'

The cat had shifted and Miranda could now make out a damp black nose, two paws and several whiskers, visible in the fridge door gap. Good sense was beckoning Miranda out the door. It was long gone five. Pete would be arriving home at any second. The dinner was yet to be defrosted. Miranda looked at the front door wistfully. The streetlights had bloomed in her absence. They blushed like lens flare on the dark glass. She imagined them sprouting from the sidewalk; bent-head tulips, highlighting her homeward route. She pictured Pete waiting on the sofa, his forehead folding in consternation. It was months since he'd found himself home alone. He would be worried. Miranda's feet refused to move. Something strong and obstinate had anchored her into the Blues' terracotta floor tiles. She could not quit. Neither could she anticipate victory. Children were notoriously difficult to talk out of their affectations and this argument, she suspected, could ricochet for weeks, pinging off the kitchen walls, gaining and losing momentum without ever coming to a satisfactory conclusion.

Miranda found herself uncomfortably wedged between a rock and a hard-faced six-year-old. She decided to humor Sorry, to play along with her story, to prove her wrong and get the hell out of the house before a significant adult appeared. 'OK,' she said. 'You win. Let's close the fridge door and see how well Mr Fluff likes it in there. If he's still content after thirty seconds he can move into your house for good. But if he goes crazy in there, he leaves for Kansas in the morning. You say goodbye and you never see him again.'

'Can she still be called Mr Fluff if I keep her?'

'Sure thing, you can change his name to Mighty Mouse if you want. I don't care.'

Soren James Blue considered this proposal for a few seconds, examined the outside of the fridge from all angles, and eventually muttered 'Deal,' closing the door to seal the bargain.

Miranda was confident the cat would begin to panic. She

stepped closer for a better ear on events.

Together they counted to thirty using the old fashioned method, 'one thousand, two thousand, three thousand,' all the way up to thirty thousand, plus another three thousands just for good measure. Miranda had two fingers crossed on each hand, hoping the child's mother wouldn't arrive home and find a strange lady had locked a cat in her fridge. The fridge purred on; monolithic, competent and surprisingly calm. Around about twenty-five thousands Miranda began to worry. Mr Fluff might be dead inside, wreaking wild havoc or comatose and slumped against the breakfast juices. She was not concerned about the cat so much as the awkward moment when she would have to explain the situation to other less understanding individuals.

'Done,' said Sorry, as soon as she got to thirty-three thousands. They opened the fridge together, fists grazing momentarily on the handle. Mr Fluff was more than alive. She had used her fridge time profitably. The margarine tub now played canvas to an uncanny likeness of the President himself. 'It's nice in here,' Mr Fluff purred. 'There's a little yellow light and everything. It really helps when you're trying to draw.'

This was the first and longest conversation Mr Fluff would have with anyone aside from Soren James Blue. The situation, she reasoned, had been dire enough to justify the breaking of her own mute laws. More so, Mr Fluff was a master of comic timing and relished, for months thereafter, the look on Miranda's face; a bipartisan mix of horror and delight. Mr Fluff measured her moments carefully. Though Sorry swore blind to parents, psychiatrists and an ever-decreasing circle of incredulous friends that Mr Fluff was capable of actual, articulate conversation, no one besides herself and Miranda could verify this claim. Within twenty-four hours of the encounter Miranda was ensconced in a midsize U-Haul winging her way to Kansas with little thought of testifying. Pete followed behind with the car.

Mr Fluff and Soren James Blue had been, somewhat awkwardly, soldered together ever since.

– Chapter Nine –

Drinking and Smoking

The People's Committee for Remembering Songs was struggling to harmonize under pressure.

Whilst the ladies on the sofa, incapable of coping with real-time disaster, sought comfort in birdy little chit-chats about the latest soap opera intrigue, the men pounded the carpet, balled fists constraining their rage. They were stoic by numbers. Between them they'd soldiered through seventeen individual wars on four separate continents, lost a devastating total of nine life partners and thirteen children, conquered six different types of cancer and survived fifteen or more presidential elections, not to mention Civil Rights, Watergate, the Great Depression, McCarthyism and the onslaught of MTV. They were not about to be intimidated by a teenage girl.

Bill was the first to take charge of the situation. He proposed marching straight to the Director's office to lodge an official complaint about the girl.

'We'll say,' he announced to the room, 'that she hit Irene with an umbrella in the face. They'll have to take an actual assault seriously. We'll agree our stories before we go and if everyone says the same thing, well, they'll be legally responsible to act on it. They'll have to get rid of the little devil.'

'Hopefully they'll throw her in jail,' added Clary O'Hare and launched into a meandering anecdote about a Japanese prisoner of war camp and a goat, an army pal from Tennessee and the incredible benefits of knowing Morse code in such a situation.

'Never mind jail,' hissed Roger Heinz, incapable of containing the rage any longer, 'the bitch deserves to be hung, drawn and quartered if you ask me.'

'No one's asking you. No one's ever asking you, Roger,' snapped Bill. He was not the sort of man given to alligator impulses. However, Sorry's departure had knocked the civility right out of him.

The two men glared at each other from either side of the Oriental rug. Averagely built and erring on the cautious side of short, Roger Heinz had a face like a brick shit wall. It was six years since he'd last been reprimanded. The unlucky idiot unfortunate enough to question Heinz's right to the only empty booth at the IHOP on 82nd had eaten his pancakes pureed for the next fortnight. Short order cooks and oil change guys from east coast to west could recount similar outbreaks of inappropriate violence. The military had planted an uncommon rage in Roger Heinz. Whilst other men favored the penis, Roger Heinz did his best thinking in his fists, finding they automatically curled and rose like a perfect pair of divining rods at the first inkling twitch of anger. Approaching eighty, his arms were not what they'd once been. Rising into an argument he felt them sag at the elbow like cheese strings left too long in the sun. The rage was not diminished, however, and more and more Roger Heinz found himself attacking with words and occasionally small weapons – salad forks or flick knives – which could be pocketed, or at a pinch secreted in his armpit.

Cornered now, he searched his tracksuit pockets for a spare

soupspoon, and finding himself entirely unarmed, fell back on his well-maintained arsenal of insults.

'Screw you all and your shitty songs,' he yelled and stomped out the front door. Within Baptist Retirement circles, Roger Heinz's exits were legendary. His anger could be contained for only so long before, like an over-blown air mattress, he exploded, scattering insults and terse expletives in his wake. Whilst exiting, the red mist lifted briefly, allowing him to scoop the remainder of the oatmeal cookies into his pocket. If nothing else, war had taught Roger Heinz to put the stomach's needs before all other loftier causes. The door slammed behind his back, screen rattling as it settled.

'He'll be back,' muttered Nate Grubbs.

'More's the pity,' replied Bill, who'd held a secret grudge against his neighbor since the night he'd caught Irene eyeing up Roger Heinz's surprisingly pert backside, bending to load the post-practice coffee mugs into the dishwasher. Though his wife was clearly insane and could not be held responsible for which behind she chose to ogle (or fondle, as Bill had begun to suspect), he resented the fact that she'd landed upon such a very loud-mouthed, obnoxious backside. It was, he calculated, almost five years since she'd last made moves upon his own ample posterior and it was this realization, more than anything, which smarted and fueled his dislike of Roger Heinz.

The room fell impatiently silent in the wake of Heinz's departure. Momentum was fading. Mrs Kellerman, exhibiting the early signs of Alzheimer's, had no recollection of Soren's departure or, for that matter, her unexpected arrival. Lately Mrs Kellerman had been struggling to form a sharp recollection of anything after the year 1963. All but the youngest of the People's Committee began to anticipate the need for an afternoon nap. On the sofa, sandwiched between two substantially cardiganed ladies, Mrs Huxley was already beginning to nod off.

'So we're going with the umbrella story,' pronounced Nate Grubbs confidently, assuming authority for the group. 'We should get our story down on paper, to make sure we have all the facts straight.'

From the inner pocket of his sports jacket he produced a tatty notebook and carpenter's pencil and beckoned the men to gather round. The women watched on from the plush seats. The sofa was their territory. They moved only for kitchen duties, for ambulances and natural disasters. They were the kind of women accustomed to being ignored. A series of fathers, husbands and lately sons had made decisions on their behalf, informing them after the event of vacations, separations, relocations and home improvements. They had, over the years, come to realize that failing a kitchen strike, a raised voice was the only way to make their presence known.

'Write down that she uses terrible profanity,' shouted Mrs Huxley, anxious to add her penny's worth.

'And smokes cigarettes,' hollered Mrs Kellerman, unsure as to whom they were speaking of, but convinced, as she had been from her earliest Baptist days, that only the commonest kind of people and sluts smoked cigarettes.

'And she turned Malcolm against us,' spat Clary O'Hare. A round room's worth of assenting nods and yeahs confirmed his suspicions.

'And that she hit Irene in the face with an enormous golf umbrella,' concluded Miss Pamela Richardson, taking the opportunity to further embellish the lie.

In the corner, by the spider plant, Irene began to cry softly, tracing a single finger backwards and forwards across her papery cheek as if attempting to locate the imaginary spot where she'd been struck.

'I don't like that girl,' she whispered. 'It's bad luck to bring an umbrella indoors.'

No one blamed Malcolm directly, but the ghost of his rebellion was a grave cloud looming over the living room ceiling, constraining all their thoughts and deliberations. In the kitchen dinette with a cup of scorched coffee cooling in his hand, Cunningham Holt listened carefully and held his tongue. He neither agreed nor disagreed with the People's Committee for Remembering Songs. He was a moderate man and rarely took sides. Despite his betting past, organized sports were wasted on Cunningham Holt for he found himself rooting, on every occasion, for a measured draw, a result which would favor no man over the other. Yet Malcolm Orange had taken the trouble to tie him down and with this small gesture, an act of kindness unrivalled in Cunningham Holt's entire sinking existence, the old man felt himself forever bound to the boy.

For seventy years, Cunningham Holt had been entirely dependent on the arms, the shoulders and kindly gestures of others. Though he sponsored several black children in unfortunate countries and was first to subsidize the Annual Thanksgiving Turkey and Tipples Tea Dance when the cutbacks set in – using his small fortune to bless the needy – he had never once had the opportunity to help another individual.

Each evening when night descended upon the cul-de-sac and the residents turned their attention to sleep, to sexual activities and earnest prayer, Cunningham Holt lay back on his collapsible table bed and consoled himself with a series of fervent superhero fantasies. In each of these vignettes he would imagine himself a much younger man, wide-eyed and blessed with above average intelligence, coming to the aid of ordinary people in jeopardy. Not for Cunningham Holt the anonymity of the mask or clichéd cape. He felt no need to assume superhuman strength or powers. He simply strode through these imaginary situations, mundane as an office worker, in corduroys and well-worn Hush Puppies, adjusting satellite television aerials, fixing burst water mains and escorting elderly ladies from one side of Fred Meyer's parking lot to the other. Having been catapulted into a lifetime of dependency, it was Cunningham Holt's holiest, miracle dream that he would one day be allowed the pleasure of helping someone do something they could not do by themselves.

Malcolm Orange was not himself. Cunningham Holt could hear this in the cut of his voice. Malcolm was disappearing and Cunningham Holt felt it his incumbent duty to interfere. Whilst the debate ricocheted round the People's Committee, fluctuating between petitions, protests and old-fashioned lynchings, he took the opportunity to tip the dregs of his coffee into the waste disposal and slip, unnoticed, out the back door.

No one noticed Cunningham Holt leave. Ninety minutes earlier, assisted by an ancient cane, no one had noticed him arrive. Edging from one garden to the next, with nothing more than a memory map to guide him, the old man began to circumvent the cul-de-sac's edge in pursuit of Malcolm Orange.

On the other side of the cul-de-sac, crouching between the recycling bin and a long-abandoned fridge-freezer, Soren James Blue was trying to recall the best way to break into a house.

Soren James Blue was enormously angry. The People's Committee for Remembering Songs had reminded her of her parents; ordering, organizing, coming upon her suddenly like a too-tight sweater. Soren James Blue could not stand to be restrained. All summer, subjected to the trials and treatments of the Center, walled up in the Baptist Retirement Village with her insides tumbling out, she hadn't been able to muster the energy for an enormous anger. This morning she'd felt stronger, strong enough to order someone else into submission. Malcolm Orange had been a miracle find. She fully intended to torture him mercilessly, correcting the imbalance in her self-defined power structure, for the remainder of the summer.

The People's Committee had not been part of her plan. Groups made Soren James Blue edgy and claustrophobic. She would never be the sort of dictator interested in a co-op. Standing on Irene's oriental rug, the anger had come bubbling out of her like a suppressed sneeze. She wanted nothing to do with the old folk. She wanted to destroy each one of them, individually. She wanted to wreak havoc on their homes and gardens, torturing them into taking her seriously.

Soren James Blue wanted to give the People's Committee a proper, quantifiable reason to dislike her; something more immediate than a nose ring, more personal than a mistrust of her father, more reassuring than the faint assumption, present from the age of three, that she was simply one of those thoroughly unlovable little girls. Burglary seemed a natural place to begin her reign of terror.

A lifetime of parental indifference had allowed Sorry more than adequate exposure to the sort of movies which gave graphic guidance on how to kill zombies, blow shit up, pleasure men (and also women), ingest ungodly amounts of habit-forming drugs and, most importantly, vandalize other people's property. As she crouched beside the bin, the stench of moldering vegetable scraps turning her stomach, Sorry made a mental list of every burglary she'd ever witnessed. A glasscutter and suction device were her weapons of choice. However, there was also the distinct, ill-defined understanding that something could be done with a credit card or hairpin, twiddled in just the right fashion. Semtex, of course, was an option, or the mundane possibility of wriggling forehead first through an open bathroom window. With little in the way of burglarizing equipment and all windows frustratingly sealed, Soren James Blue had just settled upon the notion of instigating an old-fashioned smash and grab, when she caught sight of a pair of rubber-tipped sneakers peering around the corner of Chalet 5.

'I can see you Malcolm!' she whispered furiously. 'Are you perving on me again?'

Malcolm Orange took two urgent steps backwards, dragging his sneakered toes behind him and, for the third time that day, accidentally thumped his head off the wall, hard enough to induce nausea. Chalet 5 swam in front of him, a brick and plasterboard cloud, coming and going before his eyes. He folded in two, grabbing his ankles for balance, and threw up on the gravel path. The vomit tasted of chocolate and vinegar. It caught him smartly in the back of the nose. He kept his head tucked between his knees for a good few seconds. Whilst bent, in pursuit of gravity's centre, Malcolm examined the enormous gaps, blooming now like Holy Jesus stigmata in both wrists and ankles. Through the absence in his left wrist he could see a cockroach clambering across the hot gravel. The sensation of peering through his own bones caused him to vomit a second time. The cockroach disappeared, drowned in a deluge of half-digested Chips Ahoy.

'Holy shit, Orange,' exclaimed Sorry, 'you're like a barf fountain. I could learn a thing or two about puking from you.'

Malcolm Orange stood up and wiped his mouth on the back of his hand. He dropped his arms so they dragged dully against the edge of his thighs and glared at Soren James Blue. From this distance, with the taste of vomit settling on his tongue, she looked like a really bad idea. Though he couldn't explain his own feet, the need to follow her, dashing from Bill's doorway, across the turn circle and round the back of Chalet 5, had been irresistible. Malcolm Orange had never been in a gang before, and while he was not entirely clear if a fourteen-year-old girl and her cat equated to a proper gang, he'd been reluctant to miss out on the possibility.

Malcolm was having second thoughts now. He suspected that Sorry was about to break into Emily Fox's kitchen. This realization split him. More than anything in the world Malcolm wished to impress Sorry and yet he did not want to go to prison or to the electric chair. Big time lies and cigarettes were only sins against the Jesus God and could, with the right amount of piety, be prayed into absolution. Burglary was an actual crime against the police and Malcolm Orange had no desire to risk the repercussions.

'I'm going,' he said.

'Disappearing again?' said Sorry and laughed glibly at her own wit.

'Not funny. I'm going. I should check Ross is OK at Bill and Irene's. I have things to do.'

'Liar,' she said, 'you never do anything.'

(She was not far from the truth. Before Sorry's arrival, Malcolm Orange had allowed his days to blur inconsequentially into each other. Passing time was marked only by the advent of night, of morning and Sunday dinner, when the Oranges almost always ate Mexican.)

'Take off your shirt,' she commanded.

'No way,' said Malcolm, 'you already saw me naked once today. I'm not falling for that again.'

'Twice,' said Sorry, 'I've seen you naked twice today. Big, dumb thrill!' and began to tug at his shirtsleeve.

Though loath to admit it, Malcolm Orange found the sensation of being undressed by a girl far less repulsive than he'd previously imagined. He muttered softly in objection, yet allowed himself to be disarmed and un-shirted, even ducking his head to assist with the last tug. Parts of him, previously perforated, seemed all of a sudden less problematic, warmer and inclined to flutter, like a barrel full of gin-drunk butterflies. Bare-chested, Malcolm folded his arms across the worst of the holes, and hooked his hands into his armpits. In the shadow from Chalet 5's gable wall he was painfully white; the color of brand-new tube socks.

Malcolm Orange felt like Adam, caught between the Devil and a good, true thing. The next move, he recalled from the motel movies, belonged to him.

'Take off your shirt,' he commanded, and reached for a fistful of Sorry's sleeve.

Soren James Blue threw back her head and laughed cruelly. This was not how things normally progressed on TV.

'Nice try kid,' she said, wrapped Malcolm's shirt around her right fist and punched a grapefruit sized hole in the window of Emily Fox's kitchen door. Withdrawing her fist she unrolled Malcolm's shirt, shook the excess shards onto the back doorstep and handed the glassy shirt back to him. Malcolm Orange was in shock. He could not bring his hands to grab properly. The shirt slipped from his grasp and slithered down his legs, nicking a blood-red crescent into his kneecap, before it came to rest upon his left sneaker. He kicked the shirt loose. It landed in Chalet 5's shrubbery.

'WhatareyoudoingSorry?' he asked, the sentence tumbling

out of his mouth as a single, hysterically pitched word.

'What does it look like I'm doing?' Sorry fired back, already grabbing around for a door latch.

'You can't break into Emily's house.'

'Why not? You got me curious about the fat bitch. I wanted to see what sort of house a sixty-ton woman lived in. Maybe raid her deep freeze if I got a chance.'

'Don't talk about Emily like that.'

'Why not? You said you were terrified she was going to squash you. You said she was so fat she couldn't sit up properly.'

'She's a nice lady,' Malcolm argued half-heartedly. 'She's really kind.'

'It's disgusting to let yourself go like that; eating 'til you're too fat to stand up. My dad says people like her make America look bad.'

Malcolm could think of no suitable comeback. Good people, people like Jesus, Martin Luther King and Wolverine, always spoke out against injustice. Good people did not stand on the edge of a bad thing, chewing a thumbnail and wondering what to do next. Good people got involved, or at very least called the police.

'Coming, Malcolm?' she asked, hesitating with one foot inside the chalet, already committed to the act of burglary.

'No,' said Malcolm Orange with great determination and took three Judas steps towards her. Deep inside the bones and sinews of his legs, which wished to retreat yet drew, like dumb magnets, towards the back doorstep, Malcolm understood that he was not entirely a good person. Malcolm was a mess of good intentions and disappearing resolve. It was not his fault, he reasoned. One half of his whole belonged to his father and the other, maternal slice, was more inclined to weep and mumble Spanish curses than take a stand on anything important. With such a complicated genetic make-up, it was no surprise that Malcolm had begun to disappear.

'I'm only coming because someone needs to stop you,' he whispered. It was a prayer of supplication.

Malcolm took an enormous breath and followed Soren James Blue into the kitchen of Chalet 5. Mr Fluff stood guard by the recycling bin and, when both were safely inside, picked her way through the glass shards to join them. The kitchen was gloomy. On the cul-de-sac a rumor had lately circulated that ordinary beds could no longer contain Emily Fox's massive bulk and consequently the entire bedroom had been padded to cushion her, forming a room-sized sleeping compartment. This rumor was entirely untrue, as was the rumor about the cement mixer she used to blend her meals and the nurse who came to hose her down twice weekly. However, Emily Fox suspected the other residents of the cul-de-sac were spying on her, peering through the air conditioning vents and keyholes in the hope of confirming these grotesque myths.

Emily Fox had never invited her neighbors round to visit.

It was not embarrassment which kept the blinds drawn but rather the understanding that life had more than enough compulsory nuisances without inviting the neighbors' attention. Healthcare professionals visited twice weekly, as did the official representatives of the Baptist Retirement Village; regular supervision was one of the prescribed 'perks' for cul-de-sac residents. A Vancouver-based nephew faithfully delivered the weekend papers each Sunday morning, lingering on the stoop until Emily stumbled to the front door, confirming she had not yet wobbled off the mortal coil. Meals on Wheels arrived three times daily, depositing sealed trays of steaming gloop on the welcome mat and pinging the doorbell for attention. The Vietnamese hairdresser made a bimonthly pilgrimage to the cul-de-sac and, in anticipation of a good, close trim, Emily Fox raised the blinds in the back bedroom and bid eight inches of sunlight permission to enter her home.

Emily Fox had never invited her neighbors round to visit and yet she was not an unsociable lady.

She left the chalet at every given opportunity, waddling slowly to Bill and Irene's for the People's Committee, vacationing every time an out-of-state relative invited, and wedging herself into the Center's minibus for annual outings to the Rose Parade, the Zoo Lights and the casino at Lincoln City. Emily Fox enjoyed people immensely. She ate them up in conversation, replaying their quirks and foibles for company as she fell asleep in her absolutely ordinary bed. She enjoyed children, particularly best of all. Children demanded nothing of her. Emily Fox had never appreciated demanding people.

Emily Fox had not always been a larger lady. On the eve of her debutante cotillion, her mother had laced her into a teal green frock and, taking her hands, spanned the entire breadth of young Emily's waist between fingers and thumbs.

'That's what a nice young man goes for, Emily,' she'd announced to her daughter, 'a waist like an egg timer and breasts like a pair of ripe cantaloupes.'

It was with a kind of suppressed, stammering horror that the seventeen-year-old Emily stood fast in her stockinged soles whilst her mother cupped a hand beneath each breast and jiggled them for weight, like a greengrocer deliberating between a pair of honeydews.

'Those will do very nicely, darling,' she'd said. 'You're not as well-endowed as I was but the fashion is for flatter girls these days. Be sure to dance with the Anderson boy. Your father is terribly keen for a match with the Anderson boy. You'll make a wonderful wife for him if you keep the weight off. No respectable man wants a piglet for a bride.'

Slapping her daughter firmly on the backside, Mrs Fox had ushered Emily out the bedroom door, down the swooping staircase and straight into the embrace of the dessert cart. She'd spent the evening surreptitiously downing chocolate eclairs and French fancies, doing her best to avoid making an accidental match with any of the young, or not so young, Nashville gentlemen in attendance.

The next five years were war.

Emily Fox was horrified by the possibility of marrying into a lifetime of dietary restriction and further devastated to admit that the wispy blonde debutantes who primped and powdered, assisting with her corset strings in the dressing rooms of Nashville's mansion homes, had stirred something shocking and illicit within her. Emily knew well enough to say nothing of the desire to press her palms flat against the peached blush of their naked backs or the joy of watching them dress and undress, reflected in conspiratorial mirrors. She placed a silent wall around the afternoon when she'd turned purposefully into a school friend's kiss, feeling their lipstick catch and pucker like crème brûlée cracking in anticipation. She kept all these things secret inside her, gooey sweet and sinful as a fondant crème. She knew her parents would not permit such a shameful thing in Nashville.

Emily ate to keep the brute boys away from her door.

Emily ate in secret, stealing down to the pantry in the early hours of the morning to stuff her puffing face full of devil's food cake and corn bread. Emily expanded. Mrs Fox, horrified by her daughter's creeping middle, starved her at the dining table; tied her with ropes and made her run for miles, up and down the driveway, behind the family's creeping sedan; weighed her nightly on a set of butcher's scales and could not understand why the needle continued to bear due southwest. Determined to be rid of the girl before she was too heavy to shift, Mrs Fox kept a steady circuit of increasingly elderly gentleman suitors trundling through the front parlor.

'We'll have to lower our standards, darling,' she'd explained, her voice thick with end-of-season disappointment. 'An older gentleman is probably our best bet. They're less likely to be able to see you clearly.'

Emily Fox did not care for gentlemen suitors. She could not stand their summer suits, their well-oiled mustaches and cologne, their tall tales of boats and cars and business advances. She ate sandwiches and cream cakes by the handful and watched their faces curdle in disgust. By the age of twenty-five Emily Fox weighed more than the all-state quarterback. Mrs Fox gave up. She was a sensible woman, capable of admitting her own limitations. She put the butcher's scales out to retire and shifted her attentions to the next daughter down; a docile girl of sixteen, blessed with slipstream legs and eyes like a newborn donkey.

Emily Fox watched all of her sisters court and marry, their middles expanding and contracting as they squeezed nineteen little nieces and nephews into the Nashville sun. She grew in girth annually, bursting like a split sausage from a series of pastel-colored bridesmaids dresses until the sister before last pronounced Emily a family embarrassment and she was no longer subjected to such pageantry. She passed her adult life in the guest bedroom at her parents' house, ghost-writing romance novels for a publishing company which specialized in Civil War-era love stories.

She ventured out for church on Sundays and twice weekly for her Bridge class. She took three vacations a year, accompanying various elderly relatives to various seaside resorts designed for the safe accommodation of older ladies and gentlemen. This lifestyle provided quite enough people for Emily Fox. She remained terrified that some man would see through the glutinous layers of flab now stuck to her face and arms, and find there a beauty still deserving of pursuit.

Never once, in sixty years, did it occur to Emily Fox that she could simply say no to such advances. She was a Nashville girl, raised on the notion that any gentleman who asked politely deserved her acquiescence. Even now, seventy-eight and suffering from protruding veins and cholesterol and diabetic episodes, Emily Fox kept herself well insulated against the advances of the outside world. She would have liked a child, possibly two, but such things were not possible without a man.

Malcolm Orange, as he advanced towards the sitting room of Chalet 5, knew nothing of Emily Fox's upbringing. His memories of Miss Fox were entirely sensory: the talcum and rose scent of her carefully folded hair, the press of her arms, like overblown water wings constraining his lungs each time they came in for a hug, the oil and chocolate sound of her laughter, Tennessee South leaking through the gaps in her words.

Malcolm Orange prided himself on observing people but he wasn't the best with places or spaces. Meanwhile his mother could recall, with searing exactitude, the cut and clash of every room she'd ever entered. Beginning with the hospital room in which she'd spent her first huffering moments, and concluding with the five squat rooms of Chalet 13, Martha Orange could remember hundreds and thousands of individually specific rooms. This number was notwithstanding waiting rooms, offices, stationery closets and hotel rooms, which were religiously uniform in their placement of beds, trouser presses and replica Van Gogh prints. Her parents' bedroom provided a backdrop for dreaming. The kindergarten classroom in which she'd first learnt to curl her 8s, rose in her nostrils, gingerbread warm. Her grandmother's good room with its wood-stacked hearth laughed long and rollicking loud inside her ribcage.

Malcolm Orange was not his mother. He was barely aware of his own bedroom closet and yet Emily Fox's sitting room sang to him; a long, sad song, morose as a church hymn. The carpet was lonely for friendly feet. The sofa cried out for a brace of well-padded elderly backsides. The curtains could barely contain their own unhappiness. The room was sad. Malcolm Orange felt reluctant to bring it any further sorrow.

'Let's go, Sorry,' he said, 'I don't feel so good.'

'Of course you don't,' she fired back sarcastically, 'you're disappearing. I'll bet you feel like shit.'

'We need to go now, before the police get here.'

For the first time since the disappearing started, Malcolm Orange felt actual, hurting pain. The holes in his back and belly began to throb as if contracting and dilating. He let his gaze drop and noted, to his horror, the gaps finally gaining the advantage. From such a height Malcolm Orange appeared less boy and more space. He placed one hand behind his back, one on his belly and pressed firmly, trying to hold himself together. The gaps in his torso were enormous now, merging with other gaps to form caverns and tunnels. Light gushed from his middle in bold, blond beams.

There was little left to lose and yet the thought of robbing Emily Fox felt like an enormous soup spoon scooping out his insides.

'Sorry,' he shouted, panicking, 'I'm going NOW!'

'Hold your horses Malcolm, I'm looking for something that might help.'

Abandoning the television cabinet which was now splayed wide open, video cassettes, magazines and remote controls scattered across the rug, Sorry leapt to her feet and made a mad dash for the bathroom cupboard. From his position, frozen in the doorway between sitting room and kitchen, Malcolm could hear her pop the medicine cabinet's glass-fronted door and begin rifling through Emily Fox's toiletries. A half minute later her head appeared suddenly, peeking round the door frame.

'Try these,' she said. 'My mom used to take them all the time when she was on a downer. Two of these and you won't even remember you're disappearing.'

A plastic tube of pills came sailing towards Malcolm's head. He missed the catch. He almost always missed the catch. Malcolm, his father repeatedly told him, had hands like a pair of peeled bananas. Conversely, Jimmy Orange had been blessed with a pair of perfect pitch and catch mitts. In the almost twelve years of their mutual existence, Malcolm Orange had seen his father single-handedly dominate speeding frisbees, footballs and misguided hockey pucks. Full-grown families, Malcolm had lately come to conclude, were obviously much harder to hold on to.

Malcolm Orange dropped to his knees and groped around in the gray light. The pill container had spilled its shiny guts across the living room carpet. He scooped handfuls of the little blue capsules back into the tube, and sealed the lid.

'Knock them back, kid,' said Sorry, appearing behind his shoulder. 'You won't be so boring once you've got a couple of those bad boys in you.'

'No way,' said Malcolm bluntly, pushing the happy pills into

Sorry's hand. 'I don't do drugs. I'm probably not even doing cigarettes seriously until I'm about thirty.'

'I'll hold you to that, son,' cried the booming voice of Cunningham Holt; an odd phenomenon, for the old man was nowhere to be seen.

Malcolm Orange fumbled to the wall and flicked the lights on. The room was suddenly unfiltered; muted, crimson carpet blooming a furious pink, wallpaper flowering in shameless, shocking mauves and limes. Malcolm made a quick scan of all the places capable of concealing an adult person. There was no sign of Cunningham Holt anywhere.

'Turn the lights out before someone sees them, Malcolm!' shouted Sorry, depositing an armful of toiletries and medication on the living room sofa.

'I'm looking for Cunningham Holt.'

'Is your brain disappearing now too? It's not like he's going to be hiding under the sofa. The old fart's at the front door.'

Malcolm Orange felt a wave of lukewarm relief, liberating as the first breath after a coughing fit. It was a joy of sorts to be caught red-handed, to be intercepted before things could get any worse, to defer consequences to a responsible adult.

'Cunningham,' he said, 'I'm so sorry. I didn't mean for any of this to happen.'

'I know you didn't, Malcolm. We all know you're a bit out of sorts these days.'

'I'm all muddled up in my middle, Cunningham.'

'And the girl's making you even more muddled I imagine.'

Malcolm Orange blushed fuchsia pink with embarrassment. Sorry had not heard. She was preoccupied with stuffing Emily Fox's medication into a grocery sack for later consumption.

'I wish things would just be normal again,' whispered

Malcolm and came to a halt at Chalet 5's front door.

'Me too,' answered Cunningham Holt, shouting, as he had been, through the letterbox. 'But I don't remember what normal looks like anymore.'

Malcolm Orange opened the front door of Chalet 5 and threw his arms around Cunningham Holt's diminishing middle. To his great embarrassment he began to cry, salted tears soaking into the old man's corduroy thighs. Sensitive to the sobbing oscillations of the boy's grief, the old man placed a reassuring hand on Malcolm's head and muttered a selection of comforting sentiments. 'There, there, son.' 'Things will look better in the morning.' 'It's not the end of the world.' None of these platitudes rang true for either party but the pronouncement of such sentiment seemed part of the ritual, like English breakfast tea in the face of a natural disaster.

Whilst the two men embraced on the front step, the younger raised on tippy toes for leverage, the elder bent double like a garlic press, their minds wandered round and round the cul-de-sac's turn circle, searching for a good spot to unravel. Malcolm, as he hugged, kept one eye on his own clasped wrists, examining through the empty holes the Fair Isle yarn of the older man's sweater. Concerned as he was with Malcolm's spiraling breakdown, Cunningham Holt's immediate thoughts were preoccupied by the sensation of damp warmth emanating from the area of his groin and spreading across the uppermost section of his left thigh. Lately the old man had noticed the need to empty his bladder no longer came upon him gradually like the progressive twitch of a headache, but rather rushed him, siren-like, allowing little or no time to locate a bathroom.

He removed Malcolm, unclasping his hands like a belt buckle and held him at arm's length.

'Sorry, son,' he said, head bent in shame. 'I think I've pissed myself. I don't want to get it on you.'

Malcolm Orange risked a small laugh. It stuck in his throat like a mouthful of soda. 'It wasn't you, Cunningham. It was me.'

'You pissed yourself?'

'No, no, I cried on your leg. Sorry.'

Cunningham Holt laughed. Malcolm Orange laughed. For a moment they forgot themselves and all their latest disappearings. Soren James Blue brought them back to earth with a grounding thump.

'How'd you know we'd be here?' she asked, appearing over Malcolm's shoulder to stab an accusatory finger into Cunningham Holt's shoulder. 'It's really friggin' creepy to have a blind dude stalking us.'

Malcolm Orange stepped back to deliver his customary chiding slap and in doing so left Cunningham Holt open to attack. Sorry instantly noticed the wet patch on his pants, spreading now towards the knee and, rolling her eyes to the streetlamps, inserted two fingers into her mouth and made the sign for vomit-inducing disgust.

'He didn't piss himself,' yelled Malcolm, leaping to his friend's defense. 'I just cried and it got on his pants.'

'And I'm not a big one for stalking,' added Cunningham. 'I've listened through the letter boxes of six other chalets before I found you.'

'Bloody hell, you two are a pair of prime weirdos,' concluded Sorry.

'I'm just worried about Malcolm. It's not like him to make such a scene. I wanted to see if there was anything I could do to help. I could maybe call an ambulance or something, see if they can do anything about the disappearing. I've got insurance if he needs it.'

'Sounds like a plan, gramps. I'm guessing the ER people don't see that many disappearing children. Malcolm'll be a bit of a novelty for them.'

'Or,' continued Cunningham Holt, ignoring Sorry, 'I had another idea. Something I heard back in the big smoke. It's a long shot, of course, but anything's worth a try. We'd have to get Malcolm really drunk and—'

'Now you're talking!' exclaimed Sorry and with little regard for his crumbling joints, dragged Cunningham Holt sharply by the elbow deep into the darkened belly of Chalet 5. Malcolm Orange, who remained adamantly and personally opposed to teenage drinking for any reason, even the purely medicinal, followed reluctantly, closing the door behind them. He took a cautious seat on the carpet at Cunningham Holt's feet. Mr Fluff curled around his naked heels like a bad-tempered foot-warmer. Soren James Blue positioned herself on the sofa beside the older man and demanded to be told everything, especially the bit about getting really drunk. As the details emerged, Sorry quickly lost her skepticism, switching stance from an adamant denial of Malcolm's condition to an unshakeable belief that all three should, with extreme urgency, partake in Cunningham Holt's cure, lest Malcolm disappear entirely. As the old man's story unfurled, Malcolm Orange, realizing that the proposed cure was simply an adaptation of his own Scientific Investigative Research, became more and more willing to give it a go.

'It's like this,' began Cunningham Holt, positioning a sofa cushion on his dampened lap, lest he piss himself for real in excitement. 'I used to know this fella back in New York. He went by the name of Haircut Molloy, though I think his real name was Harold, or possibly Henry, something starting with a letter H anyway.'

'Get on with it, gramps,' urged Sorry, once more prodding him deliberately in the shoulder.

'Anyway, Haircut Molloy was a bit of a legend on our block. He lived in the apartment directly above mine, used to come down every Friday evening for the weekend tips. Brought a six pack with him most every time. He was a good sort, old Haircut. We became real tight pals. So after a few months of passing on the tips and drinking his Bud I got up the guts to ask after his name. "Where'd you get a name like Haircut from? Was your pappy a barber or something?" I asked. "No sir," he says to me. "My pappy was a lot of things to a lot of folk but never a hair man. I'm the only Haircut in the family." "Oh," I said, suddenly catching on. "Is it on account of some crazy hairdo you have? Or maybe a joke, like you're bald as a coot? Something that a blind fella might miss." Haircut Molloy grabbed my hand and pulled it to his head, forcing my fingers from the tip of his crown all the way down his back to his waist. "Did you ever feel anything like that before Mr Holt?" he asked. "Four foot of jet black hair and I've not even got an ounce of Indian blood in me." It was a rare thing to feel, Malcolm. The man had hair like a rope, thicker and longer and, by my imagining, shinier than a high school girl's.

'"So that's why they call you Haircut, on account of your long locks," I said. Haircut Molloy laughs back at me and I can hear the swoosh of him flicking his hair behind his ears. "Oh, it's a lot more complicated than that, Mr Holt," he says. "It starts way back in the good old days before the Depression. My pappy ran a sideshow outfit down in Atlantic City: bearded ladies, Siamese twins, girls that lived in tanks of water, all the usual stuff. He was a great man for the magic too. Pappy's own act was the talk of the town. It wasn't trickery or hand sleight stuff. It was actual proper, honest-to-God magic. He'd done all this reading up on psychology and how the head works and got to believing that the mind was a heck of a lot more powerful than the body ever would be. By the time I was toddling about the sideshow in short pants my pappy had trained himself to walk on fire and lie on nails and stick a fencing sword right through his belly and out the other side. It wasn't rocket science. It was all mind over matter stuff. He trained hard to get his head to work a certain way and then made a fortune fleecing the folks that came to see him.

"When I was about five years old pappy upped his game. Another fella in town had cashed in on our success and was eating light bulbs and hanging off the pier by his ponytail. Pappy needed a new gimmick. He knew it would work in theory but the first night he actually done it in public my mama clean passed out with the nerves. In front of a crowd of two hundred vacationing folks and locals pappy took a butcher's knife and chopped off his wedding finger. Holding it up to the audience, still dripping blood he shouts, 'mind over matter folks! Tonight I'll take a long hard look at my good hand before I fall asleep and I'll dream me up a brand-new finger. Come back tomorrow evening and see for yourself, Old Magic Molloy's nobody's liar.' Well it took a stiff drink or six to get my pappy to sleep that night on account of the throbbing where his finger had been and mama fairly gave him the sharp end of her tongue, but when I woke up the next morning he had two full sets of completely functioning fingers and my mama had the old finger on ice to prove it was no gimmick.

"We made a fortune that summer. Pappy chopped each of his fingers off in turn, downed a bottle of Jack and dreamt them back into being by six o'clock the next morning. By the time school started that fall we had enough money for the down payment on a Model T and pappy couldn't get past breakfast without a pint of whiskey. On the first October, three weeks before my sixth birthday, pappy was three sheets to the wind with the butcher's knife, missed his baby finger and went right through the artery on his right hand. Though my mama held their wedding photo in front of his nose as he drifted out of consciousness, and kept on yelling, 'Look Davy, look you old bastard, dream yourself back to normal,' he never woke up. Mama got me through junior school eking out the last of my pappy's savings and loaning the bearded lady out to the five and dime set-ups down by the casino. It wasn't glamorous living but we got by. When I turned thirteen she gave me a butcher's knife and I knew it was my turn to start pulling my weight. I couldn't bring myself to do a finger but I found folks were just as taken with the hair. I'd chop it up to my ears each evening, go to bed with a bottle of Bushmills and a picture of Rapunzel cut out of a library book, and each morning I'd be swimming in my own hair. It wasn't long before I got the name Haircut."

"'Good Lord,' I said. It was a fantastic story but I didn't believe a word of it. "Fantastic story, Haircut," I said. "But I don't believe a damn word of it. You've to be wild skeptical about miracles when you can't see for yourself." "I understand, Mr Holt," says he, "I am in retirement now, but for you, seeing as you've been so generous with your tips, I'll get the butcher's knife out one more time." Off he runs upstairs and comes back five minutes later with four foot of hair in one hand and a dome like a plucked turkey. I had a good old rub of his head just to be sure he wasn't duping me. "I'll come back tomorrow morning and let you feel for yourself," he says and sure enough the next morning he's back on my sofa with a thing like a lion's mane pouring over his forehead. "What do you think of that, Mr Holt?" he asked. "The Lord giveth and the Lord taketh away," said I, quick as you like. "And don't it look like the Lord gone and giveth it all back again while you were sleeping." "More's the pity it wouldn't work for you, Mr

Holt." "Why's that, Haircut?" "Well you've not the eyes to be looking at any pictures before you go to sleep. It only works if you dream about getting fixed and the only sure fire way to set your dreams is to look at a picture before you go to sleep."

'Seems old Haircut Molloy was right, Malcolm. Mind over matter doesn't work so good if you can't picture what you're after. But for you, son,' concluded Cunningham Holt, 'it might be just the ticket, you know, for fixing the disappearing bits.'

It was a long speech for a reasonably silent man and the delivery had sucked the pith right out of him. He settled back on the living room sofa and sandwiched the cushion against his rib cage, clutching it like a last-ditch life preserver.

'What do you think, Malcolm?' he asked hesitantly.

'Let's get wasted!' whooped Soren James Blue. Cunningham Holt ignored her enthusiasm.

'What do *you* think, Malcolm?' he repeated.

Though the afternoon's events had turned Malcolm Orange skeptic as a lapsed Presbyterian, he truly, honestly wished to believe everything that Cunningham Holt had said.

'What the hell,' he replied. 'I'd already started thinking about dreaming myself better. Maybe the whiskey will make it happen quicker.'

'And the pair of us will get drunk for moral support,' added Sorry, who was all of a sudden overenthusiastically anxious to ally herself with Malcolm's cause. 'Nobody likes to get drunk by themselves. You just feel tragic.' This last sentiment, Malcolm suspected, was spoken from recent experience.

'Well, Malcolm, if you're up for it, there's no time like the present. I'll just go and get the beer,' suggested Cunningham. 'I'm afraid the funds don't stretch to whiskey these days but I have a shitload of Corona Light I got cheap with coupons. It'll do the same job if we drink enough of it.'

'Right,' said Sorry, standing to take control of the situation. 'You get the beer, and cigarettes if you could stretch to it, I can't drink on an empty stomach. I'll round up a few pillows from the fat woman's bedroom – make it look like a proper burglary if I can – Malcolm, you run back to yours for a picture of yourself without holes, preferably naked if you have one, and we'll meet back in the middle in five.'

Thus it came to be that Martha Orange, returning from her afternoon shift at the Center, stumbled across her eldest son, piss drunk and snoring over a paisley scatter cushion in the middle of the cul-de-sac's turn circle. To his left sat Soren James Blue, cross-legged and coercing the last dregs from a Marlboro Light, slightly tipsy but nonetheless awake, for, even at fourteen, her tolerance for alcohol was ungodly. To his right Cunningham Holt slept thickly with Mr Fluff curled like a bicycle clip about his ankle. A dark wet patch was drifting from his groin, due south in the direction of his knee, gaining ground with every second. Martha Orange placed her hands on her hips and observed the situation from a distance of fifteen feet. The inclination to bolt was strong but Sorry had already spotted her. Holding Mrs Orange's gaze with what the older lady wrongly assumed to be an alcohol-induced bravado, the girl rose unsteadily to her feet.

'Poof,' she said, flinging her arms to the sky with the exaggerated swoop of a magician's assistant. 'I've made him disappear.'

And Martha Orange, noting the absence of her younger son, quite naturally assumed she meant Ross. The relief was palpable.

– Chapter Ten –

Junior Button

Martha Orange no longer believed in anything higher than the Portland City Grill. However, the moment found her, backside wedged against the Rite Aid bus shelter, formulating a prayer of absolution.

'Forgive me my trespasses,' she began. The trespasses lay heavy on her tongue, a set of second-hand shackles she could no longer claim nor carry.

She switched tactics. 'Forgive *him his* trespasses,' and, having let the sentiment settle in silence, clarified, 'I mean Jimmy of course, not Malcolm, though I could scalp the boy for his stupidity.'

With consideration she withdrew the request. 'That bastard doesn't deserve forgiveness,' she muttered and, as the number 39 appeared on the horizon, front grill grinning like an orthodontist's nightmare, offered up a mouthful of frantic little prayerlets.

'It's not my fault.'

'They'll be better off without me.'

'It's him you should be hounding, not me.'

The three steps ascending to the driver's feet formed a kind of altar. Martha Orange climbed wearily. She shoved her monthly pass under the driver's chin and, looking into his sun-blushed face, begged, if not for forgiveness, then the smallest condescending flicker of grace.

'Expired yesterday,' he barked. 'Dollar fifteen or get off my bus.'

Martha Orange set her bags carefully on the floor; a pair of grocery sacks containing the vague necessities required for a weekend away. The doors swooshed closed and as the bus, without so much as a whispered warning, began its rickety stagger through the rush hour traffic, both bags toppled, belching pantyhose and make-up remover, tampons, shower gel and a single mandarin orange across the dirty laminate floor. Martha Orange buckled. Even the details were conspiring against her now. On hands and knees, stuffing underwear and toiletries into a Fred Meyer grocery sack, she felt for a moment the deep mortification of a repentant soul. Rising, she thrust a handful of shrapnel – far too many coins for a single fare – into the driver's lap and without pausing to retrieve her ticket, took the only free seat in the front section of the bus.

'Cheer up,' said the man sitting to her left, 'it might never happen.' She did not punch him. Retaliation required energy and Martha Orange was spent. Wedged as he was against her thigh, she observed the man in profile, noting the faintest shadow of beard, the nauseating stench of patchouli oil and a Jesus fish bracelet belted around his hairy wrist. He was exactly the kind of man she found easiest to despise.

'It's not my fault,' she snapped defensively and the man, well used to the meth addicts and un-housed crazies who rode the Trimet, managed to maneuver his arm into a cold shoulder. Martha Orange had long since quit worrying about the opinions of others. Whilst the number 39's passengers passed silent judgment and the man to her left raged like an icehouse wall, Martha

Orange quietly got on with the process of unraveling. Pinching her worldly possessions between her ankles, she fished a Kleenex from the sleeve of her work shirt and began to sob vociferously. Neither grief nor guilt could be blamed for the deluge. Martha Orange wept a waterfall of sheer, undiluted relief.

Malcolm was drunk on a turn circle. Ross was asleep in his sports bag under Bill and Irene's coffee table, a formula-filled bottle tucked into the waistband of his diaper. And Jimmy, well God only knew which far-flung drinking parlor Jimmy Orange was currently calling home. Standing on the edge of the Baptist Retirement Village, Martha Orange had seen her exit sign flash like a last-chance Texaco and, with little consideration for the binding ties, had taken the opportunity to bolt. She was neither surprised nor particularly bothered by the ease with which she'd unstitched herself. Martha Orange had been anticipating this moment for a terribly long time. The act of holding still – three months resident and bound to a four-walled house with closing doors and children – had almost killed her. Cul-de-sac living had been a crucifixion of sorts and she was immensely proud of her own perseverance.

Martha Orange was not built for permanence. She had been itchy since the point of conception. For thirty-seven years she'd carried her feet like a pair of nervous pigeons, compliant for the most part, permanently coiled in anticipation of flight. Lately this itch had intensified. She'd dreamt of trains and boats and state borders as slight and steppable as a sidewalk cracks. With Jimmy's departure the need to bolt had grown volcanic. Though she'd resented the Volvo – and the pay by the week motels with their itchy blankets and wall-mounted televisions had come to feel like an iron lung – the static world had forced Martha Orange to admit she felt closest to possible in the open spaces between departure and arrival. The fleeting road offered a clarity she could not approximate in stillness.

Lately life had begun to unravel. She'd felt the nauseating thrill of a floating thing – a Zeppelin or submarine – suddenly untethered. The children were not the anchors they'd once been. Television had become preferable to conversation. Words failed her. Occasionally she forgot the English word for certain things, mostly emotions, and was not yet fluent enough to substitute the Spanish. Everything, even expensive restaurant dinners, had begun to taste exactly like ramen noodles. Sex, when she very occasionally remembered its existence, seemed like a ludicrous thing for one person to do to another. Every day the weighted drag of good sense seemed a little lighter, a little less inclined to succeed.

For the sake of saving face and Malcolm, Martha Orange had battled through her first six Portland weeks, resisting the temptation to take off. The need to fly never once quit pinching. She drowned it daily, prescribing black coffee and Mexican soap operas for all her flightiest thoughts. On the seventh week things took a turn for the bolt, blue sky. Oklahoma finally caught up with Martha Orange and though she'd dreaded this moment for almost fifteen years, the reunion was just the justification she'd been hoping for.

On the Sunday morning of Martha Orange's seventh week at the Baptist Retirement Village, an elderly black man had been admitted to the Center. His name was Junior Button; a middling sort of name for a man built like the un-sunk Titanic. The Center's standard issue beds could not contain him and, as all the outsize beds were already occupied by morbidly obese patients,

Junior Button had been folded into an ordinary bed, knees drawn into the recovery position like a baby giant busting to get born. His medical notes were limited. Two Post-it notes and a single file page informed the Center staff that Junior had arrived on their doorstep via the Good Shepherd Mission and previously the Burnside Bridge; that he either could not, or would not, recall a permanent address; appeared to be allergic to mushrooms and penicillin; and suffered from both diabetes and various diabetes-related complications, no doubt exacerbated by his penchant for Irish stout.

Should the Center's medical staff have taken the time to examine the reverse of the second Post-it note, they might have noted a brief, handwritten memo: 'Don't believe a word he says,' magic-markered in the spidery hand of the ambulance driver responsible for his delivery. However, the Center's medical staff barely took the time to note their patients' names. Later that afternoon as she folded and stacked Junior Button's clean pajamas, Martha Orange discovered the Post-it note. Unable to find the correct cell in which to input speculation on a patient's trustworthiness, she compromised with a question mark doodled beside his name. Thereafter Junior Button – a fibber of transatlantic renown – found himself all of a sudden believable as the Bible, yet constantly interrogated about his name.

(Though inconsequential to the life and times of Martha Orange, it should be noted that Junior Button, fifth generation freeman and purveyor of top-quality dental products, had inherited this surname from his great-great-granddaddy.

Elias Button had been a peculiarly silent man, gangly tall and bent like an old-fashioned lamppost. He'd spent forty-eight of his most formative years picking cotton for a Kentucky-based landowner with naught but a Christian name to differentiate him from all the other poor souls tending field. On the Christmas Day previous to Elias's fifty-fourth birthday the Kentucky-based landowner, motivated in part by his youngest daughter's dangerous obsession with the New Testament and partially by the new thinking swooping in from the east coast, suffered an uncharacteristic fit of benevolence and offered all his slaves three days' holiday, a copy of the Holy Bible (incomprehensible to all but the household servants), and the opportunity to choose for themselves a family name with which to mark their births and deaths.

Whilst the other fieldworkers picked names as exotic and unachievable as continental holiday resorts – Honest and Capable, Steadfast and Temperance – Elias chose Button. Decades passed, and many years after Elias had worked his way to freedom and then – five short months later – the family plot in the paupers' graveyard, his second son, a grandfather now himself, asked the question, 'Why Button?' And his mother, already fading the goose-grey color of death, had smiled and answered as best she remembered, 'When your daddy was a small little thing in the fields, the preacher come and read from the Word of the Lord on the Sabbath day and he always beginned his readings with the book of Genesis, "But on the Sabbath day thou shalt rest."

'Well your daddy had no more sense than a wild buck rabbit, he never done no schooling, never learned to figure or read the Word for hisself and when the preacher man readed about the Sabbath all he heard was, "Button, the Sabbath day thou shalt rest," and he figured that this here fella Button was on to a good sure thing, having the Lord hisself urging for him to put his feet up. Your daddy worked forty-odd years for Mr Williams, sweated salt and blood six days a week in them fields, but he never did forget about that fella, Button. One particular Christmas Day Mr

Williams gathered all us pickers up in the back barn and says, bold as parlor brass, "Choose you this day what you and your folks will be known as." Your daddy turns to me, quick as Christ and says, "Button. We'll be the Buttons from this day on, and if the Lord Almighty is tellin' me to put my feet up, ain't no white man in Kentucky gonna make me work." Buttons we were, from that day on.'

By the time he'd turned twelve Junior Button could retell this particular family legend with the pinching exactitude of a Benedictine monk reciting the Pater Noster. He was the fifth in an awkward line of Elias Buttons, going by Junior for his own grandfather had claimed Senior Button, and his father was simply Elias, born fourth and fortunate enough to be free from the need for alias. Though both men were dead before he hit his teenage years and he'd produced no further baby Buttons, Junior was far too uncomfortable with the responsibilities of maturity to risk a name upgrade. Junior Button bobbled through seventy-eight years of small-town living ill-disposed to grow up, a giant man with a name like a tip-toed pixie.)

By Wednesday of his first week in the Center, the last of the Guinness had dribbled its way out of Junior Button's system and his insulin levels were finally balancing out. The old man, sobering up for the first time in almost six months, became slowly aware of his surroundings. First the pastel-blue curtains came under his scrutiny, then the carpet, the 'damn coffin of a bed' and the 'God-awful vomit you folks call art', gilt-framed and globby on three out of four bedroom walls. On Wednesday evening, bored with the aesthetics, he turned his attention to the young woman who'd been bringing his meals three to five times a day.

'You been sucking lemons, girl?' he asked as Martha Orange positioned a plate of lukewarm cannelloni on his lap tray.

Martha Orange ignored him. She noted his dinner choice on the information chart, faked his vitals in blue ink and hung the clipboard from the foot of the bed.

'Look at me when I'm speaking to you, girl,' he continued. 'You look miserable as sin.'

She paused by the end of the bed and offered Junior Button a watery smile. It was easier, Martha Orange had found, just to smile, to laugh or permit the residents to call her all the spiteful names of the day.

'Sorry,' she said, 'long day. I'm just a little tired.' She turned to go, grabbing as she left an armful of used towels, hoping this might save her the after dinner laundry run. At the sound of her voice, diluted though it was by fifteen years of hard travel, Junior Button sat bolt upright in his bed. 'Hold your horses,' he said. The cannelloni made a break for it, slipping first from the tray, then the plate, and finally his lap, so it landed in a glutinous, bloody lump on the carpet. Martha Orange dropped to her knees by his bed and utilizing the damp laundry began to scoop the worst of the pasta off the floor.

'You're an Oklahoma girl?' he asked, making no effort to assist her.

'Uh-huh,' replied Martha Orange, still scooping cannelloni into a wash cloth. 'Haven't been home for years, though.'

'What part?'

'You wouldn't know it. Tiny little town in Grant County.'

'Try me, sweetheart. I'm an Oklahoma guy, born and raised. I know that state like the back of my own hand.'

'My daddy had a homestead three miles out of Jefferson. Like I said though, I haven't been home for almost fifteen years.'

Junior Button swung his legs sideways so they escaped from the crumpled bed sheets. His naked feet dangled like a pair of polished prunes, toes just brushing the carpet. Upright now, he bent slowly forward and using a single finger tilted Martha Orange's chin towards his face. It was an oddly intimate gesture. For a moment she thought he might try to kiss her. It was weeks since she'd last been touched with such obvious intent. She dropped the soiled washing, leaving a secondary tomato stain on the carpet, and drew back.

'Sweet Jesus, you're Marcy Underdown's kid, aren't you?'

Martha Orange felt the room fold in upon her; lampshade, curtains and flower-print wallpaper, pounding like piston fists on the dome of her head.

'Course not, you can't be more than thirty-five.'

'Thirty-seven,' she found herself correcting.

'You're much too young to be Martha's kid. You're some sort of kin though. You're the cut of her.'

'She was my grandmother,' Martha Orange mumbled. 'I'm Marion's kid. How did you know? I don't think I look that much like her.'

The old man smiled and placed his hands, open-palmed, upon his pajama-clad thighs. He seemed terribly satisfied with himself.

'I can see you've the flight in you too,' he said. 'Am I right, girl?'

And though she could not have explained exactly what Junior Button meant by the flight and that Post-It note warning had risen like a shipping flare, flaming at the back of her mind, and she wanted more than anything to get the laundry done and be home in time for the Mexican soaps, Martha Orange found herself nodding greedy assent.

'I can see that,' he said. 'I seen it in your mama too though she did her best to swallow it.'

Martha Orange dropped her laundry at the foot of the bed.

She slipped her feet clean of the dirty white Keds she kept for work and perched on the edge of Junior Button's bed. Their feet, resting side by side on the stained carpet, formed a set of empty quotation marks. Neither party turned to face the other. Without speaking Martha Orange reached into her overall pocket for a stick of the nicotine gum she'd been chewing for the last six weeks. Rarely a smoker, the untimely departure of Jimmy Orange had left her hankering after an addiction. Gum was far less expensive than cigarettes. She levered a stick free with her thumb, ripped it in half and silently passed the larger section to Junior Button. The old man, a hoarder by birth and habit, slipped the gum into his pajama pocket and nibbled on a hanging fingernail. Martha Orange chewed her gum into a rubbery paste before breaking the silence.

'Did you know my mama well?' she asked. There were other questions, larger and less likely to attract answers, which she wished to ask and yet instinctively knew not to. These questions were not yet ready to be coerced into words. They dwelt in the pit of her lungs; insecurities as slight and dewy as the odd urges which never let her be. If pushed she might have asked, 'why can't I hold still?' or 'what's the matter with me?' and perhaps the older man could have fashioned a kind of answer and yet she knew, with ungrounded certainty, that no such answer would fully satisfy. This was not a conversation for words.

'Do you remember my mama?' she asked, approaching the question in reverse.

Junior Button raised a single hand, putty pink and creased as an elephant ear.

'Enough for today,' he said, 'I gotta sleep,' and without further explanation or warning, fell fastly asleep bolt upright on the edge of his bed. Martha Orange was disappointed. People died in the

Center every day, unexpectedly. The inclination to shake Junior Button out of his sleep and interrogate the answers out of him was overwhelming. However, six weeks of senior care had taught Martha Orange that the very elderly, like other flighty creatures – cats and sheep for example – could not be forced, only coaxed and occasionally bribed. She tried to swing his legs sideways but could not maneuver him into the tiny bed. The weight of him was too much for her. She was a slight woman, her muscles wasted from a full decade of Volvo living, and could barely open a screw-top jar unassisted. Arms aching with the effort, she tucked the comforter around Junior Button's knees and left him dozing on the bed's edge. It was Center policy to raise the residents' bed rails at night but Martha Orange had neither the strength nor the inclination to bother.

Returning the next morning with the breakfast tray, Martha Orange was shocked to discover Junior Button, backside thrust to the ceiling, face crumpled into the carpet. She presumed him dead on discovery but quickly noted his buttocks rising and lowering with each shallow breath. Her first thought was self-preservation, her second the reassuring suspicion that the night shift had not been carrying out their hourly obs. She tugged on the emergency cord and when the doctor on call arrived, huffing down the corridor with a cardiac arrest trolley, quickly exonerated herself.

'He was fine when I left him last night, all tucked up in bed. He must have tried to climb out by himself.'

Junior Button was too dazed to elaborate further. It required three grown men to hoist him back onto the bed. Though no permanent damage had been done he was in no mean mood for reminiscing. From Thursday to Sunday he refused to utter a single word. He ate and slept, groped his way to the downstairs bathroom and endured, with tight-lipped stoicism, the daily humiliations of senior care. Martha Orange kept up a constant barrage of chatter; a running commentary which left her thoroughly shriveled by the end of each shift. She made little progress. Each time she attempted to steer the subject homewards, the old man would stroke his bruised face tenderly and groan as if she was somehow to blame for all life's latest misfortunes.

Junior Button was a determined old goat. For four days he perched on the edge of his bed and stared intently at the tomato-colored stain blooming beneath his toes like the bloody reminder of a car crash. His mouth set in thundering rage, yet he said nothing. Such behavior would have worn down a weaker woman but Martha Orange was cut from grit and iron. At first she suspected some kind of stroke. She clipped her consonants, elongated her vowels and delivered every sentence with the sort of patronizing volume usually reserved for the deaf or internationally foreign. By the third morning she recognized in Junior Button the smug resolve of the pig-thick stubborn. She formulated a fresh plan of attack. Though far from mean, Martha Orange was not adverse to a little torture, correctly administered for the good of the whole.

On Friday she withheld Junior Button's meals, scooping them, right in front of his wide-eyed face, into a black garbage sack. On Saturday she hid his comforter and flicked the air conditioning into overdrive. Visibly shivering, he refused to complain yet fell asleep wrapped in a pair of slightly damp bath towels. On Sunday, though she had no intention of following through, she dangled his insulin shot from the open window and held it there, drooping slightly, until the battle was finally won.

'OK,' he huffed, 'I give up.' Lowering the waistband of his pajama pants he winced slightly as the needle went in. Martha

Orange tossed the syringe into the sharps bin, washed her hands with antiseptic soap and perched beside him on the bed's edge.

'Nicotine gum?' she asked, splitting a stick in half.

'Sure,' he replied, pocketing his share.

'Do you know why I can't hold still?'

He nodded slowly and the action seemed to exhaust him. His head and shoulders slid sideways, toppling like a drunken skittle to meet the pillow. His legs continued to dangle awkwardly over the bed's edge. He looked painfully twisted in the middle. She felt bad about the food and the comforter, worse still about the insulin.

'Sorry about your face,' she began. 'I should have tucked you in properly. I really am sorry. You won't tell the Director, will you?'

Junior Button did not seem to hear. His eyes were already closed.

'I'm tired,' he said. 'It's too big a story for one telling. Come back tomorrow when I'm not so done in and I'll start in the old days.'

Junior Button was a meticulous storyteller. Five sittings in, the mystery was only beginning to take shape. The old man's capacity for distraction was awe-inspiring. Whilst Martha Orange did her best to hold him to the highway, he favored the by-ways and cul-de-sacs, molding myths around minor characters, formulating legends from the footnotes, dwelling for hours on loosely related anecdotes. Averse to out-and-out lies, he took great pains to embellish. It was difficult at times to tell truth from over-leaping imagination.

Martha Orange grew thick on the stories.

Rushing through her other duties, she spent lunch breaks, evenings and every free moment chewing nicotine gum at the end of Junior Button's bed. She neglected the children, emotionally and then nutritionally. (By the week's end breakfast cereal formed the bulk of the Oranges' meals, and Malcolm had all but wiped the troubling memory of vegetables from his mind.) She let the laundry pile up in enormous flannel mountains. She wore a hat to work, concealing her hair as it cruised towards its second unwashed week.

As she listened some things slid, others settled. The religion of Church and Bible remained infinitely problematic. Eternity was an implausible concept and, if true, less reward than never-ending punishment. God, she assumed, had long since run out of patience with the folks who kept trying to get away. The Heaven of Martha Orange's imagining floated unanchored somewhere just above the cloud line, liable to bolt at the slightest provocation. However, Junior Button's long-labored stories offered her a brand-new religion, a realm of possibility beyond the unyielding stasis of her own experience. Martha Orange had never felt more inclined to believe.

Whilst the old man talked she scribbled notes at the back of the Gideon's Bible which had languished in his bedside locker, untouched by the room's last five residents: names and dates and bullet-point anecdotes. She laid her questions like fishing nets, carefully cutting him off in full stream, clarifying the details, untangling facts from the fauna, tracing a breadcrumb trail through his meandering rambles. Nights were different now. Though Martha Orange sat open-mouthed in front of her Mexican soaps, her mind twitched constantly, sewing Junior Button's cul-de-sac mumblings into a single, start to finish story.

On the tenth day, when the old man paused to contemplate a conclusion, Martha Orange finally admitted that this was her story too. A line, as long and lost as the Arkansas River bed, kept her bound to the folks who'd flown previous and those who'd pierce the sweet hereafter. Martha Orange could not be held responsible. She was not, as she'd always suspected, a bad mother or a negligent friend. Martha Orange was ill with a flying disease. The need to bolt ran in her blood, a parasite passed from one generation to the next: latent in her mother, loud as hell in her own thundering heels.

Where she'd understood in part, Martha Orange now knew in glorious technicolor. Salvation sank its feathered teeth into her shoulders. It was not long before she flew.

Junior Button was not surprised. He had always seen the number 39 coming. If it had not been a bus it would have been a taxi, a plane, a single person pedal bike or a steamboat, churning through the gloomy Willamette. Martha Orange would always leave. He'd forecast an early departure in the very particular way she entered a room, feet betraying her love of retreat. The flight was heavy on her, and as Junior Button picked his way through her family tree, tossing out stories and anecdotes like advent calendar candies, he led her closer and closer to the unavoidable moment when she herself was bound to fly. There was nothing triumphant about bolting, but Martha Orange's folks had been making a name out of it for the last two hundred years. Reviewing the story as he spoke, Junior Button found himself amazed that Martha had managed to avoid the number 39 for so long.

The beginning of her story was somewhat hazy. Junior Button was already folding into dotage and the recollection of names, places and dates that had occurred over a hundred years before his birth left him somewhat pickled. He offered everything he could recall and embellished the rest, drawing heavily from his somewhat rusty remembrances of the Old Testament, Greek mythology and the British science fiction show *Dr Who*, which he'd been briefly infatuated with during the mid-eighties. 'It's like this,' he'd said, beginning somewhere south of the start, 'you're from a long line of flying children, girl. Littl'uns with wings that could fly as soon as they learned to walk.' Martha Orange had laughed then, the sort of slack-jawed chortle she reserved for the truly senile patients: warm and generous and carefully aloof. Junior Button had not laughed nor even smiled. His seriousness had frightened her. She'd begun to realize that he actually believed in flying children and less than ten minutes later as he'd encouraged her to remove the top two buttons of her work blouse, to slide her hand inside her shirt and feel, on the straining blade of each shoulder, a raised scar where there'd once been a wing, she'd slowly come to admit that she too believed in flying children.

The children of Jefferson, Oklahoma had been flying for longer than folks had been remembering. Down the generations their legends, improbable as Old Testament plagues, had been faithfully recorded in vellum-bound scrapbooks and passed from one deathbed confessional to the next. None of the residents of Jefferson could remember a time before the flying children. In Jefferson, children had always flown, though flight was not an absolute given. With the blessed exception of twins and triplets, a family could only expect one winged child per generation. The emergence of a second newborn sporting a set of stubby, soon-to-be feathered protrusions was ample cause for speculation regarding its paternity.

The town's elders – including, over the years, a discerning gaggle of silver-haired Lutheran clergymen, two Anglicans and a solitary Jesuit priest (unpopular enough to pronounce Oklahoma unconvertible and retreat, in a matter of months, to the papist sanctuary of inner-city Chicago) had yet to deliver judgment on this peculiar phenomenon. Whilst it was gravely noted that the Angels of the Lord were winged to facilitate eternal hovering about the Almighty's throne, it was also noted that Satan himself had once been equipped with a pair of flying wings. For two centuries the people of Jefferson debated, prayerfully and under influence of strong liquor, the age-old question, more pertinent with the disappearance of each flying child: were they peculiarly blessed, peculiarly cursed, or, as the oldest and wisest dared to suggest, caught in Job's headlock, cursed to be supremely blessed and blessed to be supremely cursed?

Afraid of becoming a spectacle, all but the senile and halfwit cousins knew not to speak of such splintered miracles outside the Jefferson city limits. However, in the name of necessity, Jefferson's flying children twice sacrificed their anonymity for the greater good.

During the Civil War years the children were recruited alongside the adult soldiers, scuttling between one Union safe hold and the next with notes and candy and double-wrapped pouches of gunpowder tucked into their stockings; anything to encourage the boys at the frontline. On July 7th, 1863 they hung low in the marl-grey sky over Honey Springs, tucking scuffed knees to chins as they struggled to avoid stray bullets. The flying children, many of whom were too small to understand the complexities of Union versus Confederate, rode the thermals, graceful as turtle doves as they peered through the gunpowder clouds, audience to an unholy playground skirmish. And when an untimely summer downpour left the Confederate gunpowder barrels damp as river sand, they swooped low, replenishing the Union stocks with pockets full of bone-dry powder. Later, when the battle was won and

Cooper's boys lay disarmed and bloody on Indian land, they flew home carrying news of Union triumph like fresh feathers for their infant wings. They had little clue which side they belonged to, for both armies were as black, white and sleek-haired brown as their own mottled ranks. They flew for dimes and boiled candy and the darkling suspicion that the grown-ups depended upon them.

Almost eighty years later a handful of flying children – seven in total: six boys and a solitary, blunt-banged girl – were drafted, without permission or proper understanding, into the European war effort. A punt-faced commander, having caught a rumor of flying children as it circulated round the bunk houses at Fort Sill, arrived in Jefferson, Oklahoma early in the morning of Christmas Day 1941. Promising a smorgasbord of festive blessings – an Ivy League education for every Jefferson child, a new schoolhouse, various larger items of farm equipment and the safe return of every child – he talked the townsfolk into lending seven children for the war effort. 'It's like this, kids,' he yelled at the terrified children as they lurched and sniffled their way back to Fort Hill in an army Jeep. 'That bastard Hitler is frying littl'uns younger than you lot and gassing old folks and doing Lord only knows what experiments on mutants like you. Quit your sniveling. You should be thankful for a chance to help cut that SOB down.'

Trailing the troop ships across the Atlantic, the flying children soon forgot Jefferson. They looped the stratosphere, swinging low to brush the bearded undulations of the waves and, like Noah's raven, returned by night to sleep as kidney beans curled together in one of the ship's many lifeboats. Only the highest in command had been informed of their existence. The ordinary soldiers, many of whom had never before crossed state lines, excused the children when they appeared in telescopes and binocular sights as strange birds, peculiar to the continental drift.

The children reveled in the open sky. They flew like fighter pilots and dined like demigods on tinned fruit and Hershey bars. Recalling the claustrophobic fields and streets of Jefferson, Oklahoma, they could only conclude that their parents were selfish creatures, denying them the full breadth of their prodigal wings. By the time they hit Europe all seven children had lost their instinct to return home.

The ships docked in Belfast on January 26th, 1942, and while the regular troops trooped through the city exploring the public houses and dance halls, the children made darting, exploratory flights through the Glens of Antrim and the Newry Hills, thrilled by the jungling foliage and lush greens. Accustomed to the flat Oklahoma plains, everything seemed damp, pocket-sized and saturated in color. Such a small island, the children mused, no bigger than a single state. Yet this tiny teaspoonful of a tiny continent served to whet their appetites for further adventures. In the early days Europe felt like a homecoming for the children. The streets ran thick with mythical stories: monsters, angels, immortal beings. For one short instance the flying children felt almost acceptable. America was a youngster, too efficient to argue after unbelievable legends. No one had ever celebrated the children for their oddities. Huddling for the night in barns and rural barracks, they began to speak healing words over each other, 'lucky' and 'blessed' and 'terribly, terribly fortunate'; the squat syllables rocking them into deep, satisfying sleep.

It was only many months later, flying low over Dachau and Buchenwald and Auschwitz, that the children came to understand the dark mission which had drawn them so far from home. They began to re-imagine their parents as saints and prophets; their small, suffocating town, a haven of quiet sense. Eyes full of impossible suffering, they hid behind their camera lenses, snapping children, adults and old people reduced to bone and paper. Each silent flight became an opportunity to repent. No longer blessed, no longer lucky, no longer baptized by good, good fortune, the children grew heavier with every sad mission. Afterwards, without consulting, two of the seven attempted to claw themselves free of their wings. A third, under the mistaken assumption that this might instigate blindness, rubbed vinegar in her own eyes. All but the child given to localized hysterics lost the ability to laugh audibly. All sacrificed their teenage years, tripping straight from child to adult. There were sights and smells so horrific they could never be flown away from.

The war ruined the people of Jefferson, Oklahoma. When the prodigal seven were returned, unceremoniously dumped from a speeding Landrover, they spiraled into the backfields like wilted sycamore seeds, too limp-winged and exhausted to soar. Over the coming weeks these children seemed to shrivel into themselves. They suffered from nightmares and panic attacks, dry skin and migraine headaches. Though fully capable of flight they had no appetite for the heavens. For years they dragged their unfurled wings behind them, shameful things drooping like the living room curtains from each shoulder. These children amounted to nothing and passed away in early adulthood, too tired to rise in a world so unbearably heavy. The mothers and fathers kicked themselves for their stupidity. They took up arms and rebuilt their defenses. Jefferson, Oklahoma became a cold shoulder for strangers, a safe hold for its own.

The town adapted to its flying children. Trampolines and straw-stuffed mattresses bloomed at regular intervals along the High Street, rain-soaked and ready to cushion the faltering infant fliers. The schoolhouse went unroofed for generations. Impervious to the odd Oklahoma downpour, the classroom ceiling was removed to save the grazed heads and bruised wings of those children too sky sung to keep their seats for an entire lesson. Younger children, not yet capable of controlling their flighty urges, were often corralled, bound to their bunk beds with belts and laces for their own safety. Locally, such behavior was considered more prudent than cruel. The modern world, even the idle armpit of Oklahoma, was not best suited to flying children. Dangers lurked in the eaves of taller buildings and overhanging trees. Tragic tales were passed like good luck charms from one generation to the next, keeping even the most formidable kids local and grounded long after the migratory urges kicked in.

Telegraph wires, the children were told, had been outlawed in 1948 after the untimely death of a local teenager. The effeminate fourth-born of Jefferson's only practicing butcher had been burdened at birth with a pair of fully formed wings and the unfortunate name of Frances Farley. (This name, though not particularly ridiculous in and of itself, was unfortunate by association for it was also his mother's name, which she, desperate for a daughter and just turned forty-two, had decided to bestow upon her fourth son.)

By his seventh birthday Frances Farley could fly for up to three hours unaided. On warm afternoons he hovered above the county high school's gym hall, spying on the older boys as they sweated into their vests and wrestling leotards. Later, when a testosterone spurt turned him particularly bold, he began to favor the changing room skylights where for up to an hour at a time he watched their naked torsos and buttocks surf the shower room steam like lumbering, pink-skinned gorillas. On such occasions Frances Farley was a teeter-totter torn between rapture and Christian consequence. Though he had no desire to emulate the ordinary, young Frances knew better than to speak of such dark pleasures. His brothers – three brutish lads with feet like backyard anchors – repulsed him with their talk of God and next-door girls and bloody, butchering futures. Frances Farley was built for higher things. He flew to court the angel's share, to shirk the parched reality of butcher brothers and Jefferson, Oklahoma. Even in flight the town dragged on his heels, holding him captive by skylights and uncurtained windows; one part angel, two parts teenage boy.

His parents knew nothing of Frances's expeditions. Having birthed three perfectly ordinary, unwinged sons, his mother presumed Frances's solitude a natural side-effect of flight. The boy's feminine affectations went unnoticed in a house where the manly stench of meat and cleaver made even his slight-hipped mother seem faintly masculine. Frances Farley did his best to fake an interest in steak and football. He intended to grow a mustache before the people of Jefferson grew suspicious. The mustache never surfaced. During one of his afternoon excursions, preoccupied by desire and a growing sense of curdling guilt (having lately found himself attracted to the middle-aged man who mowed his father's lawns), Frances Farley flew straight into a telegraph wire, became entangled and hung himself by the neck in full view of his three older brothers.

The implications were twofold. Watching from the meeting house steps as they paced the dead hour between baseball practice and midweek Bible study, all three elder brothers spontaneously lost their faith. In the coming years butchery would serve as substitute religion in the Farley household. Meanwhile, every resident in a six-mile radius simultaneously lost telephone service for over an hour as the authorities untangled and removed the twisted remains of Frances Farley. To this day Frances Farley's legacy remains as a permanent kink in the wires operating the home telephones of Jefferson, Oklahoma. Half curse, half blessing, this almost unnoticeable knot automatically censors away all the villagers' talk of miracles, both domestic and divine.

The people of Jefferson, Oklahoma could never settle on the issue of flying children. To glory in the unrestrained beauty of a swooping, looping child was one thing. To lose that child to the wider skies, another thing entirely. The parents of Jefferson lived in constant dread of the moment, around the age of twelve or thirteen, when their children would begin to flirt with the dead air around the city limits. Questions as innocuous as, 'is New York really that big?' and 'how wide is the Atlantic ocean?' would take on a peculiarly sinister significance as the children became aware of a world beyond their backyard fence. By the time their sixteenth birthdays rolled round, all but the most timid had migrated: west to California, east to the big city, far, far away to over-ocean countries and continents torn from the pages of the children's encyclopedia. Flying children did not return. Neither were they inclined to write home or, when the advent of telephones made such communication possible, call on birthdays or anniversaries. Flying children were temporary creatures like wasps or bluebottles, born for a single season of flight and suddenly lost.

The mothers of Jefferson, Oklahoma were not like other American mothers. They loved their children harder and faster than most, squeezing extra birthdays, extra treats and memories into their sixteen short years. Their hearts, when examined by scientific men with scalpels and microscopes, were around one-third thicker and more elastic than any American heart previously examined in laboratory conditions. Jefferson mothers were long-suffering women who lost in public, grieved in private and never once blamed God for all his jealous takings.

In 1945 the flying children returned from the war, wilted slips of their former glory. In 1947, five flying children formed a leaving pact and, with little regard for their parents or siblings, skipped town en masse; a flock of migrating teenagers, bobby socks twinkling like tiny stars in the drawing dusk. In 1948 Frances Farley unceremoniously hung himself from the telephone wires and on Thanksgiving evening, 1950, temporarily unhinged by the discovery of a North African map secreted beneath his son's bed, the Baptist pastor took a shotgun to his fourteen-year-old son. 'Better dead and buried,' he explained to the local sheriff, 'than disappearing some evening. A thing like that'll break a mother's heart real slow.' Three centuries of loss had worn the good folks of Jefferson, Oklahoma thin around the edges. The women were gaunt, the men morose and prone to premature balding. Young couples, previously magnetic, turned celibate on their honeymoon night, terrified by the possibility of conceiving a short-loan baby. The joy had long since split the blessing, and most every resident of Jefferson now believed themselves cursed above all middling American towns.

On February 7th, 1951, a secret meeting was called in the Newhalls' hayshed and by a universal consensus of all but three, the people of Jefferson voted to end the flying era. Babies born winged would come under the knife. On the third day of their existence, regardless of background or parental whim, the local physician would take a scalpel to each shoulder and circumcise the flight from the mewling infant. Though somewhat barbaric, the operation would keep Jefferson's children ordinary and grounded right through their teenage years. The children, it was decided, should never be told of the special blessing which had cursed them from birth.

By Easter of 1951 circumcision was a standardized practice in Jefferson, Oklahoma. Older children, already accustomed to flight, were given a choice: succumb to the knife or skip town before they upset the younger ones. Even in backwater Oklahoma peer pressure proved a powerful force and most children chose amputation. Afterwards they attended homecoming dances and Sunday school picnics unencumbered by the weight of wings. The sky lust had not left them but flight was no longer within their reach. They felt inexplicably clumsy in their fancy clothes, ill-inclined to dance or date. Several took shotguns to their misery whilst the rest found more mundane ways to skip town – pickup trucks and Greyhound buses and bicycles cycling them across the United States, obedient to their migratory urges.

Forty-five years mumbled past. Children no longer flew in Jefferson, Oklahoma. Only the elders could recall with any clarity the image of a child caught in actual soaring flight. Flying children were still being conceived on a bimonthly basis. Responsibility for controlling the problem now rested upon the county midwives, a group of stout-armed women who could be trusted to remain both firm and discreet when faced with a hysterical new mother. 'Tell no one,' they urged generation after generation of horrified young girls. 'You don't want your baby growing up a freak. It's best to deal with this now before the rumors start.'

Over the years the maternity hospital incinerator saw dozens of not-yet-feathered wings, delicate as infant hands, reduced to ash clouds and returned to the heavens. The people of Jefferson, Oklahoma did not speak of such sharp sorrow. They were a stoic breed, inclined to persevere in the face of drought and great sadness. However, the flight could not be cut out of Jefferson's children. As time passed they found increasingly elaborate ways to bolt. With no good explanation for the strings and magnets which drew them any which way but Oklahoma, these children believed themselves bad mothers and friends, unworthy sons and daughters, inadequate students. They itched through their early years and, at the first opportunity, took the one straight road out of Jefferson, Oklahoma and never came back.

Junior Button was only two days into his story when Martha Orange began to recognize shades of her own anxiety in each of the flying children. This was no hillbilly parable. The pinkish circles on each of her shoulder blades, wounds as slight and negligible as acne scars, bore loud witness each time she took a shower. By the weekend of the second week she'd gathered all the justification she needed. On Monday she followed the flight out the front door of Chalet 13, over the turn circle and through the unforgiving gates of the Baptist Retirement Village. Martha Orange had no intention of returning. Neither did she feel the need to indulge in guilt. That evening Junior Button took a second tumble from his bed and the night shift, atypical in their negligence, found him five hours later, stiffly dead on the bedroom carpet. The coroner's report favored diabetic coma and noted, as an afterthought, two small scars on the old man's shoulder blades and the peculiar way his arms had set, straining upwards and outwards like a large bird angling for takeoff.

– Chapter Eleven –

Guns

Malcolm Orange dreamt thickly and woke to the worrying realization that he was not in his own bed. The comforter tucked beneath his chin was inconsiderately itchy and the bed, he suspected, more of a floor than an actual bed. He turned to his left and found Sorry fastly asleep, Mr Fluff cradling her forehead like a coonskin cap. The light was a toothache in his eyes. It hurt to turn his head. The previous evening's adventures came back in hiccups, although the final movement from turn circle to unmade bed was somewhat hazy. Perhaps he had crawled or, more likely, been carried. Given the week's events, the possibility of teleportation was no longer beyond the realms of possibility. Malcolm Orange could recall little beyond his third beer.

He turned a second time towards Sorry and wondered if the drunkenness had led to sexual intercourse or prolonged kissing. The movies had taught him that on the rare occasions when alcohol consumption did not end in physical violence it inevitably led to unplanned sex. Malcolm Orange hoped Sorry wasn't pregnant. Ross was barely out of the sock drawer. The last thing he needed was a second baby. It was too early in the morning to contemplate another disaster so Malcolm Orange lowered his eyes and feigned sleep. Half an hour passed in migrainous silence. In the shadowy corners of his consciousness Malcolm was aware of feet approaching and receding, mumbled conversation and the unmistakable aroma of frying bacon. He woke to the cut of Bill standing over him with a dinner plate in one hand and a skillet in the other.

'Sleeping Beauty's back in the land of the living,' the old man yelled over his shoulder and then, directing his attention towards Malcolm, 'Would you like some bacon, son? It's almost eleven. We don't have much time so I took the liberty of fixing you both a spot of brunch.'

As he raised his head slowly, setting off a small volcano at the base of his skull, Malcolm Orange observed Sorry, cross-legged on Irene's good sofa, chomping through a short stack of pancakes. A rivulet of maple syrup had dribbled down her chin, forming a sticky reservoir on her T-shirt. Malcolm made a superhuman effort to sit up. His head hammered in objection. He felt like an outline of himself and, looking down at his naked forearms braced against the carpet, noted with horror that there was very little arm actually left.

'No breakfast,' he said meekly. 'It would only go right through me, Bill.'

The old man laughed, misunderstanding Malcolm's fear. 'Aye, son, that's what the demon drink'll do to you. Nate and I scraped you off the road last night. You were so drunk you didn't even wake up. Cunningham's no better. He's sleeping it off in the RV. Irene thought it best to bring you here and, needless to say, we couldn't send 'you know who' back home in that state. The Director would have murdered her.'

'I'll bet he hasn't even noticed I'm gone,' interjected Sorry.

'Probably glad to be rid of you, you little bitch,' yelled the disembodied voice of Roger Heinz, rumbling from the back kitchen where he was preoccupied with fixing the coffee whilst mentally removing Irene's bathrobe.

The room was rounding like a bicycle wheel and Malcolm Orange had very little idea what was going on. Shuffling himself butt-first onto Irene's everyday sofa, he turned towards Sorry, hoping she might have some answers.

'Still disappearing?' she asked.

Malcolm huffed his shoulders grouchily, 'Looks like it.'

'Never mind, Malcolm. It was a good excuse to get wasted. I guess you don't remember any of it. You were pretty far gone on your three Coronas.'

'We didn't, you know, do anything we might regret later?'

'Well the old guy pissed himself and you fell asleep in the street.'

'I mean, did *we* do anything we might regret, you know, together?'

'Like make out?'

'Yeah, I know it sometimes happens when two people are very drunk. There's no chance you could be pregnant? It's not that I wouldn't be there for you, Sorry, but I can't really handle another baby at the minute, at least not until Ross is out of diapers.'

Soren James Blue looked like she'd swallowed a whole half-pound of last week's lemons. She made a vomit face and threw an armful of Irene's best scatter cushions at Malcolm's head.

'Urrgghhhh, gross, Malcolm. I think I just threw up in my mouth.'

'Great,' said Malcolm Orange, reassured to discover he would not be experiencing fatherhood before his thirteenth birthday. It was the first good news in a fortnight. 'So, you're not pregnant. We all got drunk. Cunningham pissed himself and I'm still disappearing. Anything else I missed while I was sleeping?'

'Your mom left,' said Sorry. 'I guess it was your fault. She found you on the road.'

Malcolm Orange turned inside out. This sort of feeling could not be measured or quantified by Scientific Investigative Research. He wanted to kill someone, specifically God, and also his father; holding them jointly responsible for this latest loss. Malcolm Orange could not think of words or questions. Out of his mouth came a noise which he was neither making nor permitting to be made. It sounded like a dinosaur becoming extinct. Bill abandoned the bacon skillet on the edge of Irene's good coffee table. The heat left a ring. (Later that evening Irene would discover the burn and strike Bill twice in quick succession, her pounding fists marking the next movement in a progression which would see the dementia leave her quickly violent and occasionally vulgar.)

Without asking permission Bill sat down on the everyday sofa and slipped an arm around Malcolm's shoulder. Malcolm did not fight him off. It felt good to be anchored to something which hadn't disappeared yet. The ungodly noise quit coming out of his mouth. It was a relief of sorts to feel once again self-contained. Ordinary words were still far beyond him. Malcolm's insides felt almost as empty as his outsides. He began to cry, shoulders heaving up and down like a pump-action soap dispenser. Bill's arm increased its grip. Between Bill's arms and the involuntary sobbing, the disappearings and the awareness of Sorry, glaring from the good sofa, Malcolm Orange was finding it increasingly hard to breathe.

'That's alright, son,' the old man murmured. 'You let it out. It's an awful thing to lose your mother. Sure, I remember the day my mother passed away. Irene'll tell you, I cried for a week and I was a grown man.'

'She's not dead,' whispered Malcolm through the sobs.

'And even now, every year on the anniversary, well, I don't feel greatly inclined to do anything but mope about the house.'

'She's not dead,' said Malcolm, louder now, in competition with the air conditioning unit.

'Aye, it's a terrible thing for a young boy, two young boys really, to lose their mother.'

'SHE'S NOT DEAD!' yelled Malcolm Orange. 'She's just left us.'

'That's way worse,' said Sorry, and before anyone could chastise her, slipped out the front door for a surreptitious cigarette. Mr Fluff snaked behind her heels, leaving a feathery circle of orange hairs hovering above the plush fabric of Irene's good sofa. Sensing the possibility of a good argument, Roger Heinz appeared in the living room, made a rude sign at Sorry's retreating back and pulled up a dining chair. Removing a veritable arsenal of craft knives, water pistols and cutlery from his pants pockets, he arranged his weapons on the coffee table before leaning back in his chair, arms crossed like a squat Buddha.

'Son,' he said, 'if the army taught me nothing else, it sure as hell taught me this one thing. When the shit hits the fan, it's every man for himself. Your ma's upped and run off, most likely she's banging some new man now your daddy's left town. Women are like that, Malcolm. It's not ideal but there's no point sitting here crying like a pussy. You've got to man up and get on with taking care of business. Ain't nobody else going to look out for you if you don't look out for yourself.'

Roger Heinz leaned back in the dining chair and tucked a dessert fork behind his left ear in preparation for imminent attack.

'Choose your weapon, Malcolm,' he said, sweeping his hand across the aluminum arsenal displayed on the coffee table. 'You're all alone now. You're going to need to be able to defend yourself.'

'Bullshit,' said Bill, left arm still draped around Malcolm's shoulders. 'Malcolm's not on his own, Roger. He's got us.'

'Exactly,' echoed Irene, who'd suddenly appeared from the kitchen with Ross in one hand and a steaming coffee pot drooping in the other. 'Malcolm belongs right here on the cul-de-sac with us.'

'And I'll be damned,' continued Bill, 'if we don't help the boy out.'

Within half an hour an emergency meeting of the People's Committee for Remembering Songs had assembled in Bill and Irene's front room. The promise of imminent danger and peach schnapps had coerced them into meeting on their day off. Nate Grubbs brought the meeting to attention with an authoritative cough. 'No time for singing today,' he announced. 'Cunningham Holt has important news to share with us. This is an emergency situation and I ask for your undivided attention.' A mood of great solemnity descended upon the room. The ladies residing on Irene's good sofa quit pecking at their breakfast pastries and turned to stare at Cunningham. Bill rose as if preparing to receive the national anthem. Clary O'Hare did Morse code on his knee with a tea spoon and Roger Heinz, secretly delighted by the possibility of an actual emergency mission, sat in the corner feigning disinterest whilst polishing his cutlery arsenal. Malcolm and Sorry were positioned side by side on the living room rug, outstretched legs running parallel like spindly railroad slats. Sorry's ankles cupped a dozing Mr Fluff, whilst Ross slept deeply in his duffel bag between the rubbery heels of Malcolm's sneakers.

Cunningham Holt kept his seat. Not much of a drinker, the previous evening's antics had left him the sappy color of lukewarm porridge. Though few of the assembled Committee members knew it, Cunningham had struggled to make the short journey from his RV to Bill and Irene's front door. The final few yards had seen the older man half-dragged, half-carried by Bill and Nate. The two men had been concerned enough by Cunningham's grisly pallor to put their own angina-rippled hearts at risk. Once successfully settled in Bill's favorite armchair, Cunningham Holt had discreetly asked his two friends not to mention his faltering health. The main thing, he assured them, was Malcolm Orange's situation. All else could be addressed tomorrow or the day after.

The People's Committee were old enough to know better. Cunningham's grey marbles were not wasted on them. His mouth had, almost overnight, begun to droop like an undrawn purse. His trembling hands betrayed the fact that Cunningham Holt was finally beginning to sink. The People's Committee said nothing for they knew he could no sooner be cautioned than halted. Even in his dotage Cunningham Holt was a steamroller. When all were circled and grazing on breakfast pastries and peach schnapps, he raised a hand to beg silence and the already somber room settled reverently around him.

'It's like this,' he said. 'Malcolm's disappearing.'

'And his mama already disappeared,' added Irene angrily. 'And I don't want that mean hitting girl in my house. And Bill's getting really fat. And we won't be allowed to do the singing anymore.'

'Those are all perfectly legitimate concerns Irene, but today we're focusing on Malcolm. If we don't do something quickly he might not be here tomorrow. Show them Malcolm.'

Malcolm Orange extricated Ross from between his heels and stood slowly. He stepped into the middle of the room and, though he'd previously encountered nightmares very similar, slipped his shirt over his head and dropped his shorts so he stood in the centre of Bill and Irene's living room naked, save for sneakers and a pair of skimpy X-Men boxer shorts. The People's Committee for Remembering Songs took a quick, collective glance around the room and, having gauged the mood, let out a theatrical gasp.

'See?' said Cunningham Holt. 'The boy is covered in holes.'

'They're getting bigger every couple of hours,' added Malcolm, pointing out the largest of the perforations, a cavern of some ten centimeters in diameter, currently substituting for his belly button and lower torso.

'Oh my,' said Mrs Hunter Huxley and Mrs George Kellerman in unison. Though their Baptist upbringings had exposed them to all manner of miraculous miracles – snake handlings, healings and angelic choirs – they'd never once come across a disappearing boy.

'Have you been fiddling with yourself, son?' asked Roger Heinz and as Malcolm Orange turned the livid colour of cheap ketchup, persisted, 'Most boys go blind when they fiddle with themselves. I've never seen a boy disappear before but maybe you're at it more than most.'

'It's a terrible situation,' continued Cunningham Holt, choosing, as usual, to ignore Roger Heinz. 'Last night we tried to fix Malcolm by dreaming him back to normal. It was a misguided plan and, as you can see, it didn't work.'

'He looks fine to me,' shouted Irene, who was too fumble-minded to understand the importance of indulging Cunningham Holt.

'*Ssshhh*,' hissed her husband, 'MALCOLM'S DISAPPEARING AND CUNNINGHAM WANTS TO HELP and that means we're all going to help too.'

'Speak up, Irene,' hollered Sorry. 'You're the only one in the room insane enough to tell the truth. There's nothing wrong with Malcolm. He's just been around you all so long he's starting to act crazy too.'

An offer of allegiance from Soren James Blue was enough to turn Irene. She slipped on her reading glasses, squinted into the centre of the living room and confessed that she too could now see that Malcolm was definitely disappearing and would he like a nice pastrami sandwich to sustain him for the trials ahead? Malcolm declined. It was days since he'd last felt honestly hungry. Quickly redressing, he took his usual place in the circle, cross-legged at Cunningham Holt's feet, and waited to see what advice they could offer.

'We could hold a prayer meeting,' suggested Mrs Hunter Huxley, and by proxy Mrs George Kellerman, who had already dropped her eyelids and clasped her hands in grateful anticipation. 'Prayer changes things.'

'I think we should do something a little more practical, Mrs H,' suggested Cunningham Holt. 'Though you are of course more than welcome to pray before, after and during our practical response. Just so long as you do it quietly.'

'And no tongues,' added Bill. 'Last time you two did your praying in tongues Clary mistook it for Morse and went a bit mad when he couldn't translate.'

'Did someone say we should use Morse code?' piped up Clary O'Hare, fingers already tapping out a distress signal.

'Shut up, you old fart,' snapped Roger Heinz. 'You and your Morse code belong in a museum. If you ask me, we need to storm the Center. This is a medical matter and all the drugs are locked up in there. We need to get inside. We'll need weapons of course, and a plan. It won't be easy but Malcolm's only hope is to get into the Center.'

'Dumbest plan I ever heard,' muttered Bill. 'The Director'll have us all thrown out of the retirement village, and for what reason? We don't even know what's wrong with Malcolm. How are we going to work out how to help him? I suggest we take him to the ER and let the professionals deal with it.'

A low, murmurous grumble began to spread around the People's Committee as the members debated, in twos and timid threes, the best plan of action. After a few moments Nate Grubbs cleared his throat and carefully coerced the conversation back on track.

'I hate to agree with Roger,' he admitted, fully utilizing the authoritative tone which had, over the years, talked him into leadership of various clubs, societies and sporting associations, 'but it does seem ridiculous to drag the boy all the way across Portland when there's a perfectly adequate medical facility right here on our doorstep.'

'And Mrs Orange did work in the Center,' added Mrs Hunter Hoxley. 'The Director might look kindly on treating the boy, because of his mother.'

'Like hell he will,' snapped Roger Heinz. 'The young floozy's skipped town, probably raided the drugs cabinet before she left. The Director's not going to let us into the Center. That's why we need weapons.'

Whilst the People's Committee were preoccupied weighing up Malcolm's options, Soren James Blue had taken the opportunity to slip several of Irene's best crystal ornaments into her jeans pockets. Thievery was not one of her specialist sins. She had always been more of an arson girl. However, all this talk of sneaking into the Center had left her nervous and itching for a distraction. An opportunity to do the right thing was hovering just in front of her nose and Soren James Blue was determined to avoid it at all costs.

Sorry was just contemplating an emergency exit when Mr Fluff began to claw mercilessly at the bare flesh of her left leg. This was no mean coincidence. The cat was trying to get her attention. Shoving the Mr Fluff aside, Sorry tried to ignore the persistent pinch of a guilty conscience. Mr Fluff continued to claw. As the cat's claws needled in and out of her leg, leaving tiny pinprick indentations, Sorry realized that Mr Fluff was a time bomb waiting to go off. The cat knew too much. Over the past few months, Soren James Blue had exclusively confided in Mr Fluff. This one-sided arrangement had been ongoing for most of Sorry's internment in the Baptist Retirement Village. Though lonelier than she'd ever been, it was not necessity so much as the unshakeable suspicion that Mr Fluff was much wiser than most human confidantes which had kept this conversation going. Mr Fluff knew everything and, having watched the drama unfold over the last few days, now felt greatly inclined to help.

Sinking her claws into Sorry's leg for a final time and finding the girl unresponsive, Mr Fluff felt forced into an alternative plan of action. It was not her intention to shock but the situation required something abnormal. The cat untangled herself from Sorry's legs and waddled into the circle's centre, whereupon she opened her mouth and forced her vocal chords – previously inclined to produce succulent purrs and predatory hisses – to squeeze five, fat, human syllables into the room.

Sorry was not expecting Mr Fluff to speak, neither was she particularly shocked when the cat did. As a child she'd often heard Mr Fluff singing from the sanctuary of the condiment shelf in the fridge. On several occasions the cat had spoken directly to her; chiding, encouraging and instructing in a tone Sorry had come to associate with European nannies, the kind who wore uniforms and disciplined lavishly and made better parents than the two inferior adults assigned to her care. However, over the years she'd convinced herself that belief in a speaking cat should be listed alongside the other side effects of a troubled childhood: bulimia, vandalism and localized arson to catalogue her own particular obsessions. The sound of Mr Fluff speaking directly to the People's Committee was stronger than déjà vu; the moment was an old nursery rhyme, long forgotten, and now recalled with searing exactitude. Certain childish smells – laundry, licquorice and pipe smoke – rose comfortingly in Sorry's nostrils and, against all usual standards, she permitted herself an unsolicited smile.

Mr Fluff had never before and would never again address a crowd. Though she had over the years drafted, in preparation for her glory moment, a speech as eloquent and universal as the Sermon on the Mount, she was fully prepared to sacrifice her spotlight for the greater good. Mr Fluff was absolutely certain that this was exactly the correct instance to release her four words of wisdom upon an unsuspecting audience.

'Tell the truth, Soren,' announced Mr Fluff, loud enough for the entire People's Committee to hear and turn, as quickly as their various elderly ailments would permit. Mrs Huxley let out a sharp, rickety breath; Roger Heinz reached for a cheese knife; and Irene, too daft to ignore the obvious, giggled like a schoolgirl as she shrieked, 'The cat just spoke!' In response to their curious glares, Mr Fluff emitted a brief, pretentious meow. It stuck in her throat like a make-believe accent. She could no longer do a passable impression of an ordinary cat. For a brief, breath-held moment the People's Committee froze, tottering between awe and disgust. Then the room began to riot as all those capable of voluntary movement rushed towards Sorry and Mr Fluff. Like Pentecost unleashed, each one spoke loudly, at once, with various accentual affectations. Sorry found herself suddenly and without warning the center point in a circle of rabbling old people. She kept her seat on the carpet and from this dizzying angle attempted to field their frantic questions.

Yes, Mr Fluff had spoken.

No, she wasn't particularly surprised, for she'd always known the cat could speak.

Yes, the cat was possessed, or maybe she was possessed. It was hard to tell. Perhaps, after lunch, Mrs Huxley could have a go at casting out their collective demons.

Yes, she would apologize to Mrs Huxley for her blatant impertinence.

No, she did not expect the cat to speak again and could they all piss off and leave her alone. The sight of so many old coots hovering overhead was beginning to make her dizzy.

As the circle began to look more and more like a lynch mob, Nate Grubbs intervened. Brandishing his coffee mug like a truncheon, he pressed for calm and the immediate return to matters more urgent. Unappeased but exhausted from the strain of standing upright for almost three consecutive minutes, the People's Committee retired to their chairs and sofas, still mumbling into their shirt sleeves. One elderly individual reporting a speaking cat might be excused as Alzheimer's; two, hysteria. A dozen simultaneous, identical hallucinations suggested the apparition was worryingly real. The cat had spoken four audible words of American English. Almost everyone had heard, though Simeon Klein, profoundly deaf but determined not to miss an emergency meeting, had only experienced the resulting commotion and a clumsily signed explanation leading him to believe the cat had eaten Mrs Kellerman's knitting. The People's Committee for Remembering Songs fell silent. As the silence grew louder it took on shapes: clouds and squares and entire rooms, ill-equipped with exits or entrances. No one felt much like speaking. Though, collectively and individually, the People's Committee had weathered all manner of wars, tragedies and homegrown miracles, no one knew how to approach a situation suddenly populated with speaking cats and disappearing children.

Sensing her presence to be something of a distraction, Mr Fluff made a discreet exit, retreating to the comforting sanctuary of Irene's fridge. She spent the next hour sucking her tail and leaving hairballs in the butter dish. It was years since Mr Fluff had last required a fridge. She returned to it now like a backslidden thumbsucker and the halogen-lit stillness helped to nurse her loss. She did not regret speaking out. Such outbursts were occasionally necessary. It had been good to hear her own voice again, to see her words evoke such flattering hysteria. However, like a wasp, once stung, she knew the power had now left her. Further voicings would turn her into a sideshow anecdote. Mr Fluff was a proud creature and the prospect of widespread infamy terrified her. So she settled into the cold meats shelf and quietly grew acclimatized to the idea of passing her remaining years as an ordinary cat.

In her absence Cunningham Holt spoke first. He felt it prudent to ignore Mr Fluff. The People's Committee was tottering on the brink of hysterics and it was up to him to hold their focus. Further interrogation of the cat would leave them circling for hours on a subject secondary to Malcolm's disappearance. 'Is there something you want to tell us, Soren?' he asked.

'No,' said Sorry.

'I think there is,' replied Cunningham Holt. 'I think you've got something important to tell us. I think you know something that could help Malcolm and I think you're going to share everything you know because at the bottom of it all, you're a much nicer little girl than you'd like us to believe.'

'And,' added Roger Heinz, 'if you don't tell us, I'll run you through with Irene's electric carving knife.'

Soren James Blue opened her mouth to retaliate and a thin, wavering sob, impotent as a length of damp toilet paper, leaked out. Sorry cried, eyes betraying the softer sentiments trapped behind her face. The threat of carving knives was wasted on her. Over the last six years she'd fielded insults – both ill-founded and conclusive – with the kind of unswerving forbearance usually found in a pro tennis player. Ugly words could rarely catch her, but the realization that Cunningham Holt saw, buried beneath the prickly pallor, a nice little girl, still redeemable, sliced her straight down the middle.

'It's alright, child,' whispered Mrs Hunter Huxley, passing her an unused Kleenex, recently fished from the cavernous interior of Mrs George Kellerman's Sunday go-to-meeting purse. 'A good cry will do you the world of good. You just tell us in your own time.'

And so, whilst Roger Heinz pounded around Bill and Irene's living room, muttering suspiciously about double bluffs and untrustworthy sources, Soren James Blue nursed a glass of peach schnapps and in a quavering voice, which did not seem to belong to her, shared the humbling details of her summer in the Center. The People's Committee were furniture for the telling. They neither spoke nor moved, nor felt the inclination to interrupt, and when the final revelation of the Treatment Room proved a little complex for the more elderly members to fully comprehend, Nate Grubbs raised his hand cautiously and asked if a further explanation might be possible. Sorry, for her previous sins, settled easily into the role of confessor. She was a natural storyteller, capable of embellishing where excess proved helpful and at other times clipping the unnecessary to create a streamlined progression from beginning to end. She was not funny. It was not a story which lent itself to humor. The People's Committee for Remembering Songs appreciated her somber tone; they were not in the mood for comedy.

'Well,' announced Bill, when Sorry's story had finally concluded. 'Looks to me like we need to get Malcolm into the Director's Treatment Room.'

The People's Committee mumbled in general approval.

'We can't just walk in there,' Sorry said. 'My dad will kill me. No one's supposed to know about the Treatment Room. He makes the patients sign a contract saying they won't speak about it. He will actually, physically kill me if he catches me in there with you lot.'

'Well, we'll just have to make sure he doesn't catch us then.'

'Or we could shoot him,' proposed Roger Heinz. 'We'd have the run of the Center for ten minutes if we shot him. That would be more than enough time to get Malcolm sorted out and if we get Irene to do it she can plead insanity; she probably wouldn't even do prison time.'

'We could use Nate's gun,' added Irene. In her younger years she'd spent summer vacations trekking the Oregon wilderness with the Girl Scouts of America. Six consecutive summers of survival training had left her above averagely adept with an air rifle and prone to inappropriate outbursts of bloodlust. The prospect of murdering the Director had excited Irene in a fashion Bill had neither seen nor experienced in all their decades of marriage.

'We can't go round shooting people,' Bill stated bluntly. His wife's willingness to assassinate the Director had thrown him. Lately he'd begun to wonder if Irene was the same woman he'd first embraced on her parents' porch in 1946. Frequently he woke to the creeping suspicion that a changeling wife was now occupying the left side of their king-size bed. He said nothing for fear of upsetting the delicate balance of their comings and goings. The previous spring, however, he'd taken up vegetable gardening as a means of legitimate and daily escape.

'You're right Bill,' agreed Cunningham Holt. 'But we could use Nate's gun for a distraction.'

The prospect of a tactical diversion served to satisfy everyone. Sorry, at first reluctant to become involved, seemed reassured that the Director would never know anything. The Mrs Huxley and Kellerman were collectively delighted by the prospect of something concrete and potentially life-threatening to pray about and Malcolm Orange was simply relieved to have a group of adults, albeit rather elderly adults, take responsibility for his problems. Over mugs of acrid Folgers, the People's Committee for Remembering Songs began to plot. Roger Heinz bucked democracy and voted himself Commander-in-Chief of the afternoon's operations. No one argued. On the reverse of a disposable Christmas tablecloth, he drew up a plan of attack.

The People's Committee would split into two individual units. The first unit, comprising Malcolm Orange, Soren, Cunningham Holt and Roger Heinz, would wait by the laundry room and, upon receipt of a secret signal (a shipping flare most likely), breach the Center via the fire exit doors and proceed directly to the Treatment Room. Meanwhile, the secondary unit, comprised of Bill, Irene, Nate Grubbs and Clary O'Hare, would occupy the reception area, mounting a choral singing demonstration in revolt against the planned closure of the People's Committee for Remembering Songs. If this tactical diversion was not spectacle enough to draw the entire Center staff, Director included, to the reception area, allowing unsupervised access to the rear fire exit, Irene would either faint or fire Nate Grubbs' shotgun at the ceiling. The appropriate action would be left to the discretion of Irene. (With hindsight, reliance upon Irene's good sense would prove to be the only weak link in an otherwise watertight plan.) The remaining members of the People's Committee would man base camp at Chalet 11, maintaining a round-the-clock prayer vigil, producing constant supplies of instant coffee and oatmeal cookies, and ensuring no further harm came to the infant Ross.

It was a good plan. Everyone agreed except Simeon Klein who, despite the helpful diagrams, could not quite understand why they were attacking the Center. The ladies immediately migrated towards the kitchen and began to bake furiously, offering up sanctimonious Our Fathers between the thrusting beats of Irene's food processor. With no appropriate harness for child restraint available, Ross was unceremoniously wedged into the cutlery drawer. His tiny body was clamped firmly between a selection of kitchen utensils and Julia Child's *Mastering the Art of French Cooking*. From this supine position he spent an oblivious afternoon monitoring the swirling rounds of the ceiling fan and feasting on the odd spoonful of cake mix.

Malcolm, Cunningham Holt and Nate Grubbs were dispatched to the wardrobe in the master bedroom of Chalet 3 with the express purpose of retrieving the shotgun. Regardless of Bill's reservations, the People's Committee had agreed that Irene's 'scene' in reception would be all the more attention-grabbing if accompanied by a firearm of some sort. Though Roger Heinz talked constantly of heavy artillery, his actual collection of weapons included nothing more threatening than a sharpened tin opener.

Nate Grubbs' now legendary shotgun had been borrowed

from a former colleague in the Fall of 1985 and remained the only firearm on the cul-de-sac. Late summer 1985 had been a particularly humid season. Raccoons and other wildish creatures, normally inclined to hide out under porch and attic, had been sweated onto suburban streets, for the most part ferociously unimpressed with the change of scenery. There had been a preternaturally high number of rabid possum attacks in the greater Portland area. Several small children had lost limbs and facial appendages. An elderly man in Selwood had slept soundly, anesthetized on hay fever medication, whilst a posse of marauding possums chewed right through his left wrist. The mayor had cautioned Portland's residents to arm themselves appropriately against the possibility of further violent attacks. Nate Grubbs, sixty-seven and still blessed with un-spectacled vision, had been appointed guardian of the cul-de-sac and acquired a firearm in preparation.

Though the Baptist Retirement Village had glided towards Thanksgiving without so much as a possum poop sighting, Nate Grubbs had grown accustomed to patrolling the turn circle, shotgun cocked against his shoulder, primed to protect his friends and neighbors. Originally he'd intended to return the borrowed gun once the rainy season set in and most giant rodents turned their attention towards hibernation. However, by the end of September 1985 the old man had developed a fondness for firearms and the way the cul-de-sac's ladies seemed to view him differently with a shotgun on his shoulder. He decided to hold on to the gun until absolutely forced to return it.

The situation remained unchanged until the week before Thanksgiving when Nate Grubbs, in a fit of self-pity brought on by the anniversary of his third wife's tragic death, swapped his single nightcap for half a bottle of whiskey. The following morning there were bullet holes in the bathroom ceiling and Nate could not recall if the gun had been placed in its customary storage spot – behind the pullover shelf in his wardrobe – cocked, or as was his normal custom, methodically unloaded with the safety on. With no means of ensuring the shotgun would not go off as soon as he opened the door, Nate Grubbs had determined never to open his wardrobe again. For months he'd worn the same burgundy pullover and slacks. Eventually, when practicality necessitated, he'd purchased a single set of secondary clothes which he'd been wearing in bipartisan rotation for the past six years. 'Better to lose a few pullovers than an arm,' he liked to say each time the anecdote was recounted to a fresh resident. Nate Grubbs' former colleague, under the mistaken belief that Portland was still plagued by armies of rabid possums, had yet to enquire about the return of his shotgun.

'How do we know it's safe to open the wardrobe now?' asked Malcolm Orange as the reconnaissance team shuffled across the cul-de-sac from Chalet 13 to 3.

'We don't,' replied Cunningham Holt grimly. 'All we can do is be careful and hope for the best.'

'It'll be fine,' added Nate Grubbs. Though not by birth an optimist, a series of lucky scratch cards and a dalliance with a fifty-five-year-old brunette in the parking lot of the 82nd Street Rite Aid had lately left him a great believer in good fortune. 'I'm almost sure I didn't load it.'

'Last week you said you'd put money on the damn thing being loaded.'

'It was eight years ago. You can hardly expect me to remember, Cunningham. We'll just open the door real slow and it'll be fine.'

Five minutes later the two old men found themselves standing in front of the wardrobe door. For safety's sake, they'd insisted Malcolm stand in the hallway and Malcolm, equally insistent upon risk reduction, had coerced the two old men into donning a pair of metallic mixing bowls for helmets. From a distance they looked like First World War soldiers. Up close they looked like two senile old men in mixing bowls, storming a flat-pack wardrobe.

'You take the lead, Cunningham,' urged Nate Grubbs, suddenly convinced that the shotgun was not only loaded but cocked to go off at the slightest movement.

Cunningham Holt reached for the wardrobe handle, turned it ninety-five degrees clockwise and without further ado began to slowly open the door. Through the opening door Nate Grubbs could make out a slim, ever-expanding slice of pullovers, pants and dress shirts. He was just beginning to mentally match an outfit for next year's Thanksgiving Turkey and Tipples Tea Dance when the bedroom door burst open, admitting first Malcolm and then Irene. As Irene tripped on the carpet edge, an entire tray full of coffee mugs came flinging free of her hands, hurtling towards Cunningham Holt. Most of the scalding hot coffee made contact with his face and neck whilst a smaller amount continued its trajectory, splattering the bedroom walls with a garish constellation of mud-colored teardrops. Nate Grubbs remained almost entirely protected behind the bedroom door. Malcolm was a muddle of arms and disappearing legs, tangling on the pastel-blue carpet as he tried to drag Irene back through the bedroom door. All were caught in a single moment of great stillness and then, like the beginning of the universe, everything happened suddenly, all at once, with great noise. In the ensuing melee Cunningham Holt drew back, yanking open the wardrobe door and instigating a landslide of V-neck pullovers, polyester slacks and the infamous shotgun, cocked and more than relieved to unload its contents upon impact with the bedroom floor.

The sound of a shotgun emptying into the tiny boxed room was the loudest thing Malcolm had ever heard. Instinctively he covered his eyes and ears. The smell sneaked through, sharp and metallic as a thousand fireworks recently spent. The inside of his ears clogged up with the memory of gunfire. He heard, as if through a blanket, Irene wheedling over and over, 'I thought you might want a coffee, I thought you might want a coffee,' Nate Grubbs, crumpled behind the bedroom door, screaming like a stuck child, and from the floor, directly in front of the wardrobe, the ungodly silence of Cunningham Holt. The silence was by far the worst.

Malcolm Orange opened his eyes, hands first and then eyelids, undrawing like leaden blinds. Cunningham Holt was leaking all over the bedroom carpet. A black, red hole, ragged and raging as the unplugged mouth of a volcano, had eaten up the centre of his belly. Blood was around him and over him and hovering from the ceiling in demonic constellations of dots and drags. His mouth moved up and down, in and out, as if attempting to chew on something much too big to swallow. No words came out. Malcolm Orange recognized death as it lay beside him heaving laboriously. He had, over the years, witnessed the untimely death of many, many old people. In the final instance they had all gone quietly. Blood and guns were a brand-new evil. Malcolm Orange did not know how to manage such a messy death. He placed both hands like wide-fingered butterflies over the wound and attempted to stem the bleed. After a few minutes Nate Grubbs sobered up and ran, as quickly as his lumbago would allow, to Bill and Irene's for backup. Irene remained, hovering in the corner, mopping the blood and coffee stains with a pillow slip as she continued to mutter her mantra, 'I thought you might want a coffee, I thought you might want a coffee.'

Malcolm Orange ignored her. None of this could be corrected by apportioning blame. As he held his friend's insides together he prayed to the Jesus God, a torrent of his own homemade prayers: prayers for healing and wholeness, prayers for miracles, prayers like Band-Aids for the disappearing.

Nothing changed. Each minute Cunningham Holt seemed further deflated; a snowman settling into the thaw. When the last bloody gush had left him and the burgundy halo quit expanding beneath his back, Cunningham Holt gave a little shiver, a noise as slight and insignificant as gravel settling. His left marble loosed itself and rolled down his cheek, onto the carpet and under Nate Grubbs' bed. The empty eye socket stared up at Malcolm. He could see the blood and muscles; jaundiced, white knots supporting a ham-pink cave. Malcolm Orange prayed all the louder for the empty eye. As he prayed, turning every so often to check if help had arrived, Cunningham Holt escaped through his fingers, royal red and sticky, staining his shorts and sneakers with an unwashable darkness.

It was decades before the door finally opened. The relief, when it arrived, was solid enough to swallow. In the interim the years had fallen off Malcolm Orange until he found himself a small child, desperate to defer responsibility to any consenting adult. He'd expected salvation to come in the form of an ambulance, or at very least Roger Heinz, who boasted regularly of surgical procedures performed, blind and without anesthetic, in Army field hospitals. Instead, he pivoted, arms still implanted in Cunningham Holt's stomach, to find his mother, framed in the doorway, an enormous electric wheelchair lodged in the hallway behind her. The shock caused him to topple backwards into the offending wardrobe. His mother gave him no time to recover.

'Get him in the wheelchair, Malcolm!' she said firmly.

'Where have you been, mama?' Malcolm fired back. There were a hundred thousand questions, prickling like unburst popcorn kernels, at the back of his head.

'No time for questions, Malcolm. Get Cunningham into the wheelchair, now. We need to get him out of here.'

As Malcolm, Martha and Cunningham Holt's supine corpse zipped across the cul-de-sac, the People's Committee for Remembering Songs emerged from Bill and Irene's to amble arthritically behind them. They made for an odd-looking parade; the blind, the halt, the doddering lame and the disappearing, trundling after an almost dead man in a stolen wheelchair. Their route took them past Miss Pamela Richardson as she sat, upended in the middle of the turn circle, lamenting the recent loss of her electric wheelchair. The wheelchair had been liberated minutes earlier, a sacrifice for the greater good of the group. Martha Orange had instigated the theft. This, it was later noted, was the slightest and most excusable of her recent crimes.

Having intercepted Nate Grubbs on his frantic dash from Chalet 3 to 11, Malcolm's mother had made a quick assessment of the situation. An ambulance seemed the most sensible option available. However, Martha Orange, confused by the old man's mumbled hysterics, instinctively wished to protect her eldest son from the possibility of a manslaughter charge. 'Let's not get the authorities involved,' she'd announced, utilizing every ounce of false bravado still available to a child dumper, caught in the act of flight. 'We'll take Cunningham to the Center. They'll be able to sort him out in the Center.' Nate Grubbs, who was well-aware of the kind of shit the shotgun had landed him in, readily agreed. Mere seconds later Pamela Richardson had cruised down her driveway, patchwork quilt tucked around her wizened knees in anticipation of an afternoon nap. 'We'll need something to transport Cunningham,' Martha Orange had muttered, her musings loaded with heavy insinuation. Without further ado, for his own scalp was on the line, Nate Grubbs tipped Miss Richardson into the turn circle and seized her electric wheelchair.

'It's an emergency!' he'd yelled as he fled the scene of the crime. 'I'll explain later!'

Miss Pamela Richardson was not a fortunate woman. All her life she'd suffered terribly with excessive facial hair. She was allergic to alcohol and rain, a particularly unfortunate combination for a lifetime resident of the Pacific Northwest. The years had proven her incapable of keeping a plant, pet or gentleman longer than eighteen months. Her first husband had passed away at the ungodly age of twenty-three, victim of a severe allergic reaction to cream cheese. The second husband had drowned after tripping into the touch and feel tank at Sea World, and the third, terrified by the untimely demise of husbands one and two, had run off with the mail man as soon as he caught wind of his new bride's terrible misfortune. Miss Richardson herself had lost the use of her right leg after tumbling, nose first, from the open door of a Trimet bus and two months later caught her crutch in the mechanics of a shopping mall escalator, losing the use of her left leg in the ensuing crush.

Over time Miss Pamela Richardson had come to instinctively fear the worst. Motivated by a particularly sinister session with a Mexican fortune teller at the previous year's Cinco de Mayo festival, she'd spent all sleeping moments since pivoting the turn circle with her electric wheelchair locked leftwards. 'It's like this,' she explained to all those visitors who stopped to ask or offer assistance, 'the Grim Reaper's after me. I can see him coming when I got my eyes open. As long as I keep moving while I'm sleeping the old bastard won't be able to catch up.' On the afternoon of the shotgun incident, finding herself unceremoniously grounded before the afternoon siesta could even begin, Miss Richardson lay crumpled in the middle of the turn circle, lamenting her chronic misfortune. Like the crippled kid incapable of keeping up with the Pied Piper, she fluctuated between an enormous shame and an anger, loud as the Liberty Bell, which boomed and bled against the People's Committee as they trooped past, too preoccupied to notice the left-behind.

Malcolm Orange, running to keep up with his mother as she steered the parade towards its unknown destination, permitted himself one final question.

'Where are we going, mama?'

'To the Treatment Room. It's too late for anything else.'

'Oh,' said Malcolm Orange, 'we were already going there.' A certain symmetry had taken charge of the afternoon. Like a boomerang returning home, the People's Committee had been dragged back to their original plan. Furthermore, Malcolm's mother had returned to the Baptist Retirement Village, acting the responsible adult he'd longed to see these last few months. Malcolm Orange began to believe that everything, even the disappearing, might be fixable. If the Treatment Room lived up to its promise, he might even reconsider his longstanding grudge with God. Malcolm Orange placed a hand on the small of his mother's back. He wanted to reassure her that he was not angry. He wanted to add his own spindly weight to the effort of pushing Cunningham Holt up the hill to the Center. He wanted to hold his mother together.

The sensation of Malcolm's hand, resting damply at the base

of her spine, was a lead weight on Martha Orange's shoulder, a reminder that she had not returned to the Baptist Retirement Village for love or duty. Rather, the godless pursuit of her credit card and, should the opportunity arise, her winter coat.

– Chapter 12 –

Vietnam

Trip Blue had not always been the Director of a retirement village for elderly Oregonians. Previously he'd occupied, for almost ten years, an unrivaled and exorbitantly paid position as plastic surgeon to Los Angeles's nouveau riche. Before California there had been a brief, ladder-climbing stint as the prodigious assistant to a controversial New York-based micro-surgeon, and, before this, Vietnam.

Trip Blue had never been to Vietnam himself. He'd seen pictures. The pictures were enough to put him off and the stories sealed the deal. Trip was the kind of young man who could not go without brushing his teeth before bed. He struggled to picture himself dispersing napalm or going hand-to-hand with an angry VC. Neither did he suppose himself capable of lying around for weeks in stagnant paddy fields or, in adherence to the frontline trend, smearing peanut butter on his toes in the hope that some Vietnamese rat might bestow upon him a bite infected enough to guarantee a one-way ticket back to America.

Vietnam, Trip Blue quickly concluded, was not his sort of war. Ideally, he'd prefer something more hygienic, something snappier, with less actual death. Subsequently he'd weathered the war years from the relative comfort of a prestigious east coast academic facility. Asthma, and an entirely fabricated two-week affair with a male lab technician (luridly documented for the benefit of any draft officer skeptical enough to ask questions, in six none too convincing 'love' letters and a single blurred Polaroid snapshot), ensured that Trip Blue had ample excuse to avoid the draft.

Trip Blue began his medical training in the Fall of 1971 and, as the Vietnam war dribbled catastrophically into its sixth, seventh and eighth years, he'd shut his ears to the growing American unease, ignored the sea of angry placards sprouting in front of the Student Union, and focused on his education. He'd studied the medical greats for days at a time, pouring over thousand-page manuals in the dusty upper echelons of the university library. When he'd run out of books Trip began paying the more gullible undergraduates to let him practice his doctoring; first on warts and minor abrasions and later, as his confidence grew, on diabetes, eczema, broken bones and various congenital heart conditions. He learned fast. He had few disasters.

Very occasionally one of his experiments went pear-shaped. Patients passed out or went into cardiac failure. Shoulders refused to set, even under extreme manipulation. On one notable occasion, the appendix could not be located, and when, using a cigarette lighter and sterilized salad fork, Trip had finally tracked down the infected organ, it seemed attached to the intestines by a substance as elastic and unyielding as Laffy Taffy. Some situations proved themselves beyond the capability of a DIY medical student.

Trip Blue was not yet a megalomaniac. He knew when to concede defeat and on the rare occasions when he found himself out of his depths during a procedure, simply deferred to the authorities, calling ambulances, making drive-by deposits at the local ER, and silencing his victims with a hefty bursary, siphoned from one of his father's offshore bank accounts. Many of Trip's 'unsuccessful' patients were marked for life, yet more than happy to trade a kidney or minor burn for the possibility of graduating debt-free. A code of silence settled around Trip Blue's medical research. It was not so much fear which kept his patients quiet, as an unvoiced belief that the young man was a genius; a Hippocrates or Pasteur destined to discover cures for any number of twentieth-century diseases. In lending one's armpit or uterus to his experiments, his patients could later claim a footnote in the annals of medical history. By night Trip Blue experimented in his home-constructed operating theatre. By day he played the academic overachiever, drinking in the compulsory lectures and plaguing his professors with the kind of spiraling, sycophantic questions which had them consulting their academic superiors for satisfactory answers. Whilst no one appreciated Trip Blue as a person, students and staff alike envied him his telescopic mind.

In June 1975 Trip Blue graduated top of his class, triumphing over the three hundred scalpel-wielding junior surgeons who stood squinting beside him in their class photo. These stiff-necked men and formidable young women were the cream of the medical crop, destined for a lifetime of unsociable hours, sterile scrubs and miracle-working. Each was, for the most part, obsessed with the gravity and greatness of their vocation; gladly working weekends and holidays without asking for overtime, rarely remembering the birthdays of parents or siblings and, in moments of brave honesty, confessing that people were much easier to approach once anesthetized. Trip Blue could not have cared less about any of them. Trip found the majority of people thoroughly unnecessary. He had, however, in the final term of his final year, met and married Soren James's mother.

Magda Mulaney first caught his eye in the science library

elevator. At the time she'd been carrying an armful of molecular biology textbooks, the rims of her glasses barely visible above the topmost volume. Two days later, ten minutes into their first date in the campus coffee house, he was disappointed to discover Magda a junior librarian and not the teenage genius he'd presumed. Over their first mutual cappuccino, Magda made stilted attempts at small talk whilst Trip glared furiously from the opposite end of the couch, silently battling his own conscience.

Trip Blue did not believe in love. He could not see himself at any point in the future developing a belief in love. There was simply no scientific justification for such atrocious sentimentality. Great wealth and a strong jaw line had conspired to ensure Trip Blue would have no problems, past, present or future, in gratifying his sexual whims. He did not need a wife. However, as he dredged the last frothy drops from his coffee cup, Trip concluded a wife might help to establish his reputation as a respectable professional. He was neither particularly attracted nor repulsed by Magda. On the strength of their first date she seemed ill-inclined to question anything he said. If Trip could not have a genius for a wife, an unassuming simpleton was the next best thing. The years would prove Magda formidable beyond his initial assumptions and Trip would come to realize that libraries were not the natural habitat of docile women.

On the eve of their second date Trip kissed his not-yet-wife perfunctorily by the staff parking lot. 'You'll do,' he said, observing Magda at arm's length. Magda had laughed drily, imagining this a joke, and, four weeks after their first deeply mediocre kiss, agreed to become his wife. At the time she'd seen no further than a much-needed exodus from her parents' duplex. Later, when the honeymoon blinkers fell off, Magda Blue wondered what exactly had attracted her to a man more driven, more ruthless and inconsiderate than any of the three hundred egocentric obsessives in his graduating class.

Dr and Mrs Blue began their married life by relocating to the suburbs of Harrisburg, Pennsylvania. Pennsylvania had never appealed to Magda. Born in Brooklyn and raised in downtown Chicago, she found the state excessively scenic and the people prone to engage in endless, circular contemplation of the weather, the church and, during the warmer months, baseball. She could not understand why her new husband's galloping intellect had deposited them in the most backward spot on the eastern seaboard. For three years she languished in the Harrisburg lending library, a two-story prefab crouching awkwardly in the shadow of the United Methodist Church. As she stacked and stamped a lifetime's worth of plastic-backed Mills and Boon novels (the library's most popular lends, farm manuals and the Holy Bible excepted), she read her way through the complete canon of Russian literature, special-ordered from head office, and grew fat on grilled cheese sandwiches. Though far from a provincial backwater, Harrisburg was the smallest place Magda had ever lived. She felt like Gulliver lumbering over the little people every time she stepped outside. The local women, burnt out on generations of short-loan army personnel, refused to acknowledge her. Magda did not take this personally. There was a line, impassable as the Berlin Wall, separating the locals from the army wives.

However, the wives and girlfriends of the few military men still stationed at the base also kept their distance, withholding dinner party invites and acknowledging her only when they came to borrow the latest arrival from the Romance section. Magda Blue was too mortified to challenge their standoffishness. She said nothing, though her loneliness felt like a freezing fog.

Everyone else's husband had served in Vietnam: a single tour of duty, a second or, in a handful of cases, a soul-destroying third. These men suffered from night sweats and terrifying hallucinations. Their heads were full of horror stories, impossible to share. Many were missing arms, legs and large chunks of skin. They were not the men they had been on their wedding days. Their children adapted, learning to hold their laughter still for fear of a whipping belt. Their wives wore the martyred look of beleaguered patriots even as they ran their errands and emptied their trash cans and collected their buzz-cut progeny from little league. Magda Blue could not claim membership to this club. Each time she walked down Main Street she carried the shame of her draft-dodging husband, the only non-serving civilian stationed in the town's military hospital. While it hurt to be so universally ignored, Magda refused to confront any of the women. She saw herself a traitor by marriage and could not spite the ladies their patriotic spirit. However, it was not patriotism which kept the army wives from her front door. Each of them had heard rumors of Dr Blue's 'experiments' on H Wing. Gossip traveled fast in a town as tight as Phoenixville and within three months of their arrival, Trip had been branded a latter-day Mengele, and Magda, his evil muse.

The truth was a much lonelier horror. As the months progressed Magda Blue saw less and less of her husband. She ate her meals alone, watching reruns of *I Love Lucy* on the television set she'd installed at one end of the kitchen table. The freezer was bursting with Tupperware servings of pot roast and spaghetti dinners, lovingly prepared in anticipation of a husband who never came home. After a few months, the freezer refused to swallow any more of her false hopes and Magda quit cooking. She ate grilled cheese for dinner as well as lunch and swelled to twice her normal weight. She gave up on the gloomy Russians and began thieving Mills and Boon novels from the Romance section, silently berating her own stupidity when the racy sections got her hot and bothered in an empty bed. When the loneliness became too much for Magda, she lifted the telephone and cried for hours into the handset, her sobs harmonizing with the dialing tone. The act of pressing a telephone receiver to her ear helped her pretend that someone out there was listening. On good weeks Trip came home once, maybe twice. On bad weeks Magda felt like a widow.

On the rare occasions when her husband appeared on the lawn, squinting at his own front door like an out-of-state visitor, Magda hid her fury from the neighbors, greeting him with arms and eyes and a carefully painted smile. Once she had him over the threshold Magda was a landslide. She could not help herself.

'Is it another woman?' she'd ask as Trip threw a duffel bag of laundry at her feet and fell exhausted into bed.

'Don't be ridiculous,' he'd reply.

'Drugs? Drink? Gambling?'

Labored silence.

'What then, Trip? I haven't seen you in days. What have you been doing?'

'Research,' he'd reply and immediately fall into a deep, comatose slumber, often drifting in and out of consciousness for thirty-six hours at a time. When he awoke he'd expect her to make love to him, silently and without preamble or afterthought. Whilst Trip would always instigate the physical moments of their marriage, he never seemed entirely present in the act. Squirming under the weight of her husband, Magda felt less a person and more a collection of muscles and organs, straining and constraining in strict obedience to their biological function. Every movement felt like an incision. Even their climaxes were mechanical, like factory parts, forced to release unnecessary pressure. Their exchanges began to resemble a suburban hit and run. It was impossible, she soon realized, for her husband to leave his science in the hospital.

Two hours after waking, having showered, repacked his duffel bag and consumed an enormous breakfast, Trip Blue would always be gone. Over the years Magda tried everything to make her husband talk. She hung over his breakfast plate, skillet in hand. She crossed her legs and played the miserly lover. She yelled and screamed and cried her eyelids bloody red. Yet she could not force her husband to divulge so much as a cursory overview of what his so-called 'research' entailed.

When first enlisted, Trip Blue himself had never heard of H Wing. His career compass was firmly stuck on big time success and as such he fully anticipated a lifetime of cutting-edge neurosurgery. America had other plans for Trip Blue. His futuristic grade average had attracted the attention of a specialized division of the US Army's Medical Corps. Ignoring the express advice of young Trip's academic tutor who'd noted in the boy a streak of something cold and opportunistic, this group of highly trained men, and a single, somewhat masculine woman, had summoned Trip to the Pentagon on the morning after his graduation ceremony. Trip Blue had obliged unquestioningly. He'd always known himself to be a genius and had waited years for just such a phone call. Over a three-day period, during which he was only allowed to speak to his interrogators by telephone, Trip was held in a sterile, constantly lit room and grilled mercilessly until his captors – satisfied that he was in fact the bona fide genius his resume suggested – offered him vast amounts of money to relocate to Phoenixville, Pennsylvania. Trip Blue accepted on the spot. The money meant nothing to him, the location, less; but the research project had him salivating the second it slid across the table, sandwiched inconspicuously within a manila folder, stamped 'Classified'. Returning to campus, Trip hired a U-Haul, packed up his wife, his textbooks and the few worldly possessions he'd accumulated over three years of medical school and drove through the night, arriving early the next evening at the crumbling military hospital on the outskirts of Phoenixville.

For the next four years Trip Blue sacrificed himself on the tiled corridors of H Wing. He went days without eating, allowing his hair to go unkempt and uncut for months on end. Whilst no actual infidelity ever occurred, Trip forgot about his wife. He felt like a man adrift, teetering on the edge of something tremendous. The Treatment Room consumed every second of his waking thoughts and, more often than not, left deep indentations on his dream life.

The Treatment Room nestled in the crook of H Wing's two wards. The left ward housed some twenty-four Terminal cases in four open dorms, each containing six cots arranged to afford the best angle at a solitary television set, wall-mounted. To the right, twenty-four Delusionals were kept in single-cell rooms, locked and bolted for their own safety. Each of H Wing's forty-eight residents, and the majority of the doctors and nurses, had recently returned from Vietnam. All staff members, save the cleaning staff – daily visitors from the civilian world – knew better than to mention the war. Instead they changed bandages, emptied drains and three times daily positioned a tray of nutritionally balanced gloop upon their patients' laps.

Only a handful of these trained professionals had been granted access to the Treatment Room. The others, those individuals too inexperienced or untrustworthy to handle classified information, satiated their curiosity with staff room speculation about the constant stream of patients entering and exiting the Treatment Room. An eight digit punch code ensured that all but the highest ranking staff members had no idea what was happening on the other side of the double-thick door. Despite his medical pedigree Trip Blue had been working on H Wing subservient to the whims of a particularly forbidding consultant, known locally as God, for the better part of six months before he was entrusted with the eight precious digits.

God had invented the Treatment Room. The idea had come to him during his fifth tour of duty. God had always been a soldier. Even after four visits to Vietnam he'd been unable to settle back into the civilian world of shopping malls and washing machines and had requested a transfer back to Saigon. Vietnam was no longer the draw it had been five years previously. Less than a week after approaching his commanding officer, God was back on the Ho Chi Minh trail enjoying the atmosphere. The odds were against him. Most soldiers didn't survive a second visit and God was now contemplating his fifth consecutive summer in the East.

Fate caught up with him when he was least expecting it. One minute he'd been taking a leak behind the burnt-out remains of a Vietnamese hut, the next minute, still shaking the last drops of piss from his rapidly wilting penis, he'd found himself staring into the slanty black eyes of a pair of gun-toting VC. The rest of God's unit, riddled with bullets and bayonet holes, were in various states of decease as he was dragged, cursing the entire Oriental race, to a rudimentary prisoner of war camp on the jungle's edge.

God was to spend the next eighteen months locked in a bamboo cage. With barely enough room for a single man to sit comfortably, the addition, two days after his incarceration, of an emaciated young private from Tennessee meant that the two men were forced to take turns standing and sitting. God was further frustrated to find his cellmate entirely ignorant of any conversation subject beyond the sports arena. 'Jesus, son,' the older man was often heard yelling, 'just my goddamn luck to get myself locked up with a halfwit redneck.' The boy could only shrug limply, for the bamboo roof impeded any sort of dynamic movement and, in lieu of conversation, offer to stand for an extra half hour. When he finally succumbed to the Vietnamese torture techniques and his wild, nocturnal yabberings got him shot right in front of God's eyes, the older man was somewhat relieved. Lying diagonally, he could now sleep almost fully reclined and was finally able to think, unencumbered by the teenager's constant commentary on the baseball games of his youth.

God marked the weeks in fingernail slithers and kept this rudimentary calendar in the breast pocket of his army shirt. By the third month he'd grown used to the perpetual itch of disembodied nails scratching at his rib cage. God grew thin. On an in-breath he could distinguish all but the lowest ribs protruding through his skin. He developed a perpetual leg twitch, a grimy, hacking cough, diarrhea, foot rot and an energetic colony of lice in either armpit, but he did not die. As the weeks turned to months, God became more and more convinced that Vietnam would not be his undoing. There was no justification for this belief. God was older, thinner and grumpier by far than any of his fellow prisoners, yet he remained convinced of his own immortality.

As he lay on the floor of his cell, the bamboo slats turning him slowly corrugated, God watched in horror as dozens of young Americans passed through the camp and within a matter of days, sometimes even hours, lost the will to live. Seemingly fit and healthy young bucks, half his age or less, were so terrified by the possibility of VC torture the damage was done long before the ropes or irons came out to play. Whilst God gritted his teeth through terrible beatings and deprivations, many of his fellow soldiers capitulated at the merest mention of tooth pulling. The effect, once noted, was undeniable; the correct words, even when uttered in a barely discernible pidgin English, could suck the life right out of a man. Thick-chested quarterbacks and wrestlers began to disintegrate as soon as the camp's 'welcome committee' uttered their customary speech for newcomers ('You want to die quick man . . . you want to die much slow?') whilst weedy little SOBs from the suburbs seemed impervious to all but the most brutally physical torture techniques. The mind was much more complex than God had ever imagined. Some strange connection existed between the barely perceivable blips inside a man's brain and the actual bones and muscles which kept him human from one minute to the next.

Though only moderately scientific, God began to hypothesize. The right sentiments, carefully spoken, could catch inside a man, resonating with his deepest subconscious understanding of himself. An apparently healthy man would curl up and die if the desire to admit defeat was lodged somewhere inside his subconscious. It was impossible to spot such a fault line from the outside. Cripples and crazy men appeared no more inclined to give up than the blond-blessed healthy. God began to ask questions. If death words could draw the life right out of a man, might there be other words – healing, healthy, life-rich words – which could stir the spirits up and appeal to those who had not yet made a pact with despair? He tested this theory on the men in the cell directly in front of his. Over a five-week period, all but one of these boys died, victims of the relentless cruelty of the Vietnamese guards.

The final kid, a mere slip of a nineteen-year-old, refused to join them. The left side of his body was red-raw and blistering, covered in napalm burns. His left arm hung awkwardly at an angle which suggested permanent dislocation. His eyes were saucers circulating an emaciated face and yet while the VC dragged him out daily for a fresh round of beatings, God watched on in amazement as the kid – subject to his own fledgling experiments – seemed to grow stronger each day.

Each time their captors were out of earshot God would press his face into the space between the bamboo bars of his cage and holler encouraging sentiments across the ten-foot gulf which separated his cell from the next.

'You're getting better every day, son.'

'Your skin is healing. Your bones are setting. You're growing fat as a Thanksgiving turkey.'

'You'll be one hundred percent fighting fit by the weekend.'

And the kid, without ever acknowledging assent, simply got better. His blistered skin smoothed over. His arm slipped back into the socket and began to bend like a regular arm. His cheeks, which had succumbed to the cavernous limitations of a boiled rice diet, began to fill out, exposing a handsome midwestern face, albeit positively filthy. Bolstered by this success, God began experimenting on the cells to left, right and center back. Positive results were few and far between. Three out of every four test cases ended up in the funeral pit at the back of the camp. However, the success stories were so dramatic, so unbelievably astounding, God refused to be discouraged. Blind soldiers had their sight returned. The lame, though far too cramped to leap, experienced a miraculous increase in movement. Lungs unclogged and breathed openly for the first time since they'd arrived in the East.

By the time the boys from home kicked in the gates of the camp, liberating the remaining twenty-five prisoners and allowing God to stand upright for the first time in eighteen months, he'd all but invented the Treatment Room in his head. It would take some six months of convincing to persuade the United States Army to grant research privileges to a man with no previous medical experience, and the project would require Top Secret classification to guard against the possibility of embarrassing mistakes, but the notion of post-conflict treatment which was both successful and virtually cost free was too tempting to pass over. God found himself dispatched to the armpit of Pennsylvania where he built a prototype Treatment Room: a closet-sized compartment (roughly the shape and size of his Vietnamese cell), walled on all four sides and ceiling with thick, shatterproof mirrors. Once completed, God opened the doors of his Treatment Room and welcomed in a steady stream of broken soldiers.

Oftentimes against their will, for the Treatment Room was disturbingly reminiscent of a prison cell, God locked his patients up with a 360-degree revelation of their most honest selves. Whilst they considered themselves from front, back, floor and roof, he spoke gentle yet firm words, carefully prepared. After a few weeks it became clear that the patients did not require personalized encouragements. A simple pre-recorded 'WISE UP' piped through a speaker system was enough to pique a man's deepest subconscious. These two words were bullets for the dying patients, whether they were aware of their own limited mortality or not. At the other end of the spectrum, God recorded incredible advances in the conditions of those patients not yet ready to give up.

'It's the truth,' God explained to a somewhat bewildered Trip Blue on his first day in Phoenixville. 'It's not mind control. It's not hypnotism. We're just peeling back the layers and letting them see themselves for what they really are. If a man's ready to give up, the Treatment Room'll give him the right to do it with dignity. If a man's fit to fight it out, the Treatment Room'll give him the balls to keep going.'

The results spoke for themselves. The Delusionals (H Wing slang for the soldiers who believed themselves better than they actually were) managed an average of two to three sessions before they simply closed their eyes and passed away, freeing up valuable hospital beds for the Terminals, a great group of men who, whilst physically scuppered, responded so positively to the Treatment Room they often began a session wheelchair-bound and ten minutes later waltzed out of the room, significantly mended.

'The mind,' God was wont to remind his staff at every given opportunity, 'controls the body,' and the ever-growing list of soldiers with baby skin where they'd once had burns, with legs and arms sprouting from the roots of hastily executed amputations, and bold, Magic Marker tattoos reminding them to 'wise up' scrawled on biceps and forearms, bore witness to this very fact. Trip Blue could not believe his own good fortune. He'd stumbled into the epicenter of cutting-edge medical research.

The Treatment Room did not surprise him. During his first months on H Wing, marking time as he waited on an eight-digit punch code, Trip had spent entire weekends camped out in the laundry closet wading through a Babel tower of medical textbooks and research papers. Psychological manipulation was no new phenomenon. Unscrupulous individuals and organizations had been exposing the minds of their enemies to diabolical torture techniques for centuries. Under pressure the human brain was pliable as unset Jell-O, inclined to conform to any loudly persistent message. Mind control had been around since the birth of humanity. However, the concept of manipulating the psyche to enhance or confound healing was something entirely new. Trip Blue was delighted to find himself tottering on the edge of tomorrow's world. Within a matter of weeks the Treatment Room and its prodigal patients had come to monopolize his every waking thought.

He worked forty-eight hour shifts, alternating his sleep patterns to complement God's so the Treatment Room could be manned around the clock. Science offered a framework for their research, war provided justification, and overleaping curiosity, fuel. Yet at the centre of the Treatment Room there remained a tight little miracle, impossible to quantify or explain. Medicine could claim no plausible explanation for the indefinable element which made one man susceptible to healing and the man in the next bed doomed. In the three years Trip Blue spent on H Wing, observing, collating and accumulating lever arch folders full of fastidious notes, he never once came close to understanding this mystery. Trip Blue was a logical man. Science was his religion. Not knowing bothered him dreadfully and it was this insatiable need to know which would drive him, almost twenty years after H Wing, to build his own rudimentary version of the Treatment Room and recommence his experiments on the elderly residents of the Baptist Retirement Village. Trip Blue would tell no one – neither his nursing staff, nor the middle-aged children who'd consigned their aging parents to his care, nor the doddering seniors themselves – what he was orchestrating in the Center's broom closet.

Christmas 1978 brought Trip Blue's time on H Wing to a premature halt, severing his relationship with God (whom he was beginning to hold in the sort of familial respect he'd previously assumed himself incapable of engendering) and almost destroying his medical career. The next twenty years would see him traipse from one side of the country to the other dabbling in neurosurgery and plastics, accumulating – and subsequently losing – a teenage daughter and never, not once ever (fearing the combined threats of the Armed Forces, the American Medical Association and FBI) attempting to manipulate the mind of another human being. God was dead to Trip. Post-Christmas 1978, communication between the two men was irrevocably severed and, though Trip Blue was never to hear of it, the older man hit the bottle like a back alley turncoat, pickling his liver in a record nine months and dying an anonymous, vagrant death in a Salvation Army hostel, almost one year to the day after H Wing folded. Despite a last-ditch attempt with a shaving mirror, God was incapable of healing himself. He died like an ordinary man; his final words, a hacking, phlegm-filled 'wise up'; his last coherent thought, the memory of his mother removing her hair pins in front of the bedroom dresser.

The events of Christmas 1978, consigned as they were to history and a handful of dusty confidential folders buried in the Pentagon's records department, had marked the beginning of the end for God and his erstwhile assistant. On the day before Christmas Eve, H Wing held its annual Festive Party. On the other side of town, Magda Blue, driven desperate with the loneliness, cried herself into a drunken stupor and forced her husband's best suit through the garbage disposal. Oblivious to this latest loss, Trip Blue commenced his last night on H Wing and, with little thought for the repercussions, killed a man, by accident with great deliberation.

The evening began without incident. Someone on the terminal ward was blasting *The Best of the Shangri-Las* from a portable record player whilst a handful of patients in festive party hats danced around with the junior nurses. Some danced in their wheelchairs, jerking forwards and backwards in a disco-like manner. In the far corner by the soft drinks machine two of the younger patients poked limply at a piñata. (A well-meaning orderly had spent the afternoon stuffing the piñata full of unused surgical gloves and Band-Aids. The patients, unaware and optimistic, poked on, hoping for coins, candy or at very least prescription drugs.)

An open bottle of Jack Daniels had been concealed behind the grey sofa in the dayroom. All five on-duty nurses, fully aware of the alcohol stash, had chosen to ignore their patients as they slipped noisily behind the sofa for a surreptitious slug. It was, they reminded each other behind cupped hands, a special occasion. The nurses were professionally superior. All their limbs were still attached and functional, allowing them to dance upright with no balancing aids. They wore party hats and full uniform. They were almost all called Sandra; each and every one popped from the same efficient pod. For one holy night they did not complain when the older men with hands found them on the dance floor. They pretended to love the Shangri-Las. They ate Christmas cake in cardboard dishes and made non-alcoholic punch in a bedpan. It was hilarious to serve punch in a bedpan. Everyone thought this was hilarious.

At seven o'clock Trip Blue drove into the parking lot, having left his wife sobbing on the kitchen floor, a meat cleaver clasped melodramatically in one hand. As he locked his car and strode purposefully towards H Wing, he realized that his Christmas tie was safely tucked away in the bedroom closet. He felt the lack of it dangling coolly against his shirtfront. Trip Blue did not, as a rule, acknowledge Christmas but it was important to maintain the trust of his patients and the Christmas tie, recently ordered from the Sears, Roebuck catalog, had been a calculated attempt to appear the everyman. As he absentmindedly ran his fingers along his shirtfront, Trip's eye was drawn to one of the recently admitted patients, fully dressed in civilian clothes and dashing, with suspicious alacrity, towards the camp's perimeter fence.

Up on the main ward, though someone had stood on *The Best of the Shangri-Las*, the party had not stopped for lack of music. Patients made their own music, forming whistles from catheter tubes, beating rhythm on their exposed ribs, singing folk songs with their fingers crossed. At one end of the wing a Terminal stood on an office chair shouting loudly, 'I only have three weeks to live.' This was a terrible lie. As he screamed, the office chair undulated gently, mocking his hysterical prophesies. God was not interested in joining the festivities. From his office behind the nurses' station he monitored the drowsy progression of fun and finger-picked at a limp tuna sandwich. Through the slatted blinds he watched a young nurse, hair tucked adamantly behind both ears, as she danced with a male patient. The man was missing both arms. He wore the nurse's arms draped around his neck, grasping him in an awkward, swaying headlock. Under the Christmas lights the man looked like a giant, flailing anemone. Transparent tubes and wires dripped in and out of his chest, releasing plastic bags of clear liquid and rust-red blood. Around his ankle similar bags of tea-stained liquid drained away his sins, one bladder-full at a time. This man had spent the previous two mornings in the Treatment Room and his spirits, like the gummy scars where his elbows had once been, were beginning to experience significant improvement. Had the Treatment Room lasted into the New Year, he might have greeted 1979 with a pair of perfectly functional replacement arms.

God stared at the man. He had nothing better to do. The

Treatment Room was shut down for the holidays. God watched his children like tropical fish in a Chinese restaurant. Half of them would be dead by New Year's Day. The other half, he presumed, would be waltzing again within weeks. God had come to despise them all. Where Trip Blue's scientific curiosity kept him keen on the patients, if only from a medical perspective, God had spent one Christmas too many on H Wing. He was beginning to feel the lack of an ordinary life: a wife, a family and a stack of earnest, if somewhat clumsily wrapped, Christmas gifts. The first nervous prickle of a migraine edged across the bridge of his nose. Christmas Eve 1978 would mark God's four hundred and fiftieth night shift in a row. He had begun to dream of leaving Phoenixville, Pennsylvania and moving to somewhere less miraculous; Texas most likely, or North Dakota. God had just about decided to hand in his notice when the office door was flung open, admitting a middle-aged man (either dead, drunk or unconscious), slumped sideways in a standard issue wheelchair. Milliseconds later the arms, shoulders and furious pink face of Trip Blue appeared at the helm of the wheelchair, a huge wad of classified cardboard folders tucked into his armpit like an unfurled wing.

'Bastard was running off with our research,' he puffed, struggling to contain his fury. 'So I knocked him out.'

'You hit a patient?' God asked.

'Hell no – tranquilizer dart. I keep them in my car, in case of emergencies.'

God wondered – not for the first time – what sort of a person he'd taken on as an assistant. It was not yet obvious that the man, now depositing goopy, transparent drool strands on the office carpet, would prove to be their collective undoing and so God offered Trip Blue a styrofoam cup of coffee and, perching on the edge of his desk, attempted to address the situation. In the corridor outside his window, one of the Terminals, having sacrificed the last of his inhibitions to whiskey and prescription meds, was dancing shirtless to the Rolling Stones. God would have given anything in the world to swap places with this man.

'Right,' he said, sipping from his own styrofoam cup, 'tell me the worst.'

The worst was pretty bad. A short 'conversation' in the parking lot – a conversation which God, fully aware of Trip Blue's ruthless streak, presumed to have included firearms or other 'conversational aides' – had revealed that this particular patient was not actually a patient, but rather an undercover agent, planted on H Wing to gather evidence of their research project. Trip Blue suspected Russian involvement. Thankfully the man was still in the assessment stage of Treatment and though he'd managed to seduce one of the orderlies into giving him access to the file room, had yet to see the inside of the Treatment Room.

'Thank God for that,' said God. 'We'll just hand him over to the powers that be and they can deal with him.'

'We can't do that, sir,' replied Trip. 'He's seen the files. He knows what we're doing here. He could compromise everything ... all your research. Plus, well, I might have been a little less than gentle with him in the parking lot.'

God sighed and turned the man's face gently towards the light, exposing in the unforgiving glare of his desk lamp a pair of perfectly formed boot marks. God was too tired to be furious. He felt every one of his previous four hundred and forty nine night shifts acutely. He wrapped the sodden remains of his tuna sandwich in a square of tinfoil, drained the remnants of his coffee and prepared to wash his hands of the matter. Trip Blue could be reported, the man handed over to the military police and, with a bit of luck, the whole G-D project put on ice for the foreseeable future. Of course there would be mountains of paperwork, most likely a formal warning and a black mark on his otherwise gleaming resume, but God had already begun to see the possibility peeking through the shit. This could be exactly the emergency exit he'd been waiting for.

'Don't worry, I have a plan. I'm pretty sure the guy's a Delusional. I haven't quite finished his assessment and, as you well know, he hasn't had his first session in the Treatment Room but I've got a nose for them. I can usually spot a Delusional a mile away.'

'And?' asked God, hoping to high hell and reason the younger man wasn't going to suggest what he was thinking.

'If I'm right and we give him a really strong dose in the Treatment Room, well he'll probably, you know . . . react in a way which could really help us out—'

'You mean, die?' interjected God, his voice stretching into a supersonic squeak as he watched his long-anticipated emergency exit begin to slide out of view.

'Exactly. We'll mark him down with all the other Delusional patients, put the folders back in the file room and no one will be any the wiser. It's not murder. You know as well as I do that all Delusionals want to die. We'd actually be helping him out.'

'Definitely not.'

'It's my whole career, sir. That guy'll press charges if he ever wakes up.'

'I don't give a flying shit, Trip. You screwed up, you deal with the consequences.'

'Alright God, you're going to play it like that? Then I'll be taking you down too. Matter of fact, I'll be using you to cushion my fall. It's not like there aren't corners cut round here every day of the week. We're hardly a conventional medical facility and I'll bet the Pentagon guys start stepping back quick sharp as soon as the shit hits the fan. How'd you like to spend your retirement in Fort Leavenworth?'

God felt like he'd been around since the beginning of time. There was no point in arguing with Trip Blue. He wearily removed his sports jacket, slipped his arms into the white coat which hung like a skinned ghost on the back of his office door and prepared for career suicide.

Outside the office the Christmas Party had descended into a drunken rabble. Two patients and a part-time nurse had come to blows over the last of the nacho cheese dip. They sat in opposite corners of the day room, like soiled featherweights, nursing cut lips and bloody noses as they nibbled shattered tortilla chips straight from the floor. The corridors of H Wing were littered with deflating balloons and fallen comrades, slumped and sliding down the pastel green walls in their standard issue military pajamas. Trip Blue steered the wheelchair expertly past the drunk, the despairing, and the very possibly dead (for it was not unknown for the most delicate Delusionals to pass away suddenly and without warning, in full view of their fellow patients). God shuffled behind, silently cursing the moment he'd turned down a perfectly respectable female oncologist in favor of Trip Blue's screaming genius. For the first time in his forty-nine years of existence God saw himself capable of failure, of making mistakes like an ordinary, fallible man. On any other day this realization would have been liberating.

When they reached the Treatment Room door Trip Blue reached up and, without looking, finger-punched the code. The door clicked open and with a single stride God crossed the line, dragging the unconscious man behind him. Trip Blue followed, locking the door from the inside so no one, not even curious senior staff members, could invade their privacy. It was pitch black in the Treatment Room, the darkness emphasizing the unconscious man's shallow breathing and the rubbery clip of Trip Blue's dress shoes as he fumbled around in pursuit of a light switch.

'And God said let there be light!' Trip cried, a running joke, wildly incongruous under present circumstances. The lights came blinkering on, blipping like erratic disco beats until they finally settled into a steady glare. Fully illuminated, God saw them for what they were: two lonely men and a stranger, reflected fifteen different directions of honest in the floor-to-ceiling mirrors. God had, over the years, developed a real phobia of reflection. Every reflective surface under his direct authority – H Wing bathrooms, cutlery and internal windows – had been deliberately removed or tarnished, under the fabricated assumption that encountering one's true self too early in the treatment process might stilt a patient's recovery. The truth fell closer to home. God had long since lost the ability to look directly at his own shitty self. On the rare occasions when he left the military compound he could barely bring himself to catch his own eye in the rearview mirror of his station wagon. Though he spent the better part of every day trundling patients in and out of the Treatment Room, God had perfected a peculiar way of squinting out of the side of his eyes, so he was at no time forced to deal with the fullness of his own reflection. These optical aerobics had resulted in a semi-permanent migraine and an inability to focus on anything further than six inches beyond the end of his nose.

On Christmas Eve 1978 the headache rested heavily upon God. On another day, a rare cool-headed day, he might have resisted Trip Blue's plan, but the migraine had turned his resolve to mush. Mutiny was impossible. It was all God could do to remain inside the room, comprehensively reflected and suffering from localized explosions of the skull.

'Get on with it,' he said and though he was not directly responsible for the deathblow, these four words stuck to him. In the remaining twelve months of his life God would assiduously deny his culpability, first to himself and then, as the alcohol took hold, to a growing number of down-and-out friends. Each time he proclaimed his innocence the four words would rise like a personal cockcrow to mock the distance he'd placed between himself and the act. Blood, he soon came to realize, stuck, no matter how far away you were standing.

Meanwhile, Trip Blue had already wired up the Treatment Room and, fearing the man might regain consciousness, making the whole process distinctly more unpleasant, was keen to press on. God found himself drawn elbow-first behind the shatterproof screen which protected staff members from the insidious forces emitted by the Treatment Room. Trip Blue flicked a switch. A series of red, robotic lights bubbled on, and through their protective headphones, God and his erstwhile assistant listened as a sexless voice dripped, disembodied from the wall-mounted speakers: 'WISE UP. WISE UP. WISE UP.' The man, slumped sideways in his borrowed wheelchair, drooled on, unaware and very possibly impervious to a generous American helping of the truth. A series of wires, attached at wrist and temple, connected him to the control room where his vital statistics pulsed in a red, monotonous line across a computer screen, proceeding like a symmetrical alpine range from one side of the monitor to the other. God watched the pattern, intent upon discovering an anomaly in the unbroken landscape. The man's condition remained consistently unchanged.

'I'm going to crank it up to 120,' muttered Trip Blue some ten minutes into the monotone liturgy wheedling from the speakers. 'He doesn't seem to be responding to a normal dose and we don't have time to hang around.'

Though no perceivable change in speed, pitch or volume could be noted, both men were aware that the unconscious man was now being exposed to three weeks' worth of Treatment in a single, condensed dose. And when a further ten minutes showed no sign of deterioration and the dial was cranked all the way up to 200, Trip Blue crossed the line from science into scientific research, experimenting with truth so intense and potentially corrosive it had never before made it beyond the hypothetical stage.

'I don't understand,' said Trip Blue. 'I know he's a goddamn Delusional. I've never been wrong before. This much should have killed him half an hour ago. Maybe the tranquilizers are interfering with the Treatment.'

God shrugged. 'There's not much we can do about that.'

'Like hell there isn't. I'm going in there to wake the bastard up. We've started this now and damned if I'm leaving it unfinished.'

God watched on with growing horror as Trip Blue entered the Treatment Room and started to slap the unconscious man violently around the head with his open hand. As it became clear that the man was not responding, Trip's blows turned increasingly vicious. His open palm curled into a fist and he began to pummel the man with pounding blow after blow until his nose broke, and his cheekbones fell flat, and a thin, ketchup-colored trickle of blood began to surge free of his left ear. Behind the glass, God watched passively on, noting the way Trip Blue's face had contorted into a caricature of rage, splintered and reflected like some circus horror in the Treatment Room's mirrors. Later, God would convince himself that he'd been too afraid to step in for fear that Trip's volcanic anger would turn on him. Fear was excusable, while the shrill and illicit pleasure he'd taken in watching one man batter another to death was a little harder to live with.

The man was already dead when God finally snapped out of his stupor. Without stopping to switch the machines off, he yanked the headphones from his ears and, dashing from behind the safe confine of the shatterproof glass, made halfhearted attempts at restraining Trip Blue's thundering fists. By this stage the young doctor's rage was blind. He lashed out at God, cracking ribs, lacerating his cheekbones, drawing a sudden rush of blood from his nose. God persevered, pinning Trip's arms and attempting to halt his progress in a standard issue army headlock. The realist in him knew that Trip had already killed the man but he kept wrestling. In all his Vietnamese days God had never witnessed anything as terrifying as Trip Blue's unbound fury.

By the time God had managed to drag Trip off the battered corpse and prop him up, exhausted from the act of unleashing a lifetime's worth of restrained fury, in the corner of the Treatment Room, both men had been exposed to a triple dose of condensed truth. Whilst the words had already spoken into God's subconscious despair, instigating a process of decline which would see him dead within the year, the very same words fell upon Trip Blue's stoic soul like fuel for his loudest ambitions. Trip Blue was a survivor. All things, he felt certain, would come to him, if only he had the audacity to persevere.

The next years would prove difficult. Though the Army did their best to make H Wing and all her filthy secrets disappear, Trip Blue left Pennsylvania with a blot on his resume, glaringly obvious to any consultant capable of reading between the lines. Hospitals were wary of employing him. Colleagues, having heard the rumors circulating amongst Vietnam vets, gave him a wide berth in the cafeteria. He moved often and early, quitting neurology and plastics and cardiothoracics before his over-leaping ambition could be discovered. Trip Blue never once doubted his own genius. Christmas 1978 had planted an irrevocable sense of worth deep in the darkest vault of his being. The Treatment Room hung over him like the proverbial 'one that got away' and yet Trip Blue did not dare to dust off the mirrors and continue with his research.

Instead he marked time, he saved his money scrupulously, and (though his personality preceded him) did his best to rebuild the shattered remnants of his professional reputation. Whilst most everyone who knew Trip Blue saw his move to the Baptist Retirement Village as the beginning of the end of his career, Trip himself had been planning just such a move for the better part of twenty years. By the early nineties, H Wing was almost forgotten and Trip Blue was ready to resurrect the Treatment Room, choosing a broom closet in a nursing home full of semi-delusional seniors as a perfectly anonymous setting for his latest advance on the Nobel Prize.

He told no one of his plans and, with the brave exception of his own daughter – a vile brat whom he secretly suspected to be Delusional – only permitted the most senile of residents access to this second incarnation of the Treatment Room. Any number of old-people diseases could be utilized to explain away the dead

Delusionals. The recovered Terminals often talked but their friends and family, accustomed to the wild gibberings of the senile, never believed a word they said. Had it not been for Soren James Blue – blessed as she was with three parts of her mother's gumption for every callous spoonful of her father – Trip Blue might well have made the scientific breakthrough of the century.

– Chapter 13 –

Disappear Here

Two days after beginning work at the Center, Martha Orange had experienced her first fully formed doubt about the Director. Entering the ground floor drugs closet suddenly, without knocking, she'd stumbled upon her new boss, sleeves rolled to the elbow, exposing the pink red point where a drip bag full of tinted liquid was emptying its contents into his vein. Though the Director did not acknowledge her presence as she picked her way clumsily round the room selecting the pills and potions required for the early morning rounds, Martha Orange instinctively knew he was up to no good. No one in the Center had a positive word to say about Trip Blue. His own kid – a mouthy rodent of a girl – could not bear to be in his presence. Many of the long-term residents winced visibly when he entered the room.

The Director, Martha Orange suspected, was a very nasty piece of work.

Almost two decades of marriage to Jimmy Orange had made Martha a naturally suspicious person. She did not trust easily and having noticed the Director's shifty behavior, could not help but let her suspicions multiply unchecked. Thankful for a distraction from her own absent sleaze of a husband, she'd been paying particular attention to all the Director's comings and goings for weeks. What had begun as well-intentioned curiosity had lately flourished, like all Martha Orange's best intentions, into an out-and-out obsession.

Martha Orange saw any unguarded paper, even those marked confidential, as fair game for investigation. She rifled through the trash can in the Director's office and eavesdropped (mug to ear and occasionally via the Center's prehistoric telephone system) on closed-door conversations. Over cigarettes by the laundry chute she grilled her colleagues for passing gossip and dropped the Director's name into conversation with patients, hoping for fresh, bloody revelations. People talked, hesitatingly at first, and then with bitter, hurtling abandon, so Martha Orange soon found herself privy to any number of incriminating details about Trip Blue's life.

The love of Scientific Investigative Research had descended from Martha's erstwhile father – who had in his youth nurtured ambitions of cracking unsolvable cases for the police – to herself and, via the umbilical cord, to Malcolm, who could not help but translate the incomprehensible facts of life into bar charts and diagrams. Martha Orange kept bullet point notes in an old address book and when the accumulating evidence, beginning on the page marked A, looked set to approach pages P and Q, started to analyze her discoveries by a process of grade school mathematics and scientific reason. Each point was a small, incriminating nail in the Director's coffin, which, when fully collated, Martha Orange planned to post anonymously to the Baptist Pastor who sat, somewhat flaccidly, at the head of the Board of Directors. A small sample of her research would be enough to get Trip Blue fired and, if Baptists believed in such a practice, excommunicated.

- The Director was not a nice man.
- Colonic irrigation twice monthly kept him regular as a downtown bus.
- Friday evenings he paid the girls who marked time on the corner of 82nd and Killingsworth for an increasingly humiliating set of services.
- He believed himself to be gluten intolerant but had never bothered to confirm the diagnosis.
- Three mornings a week he practiced mind control techniques on Senior Citizens in a broom closet.

The Director referred to this bizarre ritual as 'Treatment Room', and while Martha Orange noted in her carefully collated graphs a rapid decline in the health of almost every patient slipped surreptitiously into the closet, and had very little understanding of what exactly went on behind the cheap plywood doors, occasionally she had observed miraculous improvements in the patients exposed to the Treatment Room. Just last week Marcy Tillerman, though permanently paralyzed after a childhood cycling accident, had climbed out of bed and fixed herself a mug of instant hot chocolate before attempting to walk unaided to the second-floor bathroom. The Director, when confronted with Miss Tillerman's case and a selection of similarly strange recoveries (stone-deaf seniors suddenly able to hear, dementia in decline and the solitary case of a missing kidney which had, in the course of a week, managed to regenerate), had simply shrugged and put the miracles down to a dose of fluoride the Board of Directors had introduced to the Center's water pipes.

Martha Orange had her suspicions. Each one of the recently recovered had been a broom closet visitor. Over the course of a month she continued to speculate about the Treatment Room but never once saw fit to open the door and investigate further. In her most honest moments she suspected the Director of some sort of abuse, possibly sexual. Though she was not without morals, Martha Orange held back from reporting her boss. There was always more evidence to be gleaned, always further collation necessary. Caution, she told herself, was just another way of being tactical. However, in her most honest moments she admitted herself shit-scared and unlikely to ever report the Director. Martha Orange could not afford to lose her job. When the guilt got too much for her, she reordered her notebooks and reminded herself, somewhat self-righteously, that whatever dark doings were taking place in the first-floor broom closet, some patients were definitely getting better.

This afternoon, confronted with the gushing hole in Cunningham Holt's chest, Martha Orange had instinctively known that despite its tendency to usher eight out of ten Center patients towards the morgue, the Treatment Room was his only hope. She could neither explain nor dismiss this hunch. Martha Orange had missed out on Sorry's testimony. She had only the most rudimentary understanding of the Treatment Room's mechanics. However, when the People's Committee, informed as they now were, insisted upon storming the Center, she immediately agreed. Martha Orange had long since learnt to trust her gut and her gut was insisting upon the Treatment Room. As they made their way across the parking lot, Roger Heinz filled Martha in on the afternoon's misadventures, clumsily paraphrasing Sorry's summer in the Center, so by the time they arrived at the building's doors – a trail of lukewarm blood marking their progress from one side of the Retirement Village to the other – Martha Orange had all but formed a complete picture of what the Director was orchestrating inside his broom closet.

'Bastard,' she cried, loudly and with tremendous vehemence; the only time Malcolm had heard her swear openly in his father's absence. He could not help but be impressed. It was the first time in months he'd heard his mother express a conclusive opinion about anything.

Martha Orange was drawn, caught between a deep conviction that someone should take charge of this situation and a firm belief that this person should not be her. Inside her shoulder blades, something shuffled involuntarily. Phantom wings tensed in anticipation of flight, reminding Martha that she had not been built for commitment. Responsibility had always rested heavily on her shoulders and this particular responsibility, encompassing as it did a gravely ill man, more than a dozen seniors, three children and a particularly obnoxious housecat, was heavy enough to leave permanent indentations in the sidewalk.

The desire to bolt was almost overwhelming.

Martha Orange looked at Malcolm as he stood beside the wheelchair clutching Cunningham Holt's bloody hand in his own. His school sneakers were now a particularly grim shade of menstrual red. He seemed smaller, thinner, less believable for the day's events. She looked at the People's Committee. In the last blush of daylight they appeared frail and inconclusive, hesitating on their orthopedic heels. This was a collection of individuals desperately in need of leadership and Martha Orange was forced to acknowledge herself the only adult available. She took a deep breath and stepped up, deliberately defying the wings which were drawing her eagerly towards the nearest bus stop. The movement pained her physically and specifically in the region of her right lung. It felt like a pregnancy contraction.

'Right,' she said, mustering every ounce of forced confidence gleaned from the Mexican soap operas, 'we need a plan.'

'A plan,' grinned Roger Heinz, spirits suddenly lifted by the possibility of military maneuvers and covert operations. 'You're dead right, sweetheart. All morning I've been trying to tell these idiots that we need a plan. No one ever listens to me. I'll go grab the gun from Nate's bedroom. We can storm the Treatment Room.'

'No guns,' said Martha Orange and Malcolm – Cunningham's blood already forming flaky scabs on his hands and wrists – nodded in shell-shocked agreement.

'Fire throwers,' suggested Roger. 'Incendiary devices, knives?' Bound by the pacifist contingent he could see his role in the operation slowly receding to that of a mere bystander.

'Maybe knives or a big stick. A big stick would be less dangerous,' Martha Orange said. 'But on the other hand a knife would really make him jump.'

The People's Committee for Remembering Songs were horrified by the faintest suggestion of further violence. The day had already forced them into contemplation of their own crouching mortality. The cul-de-sac had heard more than enough dying talk for one day and all but the truly senile had no interest in tempting fate with further guns and knives. Death hovered over the People's Committee like the sure and settling threat of early snowfall. Without consulting one another, all but Roger Heinz – who still, even at the impossible age of eighty-three, planned to go down in a hail of enemy gunfire – aspired to a sleeping death; something soft and placid as a dimmer switch. Sudden, bloody death, of the kind now bearing down on Cunningham Holt, did not sit well with the People's Committee. The possibility of further violence was enough to make them consider a tactical retreat. However, as Malcolm's mother explained her plan – borrowing heavily from the plot of a Bruce Willis movie she'd once seen on pay-per-view – they came to understand the necessity of a sharp implement, well-placed.

'My dad's a cold-hearted monster,' reiterated Soren James Blue. 'He won't do shit for anyone unless you force him. Take a knife in there with you – two if you can.' And the People's Committee, though not by nature inclined to violence, remembered that the Director was a very nasty man; a man who had recently slashed the budget for the Annual Thanksgiving Turkey and Tipples Tea Dance and limited library privileges to once a quarter; who had, for want of an extra few gallons of winter oil, allowed Maybelle Symmons to freeze solid in her reclining chair, skirts akimbo and heels to the ceiling like an upended standard lamp; and had, on one unpleasant occasion, laughed as he telephoned the Portland Dog Pound whilst Mrs Hunter Huxley wept penitent tears for the life of a recently acquired and terribly companionable stray Westie. 'Knife the old bastard in the back,' shouted Mrs George Kellerman, bucking her Baptist morals to vocalize the opinion of the masses.

Martha Orange had no intention of knifing anyone.

Accepting the Swiss Army knife which Roger Heinz passed to her, she folded the blade into its sheath and, for an added safeguard, wrapped the entire knife in a couple of unused Kleenex. 'I've no intention of knifing anyone,' she said. 'It's just in case he needs an incentive to get his ass in gear.' Then she tucked the twice-bandaged knife into the strap of her bra, where it nestled coolly against a Chapstick, the remainders of the Kleenex pack and her left breast, already deflating from lack of Ross. Thereafter, the People's Committee for Remembering Songs split into two units and, commissioned with a hasty prayer, delivered in perfectly pitched unison by the Mrs Huxley and Kellerman, mounted a twin-pronged attack on the Center.

The Secondary Unit – acting on insider information from Mrs Orange – penetrated the building via the emergency exit by the staff room. Led by Roger Heinz and comprising of Martha Orange, Nate Grubbs, a quickly coagulating Cunningham Holt, and Malcolm (who, due to the perforations which had increased in direct correlation to his growing panic, could only reasonably be counted as half a person), the group divided upon entry. Martha Orange headed straight for the Director's office. The other four, leaving bloody wheelchair tracks in the ground-floor carpet, followed a hastily sketched map to the Director's 'special' broom closet. Following Mrs Orange's explicit instructions, they secreted themselves behind a set of floor-to-ceiling drapes (somewhat conspicuously, for they were largish men with protruding feet and a wheelchair), and waited for the prearranged signal.

The Primary Unit – a ragtag collection of the less competent Committee members – approached the Center via the main doors. In lieu of a responsible adult, Bill had stepped in to the leader's role. Bill was the sort of man who balked at responsibility. It was almost twenty-five years since he'd last led anything more taxing than a round of choral singing. Even then, most all of his leadership experiences had ended in confusion or localized disaster. Bill was fully aware of his own ineptitude and until recently, fearing further calamities, had been more than content to navigate towards the back of the room, defaulting leadership to the closest consenting adult. Irene was delighted with her husband. Previous suitors had attempted to play the alpha male, mistaking her quiet determination for submission. None had lasted longer than a month. In her prime, Irene had been a formidable woman, dominating men and women alike within her home, her workplace and the local chapter of the Women's

Institute. Before the head muddle had turned her dry wit sodden, Irene loved to watch her husband squirm as she recounted tales of mislaid Scout troops and mutinous little league teams to their equally embarrassed guests and friends. She was not a mean woman. She mocked to reassure Bill that he no longer need worry about taking the lead.

Over the years Bill had gradually defaulted control of everything – from finances and child-rearing, to the increasingly fickle movements of his penis – to Irene. And Irene, until very recently, had been happy to oblige, leading her husband from one end of the week to the next by virtue of a wall-mounted Disney calendar on which she marked all his comings and goings. This unconsciously agreed system had begun innocently enough with dental appointments and business meetings and peaked in Bill and Irene's twenty-third year of marriage with a carefully collated schedule allocating precise times and timings for bathing, teeth washing and even defecating. Bill had always found his wife's meddling a great comfort and when the dementia began to spirit away large slices of her good sense, struggled to fumble his way through a day's activities in the correct order. Forced to wear the pants, he had grown increasingly insecure in the role.

Bill was not the man he wished to be. He envied Cunningham Holt his unsinkable resolve. He envied Roger Heinz his monolithic balls. He even envied Malcolm his capacity to attract drama. It had been years since anything even faintly exciting had happened to Bill. Sitcoms and sports coverage, interspersed with his biweekly People's Committee meetings, had come to form the bedrock of Bill's existence and while he was quite content to pickle slowly, moldering into the living room sofa, he felt the pressure of his peers haranguing him towards a bolder kind of existence. Seizing the opportunity to prove himself capable, Bill had volunteered for the role of Primary Unit leader. It had seemed like an infinitely doable kind of challenge, the sort of thing Roger Heinz could do in his sleep. To all intents and purposes his was a mere cameo in the grander plan, a simple distraction affording the real heroes opportunity to save Cunningham Holt. Any idiot could have done it, but Bill had volunteered.

He was already beginning to regret his unchecked ambition. Failures past flashed through his mind: last Christmas's attempt to decorate the external walls of Chalet 11, the time he'd tried to surprise Irene with the Mediterranean cruise, the oft-recounted incident with the food processor.

Approaching the Center's reception desk, Bill ran over the nuts and bolts of Martha Orange's plan, silently rehearsing his own small part. Two feet from the counter he had his lines word perfect and embellished with appropriate gestures and yet, as soon as the Director's pinchy blonde assistant leaned over the counter to ask how she could help, he found he could no longer remember so much as a single sentence. Instead of alerting the staff to Miss Pamela Richardson's plight, upended and floundering in the cul-de-sac turn circle, thereby creating the kind of diversion which would drag all but the dog-lazy Director out of the Center, Bill discovered that his mouth had an altogether different plan.

'My wife just passed out,' he shouted, slapping the countertop in a fit of false passion so violent it caused an avalanche of fliers for the Annual Friends and Family Backyard Barbeque to shift and flutter delicately, like parachutes and leaves, around his ankles.

'No I didn't,' hissed Irene, stepping forwards to prove herself reassuringly vertical.

Bill ignored her. For the umpteenth occasion of the last year, he wished for a different wife or at least a working version of the old model.

'I didn't pass out,' reiterated Irene.

'My wife is extremely unwell,' continued Bill, raising his voice and bouncing slightly to draw attention away from Irene.

The receptionist looked confused. Confusion suited her. It complimented the poofy undulations of her fashionable haircut.

'I'm his wife,' yelled Irene, 'and I've never felt better.'

'Fall over, Irene,' whispered Soren James Blue, leaning into the elderly lady's ear for emphasis, 'we're trying to create a distraction.'

At the reception desk, Bill trawled the deepest recesses of his memory for a notion of what to do next. Too late he realized that he had never and would never be leadership material. The assistant glared ungraciously from behind a display of fliers promoting support groups for the incontinent, the diabetic and recently bereaved. 'Which one is your wife?' she asked, swooping a condescending hand across the female members of the People's Committee. 'They all look fine to me.'

Later, the People's Committee for Remembering Songs would claim they had simultaneously known exactly what to do and, acting on some otherworldly impetus, obliged their own initiatives accordingly. However, the confusion which broke out in the Center's reception area, causing a distraction on par with a medium-sized tsunami, had very little to do with telepathy or anything quite so romantic.

At the precise moment when Bill backtracked to confess in a bleating voice, 'It wasn't my wife who passed out, it was me,' and feigned a dramatic, bruise-incurring swoon upon the foyer floor, Mr Fluff – the only individual present with enough sense to keep the plan on track – sank her teeth into Irene's ankle so she toppled forwards, meeting her husband in midair like a pair of passing pine trees; and Soren James Blue quit her subtle whispering to yell, 'We've got to create a distraction!' Sensing all hell had already broken loose, the remaining upright members of the People's Committee took Sorry's words as a rallying cry and began to improvise their own peculiar distractions.

In the corner, by the potted plants, Mrs George Kellerman and Mrs Hunter Huxley launched into a rousing rendition of 'Onward Christian Soldiers', choosing to begin on different verses for maximum chaotic effect. Simeon Klein, still oblivious to the reason for the madness and reluctant to find himself once again excluded on account of his cloggy ears, removed his pullover and deck shoes and launched into a doddering striptease on the coffee table. Rose Roper grabbed the standard lamp, cradled its spindly neck in her arms and tangoed round the reception desk until her hair came loose and the emphysema caught her in mid gasp. However, it was Clary O'Hare who unintentionally caused the most effective distraction. Tapping his way round the walls of the reception area with the tablespoons he kept permanently tucked into his breast pocket, he accidentally forced his Morse code upon the fire alarm, shattering the panic glass and throwing the entire Center into a shrill, whining maelstrom.

Following protocol, the assistant, purple now with condensed rage, picked up the reception desk telephone and granted permission for a complete evacuation of the building.

'It's like *One Flew Over the Cuckoo's Nest* in here today,' she muttered as she gathered up her personal belongings and prepared to vacate the building.

Ninety seconds later the Center began to belch staff and seniors into the parking lot. Most walked, Bambi-legged on sticks and crutches. Many were evacuated against their will, protesting as they thrashed about in clunky, prehistoric wheelchairs. The remaining half-dozen patients, too far gone to contemplate consciousness, were dragged from the screeching building on emergency stretchers, and laid like plane crash corpses in the Garden of Remembrance which ran in a boggy, begonia-heavy strip down the left length of the Center.

One such octogenarian, roused by the cool rush of outside air, opened his eyes briefly and, observing the mud and the flowers bunched in clumsy, funereal puffs, presumed himself already dead and soon to be buried. Never the type to cause an undue fuss, he closed his eyes and obligingly passed away right there in the Garden of Remembrance. It was only three hours later, when his already concrete body was transported back into the Center and tucked tightly into bed, that a junior orderly noticed he was no longer breathing. Such incidents were not uncommon in the Center. Patients often died and went unnoticed for whole half days at a time. (The nursing staff, terrified of having their negligence drawn to the attention of the health care authorities, had recently discovered that an electric blanket could be applied to a cold corpse with the effect of defrosting a few hours off the time of death. Alibis were everything in a facility where value for money and sheer laziness outdid professionalism at every turn.)

The Primary Unit of the People's Committee for Remembering Songs disentangled themselves from the foyer floor and, under the nursing staff's insistence, joined the other evacuees in the parking lot. Reassured to see that the fire alarm had drawn everyone, even the catering staff, out of the building, they huddled by the goldfish pond and, in urgent whispered prayers, petitioned a variety of gods for the success and safe return of the Secondary Unit, for Malcolm's perforations and Cunningham Holt, who seemed most desperately in need of divine interference.

The Director had chosen to ignore the fire alarm. His pinchy assistant – only three weeks into the job and already au fait with her boss's telescopic wrath – had been savvy enough to phone down and assure him that, 'Yes, this is definitely a false alarm,' and, 'No, there is no need to evacuate,' and, 'Would you, by any chance, appreciate the lend of my headphones to block out the noise?' The Director declined her offer in his usual perfunctory manner, wrapped a hand towel round his head to cushion the din, and continued to collate the previous week's test results. The Director was oblivious to everything outside his own head. Swathed in his terry cloth turban, he was preoccupied with the case notes of Manuela Marguiles, a largish lady of Puerto Rican descent whose six sessions in the Treatment Room had eradicated the enormous warts that sprouted, like forest floor mushrooms, all over her face and neck, yet passed, disinterested, over the cancerous wrecking ball currently making mush of her uterus. So focused was the Director on Manuela's notes that when he paused between paragraphs, lifting his eyes to scan the opposite wall for inspiration, it came as a tremendous shock to find Martha Orange standing in front of his desk, furious-faced and brandishing what appeared to be a Swiss Army knife wrapped in a wad of tissue.

'Who are you?' he asked.

(Whilst the Director had, over the course of the last few months, enjoyed purposefully brushing against the breasts, backside and award-winning legs of Mrs Orange, it had never crossed his mind to ask for an introduction. Orderlies were a dime a dozen in the Center. They came, they lasted six to eighteen months and left in a haze of mumbled complaints about long hours, terrible pay and the wandering hands of their esteemed boss. They were a bovine breed, meagerly educated and lacking in self-esteem. Most seemed satisfied with the opportunity to slur his character. The few possessing gumption enough to threaten litigation had been silenced by virtue of the same offshore bank account which had kept Trip Blue's professional reputation clean as a Christmas turkey all the way through medical college.)

'Martha Orange,' replied Martha Orange. 'I work for you. I need you to let me and my friends into the Treatment Room.'

'The what?'

'Cut the bullshit. Everyone sees you going in and out of the broom closet. God only knows what perverted experiments you're doing on the old people in there. But I've seen that some of them are getting better and I need to get in there too.'

'Definitely not.'

'I have a knife,' threatened Martha Orange and began to unroll wads of Kleenex, exposing a shiny red Swiss Army knife no bigger than a can opener. After initially retracting the tweezers and toothpick, Martha Orange arrived at the largest blade on the knife, levered it out of the handle with a thumbnail and held it threateningly over the Director's towel-clad ear. 'I'll stab you if you don't let me in.'

The Director shrugged, unconcerned. 'Go ahead,' he said, turning towards her so the point of the blade tickled his earlobe. The Director was not afraid of death. A pragmatic scientist to the core, he did not believe in any sort of afterlife. While the unpleasantness of dying bothered him somewhat and he was no great fan of physical pain, being dead, he presumed, would be a welcome relief from the ongoing nuisance of being alive.

'I mean it. So help me God, I will kill you if you don't take me to the Treatment Room. One of the residents has been shot in the stomach. He doesn't have much time. It might be too late already.

That stupid room of yours is his only chance.'

Trip Blue heard nothing beyond the possibility of a resurrection. He had been waiting a terribly long time for an opportunity like this. He changed his mind in an instant, yet held the silence for a full minute, enjoying the way Martha Orange squirmed in front of him, shifting weight from one foot to the other. The Director's consent was a given but Martha Orange didn't know this; the situation was ripe for exploitation.

'OK,' he eventually agreed, 'I'll let you into the Treatment Room. But if I'm going to be nice to you, you're going to have to be nice to me.'

It was not the first time Trip Blue had found himself in such a position. Bracing his palms against the edge of his enormous mahogany desk, he shoved his office chair two feet backwards until the full length of his body rolled into Martha's view, pinstriped, patronizing and already bulging with ugly lust. Martha Orange knew what was expected of her. The whole situation was worryingly familiar. She recalled the haylofts and motel rooms, the broom closets and back alleys which had slowly shaped her muscles and bones into one particular position; a position as low and penitent as earnest prayer. There was little point in arguing. God moved in mysterious ways and Martha Orange was more than familiar with the brutal kindness of his grace. As she lowered herself to her knees and sped through proceedings her thoughts slipped free of her head and went galloping round the south Kentucky plains. The small incisions on her shoulder blades reopened and wept soft and low for the open sky, which seemed always, lately, ever just beyond Martha's reach.

The Director, grasping the plastic lever on the side of his office chair, reclined and with eyes soldered shut – for the smallest part of him did not wish to be reminded of just how sordid he could be – thrilled himself on the imminent possibility of raising the dead. Martha Orange's knife meant nothing to him; her earnest petition for a friend's life, even less; but the possibility of using the Treatment Room to resurrect the very recently dead had Trip Blue so excited he could barely contain himself. He laid a hand on the top of Martha Orange's bobbing head and, picturing himself on the cover of *Time* magazine, Nobel Prize in hand, felt himself explode with the ferocity of his own brilliance. Opening his eyes afterwards Trip Blue was surprised to find Martha Orange had not been obliterated. She sat before him, hunkered and wide-eyed, the cuff of her sweater sleeve covering her mouth. Her legs, he noted, tucked beneath her pert little backside, now floated about two inches off the ground. Trip Blue assumed himself responsible for this, and other miracles.

In the corridor, behind the curtain, Malcolm Orange wondered what was taking his mother so long in the Director's office. He hoped she had not killed the Director. Murder was a sin against America and the Jesus God and Malcolm Orange was pretty sure they still sent people, even moms and ladies, to the electric chair for killing. Having just retrieved his mother, Malcolm Orange had no desire to lose her again. He closed his eyes and prayed to the Jesus God that Martha would not do anything terrible in the Director's office. It was death dark behind the curtains. There was really no need to close his eyes but Malcolm wasn't convinced that the Jesus God could hear open-eyed prayers so he kept his eyes closed and the words running like looping ticker tape round the inside of his head.

It was nice behind the curtain. The smell of washing powder and cough drops had ingrained itself into the seams. Malcolm Orange had always hoped to one day live in a house saturated with such homely cleaning smells. Chalet 13, for all its permanence, had already assumed the Orange odor of fried food and incorrectly disposed diapers. Malcolm was sure that real family houses did not smell like the restrooms at the Dairy Queen. Someday he would live in a house which smelt like a detergent commercial.

Tucked behind the curtains, the heavy damask fabric brushed against Malcolm's arms and legs, reminding him that he had not yet entirely disappeared. With no light forthcoming he could not check on the progress of his perforations and might very possibly be healed. It was good to have his hysteria temporarily restrained. Sandwiched to left and right by his good friends Roger Heinz and Nate Grubbs, giddy with the realization that his mother had returned for him, Malcolm had all but decided to spend the rest of his life behind this curtain, companionable, safe and very possibly normal, when the curtains parted viciously. Blinking in the strip lights, he found himself staring into the furious face of Sorry's father.

'Out of there now!' cried the Director, and when the four members of the Secondary Unit hesitated – three from fear and the fourth too dead or dying to manage even the smallest shuffle – the Director reached behind the curtain and manhandled them into the corridor using arms, ears and loose clothing for leverage. 'We're going to the Treatment Room. It's not what I'd call the wisest decision I've ever made but let's just say your friend Martha here was very convincing.'

It was at this point that Malcolm Orange first noticed his mother, floating over the Director's shoulder. The sight of her came as something of a shock. On any other ordinary day, a floating mother would have been enough to tip Malcolm Orange over the edge into the land of explosive diarrhea. However, this afternoon, with his capacity for shock already dulled by the day's deluge of weird and wonderful happenings, Malcolm Orange merely observed his mother's latest achievement and wondered, 'What in the wild blue world might happen next?' Martha Orange's face was familiar. Her clothes were the same tired jeans and sweater she'd been wearing since Illinois, but her posture was entirely alien. Malcolm stared in horrified amazement as his mother hovered two feet off the floor, the crown of her head grazing the ceiling like a helium balloon halted in ascent.

The pressure of the last twenty-four hours had awakened in Martha Orange something ancient and prematurely lost. As the walls conspired to keep her anchored to cul-de-sac life, a thick and unquenchable longing for height had drawn the wings right out of her shoulders. Roots, clipped at birth, began to regenerate. Feathers formed from the downy hairs on her back and neck. Muscles melted into muscles, bones grafted, and in the last half hour a pair of knuckle-like protrusions had burst from the skin of her shoulders; baby wings, preparing for flight. Something had settled inside Martha Orange: a homely understanding that all would be well and if all should not be well, the opportunity to escape was still available. She felt fifteen pounds the lighter. Gravity had finally lost its hold on Martha Orange and only time would tell if this latest development was progressive or a reactionary return to her beginning days.

Malcolm Orange stared at his mother. She was not the same person she'd been yesterday. He was not sure exactly who she was. Mrs Orange blushed under her son's gaze; a teenage girl, awkward in her own blossoming skin. She looked beautiful and strange like a comic book hero just beginning to understand her own powers. Malcolm Orange was torn. His mother was real in a way he could barely remember and the happiness of this was so enormous and all-consuming he felt capable of having diarrhea right there on the corridor carpet, yet the other side of him – the twenty selfish percent inherited from his father – was jealous in a way he could neither explain nor ignore.

While his mother was unarguably more, Malcolm Orange seemed less with every passing second. His holes had never felt louder. By the time they arrived at the doors of the Treatment Room Malcolm was all but invisible, his T-shirt and shorts resting on the memory of a body. He caught his reflection in the fire exit door: mouse brown hair and the ghost of a grimace, floating, unanchored, on a five-foot shadow. The shock of confronting his own disappearance caused Malcolm to forget everything – Cunningham Holt, the Director, his lately absent parents – in a tremendous panic to pull himself together.

'Can you still see me, mama?' he cried out, holding the barely visible remains of an arm as evidence in front of his mother's hovering nose.

'Not now, Malcolm,' replied Martha Orange. 'There's no time for your nonsense right now. We've got to help Cunningham before it's too late.'

Malcolm waved his arms wildly in front of his mother with no significant effect. It was clear that Martha Orange could not or would not see her son. Malcolm suspected that she hadn't seen him properly in months. The larger losses – husbands, cars and aging parents – had taken their toll on his mother. There was very little of Martha Orange left and the slim part still in her possession seemed better equipped for flight than the everyday understandings of motherhood. Though the idea of a flying mother was inexplicably cool, Malcolm could not help but fear that the wings would prove to be yet another means of taking her away from him. Much as he loved his mother, right now Malcolm would have swapped fifteen Marthas for a single stay-at-home mom, with Laura Ashley frocks and a mean way with macaroni cheese. Malcolm Orange required an ordinary parent with arms for carrying and occasionally holding still. Instead he'd been blessed with a winged mother and a father with wheels where his feet should have been. Under such circumstances it was a two-bit wonder he hadn't disappeared earlier.

Considering the weight of evidence piling up on either side of his gene pool, there was little point in fighting the inevitable. With this realization, Malcolm Orange's insides finally evaporated in sympathy: lungs, kidneys and still-throbbing heart keeping pace with his external perforations.

Empty inside and out, Malcolm Orange disappeared.

The Director unlocked the door and ushered the Secondary Unit into the Treatment Room. It was death dark inside and terribly cramped. Martha Orange, incapable now of keeping her feet on the floor, grazed her head as she entered, leaving six blonde hairs like a Passover symbol on the doorjamb. Roger Heinz and Nate Grubbs, each holding a handle of the wheelchair for support as much as sympathy, manhandled a ghost-gray Cunningham Holt over the threshold. The Director followed, locking the door behind them. When the lights came blinking on, illuminating a square room, sparsely furnished with floor-to-ceiling mirrors, the Director did a double take.

'What happened to the kid?' he asked.

'You must have locked him out in the corridor,' replied Martha Orange, wrestling the ceiling tiles as she tried to force her feet back onto terra firma. 'It's probably for the best. Malcolm can be a bit of a handful.'

In the corner, knees crumpled over elbows like a discarded tissue, Malcolm Orange allowed himself the comfort of a single, invisible tear. It rolled down the invisible incline of his cheek and burrowed into the Treatment Room floor, where it joined in morose communion with the terrible sufferings of all those previously subjected to the Director's treatment. Whilst Malcolm Orange could still see the Secondary Unit as they fumbled and fussed around Cunningham Holt, he felt certain that they could no longer see him. The prospect of disappearing alone, unnoticed in a room full of familiars, felt like the very worst kind of end. Malcolm Orange was suddenly desperate for even the smallest acknowledgment of his existence.

Crawling on hands and knees towards the room's centre, he propped himself against Cunningham Holt's wheelchair and reached for his friend's hand. While he could no longer see his own arms, the feeling had not yet left him and, to Malcolm's amazement, Cunningham's fingers pulsed in his. The touch was barely perceivable, a medical anomaly which Scientific Investigative Research could undoubtedly have explained away, yet Malcolm Orange read in the gentle squeeze of familiar fingers an assurance that the blind man could see him far more clearly than anyone else in the room. Maneuvering himself closer to Cunningham's ear, Malcolm wrapped his arms like bandages around his friend's neck and in low whispers began to fill him in on the afternoon's adventures, beginning with the shotgun closet and concluding with a hastily whispered description of the Treatment Room and its present occupants, so hell-bent busy preparing the machines necessary for a resurrection, they hadn't noticed their corpse was conscious again.

'Am I dying?' asked Cunningham Holt, interrupting Malcolm mid-sentence. The second marble had come loose in transport and the loss-haunted sockets dominated his face, lending the old man the look of a Halloween corpse.

'I don't know,' replied Malcolm. 'You might be.'

'Malcolm,' whispered Cunningham Holt, tiny bubbles of

spit and blood bobbling at the side of his mouth. 'I don't mind dying but don't let me sink. Promise me, son, you won't let me sink.'

As he spoke, his face settling into a mask of ferocious intensity, Cunningham Holt clutched Malcolm's hand so hard he left individual fingerprints in his flesh.

'I promise,' said Malcolm Orange, unleashing a stream of invisible tears which trickled down the back of Cunningham Holt's shirt and formed a damp patch at the base of his spine. It was enough to reassure the old man. His face relaxed. His fingers unclenched. Allowing his eyelids to droop like a pair of paper blinds, Cunningham Holt fell asleep. As he slept the final sleep of his very many years he dreamt tremendous dreams – high towers and hot air balloons, mountaintops and ladders – all the solid lustings of a man confident in the ground beneath his feet. Malcolm Orange, watching the risings and raspy fallings of his friend's chest, could not help but wonder how a small boy, recently disappeared, could possibly hope to hold on to an entire adult. A promise was a promise however, and it was this promise which kept Malcolm Orange from slipping out the door when the Treatment started.

'Clear the room for Treatment,' cried the Director and without further ado Roger Heinz, Nate Grubbs and Malcolm's mother joined him behind the protective glass shield in one corner of the room. Malcolm watched over Cunningham's shoulder as the Director passed out four sets of enormous bucket headphones. It was dangerous, he concluded, for normal, healthy people to be subjected to the Treatment. The lights dimmed, illuminating Cunningham Holt in a single blond spotlight and the foggy outline of the Director and three well-cushioned spectators, insect-like in their goggles and ear protectors.

'Right,' said the Director, slipping into demonstration mode, 'seeing as the patient is most likely dead.'

'I'm not sure he's completely dead,' interrupted Roger Heinz.

'Let's take it that the patient is dead.'

'Didn't you bother to check?'

'It's simpler if he's dead.'

'What sort of quack doctor are you? You can't go round assuming that your patients are dead without checking.'

'Enough!' yelled the Director, rapidly losing patience with Roger Heinz. 'I'm going to assume he's dead, or on the way out. If he's not dead I'm not interested. He's just another crinkly geriatric and God knows I've done enough of them in the last year. The only reason I'm here is to have a stab at raising the dead. It's difficult in this place, I don't get the same access to the recently dead I used to have in my old job. People are sentimental about corpses. They don't understand that I'm not the enemy. I'm trying to help people.'

Even from a distance Malcolm could see his mother slipping away. A look of sheer, unfiltered disgust had set on her face and her wings, visible now as actual hand-sized sails, had drawn her two full feet off the floor. Opening her mouth to protest, the English words seemed to stick in her throat, and reluctant to voice such enormous disdain in beginner's Spanish, she simply said nothing, allowing the distance to grow gradually and perceivably between herself and the horror unfolding on the floor below.

'Right,' continued the Director, 'as I was saying. Seeing as the patient is already dead, I'm going to begin on a particularly high setting. I wouldn't normally administer such a condensed dose but we only have a small window of time before rigor mortis sets in and resurrection is physically impossible.'

'I'm not dead,' whispered Cunningham Holt, the furor at the

back of the room having roused him out of the best and final sleep of his life.

Malcolm Orange heard and gave his friend's shoulder a reassuring squeeze. Roger Heinz and Nate Grubbs thought they heard something but swept their suspicions aside under the excuse of wishful thinking and ill-adjusted hearing aids. Martha Orange heard but there were many voices in her head competing for attention and she'd long since developed the ability to funnel out all but the loudest. Trip Blue heard, and whilst it irked him slightly that the old man was still alive, he chose to say nothing and crank the machine up to a level just one notch lower than his last ill-fated experiment on H Wing. If he couldn't raise the dead, he reasoned, then he'd sure as hell take the opportunity to experiment on a willing victim.

'Here we go!' shouted the Director and, flicking the final switch, released a regular torrent of clipped computer voices through the wall-mounted speakers.

'WISE UP,' bleated the voices, male and female, soft, loud, melodic and harsh, in French, Spanish, Russian and Cantonese (for Trip Blue had been lately experimenting with the healing properties of foreign languages). As the speakers coated Cunningham Holt and Malcolm, crouching behind, in a brutal chorus of honesty, the floor circulated slowly beneath their feet; a turntable, forcing them to pirouette round the room in weary quarter-time. Malcolm Orange felt no discernible reaction to the Treatment. The floor beneath his feet was not yet spinning fast enough to induce nausea. The piped words were irritating but no more so than the incessant gargle of his mother's Mexican soaps which she insisted upon watching at full volume. However, Cunningham Holt was not faring so well. Three full revolutions into the Treatment with no significant change in his condition, he began to become agitated. Gripping the arms of his wheelchair, he tried to draw his wizened knees up to meet his chin as if pulling away from some imagined horror.

'It's started,' he hissed. 'I can feel the water nipping at my ankles. It's getting higher. Don't let me sink, son. Promise me now, Malcolm, promise you won't let me sink.'

'Don't worry, Cunningham,' whispered Malcolm. 'I'll hold on to you.'

Struggling to his feet, Malcolm Orange hooked his elbows under the old man's armpits and attempted to wrestle him upright. Cunningham Holt was a big man. Even in old age Malcolm guessed him to weigh something close to a two-seater sofa. It took sheer force of will and big time cursing to get Cunningham Holt approximately vertical but Malcolm managed. From behind their protective glass screen the spectators watched on in amazement as the patient appeared to rise, with great deliberation, from his wheelchair and stand unaided in the middle of the Treatment Room floor.

'It's working!' shouted the Director, permitting himself a single celebratory air punch. 'I'm going to crank it up one more notch, see if we can't get the guy walking again.'

The other three said nothing. They still didn't trust the Director. It was quite clear that he had no regard for Cunningham or any of his other patients. However, his was the only hope on offer this afternoon and they kept their concerns to themselves and tried to see the rudimentary evidence of a resurrection in the awkward way Cunningham Holt was now wobbling around the Treatment Room. This was not the miracle the People's Committee had been angling for. Even from a distance Martha and the two men could tell all was not well with their friend. Granted, he had risen unassisted from his wheelchair, but his legs now trembled frantically like overstretched piano strings. His head drooped against his chest at the most unperceivable angle and the gasping hole in the centre of his sternum continued to leak black-red blood in half-hearted trickles. Cunningham Holt seemed more than likely to die right under their noses, flat of foot and pirouetting slowly like a music box ballerina, the perfect picture of a bitter end.

'Are you sure this is a good idea?' asked Martha Orange quietly.

The longer the Treatment continued the more falteringly unsteady Cunningham appeared to be. Great drops of sweat the size and shape of boiled candy were now dripping from his brow, forming a puddled testimony around about his brogues. Martha Orange had suffered enough to recognize a fellow martyr. The compassionate part of her conscience told her to intervene. However, when all three of the men – for reasons ranging from fear to overleaping ambition – chose to disregard her, she allowed this small hiccup of compassion to dissipate. Worse things had happened in Texas. Despite the niggling notion that this was just the moment for an intervention, Martha Orange decided (with the same nonchalance that had kept her riding shotgun through the last fifteen unraveling years) that it was easier not to get involved. It was only when Malcolm began to materialize, arms and shoulders fizzling into focus like a recently tuned television set, that Martha Orange realized there would be no choice in the matter. Maternal instinct came thundering over her, defying flight and fear and long-grounded apathy. Martha Orange was compelled to come back down to earth and intervene.

– Chapter 14 –

All Things Go

Malcolm Orange had never done well with rotation.

At the age of eight, under the auspices of Scientific Investigative Research, he'd borrowed the *Usborne Book of Science Experiments for Grade Schoolers* from the children's department of the Milwaukee Central Library. When the Oranges had rolled out of town some three days before the loan expired, Malcolm found himself the semi-permanent owner of this and a selection of other age-appropriate library books. However, a lifetime of Volvo living had taught Malcolm Orange that all possessions should be held lightly. Like bicycles, dogs and sneakers past, his library books soon gave precedence to other more necessary articles. The *Usborne Book of Science Experiments for Grade Schoolers* lasted for approximately two weeks, before Mrs Orange, bound by some deeply ingrained reverence for the American library system, insisted upon returning Malcolm's books. For once Jimmy Orange, feeling the pinch of five extra items in a car already crowded with elderly relatives, cooking equipment and thrift store shirts, wholeheartedly agreed with his wife.

For the entire duration of her married life a strange logic had kept Martha Orange lending, leaving town and returning books five hundred miles or more further along the road. Martha

Orange believed in books like other people believed in God. In the early days, before the open road left her brain incapable of joining the dots between one sentence and the next, she read to escape the cramped monotony of the passenger seat. Devouring Steinbeck, Hemingway and other less worthy paperbacks, she imagined herself capable of one day leaving Jimmy Orange for a louder kind of existence. Martha Orange fervently believed that all people should read. Novels were her weapon of choice for nine out of ten concluded with the kind of optimistic ever after she'd never experienced in real life. For Martha, leaving a good book in a different town was an act of evangelism designed to spread the good news of literary escapism to all four corners of the American world. Depositing Malcolm's books in a carrier bag on the steps of the first small town library the Volvo passed by, Martha Orange had imagined future readers rejuvenated by ideas from another place. Meanwhile her son, eyebrows still singed from a failed attempt at the 'Create your own Volcano' experiment, silently mourned the loss of twenty-seven scintillating science experiments, never to be attempted.

Malcolm Orange had cursed his mother for fifteen minutes and then, distracted by a veritable epidemic of highway road kill, forgotten his fury. The loss of the *Usborne Book of Science Experiments for Grade Schoolers* was a mere blip on the landscape of larger losses. Books from the children's section were beneath him. Even at eight, Malcolm Orange had suspected himself scientifically astute on a par with a high school graduate. Experiments with soda pop and balloon static seemed a dumb preamble to the possibility of atom splitting or dabbling in genetic manipulation. Though aimed at the amateur Einstein, the *Usborne Book of Science Experiments for Grade Schoolers* had also included a fascinating chapter on centrifuges which stayed with

Malcolm long after the library book had been abandoned on the steps of some midwestern library, pages curling damply in the October drizzle.

Following the guidelines set out in Chapter 19, Malcolm had spent a happy hour in a Milwaukee rest stop, spinning a sealed pop bottle of oil and water on a shoelace until the oil rose and the water, pure as April rain, sunk to the bottle's base. Scientific Investigative Research had taught Malcolm that all good experiments had repercussions for the everyday. If centrifugal force could divide a liquid into all its separate components and the human body was almost two-thirds water, any sort of sustained spinning could have terrible medical repercussions. Almost instantly Malcolm Orange developed a horrendous fear of spinning floors, roundabouts and all such rotating devices. The idea that he might be unintentionally separated into all his indivisible, liquidy components had Malcolm suffering from the possibility of a panic attack every time the Volvo passed a playground.

The Treatment Room, with its floor-to-ceiling mirrors and its muttering robot voice, was terrifying enough for Malcolm Orange. When the floor began to circulate beneath his feet, his bowels flipped and the curdling remnants of the previous evening's Coronas made a bid for daylight. Clapping a cautionary hand across his mouth, Malcolm Orange tried, somewhat unsuccessfully, to forget all he'd ever learned about centrifugal force. (Over the years Scientific Investigative Research had introduced Malcolm Orange to a number of troubling concepts best forgotten by a young man nervous enough to hyperventilate over the distant possibility of a panic attack. With varying degrees of success Malcolm had forced himself amnesiac on the subjects of Global Warming, Nuclear Warfare and the whole worrying world of spontaneous combustion. There were enough imagined terrors in the world without allowing the kingdom of science to turn on him. Some lessons, Malcolm Orange firmly believed, were best left unlearned.)

Amnesia wasn't working for Malcolm Orange this afternoon. The fear of decanting into solid, liquid and noxious gas gripped him harder and faster with each round of the Treatment Room. Whilst he fought the desire to flee in pursuit of some place more static, concern for Cunningham Holt kept his feet bolted to the pivoting ground. His stomach churned, his head conjured up image after rebellious image of faceless human bodies, exploding under pressure, his sinus cavity screamed in reproach, and yet Malcolm could not abandon his friend. This was a first for Malcolm Orange. Selfish to the core, he could not recall a single instance in the last eleven years where he had willingly put his own comfort aside for another. It was a cut and shut kind of feeling. His insides hurt. His outsides ached. His heart was light as cotton candy.

Forgotten, disappeared, soon to be separated into all the composite elements of an eleven-year-old boy, Malcolm Orange sacrificed himself to the greater good. Planting his feet on either side of Cunningham's wheelchair, he settled in for the duration.

'I won't let you sink, Cunningham,' he repeated, as much for his own benefit as the old man's.

Weariness overwhelmed him. He felt, for the first time, so much older than his eleven small years.

For three full minutes Malcolm Orange spun slowly round the Treatment Room, acting as a pint-sized prop for Cunningham Holt. Arms full of heavy responsibility, Malcolm had no concern for, nor way of protecting his ears from, the Treatment. The piped voices rolled over his head and shoulders. They burrowed, in tremulous blasts, deep into his invisible skull, where the idea of

Malcolm Orange had not yet been fully extinguished. Without consent or comprehension the Director's Treatment began to appeal to Malcolm's resolve. Young and not yet lumbered with the world-weary acquiescence of the Delusional, Malcolm was a perfect candidate for the Treatment. Within minutes he began to respond to the truth as it blared mercilessly over his perforations. Cells and sinews, already inclined to dissolve, began to remember their true birth born purpose. Skin stretched to meet the moment, rolling across his torso like newly pressed paper; innocent and unblemished. The tiniest twist in his DNA perked its almost evaporated ear and heard the rallying call. 'WISE UP!'

Something unperceivable had shifted in the churning cavern of Malcolm Orange's guts. The mysterious trigger responsible for his disappearance flipped in timely agreement and right there on the pivoting floor of the Treatment Room, Malcolm Orange quit disappearing and prepared to return.

His arms came first. This was particularly fortunate, for the full weight of Cunningham Holt – growing heavier with each revolution – rested in the crooks of Malcolm's elbows. Face came next, revealing a look of such grim determination that his mother, staring intently from behind the protective screen, started in shock, losing two inches of hard-won air, so her head no longer challenged the ceiling tiles. Chest, legs, fingers, feet all began to drizzle back into focus, still inconclusive as afternoon fog, yet offering up a basic outline of an eleven-year-old boy. From the other side of the room, Martha Orange watched her son materialize before her astonished eyes. The effect was decidedly unsettling for it provoked in her the disturbing realization that she could not pinpoint with any precision the last time she'd actually noticed her oldest son. The guilt was an avalanche. By the time Malcolm had a middle, his mother had disentangled herself from the spaghetti soup of wires and leads which sprouted from the Director's machine and, with no thought for her own safety, dashed across the Treatment Room to join Malcolm and Cunningham.

It would be weeks, almost a month, before the last perforation sealed over and Malcolm felt confident enough to bathe without the protection of Band-Aids. However, full recovery, once instigated, was a foregone conclusion. Later, as Malcolm recollected the final moments of his disappearance, he would wonder what strange medicine he'd been exposed to. By the time the sun was drooping like a damp, poached egg over the Baptist Retirement Village, his holes had already begun to seal over. They scabbed quickly and peeled off under the insistence of an eager fingernail, revealing a body coated in clean, pink baby skin, uninterrupted by perforation or scar.

Over the weeks to come Malcolm Orange employed every facet of Scientific Investigative Research to make sense of the comings and recent goings of his body. A series of graphs and bar charts, coupled with the remnants of the Director's research (swiped by Soren from the fireplace in her father's study mere minutes before the police arrived), offered a rudimentary medical explanation for Malcolm's disappearance and subsequent reappearance. However, Scientific Investigative Research had no way of explaining why the emptiness inside Malcolm's head had all of a sudden, without permission or ceremony, sealed up. For eleven years, almost twelve, he'd carried a cavern in the pit of his belly; a sadness so universal it could not be filled with people, places or pastrami and banana sandwiches. In the weeks to come the emptiness would evaporate out of Malcolm, leaving not so much as a fingerprint outline of its memory. Malcolm Orange would settle quietly into himself so he no longer missed his father; no longer felt like an abandoned room each time he looked at his mother; no longer wished, with late night tears and cursing, that the Jesus God would uninvent dying before the members of the People's Committee for Remembering Songs got any older.

All these understandings would come later. As he stood in the Treatment Room pivoting gracefully, Malcolm Orange was so preoccupied with Cunningham Holt he barely noticed the color creeping back into the space where his arms had been. Malcolm Orange was beside himself with concern for his friend. The Treatment was too much for Cunningham Holt. The truth seemed to be dragging him down. Malcolm could have sworn his friend grew heavier with every cruel revolution. Though the floor remained reassuringly solid underfoot he was utterly convinced that Cunningham was beginning to sink. Malcolm's hesitating arms were no match for the weight of truth bleating from the speakers. By the fourth or fifth minute of Treatment he could barely hold his friend up. Unsure what to do next, Malcolm fell back on instinct. With every frantic blast of the Director's treatment, he leaned into Cunningham's ear and muttered his own two-cent take on the truth.

'I won't let you sink.'

'You are the bravest person I've ever met.'

'I wish you were my real grandpa.'

And, when the weight of death began to drive the honest-to-God, hard to tell truths right out of Malcolm Orange's still absent insides, 'I'm sorry I lied about the *X-Files.*' And, 'I wish my dad got shot instead of you.' And a further fifteen times in quick succession with barely room to draw breath, 'I won't let you sink.'

Buoyed by these kinder truths, Cunningham Holt appeared to grow lighter in his arms. A space of some three inches had appeared between the old man's heels and the linoleum floor. Malcolm pulled all the harder against the sinking, continuing his liturgy with renewed fervor. His resolve strengthened as Cunningham rose gently in his arms. Malcolm held tightly for every one of the elderly grandparents he'd left like signposts from the east coast to the west. He held for absent fathers and stolen tires, for every rusted bicycle sacrificed to the open road, for friends, flighty mothers and all the damn fool things the Jesus God had thought fit to wrestle from his grasp. 'The Lord giveth and the Lord taketh away,' he prayed in a direct parody of his final grandmother and, through gritted teeth, added his own epitaph, 'the Lord better not taketh Cunningham Holt.'

Miracles followed. For the first time in years the Jesus God seemed to be listening. Malcolm Orange could feel his holy, bleeding hands as they lifted the weight from his own. The hairs rose on the back of his perforated arms. He felt charged with fear and static electricity. Malcolm had never expected the Jesus God to turn up in person and though this was just the sort of miracle he'd always hoped for, he took great care to avert his eyes for fear of being struck down on the spot. Past disappointments were instantly forgotten as the Jesus God finally redeemed himself for all his jealous takings. It was only when his mother's voice rose to meet his own, muttering something soft and Spanish, that Malcolm Orange noticed her hands and the gnarly hands of Nate Grubbs each holding up a corner of Cunningham Holt. The Jesus God had once again deferred responsibility to human hands. Malcolm was unsure if this counted for a miracle in the traditional sense.

While Nate Grubbs, Malcolm and his mother stood in the centre of the Treatment Room, bearing the weight of Cunningham Holt, Roger Heinz slipped through the door, down the padded corridors of the Center and into the parking lot, where he quickly rounded up the remaining members of the People's Committee for Remembering Songs.

'What the hell?' cried Bill, as Roger Heinz came puffing towards them, protective headphones still balancing buggishly on his balding head.

'Cunningham needs us,' panted Roger Heinz. 'We got to go to the Treatment Room now!'

'That's not part of the plan,' interrupted Bill, who had, over the course of the afternoon, begun to settle into the role of leader and was not about to pass the baton on to Roger Heinz without some kind of fight. 'I've been appointed leader of the Primary Unit. I make the decisions and I'm not sure about this. It doesn't sound safe.'

'Suit yourself, Bill. Who's coming with me and who's staying with old play-it-safe-Billy here?'

Bill was just removing his hands from his pockets in anticipation of placing them firmly on his waist in a stance of resolute defiance when he noticed that Irene was already halfway across the parking lot. Sensing the last small jot of authority about to slip free of his grasp, he turned to face the remaining members of the Primary Unit and, in his most manly voice announced, 'On second thoughts I really think we should head over to the Treatment Room. Cunningham needs us.'

(Bill would not be required to lead anyone or anything for the better part of a decade. When, in the summer of her eighty-fifth year, Irene passed away, mistaking in her mind-addled confusion the furniture polish for her nightly glass of vermouth, Bill would be forced to step up to the plate, planning funerals, executing wills and leading his wife's funeral procession from the sanctuary of the Baptist Church they'd once attended to the municipal graveyard on the edge of town. When the occasion arose and he found himself more than capable of taking the lead, Bill would have to wonder if Irene had been holding him back all along.)

As the People's Committee for Remembering Songs gathered around Cunningham Holt, the four corners of the Treatment Room slowly filled up with cardigans and walking sticks and the overpowering scent of Yardley soap. The Director urged caution (shouting to be heard over the Treatment which, forced far beyond the recommended level, had jammed and could not be overridden or switched off). The Treatment had never been administered to multiple patients simultaneously. Though he did not give a half-hearted damn about his patients' wellbeing, the Director could not be sure how the Treatment would affect the People's Committee. Fearing a second career-crunching lawsuit, he slipped out the door and spent the next half hour chucking a lifetime's worth of research into the fireplace in his study. The police, when they arrived, found him, gas can in hand, attempting to set the Center on fire. They arrested Trip Blue on the spot for arson and the attempted murder of the staff and patients who'd just been shuffled, somewhat dazed, back to their beds and armchairs.

In the Treatment Room the People's Committee for Remembering Songs ignored the noise emanating from the wall-mounted speakers. Over one thousand years of combined experience had taught them how to disregard the kind of distractions – arthritis, income tax and petulant grandchildren, for example – that always seemed to get in the way of the important stuff. Shuffling into a wide circle, they stretched their arms out and, each grabbing an ankle, an ear or shirtsleeve, managed to lift Cunningham Holt three clean feet off the ground.

'We've got you, old chap,' barked Roger Heinz, struggling to hold back an uncharacteristic flood of tears. 'You're not sinking on our watch.'

A careful smile crept across Cunningham Holt's face. He closed his empty eyes and for the first time in over sixty years allowed himself to rest, secure in the knowledge that he would not sink. With his very last breaths he permitted himself a moment of overleaping ambition, imagining his final moments bound not to the greedy depths but rather the heights and hopes of the open sky.

'Sing to me,' he whispered, and the People's Committee for Remembering Songs unanimously agreed that this was the very least they could do.

'Ladies and gents,' Nate Grubbs began, his voice thick with gravitas, 'You heard Cunningham. Ignore the nonsense coming out of the walls. Let's send our friend off with something worth remembering. Forget about the songs you've practiced. Just open your mouths and sing all those songs you really can't forget. And if you can only manage to remember one song, then for God's sake make sure it's a good one. Lock the door, Bill. We're young. We've got all night if needs be. Let's start with Roger and move round the circle.'

Roger Heinz leaned forward, his arms forming a cantilever bridge where they met Cunningham Holt's. He cleared his throat and opened proceedings with the theme from the *Phantom of the Opera*, perfectly delivered. Once finished, Bill, marking time with a series of erratic hip thrusts, launched into a jaunty version of 'Night Fever'. Inspired by the cut of her husband's frisky pelvis, Irene attempted 'Bat out of Hell' and several of Diana Ross's more popular numbers. As they sang, the People's Committee for Remembering Songs grew in confidence. This, they realized, was what they'd been practicing for all along. Stirred by the music, non-members added their voices to the chorus. Mr Fluff forgot herself and, because a lifetime of hacking hairballs meant that rapping now came easier than singing, contributed a trilogy of Beastie Boys tunes. Martha Orange warbled her way through what appeared to be a Spanish version of 'D.I.V.O.R.C.E.', weeping openly as she struggled to reach the low notes. Clary O'Hare volunteered some Kraftwerk in Morse code. It worked, and, bolstered by the group's enthusiasm, he managed to tip tap his way through a believable version of 'Love in an Elevator'.

'That's seventy-three,' counted Nate Grubbs, and checking Cunningham's face for signs of recovery or distress found the old man still alive and smiling the effervescent grin of a homecoming queen. 'Let's keep the ball rolling.'

Mrs Hunter Huxley, and by proxy Mrs George Kellerman, took the floor and led the People's Committee in a rousing chorus of revival songs. Tongues unloosed and arms aloft, the Spirit descended, raising Cunningham Holt a further foot towards the ceiling. All those present got saved, some for the first time, and some for the second or third occasion of the evening. Suddenly full of conviction, Soren James Blue surrendered the last ounce of her cynicism and, unleashing a surprisingly sweet voice, offered 'Smells Like Teen Spirit' and 'Born in the USA'. This brought the collection up to two hundred and thirty something, and with the *Lion King* soundtrack itching at his elbows, Malcolm Orange opened his mouth and contributed almost two dozen individual Elton John songs.

The sun was beginning to descend by the time the baton arrived at Nate Grubbs' feet. Several of the older members had fallen asleep and stood slightly inclined, yet still holding tightly to the edges of Cunningham Holt's shirt. As always, Nate Grubbs approached the moment methodically and with tremendous charm. Adjusting the legs of his trousers, he cleared his throat once, twice, three times and delivered five hundred and three bona-fide, note-perfect, Bob Dylan songs. (It should be noted that there were, at the time, only five hundred Bob Dylan songs in existence. However, as he sang, Mr Wilson unconsciously composed three new Dylan songs which would later find their way into the great man's dreams, itching there until his guitar-playing fingers finally capitulated and weaved them into existence.)

As the People's Committee for Remembering Songs sang their elderly hearts out, Malcolm Orange began to notice something odd. All across the Treatment Room his friends were experiencing a subtle yet marked transformation. If Scientific Investigative Research had not given him a coolly logical mind, Malcolm Orange would have sworn that his friends were younger than they'd been two hours previously. The reality fell closer to fiction than Malcolm could have imagined. Trapped and open-eared, his friends were powerless to resist the Treatment. They could not help but hear every word escaping from the speaker system. Within seconds the words were at work. Within minutes they had infected the entire room with a double dose of blinding realism. Inspired by the gracious truths flying around, Committee members long resigned to a muted kind of existence were encountering the boldest versions of themselves and responding in kind. And while it was impossible to tell if responsibility lay with the Director's Treatment or the unleashed power of communal song, Malcolm Orange was forced to acknowledge that the People's Committee for Remembering Songs appeared to be getting healed right under his nose.

Simeon Klein, silent throughout the singing, threw back his head and launched into a note-perfect rendition of 'How Much Is

That Doggy in the Window', the very last song he could recall from his hearing years. Clary O'Hare quit fumbling about with teaspoons and, for the first time in fifty years, felt brave enough to engage in honest, wordy interaction with other human beings. The Mrs Hunter Huxley and George Kellerman, overcome by a fresh realization of their own salvation, felt the youthful exuberance of the immortal itching through arthritic fingers and knees, and began to fandango like loose-limbed teenagers round and round the Treatment Room. Irene remembered everything in an instant, and, seeing the jealous years peel from his wife's face, Bill recalled the woman he'd married and fell furiously in love all over again. Nate Grubbs, still lamenting his own stupidity, felt the shotgun guilt lift from his shoulders like a pair of sandbags, unleashed, while Soren James Blue was struck by a sudden and all-consuming awareness of her own peculiar beauty. Roger Heinz, with a sly grin, sensed an unprovoked stirring in his underpants, and, cheered by the possibility of loving the Meals on Wheels lady all by himself without pills or pumps, could barely contain his own excitement.

Emboldened by the miracles unfolding in every corner of the Treatment Room, the People's Committee for Remembering Songs whooped and hollered, raising their wrinkled chins and hands in anticipation of further healing. The noise was deafening. Only Malcolm and his mother hesitated on the edge of hysteria, unsure whether the truth should be counted a blessing, or a particularly heavy curse. Both had already begun to note slight physical changes, multiplying with each minute spent bowed beneath the speakers. While Malcolm would soon come to mark this, his moment of salvation, his mother would fluctuate for years between the thankful heart of a recovered addict and the suspicion that the Treatment Room had robbed her of something essential and irretrievable. Martha Orange would leave the Treatment Room four pounds lighter than she'd entered. Each fledgling wing accounted for a single pound of loss. The final two pounds marked the precise weight of thirty years worth of ambition, suddenly excised.

Arms beginning to ache from the weight of Cunningham Holt, Martha Orange had started to experience a fluttering sensation in her shoulder blades. The truth was singing to her soft and low and, much as it pained her, Martha could not keep her body from responding. Her baby wings, barely one hour old, began to retract, fizzling back into her flesh with stunning speed. She felt the loss like a toothache at the back of each lung and, for a moment, could not place the pain. Removing a supportive hand from Cunningham Holt's armpit, she stretched her arm over her shoulder and cupped the remains of her right wing. It pulsed in her hand like a newborn chick, frail and feathery. Martha could not bring herself to let go. As she held on to the possibility of future flight, her wing shriveled from a potato-sized handfuls, to a lemon, a marble, and finally a damply warm spot in her shirt. Malcolm's mother was disappointed but not surprised.

Standing unwinged and ordinary in the middle of the Treatment Room, Martha Orange remembered the very last story of her sessions with Junior Button. At the time it had seemed an odd sort of epitaph to a week's worth of biographical mumblings. Now it came back to bite her like a misplaced punch line.

'Girl,' the old man had said, propping himself up on one massive elbow, 'let me tell you a story about a young lady I once knowed back in my Jefferson days.'

Martha Orange, noting that his hand now trembled over his water cup and his thrice daily shots of insulin only kept him conscious for an hour at most, hopped up on the edge of Junior

Button's bed and prepared to take what she knew might well be the old man's final confession.

'Tell me all about it, Junior,' she'd said. 'I love your stories.'

'This ain't no story, child. This is God's honest truth and you'd be best fit to take heed of it. Give me a nip of the good stuff and I'll tell you the whole sorry tale.'

Passing Junior Button the bottle of Gatorade laced with liquor she'd been smuggling in and out of the Center for the last few days, Martha Orange had taken a quick swig for herself and curled into a question mark at the foot of the bed. Bent double and caught up in the stories of her childhood, she'd come to feel the years peel away like ancient scabs.

'It's like this,' he'd begun, coughing loosely as the liquor began to warm the insides of his rib cage, 'I used to be friendly with this gal called Mary-Betty Omquist. Stunning girl she was; all arms and legs and braids like boat rope. Don't mind telling you Martha, I'd a notion of wedding Mary-Betty when I got old enough. Course a girl like that is always going to be out of my sort's league. Old man Omquist would have scalped my ass if I'd so much as laid a finger on Mary-Betty, but it sure as hell didn't stop me looking and grinning at her like a great, gallumping halfwit every time I passed her on Main Street. Mary-Betty was a sweet gal and God bless her, but didn't she always beam back at me – face like a Fourth of July picnic – until I got to imagining the girl had a notion of me.

'Us flying folk has a way of knowing our own and I could see the flight hovering over Mary-Betty from five miles out. That girl had a peculiar way of carrying her feet like she could hardly bear to be touching on the sidewalk. She dandered about Jefferson with her nose turned up, eyes fixed on the heavens, 'til the other girls – evil bitches, every one of them – pronounced her uppity and pushed her out of the Sewing Circle and the Lutheran Ladies' Prayer and Bible Study. Mary-Betty was mortified. She was a humble kind of a gal, inclined to turn primrose pink at the very thought of offending another critter. It wasn't pride that kept her nose pointed to the clouds. I could tell it was the flight cause my nose was forever itching upwards too. It used to kill me to see the poor gal sitting at the soda counter in the drugstore all alone with no kids her own age to keep her company. Them there days, I was always lonesome myself. There weren't much company to be had for a black fella like myself in Grant County. Well, I don't mind telling you Martha, I got to thinking that me and old Mary-Betty had more in common than her papa might have thought. Back then I didn't know shit about wings or flying children but I knew, sure as God and all his angels were floating in the sky, that I should be up there too.

'By the first day of summer vacation I'd got my guts up to speak to Mary-Betty. I wasn't thinking of asking her out nor nothing. I just wanted to say hi, maybe tell her how pretty she was; nothing crazy. I knew better than to make moves on a white girl. But when I sat down beside her on the bench outside the store I could see she'd been crying and I couldn't help myself.

'"Why you crying?" I asked, and that was enough to really get the girl going. She went off like a broken faucet; the water wouldn't quit coming out of her.

'"Is you crying about them mean bitches from the Lutheran Ladies' Bible Study?" I asked, and she just kept right on howling so I couldn't tell if this was her particular bother or not.

'"Oh Mary-Betty," I said, cause the up-close sight of her boat rope braids was doing something funny to the inside of my belly and other parts. "Don't be getting yourself in a state. Them girls ain't worth two cents. You're better than all of them put together.

You're like me, ain't you? All your head can think about is flying far away from Jefferson."

'And Mary-Betty quit her crying in an instant and grabbed at my arm, all big eyes and G-D braids. "Do you feel it too?" she asks me. "Do you think about flying all the time, even when you're asleep?"

'What could I do, Martha? I couldn't lie to the girl. I nodded my head and when Mary-Betty reached for my hand I sure as hell didn't try to stop her. I just kept right on nodding and holding that white girl's hand and before I had the sense to stop myself I heard my mouth saying, "Mary-Betty, maybe I could fix it for you to do flying, just once, you know, so you could feel what it was like."

'That was it, Martha. I was screwed. I knew in my head that if I could get Mary-Betty up in the air, out of Jefferson, it would be a sort of miracle. And if one miracle could be done then there was every chance of another one and maybe, just maybe Mary-Betty Omquist would be my girl. Sense and reason went hot-footing it out the window. Next few weeks I spent every spare minute working on my flying plans. I done drawings on the back of my pa's newspaper. I built stuff in the backyard. I tried and failed and tried again 'til I finally got something I thought might just maybe do the business. It wasn't rocket science or magic, Martha. It was a dining room chair with a bit of rope for a seat-belt and ten dozen flapping birds bound to the back rest with parcel string. Catching them birds was a hell of a job. Binding them to the chair was another thing altogether. It took almost a week to get it right but when I finally got the last bird tied down and I saw fit to toss a handful of breadcrumbs up in the sky, well, them G-D birds all start flapping in the same direction and the chair went five clean feet off the ground.

'The very next day I grabbed Mary-Betty outside the drugstore. She was sitting on the stoop, sipping a Coke and pushing the dirt round with the toe of her sneaker.

"Hey, Junior," she said.

"Hey, Mary-Betty," I replied. "You still want to do the flying?"

"Sure," she replied.

"You gotta follow me."

'Mary-Betty didn't look none too sure of that but the girl was so frickin' lonely I guessed she'd have upped and followed the Pied Piper himself if the old devil had asked. We went round my pa's place. My pa was out. It was market morning. I'd made sure he would be out cause I knew he'd tan my ass for bringing a white girl round our place. Folks like us had got themselves lynched for less in Grant County. I could tell Mary-Betty was nervy. She didn't do as much grinning as usual. She didn't try to do holding my hand. When she saw the chair with them flappering birds she went paper white and quit smiling altogether.

"No way," she said. "No way am I getting on that chair."

"But you wanted to do flying Mary-Betty," I said. "You told me you wanted to do the flying."

"It's not safe. I could fall off."

"Safe as houses. Already been up in it myself," I said. This was a lie but my granddaddy once told me the Lord Himself was always tellin' lies for the good of mankind. "You want to be sad forever, Mary-Betty, or you want to feel real good about yourself right now? There's nothing like doing flying. Best thing I ever done."

'Mary-Betty looked mighty sad and scared so I put a hand on her shoulder and shoved her a little bit into the chair. She let me push her. She didn't even fight me. I wasn't thinking about Mary-Betty, Martha. I was thinking about myself and the way folks would look at me different and better if Mary-Betty was my girl. I might have shouted at her a bit.

"'Mary-Betty, you sit there in this G-D chair and quit your sniveling. You're going to do flying today and when you get back down after you're going to thank old Junior Button for making you happier than you ever been in your whole life."

'I belted the rope across her middle and stepped back. Them birds were flapping and swirling round her head like a prairie cyclone. One of the pigeons had gone and got itself caught in her boat rope braids. Mary-Betty looked like she was just about to shit herself in panic. Her hands were holding so hard to the chair I could see the white lumps of her bones. Her eyes were closed tight shut.

"'One, two, three,' I shouted, and chucked a couple of handfuls of breadcrumbs into the air above her head. I wasn't expecting the birds to go so quick. In a second they were whooshing up towards the clouds, dragging Mary-Betty and my ma's old dining chair with them. For one short, wonderful second I could see right up the girl's frock, then I could only see the bottom of her sneakers waving wildly like a pair of white headache pills.

"'Mary-Betty!' I yelled. "You OK?"

'But Mary-Betty was out of earshot. I couldn't hear a damn thing the girl was saying. Ninety seconds later when her fingers got un-feared enough to undo the belt she came tumbling out of my ma's dining room chair. She made no noise at all coming down. You'd have thought her to scream, wouldn't you, Martha? I'd scream if I was falling that far through the sky. No noise at all, but when she hit the ground she made a noise like eggs breaking. Hell, Martha, a noise like that stays with you. It haunts you, so it does. She was all snapped legs and arms and two dead birds caught up in her boat rope braids. I couldn't look at Mary-Betty except through my fingers. Honest to God, I thought the gal was dead.'

'And was she dead?' Martha Orange had asked, interrupting Junior Button before he could finish his story.

'No ma'am,' Junior Button had replied. 'Old Mary-Betty wasn't dead. More's the pity. The poor girl never did walk proper again though, and her pa got word of who was responsible for her busted legs and ran my ass out of Jefferson with a sawed-off shotgun.

'Don't mind telling you, Martha, I never did make no more tries at flying. Mary-Betty scared the living shit right out of me. I didn't want to end up like her, all broke up and crippled. No ma'am, I couldn't bring myself to think about flying no more. See, I got to figuring you can be content with your working lot and enjoy the two walking legs the good Lord gave you or you can be like Mary-Betty Omquist, take your shot at the big blue sky and end up losing everything that was ever important to you. Me, I went and taught myself to be contented with both feet firmly fixed to the ground. Never done me any harm far as I can see.'

'What about me?' Martha Orange had asked, her throat thick with anticipation. 'I can't seem to settle anywhere. Do you think it's OK to fly if you really can't get away from it?'

'You got to decide for yourself, child. Depends what matters most. It's a hard lot whatever you choose. Once you fix upon flying, you can't come back and expect things to be sitting the way you left them.'

The very next day Junior Button had passed away in his sleep, stretched out on the floor with a bottle of Gatorade clenched in one hand. Martha Orange had a whole world of questions waiting to ask him but the chance never arose. With no advice forthcoming, she'd packed her life into a pair of grocery sacks and jumped the first bus out of town.

Standing in the corner of the Treatment Room, suddenly bereft of both wings, Martha Orange could not help but wonder if hers was the luckiest of escapes. If the absence of a credit card and winter coat had not drawn her back to the Retirement Village into the midst of crisis, she would currently be contemplating the weekend from the far side of the Canadian border and whilst life would undoubtedly be chock-full of open roads and possibility, she would never again have the opportunity to persevere through her children's childish years. As the room turned and the People's Committee slipped their skins for younger souls, Martha Orange lingered on the last will and testament of her good friend, Junior Button:

'Once you fix upon flying, you can't come back and expect things to be sitting the way you left them.'

The wide blue sky seemed a small price to pay for a lifetime's worth of tiger hugs and tumbling love. Martha Orange screwed her feet into the spinning floor and chose to persevere: today, tomorrow and for all the dullish days to come.

Despite her reservations, the miracles continued to burst forth around Martha Orange's skeptical ankles. All over the Treatment Room wrinkles relaxed, joints loosened and the last decade's losses returned to the People's Committee in double portion. The Jesus God was surely giving in reckless abundance and his unchecked enthusiasm seemed to highlight the rather tight-lipped taking he was working upon Martha Orange. Malcolm watched on in befuddled amazement as his mother lost her wings, transforming from an angel into an ordinary woman in less than half an hour.

Later he could not resist asking Martha about the wings. Mrs

Orange refused to answer any of his questions. 'The Lord giveth and the Lord taketh away,' she'd mutter and settle into her resignation face, the same face which had watched two dozen states and any number of elderly relatives disappear in the Volvo's rearview mirror. She refused to be drawn on the specifics of flight. Malcolm Orange pestered her for weeks but his mother would not, or could not, explain the miraculous appearance and disappearance of her wings. In the end Malcolm simply gave up. In light of the last month's events he was happy just to have a semi-functional parent. Though a flying mother appealed to the little part of him which had not yet grown out of the X-Men, Malcolm Orange concluded that a stay-at-home, never-leave mother would be infinitely more useful in the long term.

The flight never quite left Martha Orange. On the occasional evenings when she allowed herself an alcoholic drink before bed, she dreamt of air currents and skylines; waking the following morning, heartsick disappointed with the metallic taste of cloud lingering in her teeth. The temptation to leave was constant and insidious. It rose to meet her over the breakfast table, mocking her maternal stumblings with the oatmeal and waffles. It tailed her to the school gates and taunted her openly on the rare occasions when she lost her temper with Malcolm. Good mothers, Martha Orange knew, did not long for the chance to abandon their children. Good mothers could not imagine an existence without them.

Martha Orange had no illusions about her capacity as a mother and yet she stayed put. She persevered through their growing years, assisting in the completion of homework, photographing Ross and Malcolm's important moments and priding herself on her faultless portrayal of a good mother. She forced herself to see each flighty urge as a false contraction. No one, not least Malcolm, ever noticed the way Martha spent an inordinate amount of her adult life ogling the open sky. Her addiction was a private thing, practiced quietly, in isolation. In place of wings Martha Orange accepted a pair of ordinary arms; elbowed, fingered and all of a sudden brave enough to balk tradition and hold her family close and safe for a very long time.

Whilst Martha Orange suffered her own small loss in the corner of the Treatment Room, miracles – medium-sized and extraordinary – were blossoming like weed flowers all across the room. In the centre of the circle, floating on the outstretched arms of the People's Committee for Remembering Songs, the truth had settled upon Cunningham Holt's face like August rain. Opening his eyes he saw the world as he'd long imagined it. Colors and shapes and kindly, familiar faces swam through the tears so when he passed away – just one full minute after his second birth – his last sight was not the darkness, nor the ground clamoring beneath his feet but a bold, white ceiling and the promise of sky beyond. No one cried. It was the sort of loss which left everyone larger for the losing. Two days after his death the People's Committee for Remembering Songs, standing in lieu of his absent family, were forced to make decisions about Cunningham Holt's funeral arrangements. When the Board of Directors pushed for a burial they insisted upon a cremation and, without waiting for assent or permission, bound the ashes to a bouquet of helium balloons, cast adrift over the Burnside Bridge.

'Damn it,' Roger Heinz would explain when the Board of Directors got wind of Cunningham Holt's unorthodox funeral arrangements, 'the old boy's circling the stratosphere as we speak, and you can't get no further from a sinking than that.'

The Board of Directors, mortified by certain gargantuan oversights in the supervision of their staff and management, chose to take the matter no further. Trip Blue, semi-permanently incarcerated in the state correctional facility for megalomaniacs and psychopaths, would eventually be replaced by a matronly lady from New Jersey, who specialized in rehabilitating arts and crafts techniques and dance programs for adults with dementia. The following year the Annual Thanksgiving Turkey and Tipples Tea Dance would have its budget increased by five hundred percent, the only prerequisite for this windfall a glowing article in the *Willamette Weekly*, penned by Nate Grubbs and featuring photos of the happy, healthy and well-treated residents of the Baptist Retirement Village.

Things settled down quickly in the cul-de-sac. Within a week the People's Committee for Remembering Songs had fallen back into its twice-weekly schedule. Though music was no longer explicitly under threat, the habit of meeting together to sing had become a kind of religion for the residents of the cul-de-sac, and all involved agreed that Cunningham Holt's memory would be best served by honoring the tradition. In the years to come Martha Orange continued to wipe butts and fix drips at the Center. Ross Orange remained unremarkable in his ability to eat, shit and sleep in dull rotation and Jimmy Orange became a constant absence running through the future days of his once-abandoned family. A postcard arrived annually on the day before Jimmy's birthday (the only anniversary he had memory enough to recall), signposting his travels across South America, Europe and Australia, coming to a sudden halt in Singapore on the eve of Malcolm's college graduation. Bound to a man who could not keep still long enough to execute a divorce, Martha Orange never married again. In her fifty-first year, Malcolm moved in with a blunt-haired girl from Tulsa and Ross began an internship with a local graphic design company, and Martha, finally feeling the maternal anchors slip from her ankles, without so much as a second thought indulged the persistent itch in each shoulder blade and booked a one-way ticket to Marrakech.

Malcolm Orange remained a remarkable and much-celebrated young man throughout his youth and early manhood. The events of his eleventh summer would stick with him, forming a bedrock for all future assumptions as impermeable and constant as landfill concrete. All things would go but the very fact that his mother had chosen to remain had bored its way into Malcolm's skull, muddling with all the lesser truths of the Treatment Room. Later, when the police and the psychiatrists and the 'helpful' people from the Board of Directors left the Baptist Retirement Village and everyone returned to their chalets, heart-heavy and elated, Malcolm would wonder why the Treatment had left him only half-healed, still perforated for many weeks to come. His mother, enfolding him in her now functional arms, would cover him with bite-sized, fluttering kisses and say, 'Don't worry, Malcolm. I'll hold you together from now on.' This, Malcolm Orange concluded, was exactly the kind of extraordinary he'd been hoping for all along.